A KNIFE
IN THE
HEART

NO LONGER PROPERTY
OF ANYTHINK
RANGEVIEW LIBRARY
DISTRICT

Look for these exciting Western series from bestselling authors
WILLIAM W. JOHNSTONE
and **J. A. JOHNSTONE**

The Mountain Man

Preacher: The First Mountain Man

Luke Jensen, Bounty Hunter

Those Jensen Boys!

The Jensen Brand

Matt Jensen

MacCallister

The Red Ryan Westerns

Perley Gates

Have Brides, Will Travel

The Hank Fallon Westerns

Will Tanner, Deputy U.S. Marshal

Shotgun Johnny

The Chuckwagon Trail

The Jackals

The Slash and Pecos Westerns

The Texas Moonshiners

AVAILABLE FROM PINNACLE BOOKS

A KNIFE IN THE HEART

A HANK FALLON WESTERN

WILLIAM W. JOHNSTONE

with J. A. Johnstone

PINNACLE BOOKS
Kensington Publishing Corp.
www.kensingtonbooks.com

PINNACLE BOOKS are published by

Kensington Publishing Corp.
119 West 40th Street
New York, NY 10018

Copyright © 2020 J. A. Johnstone

All rights reserved. No part of this book may be reproduced in any form or by any means without the prior written consent of the publisher, excepting brief quotes used in reviews.

This book is a work of fiction. Names, characters, businesses, organizations, places, events, and incidents either are the product of the author's imagination or are used fictitiously. Any resemblance to actual persons, living or dead, events, or locales is entirely coincidental. To the extent that the image or images on the cover of this book depict a person or persons, such person or persons are merely models, and are not intended to portray any character or characters featured in the book.

PUBLISHER'S NOTE
Following the death of William W. Johnstone, the Johnstone family is working with a carefully selected writer to organize and complete Mr. Johnstone's outlines and many unfinished manuscripts to create additional novels in all of his series like The Last Gunfighter, Mountain Man, and Eagles, among others. This novel was inspired by Mr. Johnstone's superb storytelling.

If you purchased this book without a cover, you should be aware that this book is stolen property. It was reported as "unsold and destroyed" to the publisher, and neither the author nor the publisher has received any payment for this "stripped book."

All Kensington titles, imprints, and distributed lines are available at special quantity discounts for bulk purchases for sales promotions, premiums, fund-raising, educational, or institutional use. Special book excerpts or customized printings can also be created to fit specific needs. For details, write or phone the office of the Kensington sales manager: Kensington Publishing Corp., 119 West 40th Street, New York, NY 10018, attn: Sales Department; phone 1-800-221-2647.

PINNACLE BOOKS, the Pinnacle logo, and the WWJ steer head logo are Reg. U.S. Pat. & TM Off.

ISBN-13: 978-0-7860-4386-6
ISBN-10: 0-7860-4386-5

First printing: October 2020

10 9 8 7 6 5 4 3 2 1

Printed in the United States of America

Electronic edition:

ISBN-13: 978-0-7860-4387-3 (e-book)
ISBN-10: 0-7860-4387-3p (e-book)

PART I

CHAPTER ONE

They come at him, just as they always do—at least six men, wearing the striped uniform of inmates. Harry Fallon can't see their faces, and even if he could, it's not like he knows these hardened lifers. He doesn't even remember the name of the prison where he has been sentenced. Joliet? Yuma? Jefferson City? Huntsville? Detroit? Alcatraz? Cañon City? Laramie? Deer Lodge? But a bad memory is the least of his problems right now.

He stands with his back against the door of six-inch cold iron, no bars, just a slit for a peek hole so the guards can check in every now and then. Ahead of him, to his left, are the cells on the fifth floor. Hands extend between the bars and rattle tin cups against the iron. The doors remain shut. Inside, prisoners chant some dirge or hum, mixed with curses and laughter, but all that proves hard to understand with the racket the cups make against the rough iron. To his right, there's a metal rail about waist-high, and beyond that, the emptiness for thirty yards to the other row of cell blocks. Five stories below, the stone floor of this hellhole called a prison. And just in front of him, the six men, faces masked, but intentions clear. The knives they have—fashioned from the metal shop, or the broom factory, or the farms where they work—wave in hands roughened by a life of crime, followed by life sentences.

"Hey!" Fallon shouts through the slit in iron, but dares not look through the opening. He can't take his eyes off the six killers. By now, they are less than ten feet from him.

"Hey!"

Nothing.

The big brute in the center of the gang laughs.

Of course, there's no guard here. Not now. Fallon has been behind the iron long enough to know that guards and prisoners have the ability to make a few deals when it comes to taking care of prisoners neither guards nor convicts like. A guard decides to head to the privy at a predetermined time, a trip that'll take a good long while, and it just happens to coincide with other guards needing to find a cigarette, or a toilet, or happening to be escorting another inmate to see the warden.

Handy.

Right now, there's probably not a guard anywhere in this particular house.

So six cons, armed with shivs, start to smile.

If only Fallon could recall where he is, what he's in for, why these men want to kill him. If only Fallon could remember *anything*.

My God, he thinks, has he been sent to prisons so many times his brain has become addled? Has he been hit on the head, suffered . . . what is it they call that . . . amnesia? Yeah. Amnesia. All right, at least he can remember some things.

He remembers something else, too.

Because one of the faceless men before him whispers a growling, "Take him," and the thug on Fallon's right charges, laughing, slashing with the blade, and Fallon leaps back, against the cold stone of the wall, feeling and hearing the tearing of cloth but not of flesh. His intestines aren't spilling out of his belly—yet.

The remaining five killers merely laugh.

The big fellow, eyes black, face pale, almost not even a face at all, pivots, cuts up with the blade, but Fallon uses his left forearm to knock hand and knife away. The man's face, or what passes for a face, seems surprised. A moment later, Fallon is driving his right hand, flattened, hard against the killer's throat. The crack is almost deafening. The man's eyes bulge in shock, and the blow drives him back, back, back, till he slams against the iron railing at the corner, the end of the passageway. Fallon tries to grab the knife, but both of the man's arms start waving as he tries to regain his balance, as he tries to remember how to breathe.

But he can't. Spittle comes between his lips. He's like a whirlwind now, and the other five men outside of the cells watch in fascination and amusement. Even those still inside their cells are transfixed. All they do is hold their tin cups outside the bars. Fingers grip other bars as they watch, laugh, hiss, joke, and pray.

The man moves farther over the rails. He opens his mouth as if to scream, but he can't scream. He can't breathe. He can't do anything but die. Fallon has learned several things in prison, including how to crush an attacker's larynx.

The shiv drops over the side. Damn. Fallon could have used that to defend himself against the other five killers.

The arms stop waving, and then the faceless man starts to slip over. His mouth opens as though to scream, but he cannot scream, either. A second later, and he's suspended in the air, prison brogans pointing toward the hard ceiling, and then there is nothing.

A long silence follows, stretching toward infinity, before the sickening crunch of a body seems to shake the prison house to its very foundation.

Fallon's heart races. He wets his lips, turns back toward the five other men. The shuddering of the passageway ends, and the man in the center, who might have a mustache and beard, although that appears to be against the prison policy—whatever house of corrections Fallon is in—walks to the edge, puts his hand on the rail, peers over. He spits saliva, which drops toward the corpse, broken and bloody, and stares sightlessly toward the impenetrable ceiling.

Fallon knows because somehow he, too, has moved to the railing, to see the man he has just killed, another kill for a onetime lawman turned killer. The man's dead eyes seem to follow Fallon as he turns back to the five men. The leader spits again, wipes his mouth, and slowly turns to stare at Fallon.

As though on cue, the tin cups resume their metallic serenade. The grinding has now been picked up across the chasm. Prisoners there have likewise resumed raking cups against the bars. And so have the prisoners on the floors below. The noise intensifies. Surely the warden can hear this from wherever his office or house is. Fallon can hear nothing else but the grinding, pounding, insane bedlam of hell.

The noise becomes deafening. Fallon breathes in deeply, watches the five men now back to staring at him. They could rush him, should rush him, for there's no room for Fallon to move, and he can't take down five men when they have knives and he has nothing but . . .

He takes a chance, steps forward quickly, and as a tin cup rattles from one bar to another, Fallon strikes hard with his left hand against the wrist. The damned fool should have kept his hand and cup inside his cell. He thinks he hears a scream, but the fingers release the handle, and somehow Fallon has the cup in his own hand.

That prompts a laugh from the leader.

"You think a cup is a match for a blade?" the big faceless man asks.

The killer closest to the cell laughs. But that stops when Fallon steps forward and smashes the man in the face with the hard, cold tin cup.

Fallon quickly steps back, taking it all in, seeing the man, his nose gushing crimson, his lips flattened and bloody, spitting out teeth and saliva, and stumbling in a wild spin. An arm hits the man nearest him and pushes him against the leader, who steps back against the fourth man, who jolts the fifth killer to the railing. And now that man is screaming, screaming out for mercy from God, but God cannot hear any prayer in a prison, especially with cups grinding cell doors after cell doors, and just like that, the fifth killer has gone over the edge, plummeting like a rocket, but he can scream, and his cries overcome the drone of metal on iron, until a sickening crunch below silences him.

But not the sound of cups.

The fourth man catches the railing, looks over, and mouths, "Oh, my, God," before turning to Fallon, and charging.

Fallon feels the blade as it cuts into his side, but his right hand rams the cup into the man's temple, and the man falls to his knees. The knife comes up, just as Fallon jabs his kneecap into the man's jaw. The blade sticks in up to its makeshift handle of hardened lye soap, deep in Fallon's thigh, and then the man goes down, tries to come up, and Fallon kicks him over the railing.

"Get him!" one of the men calls.

Fallon turns, blinks, confused and angry. Three men have been hurtled to the floor five stories below. There should be only three more inmates outside of their cells, but somehow the doors must have opened, and there are dozens, maybe hundreds. It's as though every prisoner in this whole cell block has been turned loose on the alley. Fallon rips the knife out of his leg with his left hand. Blood sprays the striped trousers of the men as they cover the few feet separating them from him. He has a short blade and a tin cup. They have knives and clubs and rocks.

He has no chance, and soon they have him, his cup and knife thrown to the floor. He smells their sweat, feeling blows against his arms, back, head, neck. Cursing them as they curse him, he tries to free his arms, his hands, his legs, but there is nothing for him to do.

A moment later, he is at the iron railing. Now he glances through the opening in the slit of the door, and he sees the faces of the guards, and the guards are laughing, too, shouting.

"Toss him overboard, boys!"

Which they do.

Fallon looks below as the stone floor rushes up to greet him. He sees the bloody, crushed, lifeless bodies of the three men he has killed on this day. Their eyes remain open, as well as their mouths, and he can hear these dead men laughing at him. One says, "Join us, Fallon . . . in hell."

And the stones are there to greet him and send him to the fiery pit.

Where Harry Fallon knows he belongs.

He screams.

CHAPTER TWO

His own scream woke him up.

Fallon tried to catch his breath, feeling suddenly freezing, and realized sweat drenched his night robe. While trying desperately to catch his breath, he noticed his right arm was up, crooked, and his clenched fist trembled. He held a pair of scissors. Fallon stared as early morning light seeped through the curtains of the parlor of his home. He waited until he stopped shaking, could breathe normally, and stared at the scissors.

Sobs came somewhere down the foyer beyond the formal parlor.

A woman's voice soon whispered, "It's all right, baby. It's all right. Papa just had another bad dream."

He lowered his hand, swung his bare feet over the chaise. Feet on the rug, he managed to swallow and gently laid the scissors down on the side table. How he had managed to find them was beyond him, but thank God, he prayed, he was sleeping in the parlor.

Sleeping in the parlor. One more time. Instead of in the bedroom with his wife.

Fallon planted his elbows on his thighs, buried his face in his hands, and waited until he stopped shaking, bits and pieces of the nightmare returning to him, but only in fragments. He didn't need to remember every single detail. It was the same damned nightmare he always had. A few things might change: the location, the number of inmates, how men were trying to kill him, or execute him. Sometimes he knew the men, the crazed killer named Monk from Yuma; the leader of the riot from Joliet; the Mole from Jefferson City; even John Wesley Hardin from Huntsville. Mostly though, they were cretins and monsters and blurs of men, often without faces, but always trying to kill him. In the worst of the dreams, they were about to succeed before he woke up. On the good nights, he woke up quickly before his own shouts awakened his family . . . one more time.

This, he knew, was no way to live. Not so much for his sake, but for Christina and the five-year-old girl, Rachel Renee.

He managed to stand, ran his fingers through his soaking hair, looked at the chaise, and tossed a blanket on it, hoping the wool would soak up the sweat. The chaise had belonged to Christina's grandmother. He would hate to ruin it, like the leather-covered sofa he had slept on one night that he had ripped apart with a paper opener he happened to find in his sleep.

As long as he didn't start sleepwalking. God, wouldn't that be awful.

He moved out of the parlor and into the hallway, stopped in the indoor bathroom to dry his face, comb his hair, drink a cup of water, and maybe make himself look halfway presentable, with luck mostly human, and then to the girl's bedroom. It was empty, her covers thrown off the little bed. Which is what usually happened.

Fallon took a few more steps before pushing open the door at the end of the hallway.

Christina Whitney Fallon sat in the four-poster bed, hugging Rachel Renee tightly, kissing the top of her dark hair. Dark hair like Fallon's, not the soft blond of his wife's.

Both stared at him in silence.

"Good morning," Fallon said, realized the absurdity of such a greeting, and sighed. "Sorry."

"It's all right, Papa." Rachel Renee's voice trembled.

"Are you all right?" Christina asked. Her voice was noncommittal, professional, like she was interviewing a witness or a suspect from her days just a few years back as an operative for the American Detective Agency in Chicago.

"Bad dream." He shrugged. "The usual."

"Were there monsters?" Rachel Renee asked.

By then, he had managed to cross the room and sat at the end of the bed. "Yeah," he said. "Daisies and licorice."

Rachel Renee laughed, and that made Fallon breathe a little easier, if not quite relax. He even thought he saw a twinkle in Christina's eyes.

"Daisies and licorice aren't monsters, Papa," the girl said with bemusement. "Those are nice things. My favorite flower. And my favorite breakfast."

"Breakfast?" Christina now laughed.

The day might be all right, Fallon thought.

The precious little girl, one of the two loves of Fallon's life these past few years, crawled from her mother and leaned against Fallon, still in the robe.

She quickly pulled away. "Oh, Papa, you stink."

Fallon tried to laugh.

"And you're all sweaty."

"That's what boys and men do, baby," Christina said.

"They're gross."

"Yes," her mother agreed. "Very much so."

"But I love you anyway, Papa." She came back and tried to hug him. Fallon put his arm around her.

"What was the nightmare really about?" Rachel Renee asked.

Fallon looked across the room. It was a nice room, extravagant by Fallon's standards, in a rented home—what Fallon would have considered a mansion back when he was a kid in Gads Hill, Missouri—in the up-scale section of Cheyenne, Wyoming. Fallon would have opted for something a little less pretentious, but the governor insisted, as did the state senators—Fallon could remember when Wyoming was just a U.S. territory. Everyone argued that the United States marshal for Wyoming needed to live in a fine house. Especially since he had a beautiful wife, and, for the past five-plus years, a lovely little daughter.

Politics.

All politics.

That's what Fallon's life had become. Politics during the day. Nightmares for the night.

A hell of a life.

"Papa?" Rachel Renee pleaded.

Fallon hugged her tightly. "Oh, I'm not too sure. Dragons, I think. Maybe a unicorn."

"Are unicorns mean?"

"This one was."

"I know dragons are evil. They spit fire."

"Yeah, the two in my bad dream spit out a lot of fire."

"Where there any Indians?"

Fallon looked down at her. "Indians aren't mean like dragons and bad unicorns, or smelly boys and sweating old men."

"Janie Ferguson says Indians are real bad."

"Janie Ferguson is wrong." He tousled her hair. "You know, back when I was just a regular old deputy marshal, back in Fort Smith, Arkansas, I worked with a lot of Indians. Lawmen. Peace officers like me. Scouts. They were always good folk. Really good folk. So I don't think I met any real bad Indians."

"Honest?"

Not really. Fallon had arrested Indians, too, but not as many as the white men who tormented the Indian Nations across the western district of Arkansas. But those times had changed, and after what happened at Wounded Knee so many years ago, Fallon had decided that he'd bring up his daughter to understand that you could find good and bad in all kinds of people, no matter their skin, no matter their beliefs.

Although Fallon had a hard time thinking that for himself. Most of the men he had dealt with were rotten to the core.

As a deputy marshal, and then as an operative for the American Detective Agency—the latter a job he had been forced into—Fallon had worked with dregs. And some of the worst of the lot were men who supposedly represented law and order, like the president of the American Detective Agency, a soulless pitiful man named Sean MacGregor.

Often Fallon blamed MacGregor for these nightmares, for keeping Harry Fallon from being able to spend a night sleeping next to his wife—without having this fear that a nightmare would seize him and he'd wake up and realize that he had killed her by accident.

No way for a man to live. No way for a daughter to grow up.

On the other hand, Fallon might be having these dreams anyway, even if Sean MacGregor had not forced Fallon to go undercover into three of the worst prisons in America: Yuma in Arizona Territory, Jefferson City in Missouri, Huntsville and its prison farms in Texas.

Because long before that, Harry Fallon had spent ten years in Joliet, Illinois—for a crime he had not committed.

"You hungry?" Fallon asked his daughter.

"I'm always hungry," Rachel Renee said.

"What time is it?"

"Five-thirty," Christina answered. She started to rise. "I'll get some . . ."

"No." Fallon pushed himself up. "You two snuggle or at least get a few minutes more of sleep. I'm wide awake. Let me make some breakfast."

Christina smiled, and the baby girl crawled back to her mother, hugged her, and Fallon pulled up the sheets and blankets over them. He kissed Rachel Renee's forehead and looked into the hard eyes of his wife.

He kissed her forehead, too, pulled back, and mouthed, "I'm sorry."

Christina just nodded.

And Fallon walked out of the bedroom and closed the door.

One more time.

If this kept up, he realized, he wouldn't have a wife or a child with him.

He could blame that on the American Detective Agency, the prison system in the United States, and the men who had framed him and tried to ruin his life.

Tried? Hell, his life was still ruined, even five years after being pardoned. After being told he was free, with an appointment as U.S. marshal for the district of Wyoming.

Fallon knew what most prisoners knew. Once you had spent time behind the iron, you never could be completely free again.

CHAPTER THREE

Situated on the high, rolling plains of southern Wyoming, Cheyenne was a nice city, although it had taken Fallon a while to get accustomed to a land where trees came hard to find. He still remembered the shade and thickness of the woods around Fort Smith—similar to his boyhood stomping grounds of Gads Hill in southern Missouri. But the city of Cheyenne itself was remarkable. The Union Pacific Railroad connected it with East and West; it had industry, cattle, the Army at Fort D. A. Russell. Mansions could be found, for once a Western man or woman found wealth, he or she saw no reason not to flaunt it. Railroad workers, cowboys, and soldiers on payday could make things difficult for the local lawmen, but drunks and brawlers were not the business of a federal lawman.

Lawman? Fallon didn't feel much like a peace officer these days. A United States marshal didn't enforce the law. That's what all the deputies he hired were for, which had been the case back in Arkansas and the Indian Territory when Judge Isaac Parker and the U.S. marshal for the Western District of Arkansas including the Indian Territory had hired a green kid, onetime cowboy and hell-raiser named Harry Fallon as a deputy marshal. In those days, Fallon risked his life to bring in whiskey runners, bank and train robbers, and more murderers than you'd find in the slums of New York or Chicago.

Keeping law and order was for young men, unmarried men mostly. Being the top lawman in the district, Fallon knew that a U.S. marshal was appointed by the president of the United States and confirmed by the U.S. Senate. His job required kissing babies, making speeches, and every now and then talking to the U.S. attorney, taking federal judges out to supper, and on the rare occasion, saying howdy and how ya doin'? to the deputies who risked their lives chasing men who had broken federal—not local—laws.

After making his family breakfast, then shaving and attempting to make himself presentable, Fallon left their home in pressed white shirt with four-ply linen collar, dress suspenders from Montgomery Ward & Co., a sateen Windsor tie of angled black and white stripes, and tailor-made suit of navy blue worsted wool, complete with a monogrammed gray silk handkerchief poking out of the breast coat pocket, and a solid gold watch stuck in the pocket of his matching vest. The whole rig had cost him what he made in a month herding cattle. His hat was a dark cream with what the hatmaker called a "velvety finish," six-and-a-half-inch crown, creased in the side and dented on the top, with three-and-half-inch curled and trimmed brim, with leather band.

The only thing he really liked were the boots, the

old Coffeyville style he had worn as a cowboy and deputy marshal, although these had been made by a saddlemaker near the depot. They fit like a glove. Even had spur ridges on the heels, although Fallon couldn't remember the last time he had been on the back of a horse. He walked from his home to the office, unless the snow came down hard and he could hire a hack to take him wherever he needed to go in town. Or the train if, for some rare reason, he needed to travel to Laramie, Rock Springs, or Washington, D.C.

Removing his hat when he stepped inside the office, he climbed the stairs to the second floor of the federal courthouse and made his way down the hall, turning in to the office.

"Good morning, Helen," he told the secretary, and moved to the coffeepot on the stove.

"Hank," she said. Only Fallon's friends called him Hank, and Helen was a good friend. "How was your weekend?"

"Fine," he lied. Filled a cup, turned, held the pot toward her. Grinning, she lifted her steaming mug, saying, "I beat you to it."

He hung his hat on the rack by the door.

"There's no need for that, Hank," Helen said.

He sipped coffee. She was a good-looking woman, not as beautiful as Christina, and Helen would make a fine U.S. marshal herself. Probably could, since Wyoming had granted women suffrage decades earlier. Helen did the paperwork, kept track of the schedules, and even helped some of the deputies with arrest reports and requests for warrants. Fallon would be lost without her.

"What am I doing today?" Fallon asked.

"Speaking to the Abraham Lincoln Academy." That was the all-male private school on the Union Mercantile Block for mostly wealthy kids, although they always brought in a few poor boys, so they would look better, especially if the poor kid could play good baseball. "Watch your language. The headmaster is a Methodist."

"Do I have time to finish my coffee?"

She held up the newspaper in her other hand. "You even have time to read the *Daily Sun-Leader.*"

An hour and a half later, Helen straightened Fallon's tie and handkerchief, dropped the newspaper in the trash, stepped back, and asked, "Can you do me a favor?"

"Probably, if it's legal."

She handed him an envelope. "Deposit my check for me."

He took the brown envelope with his left hand, looked at it suspiciously, and said, "It's payday?"

"Already. End of the month. I put yours on your desk. Did you just read the paper?" She frowned. "Tell me you did work on what you're going to tell those future lawmen at the academy."

"I saw the envelope," Fallon said. Last month, his check had remained on the desk two weeks after it had been issued, until Christina asked for some shopping money, and he realized . . . well . . . it was hard to explain to women, even men, who had never been in prison. They didn't let you have money in the pen. Men bartered with tobacco, or illegal whiskey, a handmade weapon, something to read—for those who weren't illiterate.

Helen shook her head. "Stockgrowers' National Bank," she told him as he slipped the envelope into the inside pocket of his fancy coat. "You remember where it is?"

Fallon nodded. "I've done this for you . . . how many times?"

"Usually, though you have forgotten a time or two."

"Well," he said. "That's because I'm not used to people trusting me with their money. I am an ex-convict."

"My understanding is that you were pardoned."

"Yes." He patted his coat. "But we can be led astray."

"I'll see you after your speech." Helen walked back to her desk. "Give them heck, Hank."

This was another thing hard to get used to. Back in Fallon's day, school was a *McGuffey's Reader* and a paddle with holes cut in the hindquarters-hitting part. Most of the boys didn't wear shoes in the spring and fall, because most of them didn't have shoes except during winter. Typically, there would be two or three empty seats, for some of the boys wanted to go fishing or squirrel hunting or to hang from the ties over the trestle and see who would drop into the river last when the train rumbled by. During spring planting or fall harvest, more desks would be empty, because the boys had to work.

At the Abraham Lincoln Academy, the boys were dressed in smaller versions of Grand Army of the Republic dress suits, sitting ramrod straight, heads up, paying strict attention. Usually, a Harry Fallon speech would put half the audience to sleep, and Fallon always wished he were asleep, too. But not here. The headmaster and his two teachers stood at attention, rarely blinking, and the teachers held rulers as though sabers at arms.

Eventually, Fallon finished his talk, and asked if anyone had a question.

A hand shot up from the blond boy with big ears on the front row. Once Fallon nodded to him, the boy stood, cleared his throat, and asked, "How does one become a United States marshal, sir?" He promptly sat down.

CHAPTER FOUR

How does one become a federal marshal?

Fallon grinned as he thought about how he could answer that question.

Well, son, first you ride herd with a cowboy with a wild streak and a taste of John Barleycorn. You're young, going to live forever, feeling invincible, and you drink far too much one evening in Fort Smith, Arkansas. And your pal, Josh Ryker, sees a saddle in a window that he figures he ought to have, but since he doesn't have any money, he decides to steal it. And you try to stop him, and next thing you realize is a lawman has shown up, and you're in the middle, and then Ryker is about to kill the lawman. That's right. Murder a man in cold blood—all because of one saddle. And while plenty of preachers and doctors and professors might tell you that only time will sober you up after a night of drinking forty-rod and cheap beer, you know for a fact that you are stone cold sober. And you stop Ryker. And suddenly you're in jail, and the dungeon at Fort Smith is as bad as a lot of prisons.

This you'll learn. In time, you'll become an expert on prisons.

So somehow, because you saved the life of a peace officer, and a lawman with connections, you're standing before Judge Isaac Parker, who is offering you a job. Take the badge, pin it on, and you'll be earning a living—if you aren't killed—as a federal lawman. Oh, but since you're just in your teens, you'll just drive the jail wagon. Tend to the prisoners as the real marshals make the arrests and risk their lives. Till the deputies you're tending jail for wind up getting cut down by cold-blooded killers, for murdering, heartless, soulless men populate the Indian Nations just west of Fort Smith. And something comes over you, and you're not going to let them get away with it. The next thing you're sure of is that you're bringing in the jail wagon to Fort Smith, with the dead and condemned criminals, and suddenly the U.S. marshal, the U.S. attorney, the other deputy marshals, and even Judge Parker look at you differently.

You're not just a kid. You're a man. And now a bona fide deputy marshal.

So it goes. Till you meet a lovely woman. She happens to stay in the same boardinghouse as you do. And you marry her. And she brings you the joy of your life, a daughter. And you start reading law with a highly regarded defense attorney, because even Judge Parker says that a young man with a future and a wife and a baby doesn't need to be risking his life chasing the scum of society. The West will be won by lawman, but mostly by law. And good lawyers are needed.

Sure, you still ride after the badmen, though you're never sent against the real killers. Till one day you find yourself accused of a holdup. Not enough evidence to get you on the murder charge, but you are convicted of a crime that you did not commit. Judge Parker, though, well he thinks you're not only guilty—since the jury found you guilty—but also a Judas. Throws the book at you and then some, but others must weigh in, and Parker agrees that sending a crooked lawman to the Detroit House of Corrections isn't justice.

They put you in the darkness of the Illinois pen in Joliet.

That's where you are when you learn that your wife and baby girl have been murdered.

What can you do then? Just turn hard, because you have to be hard, uncompromising, to make it out of Joliet alive. You learn what it takes to survive prison. You ask for no quarter, and you never give any quarter. Just get through one day, then live through the night, and watch it start over again. Day after day, week after week, month after month, year after year.

Until Joliet witnesses one of the bloodiest riots in U.S. history. And some guards are begging for you to help save them. You don't care a whit for these guards, most of them no better, often a whole lot worse, than the men they're keeping out of society. But there's that one thing you haven't been able to shake. Human decency. You thought you had lost it, but it comes back to haunt you. So you help the guards. Save their lives. And when the riot is over, the governor issues you a parole.

Up to Chicago, you're told, room in a boarding-house, work for a wheelwright—what the hell do you know about that?—and make sure you never break the terms of your parole, because if you do, they'll ship your bruised hide back to Joliet to serve the rest of your sentence—ten years or so—in full.

But when the hack takes you to see Lake Michigan—just because you're a partially free man and might as well do something free people can do— you're hijacked by a hood who you arrested before, a hood called Aaron Holderman who now is an employee of the American Detective Agency, headquartered in Chicago, rival of the Pinkerton National Detective Agency.

And that's where Sean MacGregor, a little redheaded Scot who likes smoking bad cigars and intimidating everyone, tells you a story. He knows who killed your wife and child, and he'll help you get revenge, or justice, but only if you help him out first. It's just a little assignment. Go to Arizona Territory—fear not, the warden and his associates at Joliet will get nothing but positive reports on your progress as a parolee—get arrested, get sentenced to the territorial pen, make friends with a brutal felon who happened to steal a fortune and cached it somewhere south in Mexico. Break out of Yuma with the cold-blooded killer. Find the stolen loot, recapture or kill Monk Quinn, and let the American Detective Agency reap the glory.

You do your job. Mostly. Survive the hellhole that is Yuma. Break out of the joint. Travel to Mexico with a hard lot of hardened criminals. And wind up back in Chicago, only somehow—because you have a sense of poetic justice—you let the Pinkertons reap the glory of returning Quinn's fortune to its rightful owners.

MacGregor gives you another assignment, and

this one is tougher than Yuma. You wind up at the Missouri state pen, more than forty acres covered in blood, and discover the perfect murder-for-hire scheme. The warden and some associates have prisoners who they'll let slip out to kill someone. Hey, who would ever suspect a man behind bars of killing people outside of the prison? And one of the men, now deranged, you realize is the hired killer who murdered your wife and daughter. But when that assignment is over, another riot has helped in the justice department, and all of the principles are dead. Including the Mole, the man who killed Rachel and Renee, but the man who also saved your life.

But there's one more job you need to do. One more payoff Sean MacGregor owes you. The Mole did the murder. But someone hired the Jefferson City swine to see that murder done. And that takes you to Huntsville, the "Walls," as nasty as a prison as you'd dream in your worst nightmare.

Inside the Walls, you learn another system, you deal with the leader of the inmates, the notorious John Wesley Hardin, and then you learn about another prison scheme. They send you to one of the farms that lease prisoners from the state to do labor. Cheap labor. And in this case, under the direction of a Confederate sympathizer, who, decades after the Rebellion, wants to start a new war, form a new Confederacy, and is using convicts to help him create an arsenal and an army.

This time, though, the American Detective Agency has given you some help. MacGregor's son, Dan, is part of the operation. So is a female operative named Christina Whitney. She'll be posing as your wife. And

Aaron Holderman has been hired as a Huntsville guard, not that you can trust Holderman.

But you survive this one, too. And you see the fiend who betrayed you, who let you read law with him, who loved your wife and wanted her for his own—and when he couldn't have her, he had your beautiful family killed.

You get more revenge, too. You see Sean MacGregor and Aaron Holderman sent to prison. You find yourself pardoned. Free. And appointed marshal of Wyoming. And when you're sitting at the train depot in Chicago, waiting to start a new life for yourself, lovely Christina Whitney sits down beside you. She has a ticket to Cheyenne, too.

But happily ever after?

Not with those nightmares. But, well, you do have a job. And that, son, is how at least one man becomes a United States marshal.

Hell of a way to get there, boy, don't you think?

CHAPTER FIVE

"In my case," Fallon answered with a smile, "I owe my appointment to Adlai Stevenson. I've never met the former vice president, but he, as a former representative from Illinois, where I spent some time . . ." Fallon grinned, wondering if the students might ask him how and where he might have spent time in the great state of Illinois. ". . . he had heard and read a lot about me. Thus, he made the recommendation to then-President Grover Cleveland, who appointed me to the position here, and the United States Senate unanimously confirmed my appointment."

He paused, smiled his politician smile, and added, "I have, by the way, briefly met our current vice president, Mr. Theodore Roosevelt, and although the appointment of a federal marshal is political, I would like to think that, as a Western man and a brave man—as seen from his actions on San Juan Hill with his Rough Riders—Mr. Roosevelt might have recommended me to President McKinley, even though they are Republicans and Mr. Stevenson and President

Cleveland were and are Democrats. We are all Americans, and we all seek justice."

Damn, Hank, he thought, these kids can't even vote. Tone it down. This isn't a campaign speech.

Another hand shot toward the ceiling.

"Yes?"

A pimply-faced redhead, shaped like an oversized string bean, stood as though at attention in front of his desk. "Sir, how dangerous is it being a United States marshal?"

And before Fallon could thank him for that question, the boy had moved back into his desk.

"Well, son . . ." Fallon shook his head. As a U.S. marshal, you might eat bad chicken, get sick from that, or have to pretend you like some representatives, even the governor. He got asked that question a lot. Maybe one day, he'd answer it honestly. But today: "I'm glad you asked that question, son, because it gives me the chance to sing out praises for the real lawmen in Wyoming, those who risk their lives to keep you children, as well as Headmaster Hendricks and your outstanding teachers, Mr. Williams and Mr. Dietrich, safe. As the U.S. marshal, I have to hire deputies, and these deputies are bringing peace across our state. From our national park in Yellowstone to Rock Springs. Laramie. Buffalo. Rawlings. Casper. You might not know how big Wyoming is . . ."

"Ninety-seven thousand square miles," one boy shouted.

"More than ninety-seven thousand and eight hundred square miles," said another.

The blond in the desk just in front of Fallon said,

"Ninety-seven thousand, eight hundred and eighteen." Turned and stuck out his tongue at his classmates.

"Well." Fallon looked at the headmaster. "You certainly have an erudite group of young men here." Clearing his throat, he hoped he wouldn't have many more questions. "That's a lot of country. My deputies are patrolling it, but they are not alone. We are responsible for only federal crimes. For local crimes, there are brave lawmen working as town constables, town marshals, and deputies, keeping the peace in our towns and cities. As well as our county sheriffs and their deputies, who have jurisdiction outside of the town or city limits. As a United States marshal, or a deputy U.S. marshal, we pursue bank and train robbers, mail thieves, kidnappers, and counterfeiters. But you boys could do me a favor, and the next time you see anyone wearing a badge, thank them for what they are doing for you. You should also thank the men working out of our fire stations. Me? I'm usually just behind a desk or in a meeting or talking to fine young people like yourselves."

Another hand, another nod, another question.

"How many men have you killed?"

"Silas," Mr. Dietrich scolded, but Fallon shook his head and said, "That's all right, sir. I get asked that question all the time." Even at church socials and women's auxiliary league meetings.

"As a U.S. marshal," Fallon told the dark-haired kid in the middle of the room, "none. And most of my deputies have wounded or killed few felons. The West is changing. Lawlessness is on the decline. Maybe by the time you boys have been graduated from the Abraham

Lincoln Academy, you won't have need of as many marshals, sheriffs, and constables as we have today."

"Or prisons," a boy sang out without raising his hand.

Fallon straightened. "Or prisons," he said. "Absolutely. Especially prisons."

He waited. "Any more questions for Marshal Fallon?" the headmaster asked.

Fallon was about to thank the boys for their attention and praise their questions when a small, dark-skinned boy in the left rear corner raised a timid hand. The headmaster appeared not to notice, because he started to tell the class to thank the marshal and show their appreciation by . . .

Fallon cut him off, "Excuse me, sir, but I think we have one more inquiry." He pointed at the small boy. "Go ahead, son."

The boy lowered his hand, swallowed, slowly rose, but kept his head down. Fallon noticed Dietrich tensing. The boy's suit didn't fit as well as the others', and his shoes weren't shined to a shining buff. He looked to be part, maybe all, Mexican, maybe half-Indian or something like that.

"Yes?" Fallon prompted.

"Could you . . . help . . . my Papa?" Fallon barely heard the lad.

He did hear Dietrich. "Carlos!"

Fallon raised his hand. "It's all right, Mr. Dietrich." Some of the students began sniggering, but Fallon cleared his throat, and that silenced the entire room.

"He is in prison," young Carlos said. Tears began rolling down his cheeks. The headmaster started for the boy, and so did the other teacher with a ruler that Fallon knew had smacked many a knuckle. But Fallon cut them off, and moved fast—spend enough time behind prison walls, and you knew how to beat a guard to a spot—and knelt on the floor. "Go on, son," he said, and looked back to make sure the adults came no closer.

"Which prison?" Fallon asked. "Laramie?"

"Yes," the boy whispered.

Fallon waited.

The boy wiped his nose and whispered. "His name is Carlos. Like me. Carlos Pablo Diego the Fourth. I am Carlos Pablo Diego the Fifth."

"All right," Fallon said. "Tell me about your papa."

The boy sniffed again. "He has been in the prison for *tres* years. Three. They said he stole a horse, but, señor marshal, he did not steal a horse. He is a good man. Can you help him, *por favor*?"

Fallon put both hands on the kid's shoulder, squeezed them, and said, "I'll see what I can do, Carlos." He guided the boy back into the desk, stared at the adults until they moved back to their respective guard towers, and began patting his pockets for a pencil and paper, but all he could find was the envelope with Helen's check. He sighed.

"Anybody got a pencil?" he asked.

The blond know-it-all at the front quickly jutted a finely sharpened pencil toward Fallon, who took it with a thank-you and wrote the prisoner's name on the envelope and the words: LARAMIE PRISON. HORSE THIEF. The pencil was returned, and Fallon found his hat.

"Any more questions?" The headmaster's tone let the boys know that if they asked anything, heads would roll.

After the unison *Thank you, Marshal Fallon,* and

clapping hands, the teachers escorted the boys out of the room to another classroom, and the headmaster came to Fallon.

"I'm sorry about Carlos Diego, Marshal. He's one of our charity cases."

"Is he an orphan?"

"No," Hendricks said. "His mother has four other kids. She washes clothes at the laundry behind the Inter-Ocean Hotel. Cooks breakfast at the café on Thirteenth. Still couldn't afford to send her son to our school, but we like to do good deeds, and we've never had a Mexican in the Academy before. Wanted to give it a try. See if we couldn't straighten him out before he follows in his papa's boots. Kid couldn't speak more than three words of English till we got him here a year ago."

"I see." Fallon slipped the envelope into his coat pocket and stared hard at Hendricks, the Methodist with the hard-shell nature of a Baptist, and a headmaster with an iron rule. "He speaks pretty good English now."

"Yes, well, I happen to head our English department. But believe me, he was a challenge." Hendricks tried to smile. "Anyway, Marshal, I'm sorry the little boy asked such an improper question for your visit. Besides, well, I'm sure every prisoner in Laramie says he is innocent."

Fallon placed his hat on his head and waited until Hendricks looked him squarely in the eye. Which did not last as soon as Fallon told him: "Well, Mr. Hendricks, sometimes an innocent man gets put in prison, you know."

He spit the gall out of his mouth and into the trashcan by the door before seeing himself out of the Abraham Lincoln Academy.

CHAPTER SIX

"Stop here, driver." Sitting in the back of the surrey, Fallon happened to see the Stockgrowers' bank as the hack clopped down the stone-paved street, another sign of Cheyenne's prosperity. There was a time when Fallon prided himself on his memory—a key attribute when you're a lawman in the Indian Territory, or a prisoner anywhere—but those instincts had faded during his years making speeches and signing his name on countless documents stuck behind a desk.

The driver pulled on the reins to stop the mule.

"I remembered I need to drop something off at the bank," he explained to the old black man and fished out some coins. "Here you go, sir."

"Wouldye like me ta wait fer ye, Marshal?"

"No need, my friend. I can walk to the courthouse from here. Thank you, and have a good day."

The driver looked at the coins, and beamed, "Thank ye kindly, Marshal."

Fallon stepped down, pulled his hat tight, and saw a man wearing a rain slicker leaning against the column of a saloon, one arm tucked inside the orange-colored material, smoking a cigarette. Fallon looked up. Not a cloud in the sky, but it had sprinkled some last night, and the cowboy did stand in front of a saloon that had not closed its doors, legend had it, for twelve and three-quarter years. Turning to cross the street, he looked back at the cowboy once more, and then waited for a buggy and a farm wagon to pass.

The hitching rail in front of the Stockgrowers was full, and another cowhand worked on the cinch of his Appaloosa gelding at the far right. He wore a linen duster, more common this time of year than a rain slicker. As Fallon started across the street, he saw another man, this one working a pocketknife on his fingernails as he leaned against the wall in the alcove of the bank. He wore a long frock coat, trail-worn from too many years either during the winter or rolled up behind a saddle.

Maybe he was a Texan, because anyone who had spent time in Wyoming wouldn't consider this cold. Fallon glanced back at the dude in the slicker as his boots clipped on the stones. He studied the rest of the street. It was a slow time of year and a slow time of day. But the bank was doing booming business.

All right, Fallon told himself. The federal and state employees had been paid. Probably some ranchers had paid their cowboys, too. But how many cowboys do you know that save any money? And how many would have an account at the Stockgrowers? A linen duster . . . that made sense? A frock coat or a rain slicker? Those could be used to hide a shotgun. Or a rifle. And even the greenest cowboy didn't take that long to cinch up a saddle. The man cursed, tried the latigo again.

Drunk. Fallon decided that would explain it. Left his horse at the bank because the rail was full in front of the saloon last night when he rode in. No. No, not if he's a cowboy. A cowboy wouldn't walk across a street. He would have found a rail at the apothecary . . . or the hotel . . . or most likely left the Appaloosa in the livery at the corner. And that horse was too well-blooded for a thirty-a-month waddie to own.

Fallon reached the boardwalk, looked down the street from the bank. Empty. His mind raced. One man with the horses. Another near the bank door. A third across the street with a rifle. Five horses tethered to the rail. Three men outside. Three in the bank. The fellow across the street would have his horse closer, and Fallon spied a brown Thoroughbred at the end of the hitching rail in front of the saloon.

His eyes raced up and down both boardwalks. Naturally, there wasn't one Cheyenne policeman to be seen.

You're getting too damned suspicious in your old age, he told himself. Jesse James was dead. The two surviving Younger brothers were behind the iron in Minnesota. One Dalton was in Lansing, and his brothers and the other gang members were all buried in Coffeyville. And that Hole in the Wall Bunch would never even try to rob a bank in Cheyenne. It was too damned big.

He waited for a gray-haired woman to stop and enter the bakery. The boardwalk on this side now empty for two blocks, Fallon turned back and headed past the hitching rail. The fellow stopped fidgeting with the saddle and let his right hand disappear inside his duster. Fallon just noticed the buckle to a belt that undoubtedly held a holster, or likely more than one.

He noticed the scabbards of three of the saddles to the mounts tethered to the rail were empty.

Then Fallon stepped into the alcove and reached for the handle to the door.

"Hey, pops," the man in the frock coat said with a smile and holding out the cigar he held in his left hand. "Can I bother you for a light?"

The man at the hitching rail stepped away from the horse, one hand still underneath the duster.

"I don't smoke," Fallon said.

"I do." The man clamped the cigar with his teeth, and held out a box of matches in the fingers of his left hand. His right hand remained underneath the heavy coat. "Light my cigar, old man."

Old man? Fallon didn't care for that. He might have been old enough to be this punk's daddy, but that didn't make Harry Fallon old.

"Light it, bub, or dance," the man said. And he let his coattail slip back just enough to reveal the sawed-off shotgun in his right hand.

Fallon stepped close, took the tiny box, and pushed it open. The first match he dropped, feigning nervousness, and stuttered an apology.

"There's plenty of matches, pops," the kid said. "Take your time. And smile. Our business will be finished directly."

"I wish," said the man by the horses, "they'd hurry up and get her done."

The match flared in Fallon's hands. Cupping the match against the wind, he brought it toward the cheap cigar.

"That's right," the man with the shotgun said. Then

he blew out the match as Fallon inched it to the stogie's tip. "Oops. Try again."

Fallon's eyes hardened, but so did the kid's.

"You ever seen what a body looks like after it's took two loads of buckshot in the belly at point-blank range?" the punk asked with a malevolent grin.

More times than you have, pup, Fallon thought, but found another match.

His mind raced. Break the punk's neck, take the shotgun, and cut loose on the man pretending he didn't know one end of a cinch from another. The horses would be rearing, probably pulling loose. He'd have one barrel left if one of the three inside the bank came out, and the horses rearing would protect him from the lookout across the street. Pick up the pistols from one of the two men he had killed, maybe a rifle if the man with the duster hid one of those, too. He'd have a chance at least, and the ruckus would bring the policemen and everyone with a gun outside their businesses. Cheyenne, Wyoming, was a major city, but most of the entrepreneurs here were westerners to their bones, and they didn't take kindly to men robbing them or their neighbors.

But . . .

Fallon struck the match.

That would leave citizens inside the bank with two, possibly three—if no one stepped outside to escape after the first bit of gunfire—hardened killers. Hardened. Fallon was sure of this. These weren't boys on a whim. This had been well-planned and completely professional. Three men inside. Three outside. On a day when the bank's vaults would be filled with cash and coin.

He had to wait until all the bank robbers were outside.

The match moved to the cigar. The punk grinned like a clown this time and let the flame come to the stinking cigar. The kid sucked, the flame grew, the tip began to smoke and glow. Fallon heard the door open.

"It ain't lit yet," the punk managed to say as he puffed and clenched his teeth. Fallon glimpsed a man in a bowler as he hurried by carrying grain sacks. Another, with a saddlebag over his shoulder. The third, last man, with a rifle pointing inside. He shot a glance at the punk and Fallon, and then warned the bank employees and any customers not to stick their heads outside.

The man held the door open.

"Throw him inside, Whit," the one with the Winchester said, and looked at Fallon. "Once that door closes, buster, it better not open or we'll riddle this building with so much lead, you'd think we had a Gatling gun."

The man hurried to his horse.

Whit, the punk, said, "You heard Mabry. Inside."

CHAPTER SEVEN

Fallon brought the match down and stuck the tip against Whit's throat.

The punk yelped, and Fallon slammed the palm of his left hand against the kid's jaw, then slid the forearm past his neck to the crook of his arm. Twisting, Fallon pulled Whit against his body. The shotgun clopped onto the wooden planks, and Fallon used his right hand to reach down, found a belted revolver, and he pulled it, thumbed back the hammer, and saw Mabry turning around, cursing.

The .45 bucked in Fallon's hand, and crimson exploded from the gray vest the outlaw wore, just above his waistband. Two of the men were already mounted, and as Mabry twisted from the impact of a lead slug in his belly, he triggered the Winchester, the bullet splintering the post of the hitching rail. That sent the horses screaming and the two already carrying riders bucking.

Mabry was down on a knee, head bent, blood pouring from his mouth. The one who had been pretending to cinch the horses ran toward Fallon, pulling a double-action Smith & Wesson from his holster and dropping his Winchester.

"Nooooo!" Whit tried to scream, and Fallon shoved him toward the duster-wearing horse holder as the .44 bucked three times, turning Whit around, and another slug shattered his spine. Fallon was diving now, triggering the Colt, hitting the horse holder in the shoulder and sending him stumbling into the street. Two of the horses had broken their tethers and stormed down the street. Fallon landed, came up to his knees, grabbed the shotgun, and eared back the hammers.

A bullet tore through the crown of his hat, knocking it off. Fallon caught a glimpse of one of the men shooting recklessly from the saddle of his bucking horse. He saw the other had managed to get his horse under control. That's the one Fallon drew a bead on and touched one of the triggers to the scattergun. The man was blown out of the saddle, his arm slamming the other rider somehow in the face, and sending him crashing to the pavement. Then both men disappeared underneath horseflesh and the acrid, biting white smoke from the shotgun. The horses ran, the one belonging to the man Fallon had killed heading up the street, toward the courthouse, leaving a bloody corpse on the pavement. The other horse, a black Thoroughbred, galloped the other way, out of town, dragging its rider—his left foot hung up in the stirrup—behind him for two blocks, leaving a trail of blood and gore until the socked foot slipped out of the boot, and deposited another dead man in front of Blessingame's Funeral Parlor.

Fallon sat up, bracing his back against the wall of

the Stockgrowers' bank. A bullet splintered the wood inches from Fallon, and fragments of wood stung his face. That would be from the man in the slicker, across the street. Fallon had one round left in the shotgun, but buckshot wouldn't travel that far. Fallon looked at the rifle that Mabry had carried, contemplated his chances of getting it. Two bullets hit the wood then, one shattering the window and another tearing a whole in the left sleeve of Fallon's expensive coat. Fallon saw the horse holder, standing, aiming, touching the trigger of his Smith & Wesson, realizing it was empty, and pulling another gun from a second holster. The man across the street fired again, but his bullet dug a furrow into the boardwalk. Fallon triggered the shotgun again and saw the horse holder catapulted four feet into the street.

He rolled over then, tossing the shotgun away, grabbing the Winchester, and diving as far as he could. Another bullet whined off the street. Fallon saw the man, halfway in the street, levering the rifle. Fallon came up and dived again, this time landing behind the water trough in front of the grocery next door to the bank. A bullet tore through the heavy wood, showering Fallon with water. He rolled onto his back, levered a round into Mabry's .44-40, and caught his breath.

The lookout in the slicker fired again. The plate glass window to the grocery shattered.

Fallon swallowed, tried to figure out his best action. Which side to go to or come up over the top.

Then, a woman's voice cried out, "You gol-dern hoodlum. Take this."

What sounded like a cannon roared, and then all

Fallon heard were the shrieks of men and women, and someone ringing a fire bell, and horses and feet clattering down the boardwalks and on Cheyenne's paved streets of its main business district.

Fallon used Mabry's rifle to push himself up, and he saw the man in the rain slicker lying spread-eagled on the street. Fifteen feet away, in front of the saloon, stood the owner of the saloon, red-headed and rouge-faced Ma Recknor, holding a smoking Greener shotgun in her hands, her yellow teeth clamped on her favorite brand of cheroot.

"Want a drink, Marshal?" Ma Recknor called out. "It's on the house."

Fallon tried to say, "no thanks," but nothing came out. He shook his head instead. "If you change your mind, I'll be having mine," Ma said, and pushed her way through the batwing doors.

He reached for his hat that wasn't there, leaned Mabry's rifle against the water trough, picked up his hat, stuck a finger through one of the holes the bullet had made, and examined the carnage.

Mabry was dead on the boardwalk. Three feet away lay Whit in a pool of blood. Two men were crumpled on the street in front of the bank. A trail of blood and brain matter on the stones led to the corpse in front of the funeral parlor, and the sixth was blown to pieces in front of the saloon.

What was that question one of the kids had asked at the Abraham Lincoln Academy? What had Fallon thought about answering, "I've never killed any man as a United States marshal"? . . . Well, that couldn't be his answer from here on out.

* * *

The city's street department was busy at work cleaning up the carnage. Chief of Police Derrick Mc-Gruder snuffed out his cigarette on the splintered hitching rail in front of the bank and asked, "Harry, how the hell could you kill all six of these outlaws and wind up with just a scratch on your cheek?"

Fallon sipped the coffee the banker had brought him.

"Ma killed the one across the street," Fallon told him. "Not me. I didn't kill the one the horse dragged to death, either. The fellow I blasted with the shotgun accidentally knocked him out of the saddle. The kid there, ripped to pieces with that Smith & Wesson, he got killed by his pard, but I guess I killed his pard."

"So three men instead of six?"

Fallon swallowed. "Hell, Derrick, I don't know. It happened so fast."

A deputy held a Pinkerton National Detective Agency description to Mabry's face, and looked at McGruder. "It fits Big Burl Mabry to a T, Sheriff. Man, this'll be something to tell my wife about tonight."

"Speaking of which," Fallon said, "can you send someone over to my house, let Christina know I'm all right?"

"Your wife shouldn't be worried, Harry," McGruder said. "This wasn't a job for the U.S. marshal."

"Any gunfight, Christina will likely figure I'm in the thick of it." He smiled without humor.

"Richard, go over to the marshal's house. Tell Mrs.

Fallon that her husband is fine, that there's no danger, that everything's all right."

"Should I tell her everything?" the deputy asked as he rose and handed the Pinkerton paper to his boss.

McGruder looked at Fallon, who hooked a thumb toward the Cheyenne reporters running all over the street, talking to witnesses. "She'll find out soon enough."

"You heard him," McGruder told the deputy, and added, "But tell her she has permission to shoot any newspaper reporter in the buttocks if they bother her."

The deputy was gone. McGruder shoved his hands into his pockets and shook his head. "There will be a coroner's inquest, you know. But I can assure you it'll end there. You'll be due some reward money, too."

"No," Fallon said. "Give it to Ma Recknor. Hadn't been for her, I'd be among the dead, too, most likely."

"Hell of a thing," McGruder said.

"Hell of a thing," Fallon agreed. "You done with me? I need to get back to work."

"Work?" McGruder laughed. "Harry, you're a wonder. I was thinking if it's too early to drink."

Fallon tilted his head across the street. "Ma's buying. Have one for me." He shook McGruder's hand and headed toward the courthouse.

CHAPTER EIGHT

Helen was talking into the telephone when Fallon stepped back inside his office, and as Fallon removed his hat, he heard her say, "Christina, he just walked through the door. On his own two feet." She held the earpiece to him, and Fallon closed the gap and moved closer to the big box on the wall.

Another sign of the new century about to unfold, the telephone felt strange in Fallon's hand. He cleared his throat to let his wife know he was on the other end.

"Hank." The voice didn't sound like Christina, just some mechanical crackle, and the line hummed in the background. "The Widow Walkup just rushed to the door, and told me that you were involved in a bloody gunfight in Recknor's beer hall."

Of course. The Widow Walkup. Biggest gossip in the neighborhood, probably in all of Cheyenne, perhaps the entire state of Wyoming.

"You should confirm her report with an eyewitness," Fallon said. "Mrs. Walkup being one of Carrie Nation's most ardent supporters."

"That is what I am doing now."

Fallon sighed. "Well, they were robbing the bank, not the saloon."

"Rachel Renee thought someone was shooting firecrackers, asked if it were the Fourth of July. I told her firecrackers and Roman candles only look pretty at night. And, since I can tell the difference between firecrackers and rifle, pistol, and shotgun blasts, somehow, I figured you were right in the thick of it."

"Yeah." Christina had a lot of experience with the American Detective Agency. "Is Rachel Renee all right?"

"She's coloring."

"On the walls again?"

"The floor. In her bedroom."

Fallon smiled. "Good. It's cheaper than a new rug."

The line buzzed. He could picture Christina leaning against the foyer wall. The U.S. solicitor and the governor had insisted that Fallon have a telephone installed in his home, being an important man and all. Fallon didn't even know how to work the damned thing.

"Are you all right?"

"Yes. I am fine."

"How bad?"

He drew in a deep breath, held it, exhaled, and said, "A bullet hole through my hat. One through the coat. Scratch on the cheek."

"How big is the hole in your cheek?"

"It's just a scratch. Like I cut myself shaving."

"Uh-huh."

Helen had ears like an owl. She said with a smile, "It's not even worth a bandage, Christina."

Fallon said, "Did you hear that?"

"Barely," Christina answered, "but I trust Helen."

"I asked McGruder to send a policeman over to tell you that I was all right," Fallon said.

"You could have done that yourself."

He nodded, realized she couldn't see, and said, "I know. I just didn't want to make a big fuss over this."

"Honey, the Widow Walkup said fifteen men are dead in the streets."

"I'm not that good," he said and pictured her smiling.

"I don't know, sweetheart. Remember, I've seen you at work."

"Yeah. There were six. Ma Recknor dispatched one. A frightened horse took care of another. One got in the way of his pard's gun. Which leaves three, if my math is correct."

"Yeah."

"Yeah. You didn't mention any plans to ambush a gang of bank robbers when you set off to work this morning."

"I just happened to be heading into the Stockgrowers' at the time. Pure luck."

"Luck."

"Yeah. Luck."

"Harry Fallon, I think you're the luckiest man I've ever known."

"Because I'm married to you."

Her laugh sounded musical. "Flattery will get you forgiveness. And I'll tend the cheek wound free of charge. The hat and coat, those will cost you. And remember, if I were at the bank, and not you, I wouldn't have needed a horse or a bank robber to assist me. But everyone can use Ma Recknor."

More static, then Christina said, "Well, I think

McGruder's policeman finally found where we live. Someone's banging on the door anyway. I have to go." She yelled to the front door, but Fallon couldn't make out the words.

"I'll see you tonight. What do you want for supper?"

"Bourbon," he said.

She laughed. "You don't drink."

"I've half a mind to start."

"How about mutton and potatoes?"

"That would be fine."

"Harry?"

"Yes."

"I love you."

His smile widened, and he felt warm. Helen shook her head and whispered, "Tell her the same. It won't make you less of a man."

"I love you, too," he said, glared at Helen, and hung the speaking piece into the cradle.

"That didn't hurt at all, did it, Marshal?" Helen said.

Fallon shook his head. "What's the rest of my day like?"

"There are warrants to look over. Piled high on your desk."

He turned to the office, but Helen called him back.

"Did you happen to deposit my check for me?"

"Oh." Fallon swore, apologized, and reached inside his coat pocket. "I'm sorry, Helen. But what with the—"

"Hey, darling, I'm glad you didn't. Had those boys made off with my check, my landlord would be screaming for his rent money again." Fallon was fishing out the envelope, which he laid on her stack between newspapers and her own coffee cup. "Bank's probably closed the rest of the day anyway," she said. "I'll try to drop it off on my way to work tomorrow morning."

"It might still be closed," Fallon said.

"Yeah, but I'll get to count the bullet holes with the boys skipping school."

She poured Fallon a cup of coffee, and said, "You might want to scrub the blood off your cheek before you go home, by the way."

When Fallon reached the door to his office, he turned around and called out Helen's name. When she looked up at him, he said, "If any newspaper reporter stops by . . ."

"You're not in the office, not at home, and no one knows how to reach you." She winked.

With a smile, Fallon stepped inside his ornate office, closing the door behind him.

Forty minutes later, Helen tapped on the window, and then gently opened the door. "Hank?" she called out.

Setting the pen he had been using in the holder, he waved her in, and pretended to be massaging his right wrist. "I could use a break," he said.

She grinned briefly, but then slid an envelope onto his desk. "Hank," she said, "this is the envelope that had my check in it, but I noticed your scribbling on the back."

Fallon snapped his fingers even before he glanced down. There was his unruly scrawl.

Carlos Pablo Diego IV . . . horse thief . . . Laramie prison

"Right," he said. "I almost forgot a promise."

"Well," she said, "you have had an unusual day."

Yeah, he thought, but had you known me back when I was riding for Judge Parker, you wouldn't know just how regular a day like today would have been— except for talking to schoolboys about law and order on the frontier of the United States of America.

He grabbed the pencil and wrote the name down on a pad next to the warrants and other correspondence he had been signing for what felt like all day.

His eyes went up again. "What's the name again of the new warden at the state prison in Laramie?"

"State prison." Helen shook her head. "I'll always think of it as the territorial pen."

"Wyoming has been a state since 1890," Fallon reminded her.

"I know. Jackson is the warden's name. M. C. Jackson."

Fallon thanked her and scribbled the name down underneath the name of the father of the Mexican kid from the Abraham Lincoln Academy. He looked up again and said, "I don't suppose our telephone wires stretch all the way to Laramie, eh?"

"We haven't reached the twentieth century yet, darling."

"Good." Fallon exhaled. "I know how to send a telegraph."

"But"—Helen pointed her chin at the copy of the newspaper Fallon had tossed, unread, into the wastebasket—"if you would ever take time to read the paper, *all* the paper, you might have noticed that Warden Jackson happens to be in the capital talking to our governor about the need for a new prison, perhaps in Rawlings."

"He's still in Cheyenne?" Fallon asked.

"There are meetings with legislators tomorrow, and a speech to the women's auxiliary Wednesday. I guess being a warden is a lot like being a United States marshal. Except for gunfights in front of banks."

"Do you know where Jackson is staying?" Fallon inquired.

She shrugged but said, "If I wanted to guess, I'd say the Inter-Ocean Hotel."

"You wouldn't happen to know what the phone number there is?"

"I can look it up. And, unlike you, I can even ask Mr. Bennett, our fine, upstanding operator, to ring the hotel for you. What's the message?"

CHAPTER NINE

A heavyset man with white mustache and beard, well groomed, and bald on the top of his head, M. C. Jackson pushed himself from his seat, which took great effort, because Jackson was obese, to the extent that he had to request a chair without arms to sit to his morning feast.

Fallon handed his hat to the man in the fancy suit and let another younger man, also dressed for a wedding or funeral, lead him to Jackson's table, even though that was far from necessary because Jackson was waving and booming, "Fallon. Over here. Have a seat. The bacon is worth dying for."

After thanking his guide, and shaking Jackson's clammy hand, Fallon settled into his seat, which had arms. Jackson had to ease himself down and quickly began sawing the thickest slices of bacon Fallon had ever seen while another young man in a suit appeared as if by magic at Fallon's side.

"What would monsieur like for breakfast today?" the boy asked. Monsieur? The Inter-Ocean Hotel deserved its reputation . . . for being overpriced and pretentious.

"Coffee," Fallon said. "Black."

Jackson, with a fancy napkin rammed inside his paper collar and dangling like a turkey's wattle to his waist, managed to swallow half a pig. "Fallon. Order what you want. The state prison funds will be paying for this."

"Coffee's fine," Fallon said. "Christina made my breakfast this morning."

"Very well," Jackson said, but when the waiter started to leave, he raised his head. "But I'll have two more fried eggs, son, and a big slice of toast with that huckleberry jam that tastes so divine."

Eventually, the waiter returned with Fallon's coffee, and that at least gave him something to do while the hog in front of him tackled the plates and bowls before him with great zeal. There was no break for conversation until the last morsel was finished—and before the servers returned with two more fried eggs and toast with huckleberry jam. As Jackson wiped his mouth with the napkin, Fallon set his cup on the table, a signal that he was ready to talk, too.

"Wonderful. We don't get food like that in Laramie and at the prison." He laughed.

"I trust your meetings are going well," Fallon said.

"Indeed. Now, your charming secretary yesterday said you wanted to talk to me, so here I am, at your service."

But the service had to wait because the eggs and toast arrived. It was a good thing, Fallon figured, that he didn't have anything overly important on his calendar this day.

"I hear"—Jackson began mopping up the remnants of his eggs with a chunk of toast—"that there was some sordid gunplay on the streets of Cheyenne late yesterday morning."

Fallon sipped more coffee, cold now. "I read something about it in the newspaper," he said.

Jackson swallowed, found some water, washed it down, and wiped his mouth again. "I detest newspapers. The ink gets on my fingers."

And you probably lick off the ink, Fallon thought. *Hell, buster, you'd eat anything.*

"Alas, my understanding is that those eight men won't be serving any time in Laramie. Dead. All dead. Shot down like the dirty dogs they were."

"There were only six," Fallon said.

Jackson looked up.

"According to the newspaper," Fallon said.

"Well." The last morsel of food vanished. "Be that as it may, how can I help you, Marshal?"

Fallon pulled the paper from his inside coat pocket and found a place on the table not covered with dishes. Christina had written the name in her wonderful cursive this morning before Fallon left for his meeting with the warden.

"One of the inmates at the Big House Across the River," Fallon said, using the nickname for the big stone building. "Carlos Pablo Diego the Fourth."

Jackson read the name. "Horse thief." His jowly face rose to meet Fallon's stare. "Is he wanted for some federal crime as well as stealing horses?"

"Not that I know of," Fallon said. "Just a routine investigation. I'm just looking for any information you have, trial details, the crime, what kind of prisoner he has been."

Jackson watched a waiter carrying a tray of food to another table, ran a tongue over his lips, and turned back to Fallon. "Well, you do understand that I have only been at the Wyoming State Prison for three months." He chuckled. "And we have a substantial number of convicts." The laughter resumed. "Business is good for the state prison these days, Fallon, but, well, business is always good. Otherwise men like you and I would have no job at all." Once he could control his chuckling, he said, "Let me just point out that I really do not know this Juan Chico character."

"Carlos Pablo Diego the Fourth," Fallon corrected.

"Yes. We do not have many bean-eaters in the Big House," Jackson said.

"Then you could find out a bit about him with no problem."

"You just seek the routine information. That is my understanding. Am I correct?"

"Yeah. Whatever files you might have on him. Maybe ask a guard what kind of prisoner he is."

"Well, Fallon, since I am on an expense account, I can send a telegraph after my meetings at nine-thirty, ask my assistant to relay the information directly to you. Would that be satisfactory?"

"I thank you in advance." Fallon stood, extended his hand, shook, and left the fat man to his bill.

The man at the front door was examining the bullet holes in Fallon's hat.

* * *

Rachel Renee was bouncing on Helen's knee when Fallon walked into the office after his dinner meeting—which, he thanked the Almighty, had not been with Warden M. C. Jackson.

"Papa!" his daughter exclaimed.

Fallon's face brightened. "Hey there, Tiger. What brings you to the big city?"

"Ma wanted to see you," the girl said. "Look at me. Doesn't Miss Helen make a good pony?"

Fallon didn't know quite how to answer that one, so he grinned and saw Helen pointing her chin to the office as her leg kept bouncing his daughter.

Christina sat behind Fallon's desk.

"You were lucky," she told him, and pushed herself up. "He was arrested in Laramie County. The trial was right here in Cheyenne. Three years ago."

Three years. The boy had been right. Fallon moved around the desk and saw the papers on his desk. He picked up a piece of paper, the judge's sentence, noting the date.

"You found all this out this morning?" Fallon asked.

She shrugged.

"Surely the American Detective Agency doesn't have a file on Carlos Pablo Diego."

"I doubt if the Pinkertons do, either, not for a one-time horse thief. I just sniffed around in the county courthouse. You said the boy said he'd been in prison three years, so that gave me a starting point."

Fallon wet his lips, shook his head. "I don't remember the trial."

"Why would you?" Christina said. "A routine horse thief. Like you said, it's not a federal crime, not your jurisdiction. As far as I can tell, even the *Sun-Leader* did not run any account of the trial. How was your meeting with the warden?"

"Sickening." Fallon found another paper, looked over it at Christina and said, "One more breakfast with that hog, and I'm not sure I'd ever be able to eat again."

She slid a piece of yellow paper toward Fallon. "This struck me as rather interesting."

Fallon picked it up. "He pled guilty."

Christina nodded. "Halfway through the trial."

"Ten years. Ten years for stealing one horse. And after pleading guilty." Fallon shook his head. "That must have been one hell of a horse."

"And not a hell of an attorney." She slid her finger to a name. "Remember him."

"Morrison." Fallon sighed. "A blithering idiot."

"Who doesn't speak Spanish," she whispered.

Their eyes met. Fallon understood. The headmaster yesterday had said that the boy did not speak one word of English when he started attending the Abraham Lincoln Academy. Which meant, almost without question, that Carlos Pablo Diego IV spoke exclusively Spanish during the trial.

"A plea deal," Fallon said.

"Right," Christina said. "He probably feared they would hang him for stealing a horse."

"Even though horse theft has never been a capital crime," Fallon said. "Anywhere."

"Tell that to ranchers and cowboys in Wyoming," Christina said. "Or anywhere in the West."

"Was there an interpreter in the courtroom?" Fallon wondered aloud.

"Apparently," Christina said. "They don't name him, or her, in any documents I found, but you know what court records are like. Especially at the county level. But in the loose transcript"—She picked up a stack of three pages, shuffled to the second page, and began to condense the translation—"he said he walked out of the smithy and saw this horse that had wandered out of the corral. He was bringing the horse back to the livery, thinking it might have wandered from the corral, or one of the stalls, and that's when a cowboy busted his head with the butt of a pistol."

"Did the cowboy testify?"

Christina shook her head.

"The livery owner?"

Her head moved again.

Fallon muttered a curse. "My guess," Christina said, "is that Morrison, idiot that he might be, would have had both men outside the courtroom as witnesses."

Fallon picked up the thought. "And the prosecutor and the judge decided that, so as not to risk an acquittal, they would get Diego to plead guilty."

"Probably pay Morrison a little for his troubles, too," Christina said.

He found the indictment, jotted down the name of the livery stable where the arrest had taken place, and the name of the deputy sheriff, then wrote down the names of Morrison and the judge, and started to write the prosecutor's name as well, before remembering that he had been run over by a streetcar three months earlier.

Fallon stood, kissed his wife on the lips, thanked

her, and moved to the door. "Marshal . . ." Christina said as the door opened.

When he turned, Christina said, "It's not federal business."

"I know. But I made a promise. That makes it *my* business."

CHAPTER TEN

It felt good. Real good. Fallon hadn't felt this way in years, at least, not professionally. Sure, when he had married Christina, and when Rachel Renee was born, those were wonderful times, but as a United States marshal, Fallon had been playing politics, trapped behind a desk, putting his John Hancock on documents and letters, giving speeches, playing that absurd game. Now he found himself with a purpose.

And his nightmares had stopped. He had started sleeping in his own bed again, not on the chaise. Two nights ago, after Rachel Renee had go to sleep, Fallon had made love to Christina.

Christina was helping, too, and Fallon believed she was feeling revived, motivated, more like a full-fledged contributor to society and not just a homemaker and mother. She probably had been longing to do something like this for five years. So they worked together, or separately, tracking down facts, witnesses, and documents.

Two weeks later, he sat inside his office, looking over what kind of documents he had. Helen tapped on the door, then pushed it open. "You have a visitor," she said. Her face told Fallon that it was someone he did not likely want to see. "The warden," she whispered. "And he has company, supervisor Hector French."

Fallon nodded grimly. In some ways, he had expected this call, although he expected Warden M. C. Jackson to send him a nasty telegraph and not bring in the state attorney general in as a reinforcement, so Fallon slid his papers to his left and said, "Send them in."

He stood as the fat man and the slim, erudite, distinguished gentleman with silver hair and a well-groomed mustache walked inside, with Helen closing the door behind them.

"Warden," Fallon said, extending his hand. "Hector." He shook hands with both men, waved at the jury chairs in front of his desk, and settled into his chair. "It's an honor to see you. What can I do for you?"

"You have been meddling in my affairs, sir," the fat warden said.

"Really." Fallon leaned back.

"That Mexican is not the concern of the U.S. marshal. He was convicted in a county courtroom."

"I wasn't aware there are boundaries for justice," Fallon said.

"If you want to become warden in Laramie, you will find an opening soon," Jackson said. The man's face had turned so red, Fallon thought he might keel over from a stroke or heart attack at any second. "I have put in for the job of superintendent at the federal penitentiary at Fort Leavenworth, Kansas. They are building a new prison there, you know."

"You seem to be moving from state to federal," Fallon said.

"Hank," Hector French intervened. "What do you have regarding this inmate . . ." He looked to Jackson for a name.

"Delmonico," Jackson said. "Carlos Delmonico."

"Carlos Pablo Diego," Fallon corrected. "Delmonico is a restaurant." He wasn't sure if the jab at the warden's obesity registered with M. C. Jackson, but the grin on French's face said at least one of the visitors understood.

"Yes, yes, yes. Diego." Jackson had to find a handkerchief to wipe his sweaty face.

"The Fourth," Fallon added.

"What do you have, Hank?"

Fallon slid the papers to the center of the desk. Jackson tried to stand, but couldn't without effort, and by the time he had pulled himself halfway out of the chair—it had arms, and the fat lout barely managed to squeeze between them—French had taken the stack and was finding his spectacles.

"He pled guilty, Hank." French looked over his bifocals.

"I know," Fallon conceded.

"You can argue points of law," French said, "look at improper evidence, perjury, bits of law. But a confession . . . a guilty plea. What brought all this about?"

"His kid asked me to look into it," Fallon said. "He's a student at the Abraham Lincoln Academy here in town."

"And you did, of course." French grinned, shook his head, and found another document.

"Heck," Fallon said. "To be honest with you, I thought

it would be a waste of my time. Figured I'd check it out, realize the man was behind bars for a good reason, and go about my business. But the more I looked into the matter, the more I smelled a rat."

"I resent that remark, sir," the fat man whined.

"I was not talking about you," Fallon said quietly.

"You're talking about taking away one of my prisoners!"

"Shut up," French said. He scanned the page, slid it back to the desktop, and looked at another paper.

"Have you interviewed Diego?" French asked.

The warden guffawed. "He doesn't even speak English, the damned greaser."

The room turned quiet. Hector French removed his eyeglasses and slipped them back inside his vest pocket.

"Exactly," Fallon said, and slid two signed affidavits in front of the attorney general. The spectacles came out of the vest pocket, and this time French sat down to read. When he finished, he leaned forward and put the papers back on Fallon's desk.

"These men did not testify?" French asked.

"Diego pled guilty, ending the trial."

"The interpreter?"

Fallon shook his head. "From what Christina and I have learned, you and I speak better Spanish than he does."

French grinned. "Christina's working on this one with you?"

"Once a private detective . . ." Fallon shrugged and smiled slightly.

M. C. Jackson tried to squeeze out of the chair, which Fallon hoped the fat man did not break.

"What's your next step?" French asked.

"Cross some T's and dot some I's," Fallon said. "Find an interpreter and head down to Laramie to visit Diego in the Big House. See what he has to say. If it feels right, then I bring it to you."

French nodded, then shook his head. "Ten-year sentence. For horse theft. After a guilty plea. Must have been a damned fine horse."

"That's what Christina and I thought."

French stood, helped pull the obese warden out of the chair, and shook Fallon's hand. "Keep me posted on this, Hank," French said. "I don't like thinking of innocent men behind bars." His eyes locked on Fallon. "Do you ever think about that, about the men you arrested?"

"I didn't," Fallon answered. "Until I wound up in Joliet."

"Yeah."

Jackson decided to say something. "Well, Diego won't be my problem once I get the job in Leavenworth."

"And you won't be my problem, either," French said, and moved to the door, opened it, and called out, "Let me know if you need anything, Hank. Jackson, I suppose you'll be joining me for dinner."

"By all means," the warden said, and lumbered through the door.

"My lucky day," French said, and closed the door after the fat man exited Fallon's office.

During his forced, and, thankfully, brief, employment —or imprisonment—with the American Detective

Agency, Fallon had been an undercover officer, not a detective, but now he kept putting together evidence—hoping he might have enough to present to a judge and the attorney general, and see about getting Carlos Pablo Diego IV out of the Big House Across the River in Laramie.

Four days later, he decided it was time to travel to Laramie, meet with the warden, get an interview with Diego, and see what he would tell. Christina had found an interpreter, a cook at one of the small cafés in Cheyenne that catered mostly to cowboys. Two round-trip train tickets to Laramie and back for Fallon and Señora Rodriguez. They could do this on the cook's day off, no hotel, since Fallon was paying for this on his own.

He stood before Helen in the outer office, asking his secretary if she could telephone the train depot, see about getting those tickets for Monday, when the door opened, and Attorney General Hector French removed his bowler.

"Hank," he said. "Helen." His face was grim. "Got a minute?" he asked Fallon, and already was moving to Fallon's office.

"Would you like a cup of coffee, Hec?" Helen asked.

"No."

Fallon frowned, entered his office, closed the door, and saw the yellow telegraph paper that the attorney general held out for him to read.

CHAPTER ELEVEN

"It stinks," French said. "And I hate to bring it this way. But I figured . . ." He sighed.

Fallon leaned against his desk, shaking his head.

He looked at the telegraph, read it again, felt his stomach turn over, his heart sink, and he wondered if God was playing another joke on him or cursing him.

Carlos Pablo Diego IV, Convict Number 4231, was dead. Knifed in the back, throat slashed, in the exercise yard at the state prison in Laramie on Thursday afternoon.

"It stinks, all right," Fallon said and tossed the telegraph into the wastebasket.

French straightened. "Hank, I spent all morning checking this out, exchanging telegraphs with Jackson—"

"A gutless wonder," Fallon said, and swore bitterly.

"Be that as it may, but don't think this was some conspiracy. That's the first thing I thought, too, but M. C. Jackson is a fool but not an idiot. He wouldn't do anything that would hurt his chances of getting out of Wyoming and landing that federal job at Leavenworth."

Fallon sighed. "How do you figure it?"

"Diego was Mexican," French said. "You know what prisons are like, federal or state. Even that hellhole at Fort Smith, the jail, was no different. You got your Mexicans. You got your whites. You got the Negroes. And the Chinese. And none of them mix. By all accounts, Diego had made an enemy of a white convict, Easy Emmett Tanner, murderer and cattle thief. Tanner swore he would kill Diego, and he did. Two men witnessed the affair. The guards rushed in, but it was too late. They threw Tanner in the sweatbox. But they did not check him for any other weapons. He had another homemade knife, and he used that to cut his own throat."

"God." Fallon moved to the basket and spit out the bitterness. He ran his hands through his hair, tried to control his breathing, and spit again. "What the hell did Diego do to make Tanner so mad?"

"He prayed too loudly in his cell."

Fallon cursed softly.

"I'm truly sorry, Hank," French said.

Fallon sighed, shook his head, moved to the book cases. "Diego never should have been in that prison."

"I know."

"I should have moved quicker. Gotten him out of there."

"Hank, even if you had presented all the evidence to the governor, to me, to a judge, it would have taken us two weeks, maybe longer, before we could have overturned the court actions, the sentence. Maybe . . . just maybe . . . we could have gotten Diego to a safer place, maybe out of the Big House and into a county jail. But that wasn't going to happen in a hurry. The law doesn't move that fast. Prisons don't operate that quickly. We did all we could do."

Fallon nodded. "Yeah. But it's a waste."

"Yeah."

Their eyes met, held.

"Does his son know?" Fallon asked. "His wife?"

"I don't think so," French said. "I thought I'd find a priest, take him over to the shack or the school, break the news to them."

"I'll do it," Fallon said.

"Hank, that's not your job."

"Yes," Fallon said. "It is."

Christina seldom cried, but that night she did, but only after Rachel Renee had fallen asleep. Fallon hugged his wife tightly, told her none of this was her fault, that life sometimes didn't go the way it was supposed to. He laid Christina in the bed, kissed her forehead, and pulled the sheet and blanket over her.

Then he moved out of the bedroom.

"Where are you going?" Christina asked.

"I'd better sleep in the parlor tonight," he said. He did not look back at her, merely slipped out, closed the door, and walked to the chaise. He knew the nightmares would return. He knew a raven's *kaw*, or the rustling of the wind in the trees, anything like that would have him leaping out of bed, ready to kill some imagined inmate or guard coming after him—frightening Fallon's wife and baby girl.

The only way that wouldn't happen would be if he stayed awake all night.

He didn't. The meeting with the Diego family had exhausted him. And he was right. He woke up from the first dream a little after midnight. Two hours later, he fell back asleep, and the nightmares resumed.

When Fallon sat bolt upright on the chaise around four in the morning, he wiped his brow, swallowed, and said, "Welcome back to hell." At least he wasn't screaming. At least he had not awakened his wife and daughter. There was no use in trying to sleep anymore. Fallon moved to the winter kitchen, found the coffee grinder and the can of beans, and busied himself.

Two days later, the coffin carrying the remains of Carlos Pablo Diego IV arrived at the Cheyenne depot, and the funeral mass was held that afternoon. Fallon was there, hat in hand, along with Mrs. Diego, young Carlos, his two sisters and brother, and the headmaster of the Abraham Lincoln Academy. Young Carlos shook Fallon's hand, thanked him for all he had tried to do for his late papa, and helped his sobbing mother away. Two aunts and an uncle assisted with the children. Fallon paid the priest, nodded at the headmaster, and walked back to work.

Two weeks passed. Two weeks of nightmares and anxiety.

Hector French entered Fallon's office on a Thursday afternoon, and he brought company.

"Governor." Fallon rose from his desk and shook the hands of his two visitors.

"Hank," the governor said. "Hector tells me that

you already know about the job opening for the new federal prison being built in Leavenworth, Kansas."

Fallon nodded. "And I hear that Warden Jackson down in Laramie has his eye on that job." He made himself smile.

"It's not Jackson they want," the governor said. "It's you."

Fallon stared, realized he had not misheard, understood that the governor and French were serious. He felt like sitting down, but instead he said, "I've seen enough walls and bars in my day."

The governor pulled out a newspaper, slid it onto Fallon's desk. "You heard about the execution of Slim Boris."

Fallon had heard. Everyone in Wyoming had heard. The professional hanging of a condemned killer had been botched. Hell, even the hangman at Fort Smith had left men kicking at the end of a rope, but this one had ripped off Boris's head. But that had been in Rawlings. And it had been a state matter, not federal, so Fallon had not been obligated to attend the execution.

"And did you see this?" The governor tapped another headline.

Fallon nodded. "Helen says I never read the paper, just look over the headlines, but I can read. And I do read." That article had been picked up by the Cheyenne editor from the telegraphs. In Denver, a young man named McKee had been gunned down by lawmen because he could not stand to return to prison.

"Like I said," Fallon reminded his guests, "I've spent enough time behind the iron."

"Hank," Hector French said. "The way the governor

and I figure it, Leavenworth needs you. The prisoners need you. Justice needs you."

Fallon laughed without humor. "You boys are crazy. And I don't think you do the hiring for the Leavenworth pen."

"No," the governor said. "But we know who does. And those boys have been asking about you. That Carlos Diego story made *Harper's Illustrated* and the *New York Herald*. People are starting to think something might be wrong with a prison here and there. And I think those people are right. You ... you could make a difference."

"Talk it over with Christina," French said. "You've got a couple of days to think it over."

"Otherwise," the governor said, "M. C. Jackson will most likely be moving to Leavenworth. Good for the state of Wyoming. Not so good for the boys locked up in Kansas."

"Well." Christina stirred sugar in her coffee cup. "How much does it pay?"

Fallon shrugged. "Not much more than this job."

"Well, Rachel Renee is young enough. It's not like we'd be uprooting her. Besides, she likes having adventures."

Shaking his head, Fallon twisted in his chair in the dining room and stared out the window. "I'm not sure I could be a warden."

"You weren't sure you could be a U.S. marshal, either, the way I remember it. But you have been a good one."

"Maybe," Fallon said. "But the wardens I met—"

"Were not," she interrupted, "Harry Fallon."

He smiled.

"You owe it . . ." Christina started.

Their eyes held. "To Carlos Pablo Diego?" Fallon asked.

"To Harry Fallon," she said. "I think you could make a difference. Better than Jackson."

"Well," Fallon said. "It could be the feds have already found their man."

"I think they have." Christina reached across the table, found Fallon's right hand, and gripped it. She squeezed. "And his name is Fallon."

PART II

CHAPTER TWELVE

"Is it always this windy here?" Christina asked the waitress at the quaint Leavenworth, Kansas, café near the Missouri River.

"Chil'," the gray-haired, stout woman told her, "'T'ain't even windy dis afternoon."

After they ordered coffees to start and a lemonade for Rachel Renee, the waitress walked to the kitchen.

"Don't they call Chicago the 'windy city'?" Fallon grinned. "And isn't that where you grew up and worked?"

"It's a different kind of wind." Frowning, Christina sniffed, then sneezed, and a sigh followed that.

"I thought Cheyenne was windy." Rachel Renee bounced in her seat, staring after the waitress, eagerly awaiting her lemonade.

Christina reached inside her purse and withdrew her handkerchief one more time. She blew her nose.

"Are you sick, Ma?" Rachel Renee asked.

"I think"—she sniffed again—"I think . . . I must have . . . a cold."

"It's called hay fever," Fallon said.

"It's a cold," Christina insisted.

They had arrived in Leavenworth, Kansas, late yesterday morning, found the house they had rented on the western part of town, and basically spent the day unpacking. Fallon had not even been by the federal penitentiary, either the old one or the larger one being built. He was supposed to check in on Monday. Today was Saturday. After getting the house arranged to something Christina could live with, and getting all of Rachel Renee's dolls and other toys arranged to her liking, they had decided to see what all Leavenworth had to offer.

It was bigger than Fallon remembered, but he had not been to the city in years. Like most places, it had grown. Brick buildings dominated the business district, a trend Fallon was seeing as the new century approached. Western towns had learned that wooden buildings burned, and when one caught fire, quite often the whole town went up in smoke. Red brick had replaced whitewashed facades. Many of the streets were paved. The streetlights were gas. Telephone and telegraph lines gave crows and other birds a place to watch the bustling of a thriving town.

One of the reasons Leavenworth thrived, of course, was because of the military fort—and the federal prison.

The Army and crime were always good for a booming economy.

The waitress returned with their drinks. Christina greeted her with yet another loud sneeze.

"If de cedars don't gets you, den de weeds will," the old woman said. "Dis time of year be the worse fer pure mis'ry. Dat's what dey ought to call this town. Spring Mis'ry. Best thing dat could happen would be if de river was to flood. I mean of Jesus in the wilderness proportions. Cover us underwater for thirty days and thirty nights."

"Forty," Rachel Renee corrected, and Fallon thought that Cheyenne's Bible school had come in handy.

"Even better," the waitress said. "Eat honey, ma'am," she told Christina. "Only cure we got, 'cept fer drownin'."

"You don't seem to suffer," Fallon observed.

"I eat honey. By de gallons. Ya might as well jus' call me Queen Bee. Y'all new here?"

"Yes," Fallon said. "Just moved."

"Figured. What with her askin' 'bout de wind, and now sufferin' the mis'ry of March. What would y'all care to have fer dinner?"

"Honey," Rachel Renee sang. "It's sweet."

They ordered the special, fried fish and onions, but the waitress brought out baked bread and two jars of local honey first. Rachel Renee filled up on so much bread and honey she barely touched her plate. Fallon figured his daughter was the smart, and lucky, one. The fish, at least his, was mostly bones anyway, and he could scarcely taste the onions because of all the grease. He had figured, this close to Missouri, he might have something resembling a home-cooked meal. But he had found some bad cafés in Cheyenne, too, and this was pretty much their first foray into Leavenworth. The city was big enough.

He paid his check, grabbed his hat, and escorted

his wife and daughter to the front door, which swung open, and three men entered. They blocked the exit.

"Hello, Hank," the weasel in the middle said.

Only my friends call me Hank.

The weasel was a runt, standing no taller than five-foot-five, and that included the cowboy boots he wore with their two-inch heels. He wore striped trousers, a plaid shirt, moth-eaten vest, stained bandana, and trail-worn slouch hat. The eyes were too far apart, his left earlobe was missing, his face was pitted with scars, and his nose had been broken countless times. He carried an old Colt tucked inside his waistband.

To the weasel's right stood a stout man, the kind Fallon usually saw working in a blacksmith's shop. The only thing missing was a smithy's apron. He had huge arms that strained the sleeves of his cotton shirt, a thick beard of blond hair stained on one side by years of tobacco juice. Fallon saw no gun, not even a sheathed knife, but with arms that size, he figured, this leviathan wouldn't need one.

The last man was tall, wiry, dressed better than his two pards, but nowhere near clean enough for a Kansas church. He wore a belt gun, a shiny, nickel-plated pistol holstered butt forward on his right hip. Probably a southpaw, Fallon figured, but the Smith & Wesson must not be his preferred weapon, for he held an iron rod and kept tapping one end against a calloused right palm.

The welcoming committee, Fallon thought.

"Do I know you?" Fallon asked the weasel.

The weasel's grin revealed several missing teeth and more that a dentist would consider a lost cause.

"Name's Jenkins," the weasel said. "Buster Jenkins."

Fallon's mind searched, but came up empty.

"Sorry, Buster. I don't recall the privilege of meeting you."

"Choctaw Nation. You arrested me." His left hand rose slowly, carefully, and the pointer finger traced a thin scar from the part in his hair to the center of his forehead.

He didn't look that old, Fallon thought, but it was hard to figure out the age of a man as dirty as this one.

"I arrested a lot of men," Fallon said. "But, congratulations. You're out of jail. Now, if you'll excuse me."

"Buster," the waitress called out. "I don't want y'all wreckin' dis place. Y'all take yer business outside."

The men did not move.

"What's going on, Papa?" Rachel Renee asked.

"Christina," Fallon said tightly, "go on home. I'll see you in a bit."

"You sure?" his wife said.

"Yeah." He had sized up the men. He would not need Christina's assistance with these three, and he didn't want his baby girl to see her papa at this kind of work. Fallon nodded at the weasel. "If you'll step aside, let my family go home. They have a lot of unpacking to do."

"They might wanna pack up," the burly man said, causing the thin one with the pipe to snigger.

But they did step aside, though the weasel warned Christina, "Don't go after no law dog. Just go straight home."

"I thought we were gonna see the town," Rachel Renee said. Christina scooped up the girl.

"We are," Fallon said. "After I finish my business with these . . . gentlemen. I'll be home in a jiffy."

"In a box," the weasel whispered with a malevolent grin as they stepped aside to let Fallon's wife and child leave the restaurant. The one with the pipe turned sideways to watch through the window as Christina and Renee moved down the sidewalk.

"Where they headin'?" the weasel asked.

"West," the thin one said.

"Might find a law dog down," the big brute said.

"This shouldn't take long," the weasel said.

"I'm gonna call de police," the waitress bellowed, "if ya don't take dis outside."

Fallon realized that the restaurant was empty of paying customers. The cook stepped out of the kitchen. Fallon could see him through the reflection in one of the windows with the shades partially drawn to keep out the sun. His eyes turned briefly, but this side of the street wasn't crowded. No one passed by, and Fallon realized how late they were getting out of the house. The dinner rush was long over. Not a peace officer to be found anywhere.

"Would you three like to take this matter outside?" Fallon asked, trying to sound respectful, or at least, courteous.

"Nah," the weasel said. "A copper would likely interrupt our getting-reacquainted party."

"I see." Fallon's mind began racing. "So . . . Buster Jenkins. Remind me of how we met."

"Choctaw Nation. I was runnin' whiskey."

Fallon's head bobbed. "A popular diversion."

"Yeah. So was eighteen months in Detroit."

"Well, you've been out for some time. I haven't been a deputy marshal in Fort Smith for years and years."

"We know," the weasel said. "You was a big-time law dog in Wyoming. Now you's gonna be runnin' a prison. The big one here in town."

Fallon nodded. It struck him that Buster Jenkins was not aware of what had happened to Fallon some time after Jenkins had been sent to the Detroit House of Corrections. That Fallon had spent ten years in Joliet. That Fallon had then worked as an operative in three other prisons. He figured Buster Jenkins did not even know about the gunfight Fallon had been in the middle of during the bank robbery a few weeks back.

"Been readin' 'bout you," Jenkins said.

"I didn't know you could read," Fallon said. "Did they teach you that in Detroit?"

CHAPTER THIRTEEN

The expression on Buster Jenkins's face was exactly what Fallon was hoping for. So was the laughter from the big brute. That's why Fallon threw the first punch into the jaw of the thin man with the iron bar.

That was the most dangerous man, Fallon estimated, and the one that needed to be dispatched first.

The blow sent the man turning, dropping the piece of iron on the floor, and bending over while spitting out teeth and blood. Fallon kicked him hard in the buttocks, catapulting him through the plate-glass window. Shards of glass showered the floor inside and the boardwalk outside as the man disappeared from view.

"What the hell—" was all the weasel could say before Fallon whirled, swinging a haymaker with his left that caught the side of the weasel's face and powered him over an empty table and crashing into two chairs. Body and furniture rolled over the floor.

Fallon backed up quickly, avoiding the rushed swing from the burly man, who glanced at Buster Jenkins as he tried to push himself off the floor, only to bump his head against another table. He roared in pain, in frustration, and kept rising, overturning the second table—and that one had not been cleared of its plates and glasses, which crashed into hundreds of pieces on the floor.

By then Fallon had picked up the iron bar the skinny one had dropped on his way through the broken window. Fallon shot a quick glance. That man had not emerged, but Fallon knew he would need to keep an eye out for him, for that one carried a holstered revolver—and Fallon figured he knew how to use it. Buster Jenkins also had a gun, but he was so mad, so shamed, so shocked by Fallon's initial attack, he appeared to have forgotten that he had a pistol stuck in his pants.

People across the street stared at the café.

Fallon brought the bar up, like a bat, and swung.

He could have aimed for the big man's head or neck, but Fallon had no interest in killing anyone today. This was not a prison riot, a brawl. This was not—at least for the time being—a fight with hardened men with a kill-or-be-killed attitude. This was just, well, a little welcoming party from three thugs who thought they could have a little fun, get some revenge, by whipping the arse of a former lawman. They didn't know Harry Fallon.

To men like the weasel and his pards, a deputy U.S. marshal never threw the first punch, never initiated a fight. They were paid to keep the peace, maintain law and order. They didn't start brawls, especially in respectable businesses in a thriving, law-abiding community like Leavenworth, Kansas.

They did not know Harry Fallon. Not at all. They

did not know what Fallon had been doing for much of his life. Being a federal lawman in the Indian Nations had taught Fallon a lot about staying alive—but being in Joliet, in Yuma, in Jefferson City, and in Huntsville had taught him much, much more.

The gunfight outside the Stockgrowers' in Cheyenne had revived those almost dormant instincts after all those years pushing papers and pens across his desk as a U.S. marshal. Fallon wasn't quite as rusty as he might have been.

The bone in the big man's thick arm snapped loudly. In fact, for one brief instant, Fallon thought the thin man had found his revolver and had fired a shot. But the blond-bearded giant screamed loudly and reached out with his left hand. That's when Fallon lowered the rod, tapping the floor with one end, then quickly jerked it up, catching the brute between the legs, right in that sweet spot.

His mouth widened like his eyes, and he sucked in a silent breath as what little Fallon could see of his face began to whiten. Fallon let go of the bar, stepped in close, and threw four quick punches, driving the man into the first booth on the far wall. The man fell against the bench, slipped onto the floor, and began muttering nonsensical words, basically blubbering like a baby.

"You dirty dog." Buster Jenkins was standing now. And he remembered the gun in his waistband.

The weasel had the gun out, but the hammer was not cocked, when Fallon slipped between overturned furniture and buried a left in Jenkins's stomach. Jenkins's mouth opened, the pistol dropped onto the broken dishes, and Fallon stomped on the man's left foot with the heel of his own boot. His knee then came up, again connected with the groin, and at the same time Fallon pushed the weasel's head down while his knee went up again. Jenkins's forehead connected with the knee, and Fallon shoved him, unconscious, onto the floor.

Now Fallon whirled around, glanced at the big lug underneath the booth, mumbling like some blithering idiot. Fallon moved through the door, turned to his left, and saw the thin man on his hands and knees, still spitting out blood, shaking his head, likely wondering how this day had turned out so bloody wrong. A quick glance across the streets detected no police officers in sight, so Fallon stepped off the boardwalk and came up to the thin man's side. He jerked the still-holstered revolver from the holster, spun the gun around, and brought the walnut grips down on the thin man's head. The man let out a moan and fell onto the bloody planks of the boardwalk.

A whistle shrieked, but it seemed pretty far away, so Fallon returned inside the café, laid the revolver by the cash register, picked up the weasel's gun, and set it by the thin man's revolver.

The giant kept blubbering on the floor.

Fallon stared at the cook and the waitress with the gray hair. Massaging his knuckles, he spotted a booth on the other side of the café. His boots crunched glass and shards of crockery before he slipped into the wooden bench. Again, he looked at the small man with the dirty apron and the old waitress.

"Coffee would be nice," he told them. "I'm sure the peace officers will want some, as well."

Fallon was sipping coffee when the first constable arrived.

"What's going on here?" the mustached man asked the cook in a thick Irish brogue.

The cook tilted his head toward Fallon.

"My name's Fallon," he said. "Harry Fallon. I'm the new warden here. But these three men are for you. At least, for the time being."

Christina was reading a storybook to Rachel Renee when Fallon came through the front door. He rubbed his knuckles, but they were just scraped.

"Papa!" his daughter screamed with delight.

The book closed, and Christina said, "Well?"

"I don't think we should go back to that restaurant anytime soon," Fallon said, and knelt as Rachel Renee charged toward him, leaped into his arms, and he swept her up as he rose.

"It wasn't that good anyhow, Papa," Rachel Renee said. "The waitress didn't even bring me a lemon drop."

"Did you ask for one?" Fallon asked.

"No. But I never asked for one at Kate's place in Cheyenne, and I always got one. Can we go see the town now, Papa?" Rachel Renee pleaded. "You promised."

"I don't see why not," Fallon said. "It's what we planned to do all day. Although"—he smiled at Christina—"we might stay clear of the street closest to the river."

"That's fine with me, Papa," Rachel Renee said. "I want to find a place with toys."

Fallon kissed his daughter's cheek. "Well, Rachel Renee, we can look. But I don't think you need any new toys right now. But you might see if you like anything because your birthday will be coming up in a few months. And you have plenty of toys right now." His eyes found his wife. "And we might want to skip roast beef and steaks for a while for supper. Eat rather frugally. At least till I collect my first paycheck."

"They fined you?" Christina asked.

"Just damages," Fallon said. "I mean, I couldn't argue. I threw the first punch."

"And the last one, too," Christina said.

CHAPTER FOURTEEN

Since Harry Fallon had worked as a deputy United States marshal, he understood how slowly the federal government liked to work. Back in 1895, the U.S. Congress approved the construction of three federal penitentiaries, one in Atlanta, Georgia; one at McNeil Island in Washington State, although that prison had been around for decades now; and here at Leavenworth. Since state prisons were beginning to fill up, Congress and the president figured that the time had come to send enemies of the country— whether they were counterfeiters or smugglers or whatever—to serve time in a U.S. prison. They had been sent to state prisons, usually, to serve their time. Those who committed federal crimes in the Indian Territory usually got sent to the Detroit House of Corrections, although Fallon had been sentenced to his hard labor at Joliet, Illinois.

Leavenworth, Kansas, of course, had long been holding prisoners. It got its start back in 1827, when Henry Leavenworth, colonel of the Third U.S. Infantry, decided a new military post needed to be established right here, on the banks of the Missouri River, more than twenty miles from the Kansas River, a prime location to protect travelers on the newly opened Santa Fe Trail. For decades, though, the fort had served as a supply depot to frontier posts from Kansas to the Rocky Mountains.

Soldiers often weren't the most law-abiding men on the earth, and a lot of men in uniform got into trouble with higher-ranking men in uniform. Guard houses, like post hospitals, were usually full up. And for more serious offenses, a military prison was needed. So back in 1875, the United States Military Prison, also established by Congress—back in 1874—began, starting out in an old supply building that had been fitted with cell blocks and iron bars. Three hundred inmates were incarcerated there a year later.

So when the Secretary of War decided in 1894 that the Army no longer needed a prison just for offenders of military matters, Congress transferred the overseeing of the military prison at Fort Leavenworth from the War Department to the Department of Justice.

Which could have been the end of things, but, no, then the House Judiciary Committee started meeting, and the committee said that the old structure at the fort just no longer was suitable, and that's when Congress said that a new federal penitentiary had to be built in Leavenworth. Land was allocated roughly two-and-a-half miles away.

There was a lot more going on during these meetings and votes with representative and senators and lawyers talking and dining and drinking. The Three Prisons Act did a lot to get the ball, and construction, started, but the act did not come up with any money to build those pens.

Fallon couldn't blame the citizens for that way of thinking. Imagine if the military got tired of keeping its post in Leavenworth. Army institutions, especially on the frontier, were shut down, and now that some scholar had declared the frontier of the United States officially closed back around 1893, the good folks in Leavenworth worried that if the post—the very same institution that had made many a businessman, particularly the saloon and brothel owners, wealthy since about 1827—departed, what would become of the city on the banks of the river? Would it turn into a penal colony like Australia? Would travelers across Kansas avoid it like they would a leper colony or Alcatraz?

Anyway, in 1895, the military prison became the United States Penitentiary, and embezzlers, murderers, whiskey runners on the Indian reservations, counterfeiters, perjurers (in federal cases), and men who used the mail to send naughty drawings or photographs found a hard cot and three meals a day.

Since March 1897, prisoners from the facility at the fort had been marched those two-plus miles to help with construction. It was still going after the warden got sick of it all and tendered his resignation. That opened up the job, which the warden at the state prison in Laramie, Wyoming, had his eyes on, until Harry Fallon had to open his big mouth and start the ball rolling, and found himself taking the job.

The plan was to put twelve hundred cells in the federal pen here. Five and a half feet wide, nine feet deep, ceilings about eight feet high, with a barred door and window at the front. Since the twentieth century would be dawning shortly, each cell would have water and even some of Thomas Edison's newfangled electric lights.

The United States government moved slowly. From Fallon's viewpoint, so did the prisoners building their new home. He thought about the inmates who had built most of what became the Missouri state prison in Jefferson City. There weren't nearly as many prisoners building in that hell box as there were here, but they got it done. Fallon's pa would have called that "a problem with your generation. You young whippersnappers don't know how to work anymore. If I was as lazy as your pals back when I was your age, my pa would've tanned my hide. And I'd tan yours, except you're bigger than me." He'd wink, but Fallon figured, deep down, his father was speaking exactly what he thought.

And Fallon, to be honest with himself, would likely agree with his pa. And the more he looked at the kids around him, in ten or twelve years, Fallon would be telling them exactly what his father had told him.

But not Rachel Renee, of course. Fallon's daughter was perfect.

Just like her mother.

Fallon moved over to the table where men looked down at the plans designed by a couple of architects from St. Louis. That firm had gotten the lush job of designing the federal pens at both Leavenworth and Atlanta. Fallon was already sweating, and he had to remind himself that summer had not begun. He wondered if he should have asked for the job on that island in Puget Sound. On a morning like today, waves and water sounded peaceful and cool. The Missouri River was mighty fine, but also ugly, smelly, and radiating heat and humidity.

"Is this the plan?" Fallon pointed at a blueprint spread across a table, snuff cans, scrap wood, rocks from the quarry, two hammers, and one saw placed at the proper points to keep the paper from being blown halfway to San Angelo, Texas.

A man in bifocals and bowler looked up. "Yes," he said in a nasal voice.

Fallon moved closer. He had done just a little preliminary investigating about what he was getting himself into. Now he saw the design for the prison here—if he lived to see it completed. Not that he thought he'd get killed in some riot or jailbreak. He had already helped bring back three escapees. But he might die of old age before this compound was halfway finished.

Frowning, Fallon said, "So . . . we're looking at something under a thousand acres all total."

The man pushed the spectacles up the brim of his nose.

"Seven hundred."

Fallon's head bobbed. Most of that was just land. Give the escapees plenty of land to run themselves out before they ever reached the high walls.

"This is the compound." Fallon tapped his finger on the blue print.

"Yes, sir."

"How many acres?"

"Sixteen. Give or take."

He slid closer, and looked at the design. "This is similar to Auburn," Fallon said.

The man cocked his head. "You have been to the New York state prison, sir?"

Fallon grinned. "Not that one. I put Sean MacGregor in prison before he could send me there. Or Alcatraz. Or Cañon City. Or Deer Lodge. Or . . ." He laughed in spite of himself. "But I've studied prisons, sir. From *The Count of Monte Cristo* to here."

The Auburn prison had been built even before Leavenworth became a fort. The prisons were cavernous rectangular structures. Two barracks to serve as the wall on one side, the south side, with smaller cell blocks stretching out from the rotunda like three spokes in a wagon wheel. Corridors shaped like horseshoes to connect the rear and central buildings. The theory was that would make it harder for any inmate to escape at night. Fallon looked at the walls, nodded.

The administration building would face the south, in the middle between the two long cell houses. The three radial cell blocks jutted out, coming close to the next monstrosity of buildings. Fallon tapped one.

"What's this?"

"Office and school," the man in the bowler said, and went on to show Fallon the dining hall, auditorium, commissary, kitchen, even an ice plant.

Fallon smiled. "The didn't have one of those in Joliet. Sure could have used them during the riots."

The man made himself smile and showed Fallon the storehouses and the laundry. Fallon tapped another structure.

"That's the dormitory," the man said as he moved his eyeglasses down his nose.

"Dormitory?" Fallon studied the young man. Where was he? A university like Yale or someplace?

"Solitary. You know, an isolation unit."

"Ah." Fallon shook his head. "Yes." He made himself nod. "Yes, Mister . . . ?"

"Baker, sir. Roy Baker. I work for Eames and Young." Those were the architects from St. Louis.

"Yes, Mr. Baker. Yes, I know all about solitary." His finger slid across the blueprint.

"That's the hospital." The man took charge, showing Fallon the planned powerhouse, the quarantine unit, a maintenance shop, laundry, a proposed shoe factory—Fallon knew all about those, too—and something Mr. Roy Baker of Eames & Young called "Industries." Fallon really didn't know what Industries would be, unless another place for slave labor.

"That's all there is, sir. That's all a prison needs." He grinned at his own joke.

"Very good, Mr. Baker," Fallon said, and looked at the young man. "What do you suppose we're missing?"

CHAPTER FIFTEEN

Roy Baker blinked repeatedly, looked at the blueprint, frowned, adjusted his eyeglasses, leaned closer, ran his finger all across the design, and finally, lifted his gaze, then the rest of his body, and cleared his throat.

"I don't see anything missing, sir."

Fallon nodded. "How about . . . guard towers?"

The man pushed back his bowler and looked at the blue print.

"Ummm . . ." he started.

Fallon used his finger for effect. He had always been a pretty good jabber. "Corners, obviously. There. There. There. And here. You'll want another here, in front of this gate. Not on top of the gate. About"—his finger moved—"here."

The architect, construction supervisor, foreman, whatever Roy Baker called himself, swallowed, and looked at the blueprint.

"Mr. Baker," Fallon said, authority in his voice now,

not the bemused tone of an attorney ridiculing a witness. "Don't you think you'd better mark these down?"

The young man's face paled. "Without . . . without sending a telegraph to Mr. Eames or Mr. Young?"

"Mr. Eames and Mr. Young aren't the wardens of this United States Penitentiary, young man. I am." Now the man's face revealed complete fear. "But when we are done, after you have put in the guard towers, you might want to send a telegraph to whoever is doing your job at the prison being built in Atlanta, Georgia. I don't know how the warden there wants to run his prison, but I suspect he'd like guard towers in Atlanta, too."

Fallon made one final stab with his finger. "And a guard tower here, at the front gate. But far enough from the wall." Fallon waited until Mr. Baker made the necessary adjustments—improvements—to the plan. Then he saw someone he was looking for and excused himself.

"Captain O'Connor," Fallon called out, and the big man stopped, turned, and glared. Fallon could have kept walking, but he stopped, crooked his elbow, and beckoned the big man toward him.

They had met when Fallon first arrived. Captain O'Connor, the mayor, the colonel at the fort, and the deputy warden had been in the welcoming committee at the train depot.

Fallon waited. The big brute saluted and asked in a raw voice, "What?"

"How many guards do you have?"

"Total?"

Fallon nodded.

"Fifty."

"How do you divide them up? How does the schedule work?"

"There ain't no division, sir," the man croaked. "Fifty guards. Every day. Ten get to stay at the prison. Five of them can sleep. But those five have to pull night duty. We march these fish out at dawn from the prison to here. They work twelve hours, then we march 'em back. Once they's all locked up, we rotate the men off. The five who slept get to guard the prison at night. So we move them around that way. Five sleeping. Five at the prison. The rest watching these fish."

Fallon frowned. "Days off?"

"They'll get their days off when this prison is finished."

"Captain O'Connor," Fallon said sternly. "At the rate this prison is being built, this place won't be finished for twenty or thirty years. And what are your guards making a day?"

O'Connor told him.

"We do have a budget, you understand."

"Arithmetic ain't my concern."

"It is now."

The big man tensed. His ears started turning a bright crimson.

"We're going to come up with a system, Captain, that makes it fiscally responsible." Golly, he thought, he had learned quite a lot pushing numbers and figures and pencils and erasers during that spell as U.S. marshal in Wyoming. "I'd like our men to be able to have time with their families, or at least sleep uninterrupted. And I'd like you to have time off, too."

"I don't sleep, Warden. And I ain't got no family."

"Do you drink?"

The man chuckled. "I been known to. A good porter. A better brand of rye whiskey."

"Well, Captain, since you don't have a day off, that means you're drinking ardent spirits on the job. And that's grounds for firing."

"Warden." The big man closed the gap. "You look around here, and you'll find a bunch of pettifogging gelded roosters who come here because of stupid, ignorant crimes that ought to have gotten a slap on the wrists. But you'll also find the most rotten-headed, mean, evil sons of strumpets that ever was born. Who'll slit your throat if you turn your back on them for this." His finger snapped. "I need all forty of them guards." He gestured. "Look around here, Boss Man. What do you see? Nothing but a thousand acres of Kansas prairie and prisoners just itching to light out to freedom. There ain't nothin' holdin' these boys in—except me and my men."

"I think we can fix that somewhat, Captain," Fallon said.

"How?"

"Leave that to me."

The man found a plug of tobacco and bit off a giant mouthful. As his yellowed and browned teeth went to work, his face continued to redden.

Fallon waited for Big Tim O'Connor to either explode or start the attack. Instead, two other guards came loping up on horses.

"Capt'n!" one cried. "Capt'n!" They reined up hard in front of Fallon and O'Connor.

"What is it?" the giant roared.

"Three flew the coop, Capt'n. Took off thataway."

Fallon expected O'Connor to blow up, but this news seemed to calm him down. The redness turned pink then ivory, and finally his true color. He even smiled.

"Who?"

"Loder," the first guard said.

Which widened O'Connor's grin.

"Walburn and Turner," the other guard said.

"Just now?" O'Connor asked.

"No, Captain," the first guard said. "Benson just reported to us."

"Did he know how long those three dirty curs have been gone?"

"No," the second guard said. "Last seen them two hours ago."

"Two hours," Fallon snapped. "Good God!"

O'Connor chuckled. "Boys, y'all ain't met our new warden. This here is Harry Fallon. Warden, I'd like you to meet Wilson and Raymond."

Fallon nodded at the horseback-mounted guards.

O'Connor turned toward the east. "Loder . . . Walburn . . . and . . . ?" He looked at Raymond.

"Turner," Raymond said.

"Right. Turner. Good. With maybe a two-hour jump on us?"

"That's our best guess."

O'Connor spit a pint of tobacco juice into the grass, wiped his mouth with a worn handkerchief he fished out of his pocket. "You said Benson's saddling a horse for me?"

"That's right," Wilson said.

"Well, Wilson, go make sure he does a good job. You know how particular I am about my horses, and my saddle. I'll meet you at the horse pen."

"Yes, Capt'n."

Fallon cleared his throat. "What about bloodhounds?" he asked.

The three guards stared at him.

"You mean . . ." Raymond said, "Dogs?"

"That's right."

"We ain't got no dogs, Warden Fallon," O'Connor explained. "Us being fiscally minded and all." He grinned.

Raymond and Wilson did not know, most likely, the meaning of "fiscally."

Fallon blinked. But now he remembered that when Roy Baker showed him all the structures, the outer buildings, every thing drawn onto the blueprint, there were no kennels for dogs, no corrals or barns for horses—but that made sense. You didn't want prisoners to have easy access to horses if they ever got out of the pen. But dogs? Prisons liked to have bloodhounds handy. Indians were better, especially Tonkawas in Texas and Navajos in Arizona—now that most of the Apaches had been shipped out of that territory. But dogs were good. Real good.

"You don't use dogs, bloodhounds, to run down escapees?" Fallon asked.

Big Tim O'Connor guffawed. "Warden, we don't need no dawgs. What we got's better than some ground-sniffin' dawg. We got ol' Buffalo Bones."

Fallon didn't press, did not show any curiosity about this Buffalo Bones. He spun sharply, and called out for Wilson, the young guard riding away, to stop.

"Saddle a horse for me," Fallon said. "I'll be riding out with you."

CHAPTER SIXTEEN

"Wardens don't go after escapees," Big Tim O'Connor snarled, and let a half-pint of tobacco juice spray the Kansas grass.

"This warden does," Fallon told him.

The chief guard's head was already shaking. "Unhunh," he said. "I pick the men who ride with me, and I ain't gonna be the fellow who has to answer to this idiot newspaperman"—he gestured absently toward the *Post* reporter—"when I bring your bullet-riddled corpse to the undertaking parlor."

"As far as I know, the prisoners aren't armed," Fallon told him.

"Warden, they will be, if they ain't already. That you can bank on. I know them sons of strumpets better than I know you."

"You don't know me at all. But you're going to get to know me."

"Here's one thing I do know, Warden Fallon. I know what 'em sons of strumpets are capable of."

"I'm going." He turned to the journalist. "You're

the witness here. O'Connor tried to talk me out of going. I pulled rank on him, so if this turns out badly, for me, no one can hold Captain Timothy Horatio O'Connor responsible."

The big man tensed, and he stepped just inches from Fallon, whispering with heated breath. "Nobody knows my middle name, Fallon. Nobody mentions my middle name."

"You forget," Fallon said with a grin, "who authorizes your paycheck, and who has personnel records on everyone who works for the federal pen, not just everyone who happens to be incarcerated here. Everything." He let his voice drop even softer. "Including that little sixteen-year-old in Franklin, Tennessee. And that other little thing in Shreveport, Louisiana."

The well-gnarled chaw of tobacco came out of O'Connor's mouth and landed in the grass.

"The hell you say," he whispered.

"I'm going."

"You can't blackmail me."

"I don't blackmail, O'Connor. I don't bluff. And if we don't start moving after those three men, they'll be across the Missouri River."

"They won't go across the Big Muddy," O'Connor said. "They'll head south. Try to make it to the Nations."

"How's that?"

Now O'Connor grinned, though not too wide, not after he realized how much the new warden knew about his own nefarious background. "I know these men, Fallon. Walburn can't swim. Too scared to take a bath. He won't go near the Missouri. Loder has a gal in the Cherokee Nation. Turner's from Texas."

"Then let's go bring them back."

The smile on the big man's face widened. "All right. Saddle up the black for our boss," he told the old trusty, and found Fallon again with his murderous eyes. "I'm afraid we ain't got no sidesaddle, Mister Warden, suh."

"That's all right," Fallon said. "I have every confidence that you'll be able to sit in a slick fork even at a gallop."

The old buffalo soldier scouted ahead. Two guards, Raymond and Wilson, armed with bolt-action rifles and double-action revolvers, trailed Fallon and O'Connor. They had turned south before nearing the river, cleared most of the farms, and now followed up and down the rolling hills. Two miles out of Leavenworth, O'Connor reined in his big gray. Fallon stopped the black, and once Wilson and Raymond caught up, O'Connor tore off another huge chaw of tobacco and began chewing it to shreds.

"You two ride along ahead. Till Buffalo Bones picks up their trail. If they split up, fire two shots. Otherwise, just keep houndin' 'em, but don't make no move until I catch up with you." Still holding the Greener shotgun, he swung out of the saddle, wrapping the reins around the double barrels, and laying the ten-gauge on the grass—sort of a tether for the gray. "Warden and me is gonna have us a little parley."

Both men frowned, looking at Fallon for help,

and Fallon swung out of his saddle. "Go ahead. Tell Buffalo Bones we'll be along directly." He kept the reins to the black in his left hand.

They watched the guards trot off toward the old prisoner, and when the tall grass and gentle slopes had swallowed both guards, O'Connor spit tobacco juice and unbuckled his belted gun. "Drop the reins, Warden. You'll need both hands to defend yourself."

Fallon did not obey, but stepped closer, bringing the horse with him. "No, Tom, I don't think so. If my horse ran away, that would give you all the excuse you needed."

"You're goin' back one way or the other," O'Connor said as he stepped toward Fallon. "You can ride out, or I can throw you over the saddle, or if the horse spooks, you can walk back to town when you regain consciousness. But one thing's for certain. You ain't goin' no damn furth—"

O'Connor went down hard, taking the right punch Fallon threw without warning, so fast O'Connor never even saw the fist before it flattened his ear and left him rolling over Kansas sod. Fallon stepped forward quickly, reins to the black still clenched in his left fist. The horse snorted, but offered no resistance as Fallon kicked just as O'Connor tried to push himself to his feet.

This time Big Tim O'Connor grunted as the square toe of Fallon's boot caught him in the soft spot between his jaw and throat. Again, he hit the ground, this time gagging. He rolled over, coughed, and spit out the chaw of tobacco, tried to breathe, shake some sort of sense back into his fighting mind.

Fallon was over him again. The black walked along behind him. It was O'Connor's gray horse that seemed spooked by it all, snorting and dragging the heavy shotgun a few feet in the grass.

Rolling over, O'Connor tried to kick Fallon but caught only air. But he sprang to his feet, somehow, and was spinning around, cursing vilely, then roaring. Fallon had to turn, too, and as the tough captain of guards charged, Fallon simply dropped, still getting a firm hold on the reins, and let O'Connor trip over his body. The man yelled as the grass broke his fall, and Fallon sprang up, stepped forward, and when O'Connor sat up, tried to raise his fists, Fallon kicked him hard in the center of his chest.

O'Connor lay spread-eagled on his back, fighting for breath, bleeding from split lips and a few scratches from the falls. The black followed as meekly and as mildly as Rachel Renee might walk behind her mother, obedient, and maybe a little or a lot afraid of making someone angry.

Fallon's boot lay against O'Connor's neck, not too hard, but letting the guard know what could happen, possibly would happen. Fallon spoke just to make everything clear.

"So here's the way this hand plays out, Tim." Fallon spoke slowly, enunciating every word, not sounding angry or showing even the slightest concern. "I crush your throat, and you suffocate in a matter of seconds, maybe a minute, but probably not that long. During the coroner's inquest, I will commit perjury, tell everyone for the record that that big gray of yours had you tasting gravel, and then just happened to step on your throat. It was over before I could do anything, but, certainly, the horse was not to blame. He's a good horse. He just had a rider who probably should have been in a sidesaddle, and not a slick fork."

Just in case Big Tim O'Connor figured he might want to fight to the death, Fallon brought the foot up, and let the opening between heel and sole rest against the guard's Adam's apple.

"The other way this ends, Tim, is that I step away from you, I mount my horse, and I watch you pick up your hat, buckle on your gun rig, get your shotgun, and mount your horse. And nobody knows anything about what just transpired. We ride out of here, catch up with the others, and we finish what we set out to do."

He made himself yawn. Nodding at his own originality, and put just a wee bit of pressure on O'Connor's throat. "Tom. I need an answer. All you have to do is blink twice for yes. So, do you want to do the job we set out to do?"

The eyelids shut, long and hard, opened, and shut tightly. When they opened, Fallon put his boot back on the ground.

"Good decision, Tim." Fallon turned and pulled himself into his own slick fork. "Let's catch up with, as you call them, those sons of strumpets."

Fallon rested his right hand on the butt of the revolver, and he made sure to turn his horse so that O'Connor could see his hand as the captain took the shotgun, gathered his reins, and eased into the saddle on the black. Slowly, he slid the scattergun into the scabbard and massaged his throat.

His eyes locked with Fallon's. He spit, wiped his face, and the lips moved about as he tried to figure out what to say.

"I ain't never met a warden like you," O'Connor finally said.

"I told you earlier, Tim, you don't know me at all."

O'Connor turned his horse, kicked it into a walk. Fallon caught up with him quickly, and they rode side by side.

"You ain't like most wardens," O'Connor said.

Fallon nodded. "Most wardens never spent ten years behind the iron in Joliet, Illinois," Fallon told him. "Most wardens, if any, never rode in the Nations with a federal marshal's badge pinned to the lapel of his vest. And I doubt if any warden or guard even went undercover for a detective agency, posing as a hardened inmate, in Yuma, Jefferson City, and Huntsville."

The captain of guards fished out his chaw, bit off a mouthful, and after starting to return it to his vest pocket, held it toward Fallon.

"No, thank you, Tim," Fallon said. "Might make me sick."

The guard laughed, good-naturedly and honestly, and let the chaw fall into a deep pocket. "I don't reckon it'd make you sick, Warden."

"The name," Fallon said, "is Hank." He held out his hand.

They shook, both grinning widely now, respect mutual. "You're right, Hank." O'Connor tested the name, decided he liked it, and nodded his dirty head with enthusiasm. "I don't reckon I do know you at all. But I think I'm gonna like getting to know you, sir."

"The feeling's mutual, Tim." He urged his horse a little faster. "Let's catch up with Buffalo Bones and the others."

"You bet," Big Tim O'Connor said.

And they gave their mounts plenty of rein, kicked the sides hard, loped up the hill, and felt the wind blasting their faces as the horses moved into gallops, and the rolling prairie swept past them.

CHAPTER SEVENTEEN

They sat in their saddles, Fallon, O'Connor, Wilson, and Raymond, waiting, the Kansas wind whipping their faces. Down below, Buffalo Bones knelt in the grass, his pinto pony ground-reined a few yards behind him.

"He's been there for ten minutes," Wilson whispered. "What the hell's he doin'?"

"His job," Fallon said and smiled. He did not know this Buffalo Bones, an old black man, head shaved to a shiny mahogany, feeling the land, those old eyes scanning west and south. But Fallon knew his kind. He had worked with men like this in the Indian Nations, scouts, often former slaves who had found a home with the Creeks and Seminoles, the Choctaws, but rarely with the Cherokees. Many of the Cherokees had been slaveholders before the War of the Rebellion, and a number of black men did not want anything to do with Cherokees. Fallon had even served with a former slave, a deputy marshal named Bass Reeves, the only federal lawman of his race—and, by Fallon's estimation, the best lawman who rode with Judge Parker's court. The last Fallon had heard, Bass Reeves was still wearing a badge and bringing in felons by the score. They didn't make them like that anymore. Buffalo Bones, Fallon figured, was from the same mold.

"What's he in for?" Fallon asked.

"Robbed an Army paymaster," Big Tim O'Connor said, still massaging his ear from Fallon's first blow.

Fallon looked away from the scout and locked on the captain of guards. "While he was serving in one of the Negro regiments?"

O'Connor shook his head. "Nah. He was out of the Tenth Cavalry by then. If what I recollect is true, he was a first sergeant for almost like forever, joined up with those Negro regiments was just gettin' formed sometime right after the War Between the States. Don't know exactly why he got out of the Army—if he was kicked out or left on his own accord—but he was out when he took to the owlhoot trail. Payroll was headed to Fort Sill down south in the Indian Territory. Six guards. He took it alone."

"Nobody hurt?" Fallon asked.

"Just the Army's pride. One old colored man gets the best of six white troopers, took the wagon, and left the troopers and the paymaster afoot." O'Connor chuckled. "Problem with Buffalo Bones was he didn't know what to do with the wagon. Went to a cathouse in one of them all-colored towns, left the wagon parked out front. Almost like he wanted to be caught."

"How long has he been in Leavenworth?"

"Eighteen years, if my math's right," O'Connor said. "Seven more to go."

"What's his real name?"

"I don't rightly know," the captain replied. "I've

been here twelve years, and he has always been just ol' Buffalo Bones."

"He's waving," the guard named Raymond said.

And they rode down to join the scout, who had moved from where he had studied the ground, and swung onto his black-and-white pony.

Buffalo Bones pointed east. "The fastest one took off that way."

"That'd be Walburn," O'Connor said.

"Who doesn't swim," Fallon said.

"Right."

"So why is he going toward the Missouri?"

"Pig farm," the old black man said.

The guard Raymond laughed. "He want some barbecue?"

"He wants horses," Fallon answered. "Mules. Something to ride."

The guards stared at Fallon in wonder, but Ol' Buffalo Bones grinned and let his bald head bob in agreement. "He'll take what he can get." His left hand pointed west. "Meet up with them other two probably in some trees or at the pond."

"So," Wilson said, "we ought to go after Loder and Turner. Catch them. Wait for Walburn to return."

"No," Fallon said. "We go after Walburn."

"Why?" Wilson asked.

"Because if he has a horse, or a mule, or even just a jenny ass, he might decide to give up on his pards and hightail it to the Indian Nations."

"The others are afoot," Big Tim O'Connor agreed. "They'll be easier to track down—unless they find some other homestead."

Fallon turned his horse east and kicked the black's

sides. The others joined him, moving their horses slowly but at a steady pace.

"Buffalo Bones?" Raymond asked. "How do you know there's a pig farm yonder way?"

It was Fallon who answered. "Can't you smell it?"

Ol' Buffalo Bones let out a throaty belly laugh and nudged his horse into a lope. "Y'all stay back," he called out. "Just keep restin' ya hosses. Till I signal y'all."

Leviticus Deuteronomy Johnston had Walburn covered in pig dung, while his wife, Ruth, and his kids, Ezra, Nehemiah, Esther, Job, Psalms, Proverbs, and Ecclesiastes, cheered for their pa, while piglets, sows, and hogs scurried about the large, stinking, and disgusting pen. The farmer, wearing mucking boots and stained overalls, pressed a fowling piece against Walburn's groin, then used his left boot to sink the inmate's head underneath the slop and manure.

A mule drank from a bucket in the middle of the yard, and a blind burro urinated by the gate to the pigpen, which the two oldest boys, Ezra and Nehemiah, stood in front of, staring as the posse rode into the yard.

Fallon swept off his hat and bowed to the wife, introduced himself and his guards, and turned back to the pig farmer. "Sir," he called out, "we'll be glad to take Mr. Walburn off your hands."

"He tried to steal Matthew and Mark, by golly," the farmer said. "I will kill him now and feed him to Colossians and Thessalonians." He nodded at two of the biggest hogs Fallon had ever seen.

Wife and children from the Old Testament. Animals

from the New. Fallon felt blessed that his parents had not raised pigs in eastern Kansas.

"If you shoot him," Fallon said, "they won't let you collect a reward."

The old farmer looked up. "Reward?"

Fallon nodded. "He escaped from the Leavenworth prison. Twenty-five dollars for his return. Alive."

Ten minutes later, the dung-covered Walburn was being marched by Wilson north toward Leavenworth. They had drawn lots, and Wilson had lost. He let the reeking prisoner get a good twenty yards ahead of him, and Fallon wrote out a receipt for Mr. Johnston to deliver to the comptroller of the new Leavenworth federal penitentiary the next time he brought some pork to the market.

"Thank you for your service," Fallon told the Johnstons, and he let Ol' Buffalo Bones ride west first.

Turner and Loder were not incompetent. They had managed to get about seven or eight miles from Leavenworth, and one of them had enough outdoors skills to have snared a jackrabbit. But neither, Fallon decided, had much for brains. They did not need Ol' Buffalo Bones to find the two remaining escapees. They saw the smoke from the fire where Loder and Turner roasted the rabbit wafting from the grove of trees in a small depression that caught water. They also smelled the meat.

"That's a whole lot better than pig dung," Big Tim O'Connor said. He nudged his horse closer to

Raymond's and held out his right hand. "I'll take the Mauser."

The guard pulled the bolt-action rifle from the scabbard and handed it to the big man.

"Let them eat their supper," Fallon told them. "Then we'll take them."

"Why?" O'Connor asked.

"Men think clearer when they have a full stomach," Fallon said. "Hungry men are desperate. I figure they'll be more likely to surrender after they've eaten."

The big man shook his head but laughed. "I might think clearer, too, if I had something to eat."

Fallon dismounted and opened one of the saddlebags. "You boys are in luck. My wife made me dinner for my first day on the job."

"They's kickin' out the fire," Ol' Buffalo Bones said from the crest of the small hill.

Fallon shimmied up the incline, looked over the tall grass, and studied the scene. "Getting restless," he said. "Wondering what is taking their pard so long."

The black man nodded his bald head in agreement. "They'll give up on him soon enough, boss. Start runnin' some more."

"Easiest thing to do," Big Tim O'Connor said from where their horses were hobbled. "Is for me to shoot them from here."

Fallon was already crawling down. "Yeah, that would be easy enough. But not nice."

"Nice ain't in my . . ." He paused, thinking.

Fallon ended the sentence. "Vocabulary."

The captain laughed. "I reckon. But we ain't gonna be able to get around them without them seeing us. Not enough cover. We can call out for them to surrender. And when they run, I can likely hit them."

"I have a better idea," Fallon said.

CHAPTER EIGHTEEN

Fallon removed his coat, laid it across the saddle of the scout's pinto, and then hooked his hat over the horn. When he turned to Ol' Buffalo Bones, he said, "Take off your clothes."

The old man's jaw dropped open. A moment later, he said in a dry whisper, "How's that, boss?"

"Your pants and shirt. Prison uniform. I'll put those on, lead two of our horses toward their camp."

Raymond and O'Connor exchanged glances, and before O'Connor could start to argue, Fallon explained.

"I'm the closest to Walburn's size. They see me, in a prison uniform, bringing two horses, they'll think they're about to be delivered. That'll get me close enough."

Shaking his head, O'Connor protested, "They get you, they got themselves a hostage."

"They won't get me." Fallon had his shirt off.

"They'll recognize you before you get close enough to pound their brains out," O'Connor said.

"Right. And they'll let me keep coming to them because they'll figure those two horses are their best way of getting out of the jam they find themselves in." He slipped off the suspenders while using his left foot to start prying off one boot, which he kicked toward Loder.

"They might have a gun," Loder said.

Fallon shook his head. "They haven't been to a farm."

"They certainly have a weapon," O'Connor chimed in.

"I've never met an inmate anywhere who didn't have one." He nodded at the captain and removed his pants. "You'll be up here with that Mauser. If something goes wrong, you'll get your chance to be a hero. Just don't miss your aim and hit me by mistake." He stood in his underdrawers and socks, and glared at the black trusty.

"Get out of your duds, Buffalo Bones. We're burning daylight."

"They ain't gonna fit you, boss," the old black man said.

"They'll do the job."

He took the pinto and the black, leaving Ol' Buffalo Bones's saddle and bridle behind, and slipped a hackamore around the small mare's neck to lead it. The chances of a pig farmer having two saddles seemed remote, Fallon had determined, and if the two remaining convicts had any sense, they might grow suspicious. Fallon rode the black, hatless, head bent, but eyes forward.

When he saw movement in the trees, he wet his lips, raised his right hands just enough and waved sideways, letting Loder and Turner know he was coming. He made himself look awkward on the horse, because from what he had seen about Walburn, the man didn't look like he had been on horseback too often. On the other hand, not much about an escaped convict, covered in pig manure and wailing like a newborn baby, impressed anyone back at the Johnston farm. So why had Loder and Turner sent Walburn to bring back horses?

One of the men waved back.

And that gave Fallon the answer.

"These boys," he whispered to the black gelding, "are imbeciles."

But as the black covered the distance, the one on Fallon's right pointed and said something to the other. That caused the second man, the stoutest of the two, or even three if you considered Walburn, even when the latter had been covered with manure, to step forward, and bring his left hand above his eyes to shield him from the sun. When the left hand lowered, that man said something to the short one, then let his right hand slip inside the trousers of his prison pants. The short one raised his head and began scanning the countryside.

All right, Fallon figured, so they know I'm not Walburn. He did not let the black slow its gait.

He moved into the small depression, knowing that O'Connor had a clear view from the higher ground, and likely had one of the two felons in the sights of the Mauser. The two escapees had spread apart now, and Fallon reined up, with the pinto moving a little ahead until Fallon jerked on the end of the hackamore.

The short one had his right hand inside the pocket of his prison jacket, and now he brought it up hip level so that Fallon could see the impression of a gun barrel.

"Just keep ridin', mistah," the short one said with a snarl. "Or I'll cut you down right where you sit."

"Just do like Turner says," the stout one, Loder, said, and he brought the handmade knife out of his pants pocket.

"Raise your hands," Turner said.

"I raise my hands," Fallon told them, "I drop the hackamore. And the pinto leaves you with one horse."

"You just come then." Loder beckoned him forward with the flashing knife.

Fallon let the horses bring him to the escapees, Turner on his right, Loder on the left.

"Where's Luther?" Loder asked.

Fallon said, "Last time I saw him, he was covered in crap and walking back to Leavenworth."

"I tol' you it was a dern-fool plan, Marvin," Turner said.

"Shut up." Loder waved the knife toward Fallon. "Who are you, buster? And how many is with ya?"

"My name's Fallon."

Loder took a step back, glanced at Turner, and then grinned. "The new boss of Leavenworth?"

Fallon's head bobbed.

"Horse apples," Turner said. "No warden would come out here alone."

"Boys," Fallon said. "Captain O'Connor has a Mauser trained on you right now. There's nowhere for you to run, so let's just start heading back to the prison. I'd like to be home before it gets too dark."

"If you're the warden," Loder said, "you might come in real handy." He laughed, spit, and turned to his partner. "We got ourselves a ticket to Mexico, Sylvester. Get down off that gelding, Boss Fallon. Or I let Sylvester give it to you in the belly. Ever seen a man gut-shot?"

"Just the ones whose bellies I put bullets in," Fallon said, letting go of the hackamore and the reins to the black. He dived out of the saddle, using the stirrup to boost himself like a cannonball toward Loder.

Loder raised the knife, more as a defensive measure, and Fallon's left shoulder slammed into the stout man's chest, driving him into the ground and sliding partly down the slight hill. As the man gasped for breath, Fallon came up, used his right knee to pin Loder's arm down. His left fist then smashed the man's nose. That caused Loder to release his grip on the knife, and Fallon deftly swept it up and sprang to his feet.

Turner had brought his hand out of the jacket pocket and dropped the piece of kindling he had hoped Fallon would think was a pistol. He swore and tried to find the reins to the black. That spooked the pinto, which loped back toward Ol' Buffalo Bones, O'Connor, and Raymond.

Fallon halfway expected the Mauser to open up, but the captain of guards held his fire. Perhaps he had no clear shot, not wanting to hit a horse by accident or even Fallon. Turner snagged the reins, but the black leaped back, snorting, slightly rearing, and the leather whipped out of the convict's hands, burning his palm and leaving him screaming and trying to shake the hurt out of his hand. He spun, hearing Fallon, and swung out with his left. That blow was easily deflected, and Fallon rammed his knee upward and into the man's groin. A gasp, a groan, and a whimper, and Turner slowly sank into the earth, his eyes rolled back into his head. He fell onto the guts and skins of a rabbit, and lay next to the smoldering ruins of a campfire.

Fallon turned, waved his hands over his head, and caught his breath. He glanced at the two men, then moved slowly and gathered the reins to the black. Rubbing the horse's neck, he whispered compliments to the horse, and looked up across the prairie. Ol' Buffalo Bones, in his prison undergarments and boots, ran toward the pinto that was almost to him. Raymond walked down the hill, carrying the Mauser, and Captain Big Tim O'Connor rode Raymond's mount, replacing the high-powered rifle with his favored sawed-off shotgun in his right hand.

Fallon massaged the knuckles in his right hand and assayed the damages. Loder had rolled over and was spitting out blood and snot onto the grass. Turner clutched his privates, and stared hopelessly up at Fallon.

"That"—he coughed out the words—"that . . . wasn't . . . fair." He groaned and lay whimpering.

"Life's not fair, either," Fallon told him, and while waiting for the rest of the posse to join him, he began removing the tight-fitting prison uniform of Ol' Buffalo Bones. He figured the old man would want his clothes back pretty soon, and Fallon hoped

Raymond had the good sense to bring Fallon's own duds with him.

O'Connor reached the camp and looked down at the escapees. He shoved the shotgun into the scabbard, spit tobacco juice, and wiped his mouth with his sleeve, before nodding at Fallon.

"You do pretty good work alone, Warden."

Fallon cracked a knuckle. "I've had plenty of practice, Tim. And remember, the name's Hank."

It was approaching nine o'clock by the time Fallon opened the door into his new, if rented, home.

"Papa!" Rachel Renee ran from the woodstove, leaving a toy giraffe on the top, and leaped into his arms. Fallon caught her, laughed, and let her rub her nose against him. Quickly, she jerked away.

"Ohhhh, Papa . . . you stink . . . you smell . . . horrible."

He kissed her forehead and let her down. She turned toward Christina and pinched her nose. "Papa smells bad. Real bad."

Fallon closed the door and hung his hat on the rack. "It's pretty late for a little princess to be awake," he told her, not scolding, just making a fatherly observation.

"Mama said I could stay up. To see you. To ask you how your first day on your new job was."

"It was"—Fallon slipped off his coat—"different. In some ways." He grinned at Christina. "And . . . in many ways . . . just more of the same."

"Mama baked cookies," Rachel Renee said. "I helped. Didn't I, Mama?"

Christina nodded. "You want some?" the girl called out, but not waiting for an answer, rushed toward the dining-room table. "They're lemony," she yelled from the other room.

"Don't eat them all," Christina said pleasantly but sternly. She looked at Fallon. "Did you catch them?"

"All three," Fallon said. "In solitary for now. No injuries."

Her chin jutted toward Fallon's right hand.

"That's just a scratch."

"I imagine I'll read about it in the *Post*."

"I'll tell you about it."

The girl ran back into the room, extending a cookie that had been nibbled on, but quickly slid to a stop, leaving the cookie held toward Fallon. She sniffed, pouted, and shook her head.

"You really do stink, Papa."

Laughing, Christina stepped forward, took the half-eaten cookie from her daughter's hand, and told her, "It's bedtime, Little Princess. Off you go. Now. Say your prayers, and I'll be in to tuck you in and wish you sweet dreams."

The girl yawned, blew Fallon a kiss, and raced to her room. "All right, Mama. Papa can come in, too, but maybe he can just wish me sweet dreams from the doorway. He smells . . . awful."

Fallon smiled. Christina stepped toward him, but then she also stopped.

"My word," she said. "You do reek."

"Yeah," Fallon said. "It was a pretty long day."

She stepped back.

"Pig farm," he explained. "One of the prisoners . . . well . . . and then there were a few goes at . . . fisticuffs."

"Yeah."

"You could help me fill the tub," Fallon said. "I'll let you wash my back."

She shook her head. "We're in a big city, darling. There's a Turkish bath house. And an all-night tonsorial parlor with various soaps and tonics and one of those indoor showers. The Turkish place is open twenty-four hours, too. And that's where you're going, my loving husband, while I put Rachel Renee to sleep." She turned, went into his daughter's bedroom, and looked back at him.

"I'm serious, my love. One of the bathhouses or maybe both of them. I'll see you . . . later."

The door closed.

Harry Fallon reached for his hat.

CHAPTER NINETEEN

Fallon saw the young guard staring at him as the prisoners marched forward to resume construction duties. The guard had red hair, curly, underneath his guard's cap, and what looked to be freckles. He couldn't have been much older than twenty years old and didn't look like most of the guards Fallon had know in and out of prisons. Not hardened like most of them. Eventually, the boy must have talked enough courage into himself, because the Adam's apple bobbed and the young man began crossing the construction zone. The head lowered, but he kept walking, putting one foot in front of the other, until he stopped, looked up.

Yep, Fallon was reassured, those were freckles. Green eyes, too. But now that the boy stood this close, Fallon began doubting if this kid had reached the age of twenty yet.

"Warden Fallon," the boy said.

"Yes."

"Can I speak to you?"

"That's what you're doing, son." He extended his hand. "I'm Hank Fallon."

After the boy shifted his shotgun, they shook. Fallon wondered if the kid would introduce himself. He kept wetting his lips, trying to figure out how to speak.

"And you are . . . ?" Fallon asked. Sure, it wasn't polite in the West to ask a man's name, but this was a federal pen, so politeness could be overlooked. Besides, the boy worked for Fallon, so he had a right to know his name.

"Oh." The kid blushed. "I'm Elliott Jefferson."

"It's nice to meet you, Elliott. How long have you been working here?"

"Since they got the orders to build the new pen. They hired a lot of us then."

"I see. Like your job?"

"It's all right."

"Well, Elliott, here's a piece of advice for you. No criticism. Just advice. When you walk across the prison yard, keep your head up. Don't look at your feet. Head up. Eyes open. You're carrying a loaded shotgun, with a lever action, and any inmate doing hard time or facing execution would love to get his hands on that Winchester."

The mouth dropped, and Fallon thought Elliott Jefferson would drop the twelve-gauge, maybe even break down and bawl.

Smiling, Fallon brought his hand up and squeezed the kid's shoulder. "It's all right, Elliott. I can tell from your reaction that's one mistake you'll never make again."

"I won't, Warden. I promise."

Fallon nodded, and his grin widened. "How old are you, Elliott?"

"Nineteen. I know that's young but . . ."

"Elliott." Fallon kept his smile. "I wore a deputy U.S. marshal's badge when I was younger than that. Age doesn't matter. It's the will."

The boy sighed and suddenly relaxed. "Thank you, sir."

"What can I do for you?"

Fallon kept his own eyes moving, from the boy, to the convicts, watching the guard details, seeing how they oversaw the construction. The buildings were taking shape. Mostly, he studied the inmates, those working, those resting, and those studying what the guards were doing.

"I think you knew my father," Elliott Jefferson said.

Fallon stopped looking at the prisoners. That's what guards were for, and since Big Tim O'Connor was on hand, Fallon figured the guards had everything well in hand. His eyes focused on the kid. So where had Fallon known the boy's father? Joliet? Or . . . ?

"He was a deputy marshal."

Fallon's eyes remained open, but now he didn't see young Elliott Jefferson. He remembered the blackness and the pain.

Groaning, Fallon felt hands on his shoulder, and felt his body being gently rolled over. The sunlight made his head hurt worse, and he tightened his eyelids shut, but saw orange, purple, red and yellow flashes. Then a coolness wet his lips, and his mouth opened. Water trickled in.

Something soft, cold, and damp then touched the part of his forehead that hurt so much. It felt better.

"Nice lump you got there, kid, but it's just a big-arse knot, so you might not be able to fit a hat on your noggin for a spell, but you don't require any stitches."

His eyes opened, finally, and some time later, he could see the thick, drooping red mustache and green eyes looking down at him. A battered black Stetson topped the head. The face was bronzed from the sun, stubbled with the beginnings of a mustache and beard.

"What . . . happened?" Fallon managed to say.

"I wasn't here to witness it, kid, but if I was a detective or a newspaper editor, I'd say you got clubbed by Red-Eye Huston."

Fallon pressed his left hand against the rag on the headache. The eyes closed as he nodded his head, just a tad, then said, "Yeah." Curiosity struck him, and he made himself look into the trail-worn face. "How'd you know it was Red-Eye Huston?"

The redheaded stranger's eyes turned to the left. "Arrest warrant on the ground yonder," the man said. "Red-Eye Huston don't like getting arrested. Especially since Judge Parker told him if he showed up in his court one more time, he'd rue the day he ever set foot in the Cherokee Nation or the Fort Smith federal courthouse."

The canteen came up, the man muttered something, and Fallon drank a few more swallows.

"Not too much. Don't want you to get sick. Headache's bad enough."

Fallon nodded. "It is."

"Don't mean to pry, son, but I see from your badge that you're out of Parker's court, too. Where's your jailer and the wagon?"

Every posse sent out by the U.S. marshal in Fort Smith, Arkansas, went with a jailer and a prison wagon, which would be filled with prisoners as the deputy marshals made their arrests till they returned with a load of prisoners to be tried by Judge Isaac Parker. Fallon actually had started out driving a wagon himself, until his two bosses were murdered. When Fallon tracked down the killers himself, he was rewarded with a promotion. Right about now, Fallon wished he had just let the real lawmen go after those killers. Then he would have been feeding and guarding prisoners somewhere else. And his head wouldn't feel like it had been run over by a KATY locomotive.

"Over on the Verdigris." Fallon made a feeble gesture toward the south.

"You come after Huston alone?"

Fallon started to nod, realized that movement was just tormenting him more, so he said, "Yeah. Clint Grisham went after Howie Grady."

"You drew the black bean."

"I reckon so."

"And just who are you?" the redheaded man asked.

"Fallon. Harry Fallon."

The man sat back on his haunches. "You're *the* Harry Fallon, the one everybody's talking about in Fort Smith? The jailer who brought in those cutthroats?"

Fallon tried to smile. "Same people who'll be talking

about me next week, the idiot Fallon, the dumb-arse kid who let himself get coldcocked by a whiskey runner. Judge Parker will likely ask for my badge, send me back home. Or arrest me."

The man chuckled. "Judge Parker and the U.S. solicitor and our chief marshal ain't about to do no such thing, sonny. Marshals are scarce in this country. And you ain't the first lawman to get belted by a whiskey runner." He pointed at a mangled ear. "Jordan Two Horses gave me that." His red head shook. "And I'd been lawing for two years when it happened, not just two months."

His hand lowered, and he lifted his plaid vest, high enough for Fallon to see the six-point star pinned to a torn pocket. Stamped into the tin in large black letters in the center of the star was the title:

DEPUTY
U. S.
MARSHAL

The big man extended his hand. "I was hoping to make your acquaintance long before now, Marshal Fallon. In Fort Smith, on Garrison Avenue, where I could buy you a beverage. Those lawmen you avenged, they were good friends of mine. I didn't learn about what happened till after they were buried, being out in the Creek Nation looking for Huachuca Linton. Missed the funeral and everything."

They briefly shook. The movement made Fallon's head throb even more.

"You're . . . the man . . . who killed Huachuca Linton?"

"Well, he didn't rightly give me much choice. I'd rather have seen him drop through the gallows with George Maledon's rope around his neck. But, yeah, I am that man."

He smiled. "Name's Jefferson. Edward James Robert Jefferson Junior. Deputy U.S. marshal. Same as you. Call me Eddie, though. Edward James Robert Jefferson Junior is a handful."

CHAPTER TWENTY

Fallon stared at young Elliott Jefferson. The kid had the hair and eyes, but Fallon, from what he remembered of Deputy Marshal Eddie Jefferson, figured young Elliott took after his mother.

"I should have guessed." He shook the kid's hand again, firmer, and grinned. "Your father was a good man. One of the finest lawmen I ever met. Judge Parker, everybody in the court, and especially all the deputies, admired and respected him. No better man ever pinned on a tin star."

"Thank you." The kid seemed to like the praise, but Fallon wasn't feeding the boy a bunch of tripe. He meant every word. "I don't remember that much about him. I wasn't very old when . . ."

When . . . Yeah. When Marshal Eddie Jefferson got gunned down. Killed in the line of duty. Murdered by some whiskey runner in the Choctaw Nation, not very long before Harry Fallon found himself in the Fort Smith dungeon, framed for a robbery, and about to begin what would turn out to be more than a decade behind the iron bars of prison.

"How's your mother?" Fallon made himself ask.

"Oh. She's all right. Got a letter from her two weeks ago."

"Still living in Fort Smith?"

"No, no. She stuck it out two years, but . . ." He shook his head. "It was just too painful, I guess, for her. Staying there. Seeing all those lawmen every day. And one after another coming in draped over a saddle, or atop the prison wagon."

Fallon nodded somberly. "Yeah. We all saw that too many times."

"Well, she moved—took me and my big sister with her—back to her folks' farm in Indiana. That's where I grew up. But . . . I came back to Arkansas once my schooling was done. Tried to get a job riding for the U.S. marshals, but they weren't hiring. So I drifted into Kansas. Everybody told me Leavenworth was booming. And when I read that they were hiring new guards for the new federal penitentiary, I interviewed. Got hired. It's not the same as being a deputy . . ."

"It's just as important, Elliott. Maybe even more so."

The kid looked at him questioningly.

"I know, son," Fallon said. "I have plenty of experience in prisons." His smile brightened. "More, actually, than I have riding as a federal deputy."

They looked at each other, and Fallon again studied the prisoners. At length he saw a couple that held his interest, and he did not know how long Elliott Jefferson had been talking to him.

Fallon looked again at the redheaded kid.

"What do you think, Warden? Does that sound all right? I mean, it's not out of line for me to ask, is it?"

Fallon tried to think of a way to cover his inexcusable actions of not listening to one of his guards.

"Well . . ."

"My wife, she cooks real fine, sir. Real fine. And we'd just love to have you . . . and your own wife . . . over."

Ah. Fallon nodded. The invitation to supper.

"Well, that's kind of you and your wife. We'd be honored."

"Seven o'clock, then?" The kid looked like he had managed to talk the Prince of Wales into dining with him. "Friday evening?"

"I believe we have Friday evening free, but I'll need to make sure my wife hasn't made any plans. How about if I confirm with you tomorrow?"

"That'd be dandy, sir."

"Good." He shook his hand again.

"You can bring your daughter, too, of course. My wife, Julie, she'll insist on that." He blushed. "We want to have a baby of our own. Right now, we just have a cat."

"There's a bit of a difference," Fallon said. For one, he thought, a man could not trust a cat. For another, cats made him sneeze. But, well, he could suffer for Deputy Marshal Eddie Jefferson's memory. And Rachel Renee loved cats.

"Maybe you can tell me some stories about my pa."

"I'd be honored. I'll just have to think of the good ones. Can we bring anything?"

"No."

"All right. I'll let you know tomorrow. But, now, Elliott. Not to sound like a warden, but you probably should get back to your post. Before Captain O'Connor comes down on you like a wagonload of bricks."

The boy laughed, shook Fallon's hand again, and took his lever-action shotgun back to his spot. He kept his head up, though, this time, and made himself take in everything, prisoners, guards, civilians watching the commotion, as he crossed the yard.

"He'll do," Fallon told himself. "He'll do fine. Just like his old man." Yeah, Eddie would be proud.

Fallon looked back, and then he walked toward the prisoners on their smoke break.

He would not have recognized Aaron Holderman, who had lost weight over the past few years, and with his head shaved, the beard gone. Still a brute, but a much smaller brute, and Fallon was used to seeing Holderman, the man who usually did all of Sean MacGregor's dirty work for the American Detective Agency, in trail duds or a cheap suit that did not come close to fitting.

Holderman crushed out a cigarette with the thick heels of his prison shoes and pushed himself to his feet.

"Stripes look good on you, Aaron," Fallon said, just to torment the oaf.

"You may speak, prisoner," Fallon told him, remembering the Auburn Prison System rule—*Convicts are required to be silent at all times, unless given permission to speak.* Aaron Holderman spoke his mind, briefly, clearly, concisely. His language had not been cleaned up after being sentenced to Leavenworth.

The man sitting on the rock next to him laughed.

Fallon looked down at the pathetic old man. "I do not recall giving you permission to speak."

Sean MacGregor, still a puny, pathetic man, frowned, but closed his mouth.

Fallon looked at four other prisoners, all staring at him, and noticed a few guards moving closer.

"I think you boys have been on break long enough." He nodded. "Back to work. And pick up those cigarette butts and put them in the trash. Now. We don't want to start any fires, burn down the walls, see all your hard work reduced to ashes."

He watched them stoop, picking up the remnants of their smokes, and dump them into the bucket between Sean MacGregor and Aaron Holderman. One of the guards followed the four prisoners. The other two stepped back, well out of earshot, but close enough with their shotguns to take action if needed. Fallon knew that neither Holderman nor, especially, old Sean MacGregor would do anything stupid. Not here. Not now.

"For your own edification, I thought you were sentenced to McNeil Island," Fallon told them.

Located in Puget Sound, southeast of Tacoma, Washington, McNeil Island had been a federal penitentiary since 1875, five years after the U.S. government bought the island.

"You didn't read the list of us convicts before you took the job, Fallon?" MacGregor asked in a hoarse whisper. Cigarettes, apparently, did not agree with him, but Fallon thought they sure smelled better than the filthy, cheap cigars he had smoked as president of the American Detective Agency.

"I didn't ask for the list. And with three hundred names on it, I thought I could find better things to read."

"You can always transfer us to the new joint in Atlanta, Georgia," MacGregor suggested.

"Or pardon us," Holderman added.

The two prisoners snickered, and even Fallon cracked a smile.

"You've developed a sense of humor," Fallon told them, and they turned quiet. "That's a good thing to have in a federal penitentiary. Keep it up."

MacGregor stubbed out his cigarette against the heel of his right shoe and flicked the butt into the trash can. The thin old man wasn't that active back when he ran the American Detective Agency, but those years behind bars had changed him—as Fallon knew, years behind the iron changed every man.

"Just so we understand each other," Fallon said. "The two of you are just like all the other three hundred-odd convicts housed here." He waited till they looked up. "You," he told MacGregor, "are Number Five-Zero-Nine-Eight." His eyes moved to Holderman. "And you are Number Five-One-Oh-Four." Another part of the Auburn Prison System. Inmates were numbers; they had no names. "Do your work. We get along. Raise trouble. You know what happens. I'd rather see you two men complete your sentence and get out of my sight."

MacGregor pushed himself to his feet. "Well, Warden Fallon, I'm not all that eager to see my sentence end.

Since in all likelihood I'll be dead before that term is over."

Holderman stood, too. "And, you know, Mr. Warden, that my sentence here ends when I'm dead. That's what they call life, Mr. Warden. I'm here for life."

Slowly, Fallon exhaled. "We understand each other, then," he said. "Now . . . do you have a complaint?"

Holderman sniggered.

MacGregor said, "Can we go back to work now, boss?"

Fallon nodded and watched the two men walk to the brick pile, but Holderman stopped, turned around, and looked at Fallon.

"Warden, boss, sir," he said mockingly, but then he straightened and spoke in a normal voice. "If you are serious about a complaint, it would be nice if the boys in the kitchen didn't piss in our soup."

CHAPTER TWENTY-ONE

Since the success of the New York prison at Auburn decades earlier, most states and territories had adopted what people in the business called "the Auburn Prison System."

Convicts were locked alone in cells at night, but worked—at hard labor—during the day. They were not allowed to speak to one another or a guard or prison official, either, unless given permission. Talk meant the whip, or, by this time in Leavenworth, Kansas, a wallop with a billy club. A prison would be devoid of human voices. Guards could signal which direction the prisoners were marching—always in lockstep—by tapping their canes. In the mess hall, lifting cups, spoon, fork, or plate would be the command for a refill of coffee or water, more meat—when there was meat—or bread or whatever. An inmate did not even make eye contact with another felon or a guard. Ten hours a day working hard and without conversation, in the winter. Twelve, maybe even fourteen hours in the summer.

Yet things were beginning to change this late in

the century. Over some eighty years, humanitarians had been heard. Back in 1846, the New York State Legislature put a stop to the whipping and beating of inmates, and other states followed suit. Of course, you didn't have to beat prisoners with nightsticks, butts of shotguns, or gloved fists . . .

"Captain O'Connor." Fallon's boots slogged through the water in the wall-enclosed corral that housed the brick kiln. The city of Leavenworth had provided the new pump fire engine—in case a fire spread—but the guards had found another use for it.

Big Tim O'Connor slowly lowered the dripping hose, handed it to another guard, wiped his soaking hands on his trousers, and offered a smart salute at Fallon. Ten yards away, arms strapped to two posts, slumped a naked man, shivering from the cold, hard blasts of water. His pale skin was reddened from the impact of the water.

"Yes, sir?" O'Connor said.

"Explain to me what is going on here," Fallon ordered.

O'Connor nodded. "Shower bath, sir."

"I see. I thought baths were given on Saturdays. In tubs."

"They are, sir. This is a special occasion."

"What's so special about Wednesday, Captain?"

"We heard it was his birthday."

Fallon nodded and moved through the cold water, past the fire engine, past O'Connor and the guard holding the hose, and stopped a few feet behind the shivering, pale, naked man with goose pimples all over his flesh. If he had been facing them when they cut loose with the water hose, the man would have drowned.

After introducing himself as the warden, Fallon asked the prisoner's name, and heard nothing.

"You have my permission to speak," Fallon said. "Your name." And he added, "Please."

He did not look behind him, but could picture the faces as the guards, and especially Big Tim O'Connor, rolling their eyes.

"Three-Nine-Seven-Two."

"Your name," Fallon told him. "Not your number."

His teeth kept chattering. "Lawless," he finally managed. "Ben Lawless."

Fallon moved closer, his feet already cold from the water. "*The* Ben Lawless?" This old man didn't look like the killer Harry Fallon remembered from his days riding across the Indian Nations.

"The only"—he still shivered and had trouble keeping his teeth from clattering—"only . . . Ben . . . Lawless . . . I know."

"The one who poisoned Indians?"

"Just the . . . sons of . . . bitchin' . . . Cherokees."

"They didn't hang you?"

"For riddin' the . . . world . . . of . . . maggots?" He managed to laugh.

Slowly, Ben Lawless, Number 3972, lifted his head, spit out water or saliva, and turned just enough to make eye contact with Fallon. One eye socket was empty, and the scars on his face ran deep as canyons. His hair was shorn, per prison regulations, but it was easy to see where the scalp had been lifted so many decades ago. The guards had stripped him naked, but even Big Tim O'Connor had left one item on the killer's body. He wore a chain, and hanging from the chain was a cross. It was a miracle the hose had not blasted the small, hand-carved piece of cotton-wood all the way to the Missouri River. Fallon saw something else in Ben Lawless. He saw the one good eye, a deep brown, and in that eye, he understood something about Ben Lawless.

Fallon had seen that look in a few—but certainly not many—inmates during his tours behind bars. He looked over his shoulder at the guards, felt the anger rising, but managed to calm himself, and asked Ben Lawless another question.

"What's your date of birth, Lawless?"

The inmate managed to grin. "December twenty-fourth . . . warden. I was . . . a . . . Christmas gift . . . for my mommy."

He turned away and marched back to O'Connor.

"Captain, today does not feel like Christmas Eve, does it?"

"No, sir."

"Apparently, your birthday bath was either months too late or months too early."

"Yes, sir."

"Have this man dried off. Put his clothes back on. And have him escorted to my office at the old prison."

O'Connor saluted. "Yes, sir."

Fallon then pointed to four other inmates, lined up against the four-foot high wall, the wall that eventually would be part—if Fallon remembered the blue-print right—of the maintenance shop on the northeast corner of the prison grounds.

"Is today also the birthday of those inmates?" Fallon demanded.

"I would not know, sir."

Fallon looked at the men, standing in puddles of water in their bare feet, pants still on, but shirts off, and their wrists lashed to a beam that had been placed behind their necks. Back at Joliet, Fallon remembered, they called that a yoke. Fallon's neck and shoulders hurt from the memory of it.

"If they came with birthday gifts, Captain, I don't see any."

"They probably forgot them, sir."

"I see. Maybe we should remove the yoke off those men, and have them returned to their work detail."

O'Connor's eyes moved from staring straight ahead, to locking in on Fallon. That the warden knew what a "yoke" was impressed the big man. His eyes shot back ahead. "Very good, sir."

"Is there anything else you'd like to say, Tim?" Fallon let his voice drop to a whisper. "Speak freely."

O'Connor wet his lips, considered the suggestion for a moment, and at length cleared his throat. "Lawless is the king of the coop, Hank," he said, testing the name. "We have to put him in his place. Let him know who's the boss. He controls most of the prisoners, and there are too many of them compared to the fifty guards we have. You've never seen a riot . . ."

"Oh," Fallon interrupted. "I have seen many. Been in more than my share. You might want to do a little more research about me, Tim, before you make assumptions." He then asked. "And why the witnesses?"

"Newbies," O'Connor said. "Fresh fish."

Fallon nodded. "Showing them how things are . . . rid them of any bad ideas."

"Yes, sir."

"We'll talk about this in my office, Tim. Bring Ben Lawless with you."

He walked out of the water, away from the kiln, and toward the old prison at the fort.

CHAPTER TWENTY-TWO

Fallon had never served in the military, and from his office at the United States Military Prison on the bluffs overlooking the Big Muddy, he was glad he had been spared. Prison cells were drab affairs, lacking personality, lacking light. The paint was whitewash. The arched window let in little light. The furniture was dull.

After removing his hat and hanging it on the rack, Fallon settled behind his desk and felt like he was back in Cheyenne, Wyoming, in the federal courthouse, going through papers that needed his signatures. He signed his name, and took the forms to the clerk, but reread one of the documents at the top of the file and pulled it out. "Preston," he told the clerk, "I'll keep this one for a few minutes and bring it back later. That sound fine with you?"

"Yes, sir," the tiny man said.

Fifty guards. An assistant warden. A doctor. A bookkeeper. A chaplain. Eventually, the United States Penitentiary, Leavenworth, would also hire a couple of superintendents, one in charge of industries and another in charge of transportation and the farm. Every one of them a government bureaucrat—except, he hoped, the minister. Harry sure missed Helen these days. Too bad he couldn't have talked her into leaving wind-blown Cheyenne for even windier Kansas.

He went back into his office, looked out the window, saw Big Tim O'Connor and Ben Lawless, flanked by two guards—Ben Lawless had to be a most desperate criminal—moving toward the high stone walls and ugly yellow-painted offices. Fallon picked up his empty cup, found his way to the kitchen, and returned with three steaming mugs of coffee. Army coffee, too. The kind that would put hair on your head—maybe even scalped Ben Lawless's.

Prisoner and chief guard removed their caps when they stepped into the open doorway. Fallon rose, waved them in, and motioned to the two chairs in front of his desk. "Have a seat," he told them, "and if you'd care for coffee . . ." He motioned at the tray, and both men accepted the offer before settling into their seats. The two guards stood at the doorway uncertain, and Harry smiled at them, before calling to the clerk, "Preston?"

"Yes, sir?"

"Do me a favor. Take guards Raymond and Wilson"—he smiled at his former posse members, and held out his hand, shaking with each one, telling them (and feeling like a governmental and political appointee) that it was good to see them again— "down the hall to the commissary and show them the coffeepot." He grinned at Raymond and Wilson.

"There are cookies there, too. Preston's wife is a great baker. I'll bring Captain O'Connor and the prisoner to you when our meeting is over."

It sounded like a polite dismissal. The men started away, and Fallon turned back to his office but stepped back out and called out to the clerk.

"Preston," he said, "bring a few cookies back with you. For my guests."

He waited as the men stirred sugar into their coffee, sipped, sat, and crossed their legs. Finally, Preston returned with a plate of cookies. Ben Lawless eyed his with suspicion, and did not take a bite until Big Tim O'Connor started washing down his with his coffee.

Once he bit into it, his eyes revealed enormous pleasure.

Fallon told the clerk to close the door behind him.

"Let's get down to business," Fallon said when both men stopped chewing. He looked at Lawless.

"Captain O'Connor did you a favor this morning, Ben," Fallon said. "Those fresh fish know you're a big man in this pen."

The dark brown eye of Ben Lawless stared hard at Fallon, who tried not to stare back at the empty hole. "I am," Lawless told him, "a big man."

"If you were that big, Ben, you wouldn't need the captain to hose you down."

"Mister"—Lawless leaned forward in his chair, speaking in a dry whisper—"I've been here . . ."

"Better than twenty years," Fallon told him. "And you're here till you die. You know that."

"Or I get out."

"You've tried that four times." Fallon glanced at one of the sheets before him but did not pick it up.

"In '78, '79, '85, and '91. Each time you got maybe as far away as Loder, Walburn, and Turner. And Loder, Walburn, and Turner are damned fools."

The one-eyed killer, poisoner of Cherokee men, women, children, babies, horses, and dogs, leaned back in his chair and crossed his arms. Fallon looked at O'Connor.

"Why was he given the bath, Tim?"

"He dumped his soup for supper last night on the floor."

Fallon nodded, looked back at Lawless, then again at O'Connor. "Maybe if you didn't piss in the soup . . ." He decided what Aaron Holderman had told him wasn't so far-fetched. O'Connor's reaction told Fallon that Holderman hadn't been lying at all.

"I ain't no dog," Ben Lawless said.

"The hell you aren't," Big Tim O'Connor told him.

Fallon interrupted. "And you're not king of this pen much longer." He stood, moved around the desk and came directly to Lawless, reached down, and brought the carved cross up in his hands. Lawless stiffened, but decades in stir taught him better than to react or touch the warden. "The Ben Lawless I remember back in the Indian Nations did not fear God." The cross fell against the striped shirt, and Fallon turned back, sitting on the edge of his desk now. He reached over, grabbed his cup, sipped a moment, and lowered the cup to his thigh.

"But you're an old man now, Ben. Scared of dying. Scared of what awaits you. Scared of letting someone take over your place." He looked at O'Connor. "Who would that be, Captain?"

"Bowen Hardin," O'Connor said.

Lawless laughed. "No."

Fallon smiled. "Why not?"

"Hardin will be dead before I am," the Indian murderer said.

Fallon nodded in affirmation. "That could be. Hardin faces a firing squad in . . . July?"

"Unless his lawyers get it postponed one more damned time," O'Connor said.

"They won't." Lawless's grin looked like one of those clay masks of a dead man. "They can't."

"The Supreme Court turned down the last appeal," Fallon said. "Execution is scheduled for dawn on July thirtieth."

"Then it's Indianola Anderson," O'Connor said.

Lawless guffawed and picked up his coffee cup. "He's worthless."

"So were you," Fallon told him. "It took you . . . ten years, twelve?"

Lawless leaned back. "You seem to know a lot for a pencil-pushin', yellow-livered warden."

"I know enough about prisons, Ben. I've seen you in your birthday suit, remember? And I know I have more scars on my body than you have on yours—and not those the Cherokees gave me."

"Watch it, buster." The coffee cup rattled in Lawless's hands. "You don't know what it's like to lose a wife and a kid so—"

"*You* watch it, buster," Fallon threw the words back at the killer. "You don't want to go there. Not with me."

The tone, the eyes, the still quietness of Fallon made Lawless reconsider his adversary. He chewed on his lip and slid back into the chair, before relaunching his attack, but in a milder tone.

"Well, you need to know one thing, Mister Warden, I don't belong here. I never—"

"Don't preach that dung to me, Lawless," Fallon said. "But, yeah, you don't belong here. They should have strung you up years ago. Or Judge Parker should have let the Cherokees have you."

"They killed—"

"I know what happened, Lawless." He had switched from first name to last. "That's a name you deserve, Number Three-Nine-Seven-Two. Lawless. So white whiskey runners get four Cherokee boys, in their teens, drunk on their forty-rod they're peddling. Those boys go to your place, and, yeah, what they did was horrible. Butchery. And being drunk isn't an excuse for their barbarity. Which is why the Cherokee police arrested them, which is why a Cherokee judge sentenced them, and which is why forty days after your family was murdered, those four kids were hanged in Tahlequah."

Lawless's head dropped.

Fallon caught his breath, and continued, "But you, Ben Lawless, you couldn't see that. You didn't think that was enough, that the four kids who ruined your life, who murdered your family, that they were dead. But you didn't go after the white men who ran that whiskey into the Cherokee Nation. You let those men go free. Hell, I don't believe we ever learned who they were. Maybe they wound up in Detroit. Most likely they did. Perhaps they even spent a year or two here in Leavenworth with you. You let the white men go, Ben Lawless. You went after innocent Indians." Fallon shook his head in disgust. "And, hell, Number Thirty-Nine-Seven-Two, I might have a bit of respect for you had you done it with some sort of honor. Walk in, draw a gun, shoot a man in the head. Hell, shoot a man in the back. That's one thing. But you poisoned water wells. You poisoned canteens and gourds. You poisoned pies left on a windowsill to cool. You were like a sneak thief, but instead of stealing money or silver, you stole the lives of innocent Cherokee families. And why they didn't hang you for that, why they made taxpayers keep you alive for decades . . . that's another thing about our judicial system that I can't wrap my head around."

Fallon moved back to his chair, sat down. "You disgust me, Ben Lawless. I hate your yellow-livered guts. But I'm here for you, boy. I'm here as your protector. You want absolution. Maybe you've got it. But you also want respect. From those wearing stripes like yourself. You want to be the big man. Well, from where I sit, I can help you get that. For a price, Ben. For a price. You've been in this hellhole long enough to know how things work, Ben Lawless. It's that old deal. I don't like it. But I've seen it enough in Illinois—in every other dungeon I had to stick my head into. This time, I'm here of my own accord. So I'm playing the game. I know the game. It's the game we all have to play in pieces of filth like this. We have to deal with filth in places of filth. I'm dealing with you."

He quit preaching. His mouth felt like it had been coated with gall. Finding his cup, he brought it quickly across the desk, spilling some, but not caring, and drank greedily. The coffee was cold by then. He was finished. He swallowed what he could, and spat more into the trash can. Then, leaning back in his chair, Fallon waited until Ben Lawless raised his head.

"Let's make a deal, Ben," he said, going back to the first name now. "I let Captain O'Connor spray you with water. So the fresh fish know just how dangerous you are. I keep Bowen Hardin as a nobody. I make things tougher for Indianola Anderson. You reap the profits. You're the king of Leavenworth till you die. Which, for me, can't be soon enough. What's your price?"

He waited.

Ben Lawless sat there, a wretched, pale little man, scalped years ago by drunken and foolish Indian boys. Saw his life ruined. Then ruined his own life, and the lives of many innocent Cherokees till a handful of deputy marshals finally brought him to Fort Smith. Fallon could remember watching the jail wagon as it rumbled down Garrison Avenue—and he could remember the cheers. Some of them were for the lawmen. Most had been for Ben Lawless.

That sickened him, too.

After what felt like hours, Ben Lawless cleared his throat and made his demand.

CHAPTER TWENTY-THREE

"I want," Ben Lawless said, lowering his one eye, and speaking in an arid whisper. "I want to . . . read."

Fallon's mouth opened. He leaned back in his chair and looked at Big Tim O'Connor to make sure he had heard right, but the captain's face registered as much shock as Fallon's own must have.

"You want to . . ." Fallon couldn't finish.

"Read," the little man said. "I know the Good Book from what the preacher man has been tellin' me. But I want to read it . . . for my own . . . my ownself." A tear suddenly ran down from the corner of the killer's dark, cold brown eye.

"Ma taught me some of my letters back in Tennessee. But . . . I done forget 'em." He wiped away the tear. "I'd like to be able to read the Good Book before I'm called to Glory. Or sent to the Pit. Whatever. I know I don't deserve to walk the Streets of Gold. But . . . I'd surely like to be able to read the Bible. Read my own name. Read anything. And write my own name. Before I die."

Money . . . a whore . . . whiskey, not the awful, sometimes lethal, brew the prisoners could come up with on their own . . . maybe even just a chance to fish from the banks of the river, or a carriage ride through town. Something like that. But most likely the money, prostitute, or good whiskey. That's what Fallon expected from a miserable wastrel like Ben Lawless.

Fallon glanced at the cross the man had carved, and looked again into the red-rimmed eye—the one the drunken teenagers had not carved out with Lawless's own fork.

"All right, Ben," Fallon heard himself say. "Let me see what I can do." His head turned away from the pitiful prisoner and locked on Big Tim O'Connor.

The captain stood, moved to the door, and called out for Raymond and Wilson. When the two guards appeared, Fallon rose from his seat. His back felt sweaty, drenched in water, like he had been the victim of the bath treatment from the city fire engine. "Return the inmate to his cell," Fallon instructed the guards. "His work detail is over for this day. When you have done that, report back to your stations at the work detail. Thank you, men."

Ben Lawless rose, without a word, without acknowledgment. He was back as the prisoner, finding his cap, keeping it in his hands until he was outside. His head hung down, that one eye kept trained on the floor, and he marched as though in lockstep with another prisoner, out of the office, and out of the building.

Fallon sat back down. Tim O'Connor closed the door.

"I could use a drink," O'Connor said.

Fallon whispered an answer. "Sorry, Tim. I've been off redeye for years."

"You're a smart man."

Fallon laughed. "If I was smart, I'd be looking for a bottle of rye with you." He leaned back in the chair. "Read."

"And write. Ain't that the damnedest thing?" O'Connor said, and began searching his pockets for his tobacco.

Fallon leaned forward. "How many prisoners can read and write, Tim?"

The guard had the chaw in his hand, was bringing it up to his mouth, but he stopped, and let the hand drop down to his thigh. "I wouldn't know . . . Hank."

Fallon remembered the paper he had taken from the stack on Preston's desk. He waved it toward O'Connor, then brought it before his eyes. "This is a note, from my predecessor here, a report for . . . well, that doesn't matter . . . but it says that most inmates released are destined to return to prison."

"That's true." O'Connor decided it was all right to chew his tobacco, so he bit off a mouthful and slipped the rest into the pocket of his trousers. "We turned one ol' boy out three weeks ago. Deke Reno. I told him when I shoved him through the gate that I'd keep his cell ready, that he'd be back. And he will. Though I thought he'd be back before now."

Fallon barely heard what the big man said. "It goes on to say that because of our location in the West, because most of these inmates did not grow up with all the temptations in the Eastern cities, there is a better chance of rehabilitation of these inmates. That we can do something to prevent them from returning to a life of crime."

"That's from"—O'Connor shifted the chaw to his other cheek—"the warden before you took this job."

"Yes."

O'Connor rose to bring the spittoon closer. He shook his head when he sank back into the chair. "No offense, Hank, but that son of a strumpet was off his rocker worser than you are."

Fallon started tapping just below his lower lip with the fingers on his right hand. O'Connor's juice made a pinging noise as it hit the rim of the brass cuspidor. "In every prison I was in," Fallon said, "Joliet, Yuma, Jeff City, and the Walls. Every one. There always was a library."

"We got one here, too," O'Connor told him. "Twelve books, three of them Bibles but one's for the Mormons, and newspapers when some people donate them after they've read them. Subscribe to *Harper's* and *Frank Leslie's*. But that's for the guards." He chuckled. "The guards we got that can read for themselves. We used to keep the *Police Gazette,* but the warden before the last one stopped that. Said it gave the inmates bad ideas."

Fallon stared hard at Big Tim O'Connor.

The captain wiped his mouth with the sleeve of his shirt, chewed on the tobacco with his molars, and finally said, "I can read pretty good, Warden," he said. "If that's bugging you." He pointed at the desk. "Hand me one of those papers and I'll prove it to."

"I don't question your literacy, Tim," Fallon told him. "I was just thinking. All those prisons. We had libraries. But no one ever thought about the inmates who could not read."

"We got *The Count of Monte Christo* by this guy named Dumb Ass." O'Connor snorted. "Funny name."

"Dumas," Fallon corrected after he chuckled with the captain of the guards. "A Frenchman." He took in a deep breath and let it out. "And, yes, every prison I've been in had that book in its library. I don't know how many times I've read it."

"I never read it," O'Connor said. "The prisoners we got who can read . . . they read it. Says it's a good story."

"It's about revenge," Fallon told him. "And escaping from the Bastille."

"What's that?"

"A prison. In France."

"Maybe we should ban it."

Fallon laughed. O'Connor spit.

"It's a big book," the captain said after a while. "That's why I don't read it. Haven't read it, I mean. I like the smaller books. The half-dime novels and the dime novels. But I don't even read them much."

Fallon barely heard him.

"Hank."

Three times later, Fallon realized O'Connor was talking to him. "Yes?"

"You made a bargain with Lawless. How you plan on keeping that?"

"That's what I'm trying to figure out." He resumed tapping his fingers below his lip.

"Well." O'Connor spit into the cuspidor, wiped his lips, and pushed himself out of the chair. "I think I should get back to the building site, make sure no one has lit out for the Indian Nations or Canada. Make sure none of my guards are giving somebody a bath when it ain't his birthday." He stood, waiting, hat in his hand, staring, wondering if Fallon had heard him at all.

Fallon hadn't. "How big is the library here?" Fallon asked.

O'Connor thought a moment. "Not big. Your office. Maybe with part of Mr. Preston's office. Too big a building, though, for as few books and stuff that we got."

After scratching his head, O'Connor spit again, and this time removed the plug from his mouth, and dropped it into the spittoon, even though he had barely chewed it. "Are you thinking about . . . turning the library . . . into a . . . school?"

"I'm considering it," Fallon answered without hesitation. "But the library wouldn't work. Prisoners and guards are in there too much. We need a building that doesn't get much use to serve as a—"

"School." O'Connor spit again. "Teaching murderers . . . counterfeiters . . . scum of the earth . . . to read and write."

"Some of them," Fallon said. "Lawless, certainly. Not the killers."

"Ben Lawless is a murderer, sir," O'Connor pointed out.

"He wasn't convicted of murder, though. Attempted murder. And running ardent spirits into the Indian Nations. Justice isn't always justice, you know."

"For which he got life with no chance of parole. An extreme sentence."

"Which the president of the United States allowed. That was Lawless's only chance of appeal."

"Because a lot of those jurors didn't care for Cherokees or any Indians."

Fallon sighed. "We don't sentence the men here. We don't convict them. We don't try them. We try to rehabilitate them, and that's where we have failed. And we try to keep those who can't be rehabilitated away from the public."

"Well . . ." O'Connor pulled his cap on and withdrew the tobacco from his pocket. "I'll be back in the yard, sir. You keep thinking on your dream. But where you gonna get a teacher, Hank? And don't look at me."

Fallon didn't hear the last part, either, and Big Tim O'Connor left him in the office, closing the door, and hearing Fallon say over and over: "I don't know. I just don't know."

CHAPTER TWENTY-FOUR

When Montgomery Berrien tapped on the door frame, Fallon looked up from the papers scattered across his desk and pushed back his chair, waving in the timid, tiny, bespectacled man, who was wearing the finest suit a man could find in Leavenworth, Kansas.

"Come in, Monty, come in," Fallon said, and pulled the handkerchief from his vest pocket to wipe away the ink and pencil marks staining the tips of his fingers. Paperwork left a mark on an administrator. Fallon always preferred trail dust and sweat stains on his hat.

The little man swallowed and stepped inside, finding the chair Fallon had positioned closest to the desk. He settled into that, cleared his throat, and said, "You wanted to see me, Hank?" He smiled the smile of an incredibly nervous man.

Only my friends call me Hank flashed through Fallon's mind, but he would let this slide for the time being.

After sliding back closer to his desk and shoving the handkerchief inside the pocket, Fallon reached down, picked up one of the papers, and waved it at the little man. He sort of reminded Fallon of Sean MacGregor, only not as corrupt, and smaller in size and frame and mental capacities.

"Monty," Fallon said, "I've been going over the prison's books."

The little man stopped fidgeting. "I'm the book-keeper, Hank," he said, trying to sound stern, but squawking more like a nervous hen.

"You were the bookkeeper." Fallon let the paper fall softly back to the stacks on his table. And this *Hank* stuff was ending now. "And only my friends call me Hank."

What little color was in the bookkeeper's face drained like beer from a tapped keg right after a trail crew hit the saloon. His mouth hung open, and his upper lip quivered, and he tried to say something, but it appeared that Montgomery Berrien had forgotten how to talk.

"That's a nice suit you have there, Monty," Fallon said. "Bloomingdale's?"

The man shook his head.

"I didn't think so. Tailor made?"

The head could move up and down, too.

"Yeah." Fallon opened the top drawer, found another sheet of paper, but it was yellow, and smaller, and the writing was made in a beautiful cursive, with many of the words in French. The numbers at the bottom were the most important part. "I dropped in to see Jean Baptiste Alphonse Charpentier's place downtown." Smiling pleasantly, Fallon waved the receipt. "That's a lot of name for such a tiny fellow. Charpentier, Couture de la Plus Haute Estime. I don't know what that really means, but that's what's spelled out on this receipt, on his shingle, and in real pretty letters on the plate-glass window of his suit-making shop." He stopped waving the paper. "You recognize this? It's his copy. Not yours."

The little head's movement was just perceptible.

Fallon shook his head and laid the paper on the desk. "When I rode for Judge Parker's court down in Arkansas and the Indian Nations, I could have bought twenty suits for what you paid for this one." His arms folded across his chest. "Course, that was quite a few years ago. I guess prices for suits have gone up since then."

Berrien's head nodded in ready agreement.

"But not that much." Fallon found another piece of paper. "Especially not on what the United States government pays you." He waved this sheet, too. "According to the records I have here."

"I came into some money . . ." the petite man tried.

"Inheritance?"

He had to think, finally shook his head. "No . . . it was . . ." He thought of something genius. "Gambling."

"Poker?" Fallon fired out.

"Yes. No. No. Horses."

Fallon congratulated the bookkeeper and found another paper. He flashed it toward Berrien. "You've been betting on horses a long time. According to your bank account." He smiled. "And who is this Sienna Ginevra Di Genova?"

Now the face became scarlet. "You have no right."

Fallon found another paper. "This is a warrant, Monty. Signed by a federal judge. And from more papers on my desk here, I see that Sienna Ginevra Di Genova is not your wife. That's an Italian name, isn't it?" He replaced the warrant with another paper. "Your wife is Marian Berrien. I like the rhyme."

Tears welled, then flowed, and in moments, the bookkeeper blubbered in the chair so much that Fallon tossed him the handkerchief he had been using to clean his fingers. He let the man cry. When the sobbing reduced to a sniffling, Fallon pushed his chair back against the wall and propped his boots on the edge of his desk.

"Monty, embezzlement of a substantial amount of money from a federal institution lands the embezzler in the federal penitentiary for quite a few years." The loud crying resumed. Fallon added: "With luck, Monty, your cell will be across from Ben Lawless's or Bowen Hardin's."

The man wailed like a banshee.

Fallon knew his handkerchief, if Monty Berrien didn't keep it, would be going into the trashcan. Letting the man sob relentlessly, Fallon stood, crossed his office, and stuck his head out of the doorway. Preston, the clerk, was still enjoying his dinner at the commissary. The doors to the rest of the closest offices remained closed. Fallon shut this one, too, and went back to his chair, letting the man cry for another minute.

He cleared his throat. It took a few minutes before Berrien managed to sit somewhat steadily in the chair.

"These little deductions that popped up, Monty." He nodded with approval. "To be perfectly honest with you, I don't think I ever would have noticed them. In fact, I had to take this copy of the books back home, let Christina—that's my wife, you know—go through them. And I wouldn't have done that if I hadn't noticed your suits." He found a handful of other receipts and flashed them briefly. "That struck me as, well, a bit above your means. Anyway, Christina, she has a lot of experience at these kinds of things. She was a detective before we married, you see. American Detective Agency. Out of Chicago. That's where we met. But I digress."

He propped the feet back on the desk, and leaned back. "What I was looking for, at first, was a way to get a few items in our budget. Make things easier on my guards. They work their butts off, Monty, for practically nothing. You get to go home at night. To your wife. Or"—he had to find the paper again—"Sienna Ginevra Di Genova." He grinned and shook his hand. "That's a lot of name." Then he winked. "For a lot of woman, right, Monty?"

The man was about to bawl his head off, so Fallon stopped the taunts.

He rose, grabbed the ledger, and moved to the vacant chair, which he dragged forward and settled in beside the small man with big ideas.

"Monty."

The bookkeeper wiped his nose and eyes with Fallon's silk handkerchief and, lips quavering, tried to focus.

Fallon handed the book to Berrien. "See, Christina figured out what you were doing. Or what somebody was doing. Then we did what we in the private detective business call . . . snooping. Once we had enough to bring to Judge McDowell, we sat down with him, got the warrant, did our work, and here we are. Me and you. *Mano a mano.*"

He gave Berrien a few moments to try to compose

himself before Fallon reached across and pointed at the books. "All I started out trying to do, Monty, was figure out how we could hire someone to teach school. Teach school to the inmates, I mean. Say . . . five hundred dollars a year."

The tear-filled eyes blinked.

Fallon pulled out a receipt of his own from another pocket and showed it to Berrien. "And the . . . see what it would take to buy all these supplies. For the prison. Make things easier. Make things safer. And not have to dillydally around and wait for the pencil pushers to figure out a budget for next year. I want this done"—he waved the receipt—"immediately."

Fallon leaned back. Berrien saw the receipt, wet his lips, and found a pencil in his shirt pocket.

"This . . . is . . . for . . ." Berrien looked up.

"The library. Just the materials. That number right there. And the five hundred dollars for the teacher. That's a woman teacher, you understand. A man would earn a little over a hundred dollars more per annum. We'll supply the labor from our own pool."

The little bookkeeper went to work, and when Fallon saw that this would take a while, he rose, dragged the chair back, opened the door, and went to find some coffee. Five minutes later, he was back inside, closing the door behind him, and returning to his desk. He gathered the papers, stuck those in a folder, found the *Post* and the *Sentinel*, and began to read.

Noise from the hallway told him that Preston and others had finished their dinner and were back to finish the day's work. The bookkeeper kept working, and finally, as Fallon was reading about the goings-on in a country he had never heard of, Montgomery Berrien cleared his throat.

"Warden Fallon," the little man said.

Fallon closed the *Sentinel*, laid it on his desk, and nodded.

"You don't have the money." He swallowed. "The penitentiary, I mean, does not have the money."

"Even if we added back all the money you stole?"

He thought Berrien would break down into tears again, but he maintained his dignity—whatever was left—and shook his head again after blowing his nose. "Even . . . yes . . . that's based on the . . . real . . . budget."

Fallon sighed. "I see."

The man stared at his shoes, which were new, and expensive, too. Fallon said, "I suppose, at some point, later, we would have fallen short of funds when we tried to . . . oh . . . pay for the fire engine we've been renting from the city?"

"Perhaps." Montgomery Berrien managed a quick grin. "But you know how the government works."

"Yes." Fallon laughed. "Yes, I've worked long enough for the good ol' US of A to know that route."

The little man began to pale again.

"So the prison doesn't have the money, right?" Fallon said.

"Yes. Right. The prison doesn't have the money."

Fallon nodded. "But you do. Right?"

CHAPTER TWENTY-FIVE

Fallon, Christina, and Rachel Renee found the duplex that Elliott and Janice Jefferson rented without difficulty. It had been a nice enough walk from their home to the neighborhood. Rachel Renee loved the picket fence and whitewashed gate, asked if they could have one at their own house. They let her go in and out of the gate three times before Christina said she might break it if she kept that up, and so they moved up the cobblestone walkway and climbed the steps. Fallon lifted his daughter up high enough so that she could twist the knob that rang the buzzer.

"That sounds funny," the girl said and laughed. Fallon lowered her to the porch before she could buzz the house again.

The door opened, and Elliott Jefferson, dressed as best as a prison guard could, with a black string tie hanging from underneath the paper collar buttoned to his starched white shirt, grinned widely. "Welcome to our humble abode," he said, and stuck out his hand. Fallon figured he had been practicing that often-used line over and over for the past hour and a half.

They shook, Fallon introducing his family, and stepped into the foyer, with Fallon removing his hat and Elliott Jefferson taking it.

Christina breathed in deeply. "I don't know what's for supper," she said, "but it smells divine."

Fallon smiled. For he knew his wife had been practicing that sentence during the walk from their home.

Fallon's dress hat was hung on the top hooks on the coat rack, and Elliott beckoned them down the hall and to the dining room, but showed them the parlor, the piano, and the fireplace, and the wedding-day photograph of Elliott's parents. Fallon held the tintype up close, nodding, and remembering.

"Best lawman in the Indian Nations," Fallon said as he handed the photo back to the young guard.

"It's kind of you to say that," Elliott said somberly as he returned the small photo to its place on a corner case.

"I didn't say that," Fallon said. "Those words came from Judge Isaac Parker himself. At your father's funeral." Fallon nodded, liking the way the kid's eyes beamed. Fallon added, "But I will say I agreed with Judge Parker's assessment."

That lightened the mood, and they stepped into the dining room. Elliott pulled out a chair for Christina, then one beside her for the five-year-old, and quickly slid to the sliding door, which he opened, stuck his head inside the winter—and only—kitchen and called for his wife.

She stepped out of the entryway, wiping her hands on the apron, and grinned.

Fallon found her beautiful—not the same as Christina, and certainly not as tough, but a lovely blonde with piercing eyes, freckles on her face, a young girl who looked younger than her husband.

"Elliott," Janice suggested, "why don't you offer our guests a drink?" Her eyes settled on Rachel Renee. "Would you like lemonade or milk, sweetheart?"

"Lemonade," the girl practically screamed.

Both the five-year-old and the young bride quickly looked at Christina for confirmation.

"Is that all right?" both asked the mother.

Grinning, Christina said, "Lemonade would be fine. It's a special occasion."

"I'll have a lemonade, too," Fallon said, before someone offered him bourbon or a beer.

"The same," Christina said.

"I guess that's unanimous," Elliott said.

"Can I help you?" Christina called to Janice as she slipped back into the kitchen.

"On, I'll be fine," the panicked wife of the young guard said.

Christina stood. "And I'll be fine, too, if I don't have to listen to the silly banter of these two men. Come on, Rachel Renee. It's high time you learned how to cook a fantastic supper."

And supper, Fallon had to agree, was fantastic. Braised beef, stewed cabbage, mashed potatoes so creamy each spoonful melted in your mouth, seasoned perfectly with garlic and rosemary. The baked bread, coated with slabs of butter, was what Fallon had heard a greased-mustached waiter call "a fine cleanser of your palate," and what followed was apple pie, perfected with cinnamon and served with heaping spoonfuls of rich, delectable cream.

The adults drank coffee to wash down the last remnants of dessert. Rachel Renee had milk.

"Well . . ." Fallon set his fork on the bowl. "I don't think I can fit another morsel in my mouth."

"Let me help you clear the table, Janice," Christina said, and Rachel Renee sang out, "I'll help, too."

"Excellent," a nervous but winding-down Janice Jefferson said. "You men take your cigars outside on the back porch. We'll join you when the smoke has cleared."

"Warden Fallon," Elliott Jefferson said nervously when he closed the screen door to the porch. "Well, sir, I . . . I don't smoke. No cigarettes. Not even cigars. I don't even chew tobacco."

"I don't, either, Elliott," Fallon said. They looked at each other, then laughed.

"And I haven't had much taste of wine, liquor, beer, or even cider since I wore a badge pinned on my chest," Fallon continued. They stared at each other, grinning. "But I do have a particular fondness for coffee. Black. It doesn't keep me up, either."

"I'm the same way, Warden." He was heading back toward the screen door. "There's a pot on the stove morning, noon, and night."

The sun was setting, bathing the backyard of the rented house in brilliant, warm spring light.

Rachel Renee lay sleeping in her mother's arms while Christina rocked the wicker chair gently on the wooden porch. Somewhere in Leavenworth, a dog barked, and birds chirped the last choruses of their songs. A church bell chimed. No gunshots. No curses. No whistles, shouts, breaking of glasses, windows, or heads. Leavenworth, Kansas, on this particular night, was at peace.

Fallon set the empty china cup on a saucer, looked up at Elliott and Janice, and nodded his approval. "It has been a long, long time, folks, since I've had . . . we've had . . . such a wonderful supper and such a relaxing, great evening."

"We're so glad you could come," Janice said, "and share this evening with us." She smiled down at the sleeping child. "She's adorable. And a perfect child."

Christina laughed. "Oh, you should see her when she's a tigress."

Elliott drank more coffee. "How was your day, Warden?"

"Let's make it Hank, Elliott," Fallon said, and leaned back in the comfortable chair. "I got a few things done." He thought about his accomplishments, felt satisfied, and nodded at the guard. "How about yours?"

"All prisoners accounted for."

They grinned. Janice said, "That's a start."

"Actually," Fallon said. "I think I made some headway." He nodded at the young man sitting across from him. "That might make your days and nights a little easier."

He had struck a deal with the bookkeeping swindler and embezzler—not to mention two-timing cheat—Montgomery Berrien. The bookkeeper agreed to fund two of Fallon's pet projects in return for not going to federal prison for the maximum sentence Judge McDowell could give a rake, scoundrel, and idiot. He'd even keep his job, with the understanding that if one penny turned up missing in the books, he'd become the best friend on Friday nights of Bowen Hardin.

"I'd love to see my husband," Janice said.

Fallon slid cup and saucer to the center of the table. "Well," he said, "you might." He told them his plans, his project—he did not have to explain how he had come up with enough money to cover the expenses; Christina already knew, of course, after discovering the strange, illegal, inappropriate entries in the Leavenworth pen's books.

"You mean . . . ?" Janice sounded hopeful after Fallon had given a short overview.

"I mean ten-hour shifts six days a week," Fallon said. "Seven in the morning till five in the afternoon." He liked the way that sounded. "The shifts might change. Night duty or daytime hours. The days off would have to rotate. But we'll be getting rid of these ridiculous hours, draining my men—men who are paid to be alert for anything when they're on duty. We have to do it this way. By thunder, before we know it, we'll be living in the twentieth century—and working like men were four centuries earlier."

"That's great," Christina said, though she was aware of Fallon's plan long before he had ever blackmailed Montgomery Berrien.

"And here's something else I have in mind," Fallon said. He had not even gotten the chance to tell his wife about this. "It's a possible way to help actually rehabilitate the prisoners we have, those not doomed to execution or never to be released from this prison. Education."

They stared at him.

"Eighty-three percent of the inmates here can't read or write," Fallon explained. "They can't add. They can't write their own names. *If* we can educate the prisoners, the illiterate, they might have a chance. Once they get out. It's a long shot. But it's at least . . . a chance."

"You think that's possible, Hank?" Elliott Jefferson asked.

"I'd like to think it is," Fallon conceded.

"You might be dreaming," Elliott told him. "I've worked with most of these men."

"I know. But if you can reform one man, then it's worth it."

"Maybe." Christina sounded doubtful.

Hell, Fallon couldn't blame her for that.

"Warden . . . Mr. Fallon . . ." Janice Jefferson was stuttering. She laughed, shrugged, and tried again. "You need . . . a teacher."

Fallon nodded. "Yeah. And that's the next mountain I have to climb. Find someone willing to teach men in a federal penitentiary. For five hundred dollars a year. That's where my groundbreaking idea ends."

"Maybe not."

Fallon and Elliott looked at their wives. Both had spoken those two words at the same time.

Janice started to blush. "Well." She forced a smile. "Well, before I got married, I taught school. At Pleasant Hill. Over toward Monticello."

Fallon frowned. "Why'd you quit?"

His own wife laughed. "Harry," Christina said, "most schools will not hire a female teacher unless she is not married."

Fallon studied his own wife. "You learn that from your years with the American Detective Agency?" he asked.

"I learned that when I was seventeen years old, darling," she told him. "For two and a half years, before I found another line of work, I taught school in a one-room log cabin in Pike County, Illinois."

CHAPTER TWENTY-SIX

Scrambled eggs with plenty of salt and pepper, fried bacon, wildflower jam to go on the thick slices of fresh bread—Fallon thought he could have become a chef at a fancy restaurant in some big city with the breakfast he had whipped up this Monday morning. He even plated the dishes, poured Christina a cup of coffee, and put milk into a glass for Rachel Renee before fixing his own breakfast.

They sat and Rachel Renee insisted on praying. Finally they all said, "Amen," and Fallon dropped his napkin on his lap and tested the coffee.

Even that tasted great.

"What are you doing today, Papa?" the girl asked, and Fallon grinned at her milk mustache.

"Find a place we can use for a schoolhouse," Fallon told her.

"Can I go to school?" his daughter practically screamed.

"You'll be going soon enough, sweetheart," Christina said, and bit into the eggs. Her eyes showed amazement. She turned to Fallon and nodded, "These are great."

"I had to cook for prisoners when I was just starting out as a lawman in Fort Smith," he explained. "But trust me, nothing they ate ever tasted like this."

"I want to go to Papa's school," Rachel Renee said. "I bet he can teach me gooder than anybody else could."

"Better than," Christina said. "Not *gooder* than. *Gooder* is not a word. You'll learn that in school—next year."

Fallon grinned. "You were a schoolteacher."

Christina gave him a menacing look, at least as long as she could hold it, then laughed.

"I want to go to Papa's school," their daughter continued.

Fallon shook his head. "This school won't be for little girls or even little boys," he explained with patience. "It's for the inmates—some of the prisoners—here."

"The bad men?"

"Yes, honey, the bad men. But not the meanest. Not those . . ." He had to figure out how he could get out of this. "Not the . . ."

"Only the *gooder* ones," Christina said.

Rachel Renee laughed, and Fallon joined them. "That's right. The *gooder* prisoners."

His daughter pointed her fork at him. "Mama said gooder ain't a word."

"Isn't," Christina said. "Not ain't. Remember?"

"Yes." She looked at her plate, then moved back to the glass of milk and drank again. "Is Mama going to teach the prisoners?"

"I think Mr. Jefferson's wife might be taking that job," Fallon said.

"Well, Janice might need some help."

The bacon in Fallon's mouth lost its flavor, and he swallowed, washed it down with coffee, and set the cup on the saucer. "I don't believe I was privy to that conversation."

"You were outside with Rachel Renee and Elliott," she told him. "Janice and I were doing the dishes."

"I see." He patted his mouth with his napkin.

"Janice is also a seamstress," Christina said. "She wants a day to work on the dresses she makes for Mrs. Peterson's shop, and do the hemming and things, sew buttons on shirts, and do some work for herself."

"She'd have Saturday and Sunday off," Fallon said.

"Saturday, she works in Mrs. Peterson's shop. Sunday, as you might recall, is a day of rest."

Fallon made himself drink more coffee. "So, we could hold school Monday through Thursday."

"You could. But Janice and I decided that wouldn't be good for the prisoners. So I would teach on Fridays."

"The budget Monty Berrien managed to finesse gave us only one teacher."

"Which is what you'd have. One teacher. Just filled by two highly talented women. Janice would be paid for four days' work. I would collect for just one. At a salary of five hundred dollars a year, the week of Christmas off, along with Thanksgiving, Independence Day, New Year's Eve, and New Year's Day, and the Monday after Easter, that would be ten dollars a week. Janice would take home eight dollars, and I would take home two."

"That doesn't seem worth the trouble," Fallon said.

"It's not. Especially when you take into account that had you hired a man to teach, he would be earning a hundred dollars more a year than a woman."

Fallon began to regret he had ever listened to Ben Lawless's dream.

He forked some eggs into his mouth. Too much salt. Not enough pepper. Should have used more bacon grease to get better flavor. Swallowed. Found the coffee cup again. Sipped. Scratched his head.

"Well," he said. "We'll have to see if this actually happens." He realized his wife could take that the wrong way, so he quickly added, "Having a school. For the prisoners. I have to find a place . . ."

"That should not be hard," Christina said. "There has to be a spot in the old prison. This new one won't be ready for some time."

"And then I'd have to figure out how to schedule the guards." That idea came to Fallon just then.

"What do the guards have to do with a school for prisoners?" Christina asked.

Fallon said, "Well, we'd need to have a guard in the school."

She set her knife on her plate and folded her arms. "You think we need a guard . . . to protect us from . . . embezzlers . . . counterfeiters . . . forgers?" Her eyes did her patented roll. "You said yourself, darling, that the violent men would not be attending class, with the exception of, I'm guessing, Ben Lawless."

"Ben's not a threat to anyone," Fallon said softly. "Not anymore."

"So why would we need a guard?"

"Yes, Papa," Rachel Renee said, "since only the gooder prisoners would be learning to write and read."

They have joined forces against me, Fallon thought. Women!

"For the protection of the teachers," Fallon said, and let his eyes bore into his wife's. "Whomever we may hire for that job."

A smile rose across Christina's face. "My love, do you remember a man named Justice?"

Sighing, Fallon wished he had not been feeling so noble this morning, that he had left cooking to Christina and had taken his meal either in one of the cafés on his way to work or even at the prison dining hall.

"Yes, sweetheart, I do."

Justice. The insane Southern plantation owner from Louisiana and Texas who had tried to relaunch the Civil War—before Fallon and other agents had thwarted that conspiracy. One of those agents, he knew, had been Christina.

"Well, now, if I could handle that renegade and butcher, I think I can take care of myself against an artist who makes fake money or an old butcher like Ben Lawless. Before we ever met, my love, I'll have you know that I worked right alongside a bunch of anarchists who planned to bomb Union Station. And the Elton gang, operating along the Ohio–Pennsylvania border . . . do you remember them?"

"Yes."

"They haven't robbed any federal paymasters in ten years, my love, because I arrested all three of them, testified at their trial, and saw them off to prison."

"You did all those things, Mommy?" Rachel Renee asked.

"She did," Fallon answered, "and more than that."

"Wow." The five-year-old jumped down from her chair, and ran to her mother to give her a hug. "You're the bravest mommy who ever lived. I'm so proud of you."

"So am I," Fallon said.

Rachel Renee looked over the tabletop at her father. "What did you do, Papa?"

"Not a whole lot, honey."

"He's fibbing, Rachel Renee," Christina said. "Your father is the bravest man I've ever known. When you're old enough, I'll show you some of the men he brought to justice. They should be writing dime novels about him, not Kit Carson, Buffalo Bill, and Jesse James."

"Is that true, Papa?"

"It's true," Christina answered for him. "It's hard to believe, seeing what a sweetheart he is around the house."

"All right," Fallon said. "Let's finish eating. I have to get to work."

"What will you be doing today?" his daughter asked.

"Finding a school?" Christina inquired. "Since you've already, obviously, found your two teachers."

"No," Fallon said. "I have to figure out something

else today. But the school will happen. And, yeah, I know two perfectly capable women who will get that job."

Christina grinned. "Without guards, right?"

"Wrong." He raised his cup of coffee, drank, and smiled. "Honey," he said, "some of those guards need teaching worse than many of the prisoners."

CHAPTER TWENTY-SEVEN

He tapped on the door, and Montgomery Berrien looked up over his spectacles and immediately turned whiter than one of Fallon's mother's sheets after she'd done her spring cleaning. "Bring your notepad, the ledger, and some pencils," Fallon said, beckoning him with a crooked finger. "To my office." Stepping back into the hallway, he roamed down to the hall, where most of the guards were finishing their chuck. Unlike prisoners, guards could talk when they ate, and Fallon's ears hurt from the boisterous laughter, farts, and profanity until he found Big Tim O'Connor, who wasn't talking, just drinking coffee and tapping a new plug of tobacco against his empty plate.

"Before you head to the new prison," Fallon said, "stop by my office."

O'Connor's big head nodded, and Fallon walked back out.

Berrien was already seated in his chair across from Fallon's desk, which Fallon began cleaning off. He turned, nodded politely at the timid number pusher, and happened to see Elliott Jefferson walking down the hall, on his way outside to start another shift. That triggered another idea, so Fallon moved back out and called the young man's name.

"I need you in my office for about ten minutes," Fallon told him. He looked at the big guard who had been walking out with Jefferson. "Can you handle things without Elliott for a bit, Hans?" The German's eyes shone with glee, and he muttered an answer that sounded musical for the big Hun.

Fallon was stretching another blueprint of the new prison when O'Connor came inside.

"All right, gentlemen," Fallon said. "Gather around."

The four men stood close to the desk, and Fallon tapped on the blueprint.

"I think I've come up with a way that can cut down on the number of guards we use—and the hours they work," he said and picked up a pencil and tapped the map. "Barbed wire," he said.

"What?" O'Connor asked.

"Barbed wire. Thirty-some-odd years ago this farmer named Glidden got a patent—"

"I know what bob wire is," the big man said, mispronouncing the name of the invention as many people were prone to do. "But we don't have the money . . ."

"Mr. Berrien assures me that we do," Fallon said.

"You mean to tell me that you're gonna put up a strand of . . ."

"A fence," Fallon said. "Not just one strand. A fence of barbed wire."

"How high?" Elliott Jefferson asked.

A good question. Fallon said, "Seven feet. Six strands tight at the top, in case some hooligan climbs up that far without ripping his palms to shreds or tearing his striped britches off."

"Bob wire won't keep a jackrabbit out," O'Connor protested.

"I don't care how many jackrabbits get out, or in," Fallon said. "As long as no convicts make it out."

"They'll just cut the wire," O'Connor said. "You need a stone wall."

"The stone wall's going up. Along with the first cell block," Fallon said, shaking his head. "I know a barbed wire fence won't stop any determined man from getting out, but it will slow him down enough that guards will be able to stop him. I didn't say we'd be eliminating any of the fifty guards we have on the payroll, Tim. We'll still need men, lots of them, but not working them to death the way we have been doing."

O'Connor and Jefferson stared at the blueprint. O'Connor pulled the new plug from his trouser pocket and tore off a big chunk with his tobacco-stained teeth. As his mouth worked on the hunk, he turned to stare at the bookkeeper. "You think this is a good idea?"

"Well . . ." the little man said and started sweating.

Then O'Connor found the trash can and spit, wiped his mouth, and faced Fallon again. "This place is gonna be seven hundred acres, Hank. That's bigger than a section, more than one square mile. You can't fence all that . . ."

"We won't fence all seven hundred acres, Tim," Fallon said. "We don't guard all seven hundred acres now." He tapped on the blueprint. "That's the shoe factory, proposed shoe factory I should say, and this is the maintenance facility. Foundations haven't even been dug yet for those—and by my reckoning, they won't even be started before you and I are sitting in our rocking chairs, with wooden teeth, and nothing to do but tell our grandkids stories about what it was like in our youth." Now he turned the pencil around, and drew a line, eventually making a rectangle box.

"This is where we're working right now. Mostly on the first cell block. That's all we really have to enclose. Guards will be posted outside and inside the fence." Fallon marked places for the best positioning, then pointed out a place with easy access. "The gate will be here. The only gate. That's where prisoners march in and out, and we can also deliver supplies as needed. Extra guards will be put at the gate." He looked into the faces of O'Connor and Jefferson, liking their reaction. So Fallon continued. "We'll construct a temporary guard tower here." He drew a circle. "Twelve feet high. The guard will have a clear view of the whole zone where we'll be working." He made another circle on the other side, catty-corner from the first. "Another here. When we move locations, start work on say . . . here . . ." He tapped the spot where the hospital would be built. "All we have to do is move the fence." And Fallon showed where the next fence would be put.

"We just keep this up," Fallon said. "Till we're done. And then we can move the barbed wire to help cover those seven hundred acres that will be fenced in according to the blueprint. Just with fences much higher than what we'll have here."

Stepping back, he waited. O'Connor looked up, glanced at young Elliott Jefferson, and spit again into the trash can. He quickly spun to the bookkeeper and asked, "Well, how much will it cost to get all this stuff?"

Fallon already had the paper on his desk. He grabbed it and stepped around, showing it to the captain of guards, but letting Jefferson see the figures and budget, too.

"Here's what we need, and the prices from the merchant in town who got me the best deal. John Halleck, at Halleck's Mercantile, Hardware, and Sundries. Mr. Berrien says if we buy this many spools of this brand of wire, we should be good." He ran his finger under the name of the wire. "This brand. Don't get any other. This wire has enough barbs to strike fear into the heart of even Ben Lawless, and it's cheaper than other brands."

He tapped at another line entry. "This is the wood we'll need." He moved up and down the other materials that would be required—kegs of nails, mortar to secure the foundation of the guard towers, hammers, saws, and lumber. And at last, he showed both O'Connor and Jefferson the cost of the project.

O'Connor swallowed and looked grimly at Fallon. "That's still a lot of money." He turned to the paling bookkeeper. "Mr. Berrien, are you sure we can afford the cost of this?"

"Well . . ." The man appeared to be about to wet his pants.

Fallon spoke up. "Mr. Berrien has found us a generous donor. The donor, who asks for anonymity, has agreed to foot the whole bill."

After shifting the tobacco to his other cheek, O'Connor slowly started moving his head up and down and finally grinned. "Well, if we could do that, it would make all us guards a whole lot less ornery." He lifted his right hand and clamped down hard on Fallon's shoulder. "Boss, Hank, by golly, you're not only a hell of a fighter, you got brains, too. Brains no other warden I ever worked for had."

"I'm glad you think so." Fallon faced Montgomery Berrien. "Do you think our donor could fund this project immediately?"

The crook nodded in a hurry, and stuttered, sweating even more profusely, "I'm . . . c-c-c-certain . . . h-h-h-he . . . Y-y-yes." The speech impediment stopped. "In fact, I shall go . . . call . . . yes . . . call upon him . . . and I'll be back . . . in forty minutes."

"Good," Fallon said. "Forty minutes. And there's no need for you to go to the railroad station or the stagecoach station or the livery stables, Monty. We'll see you back here in forty minutes. Forty."

Montgomery Berrien hurried through the door.

"What was that about?" young Jefferson asked. "Railroads and liveries and all that?"

"A private joke." Fallon laughed, and began rolling up the blueprint. "Well, gentlemen, I've kept you from your work long enough."

"Yeah," the big Irishman said. He spit, wiped his mouth, and headed for the door.

"But," Fallon called out, "there's just one more thing I'd like you two to think on."

They stared at him.

"Where can we open up a school inside the old prison?"

CHAPTER TWENTY-EIGHT

"You still thinking school?" O'Connor asked. "For them sons of strumpets serving time here?"

"Yes," Fallon said. "Teaching those who are illiterate how to read and write. How to do arithmetic. Preparing them for a chance at a normal life when they have finished their sentences. So they might not come back here or another prison."

O'Connor looked at Fallon as if questioning the sanity of the new warden.

"I told you before, Tim, not the Bowen Hardins, men like that," Fallon said. "The ones who have shown good behavior, are minimal risk for trying to escape or cause any sort of disturbance."

"Like a . . . counterfeiter?"

Fallon smiled. "Well, I would assume that a man with the brains to make plates that can duplicate federal currency is probably fairly well-educated."

"If he was that smart," O'Connor counted, "he wouldn't be incarcerated at Leavenworth."

With a smile, Fallon nodded his acceptance of the captain's counterpoint.

"How many inmates would you be teaching?" O'Connor asked.

Fallon thought back to the subscription school at Gads Hill, Missouri, and of the various schools he had been forced to give talks to in Cheyenne and other towns and cities in Wyoming. "Fifteen," he guessed. "To start off with. Maybe twenty." He turned to Elliott Jefferson for confirmation.

"That'd be about right," the young guard said.

"If they're minimum risks," O'Connor said, "I'd guess two guards." He grinned. "Maybe some boys who need a little reminder of how to cross their t's and do long division."

"That's what we were thinking, too." Fallon liked how this was going, and he hated to bring up the next fact. "One of the inmates who'll be going to our school will be Ben Lawless."

The guard's face turned to stone. He let that sink in for almost a full minute before he said, "You said minimum security."

"I did."

"You bring Lawless into that classroom, you'll need thirty guards."

"I don't think so, Tim."

The big man shook his head. "You willing to bet on that, Hank?"

"I'm not a gambling man, Tim. Ben's an old man. Remember: He's the one who actually gave me the idea."

"Likely so he can figure out a way to escape. Who's gonna be foolish enough to teach these ignorant brigands? Someone from one of the crazy houses. Something like that?"

"Our wives," Elliott Jefferson said. "My Janice." He nodded at Fallon. "His wife, Christina."

"They'd make fine hostages," O'Connor said when he realized they were serious.

"That's why you'll have two guards in the room with them," Fallon told him.

"You two boys hate your women so much you want to put them in the same room with the scum of our United States?" O'Connor practically shouted.

"I'm not putting them in with Indianola Anderson, Tim."

"Ben Lawless is just as bad."

"Twenty years ago, maybe. Today, I don't think so."

O'Connor opened his mouth to start another attack, but Fallon raised his hand to stop that. "We're doing this, Tim. We're going to start a school for the prisoners who want to learn, who don't want to return to prison when they walk out of the gates. Twenty prisoners. Two guards. One teacher. Christina will only be doing this on Fridays or if Janice has something come up. Five days a week. Say six hours a day. So where can we find a classroom that will work?"

It was Elliott Jefferson who made the suggestion.

"What about the chapel?"

Looking at the young guard, Fallon considered that idea, and while he was debating the merits, O'Connor said, "It don't get much use except on Sundays and Wednesday nights."

"What happens on Wednesday nights?" Fallon asked.

"We got some boys who think they can carry a tune. They can't. But they go to the chapel to sing songs from six to seven each Wednesday evening. The chaplain leads 'em."

"I've never heard them," Fallon said.

"You're lucky. You go home at five or thereabouts."

Jefferson added: "The Reverend Pigate has an office. Sometimes he'll meet with one of the convicts in there if they want to confess or pray or something. That doesn't happen very often, but he can take them in his office. It shouldn't interfere with any schooling."

"Good." Fallon liked the idea.

"I bet we got more than twenty convicts who need some schoolin'," O'Connor said.

"Well," Fallon said, "I don't want more than twenty men in with those women—even with two guards." The idea struck him almost as soon as he finished the sentence. "But . . . if we do . . . have men who really want to learn, maybe we could have two classes. Not the same day. That's too much work. But send twenty men to school on Monday, Wednesday, and Friday. And another class of students on Tuesday and Thursday."

The guards looked at each other, shrugged, and turned back to Fallon. Jefferson grinned and said, "They might write you up in *Harper's*."

"Or the *National Police Gazette* if this goes wrong on you," O'Connor said.

"I'll speak to the Reverend Pigate," Fallon said. "But I've kept you two from your duties long enough." He thanked them, shook their hands, and walked them to the door. Then he went back to his desk to work.

* * *

The first interruption came ten minutes later when guards Raymond and Wilson brought in four prisoners, all medium-sized men, three white, one black, heads bowed, holding their ugly prison caps in their shackled hands.

"Warden," Raymond said, "we caught these men rolling dice behind the walls to one of the cells being built in the first cell block."

"Boys," Fallon said as a tough father addressing kids who had yet to reach their thirteenth birthdays. "Were you gambling?"

"No, Warden Fallon," one of the men whispered. "We was jus' . . . exercisin'."

"Yeah." Wilson reached into his trousers pocket and withdrew a wad of bills and laid them on Fallon's desk, spreading them out so that he got a good look at the currency and the denominations of the bills.

Fallon's eyes widened, and he leaned forward, picked up what looked to be a freshly minted ten-dollar note. He expected the men to be shooting craps for cigarettes or snuff but . . . Fallon made a rough guess that he had more than one hundred and sixty dollars in front of him.

"Where did you get this money?" He spoke sharply, and his eyes opened. "Heads up. Eyes front. Now where did you get this money?"

None answered.

"Having currency is forbidden. We keep all money in your accounts. You may draw it out once a week to buy certain items—but you know better than to have cash on your persons. Now, I'll ask you again. Where did you get this money?"

They were mute. If one had spoken, Fallon would

have been disappointed. That was the ex-convict that ran through his veins. You never told a guard or warden or anyone anything. Once you became a rat, your life inside a prison was worthless. The guards wouldn't give you any respect. Your fellow inmates would likely try to murder you.

"Solitary," Fallon told Raymond and Wilson. "Five days. All privileges revoked for one month. When they are out of solitary, put them to work in the quarry."

Montgomery Berrien was Fallon's next visitor, exactly forty minutes after he had departed—the man was punctual, Fallon had to concede—but his face had turned a yellowish tint, as though he had been stricken with jaundice.

"Warden Fallon," the man said meekly, "we have a problem."

Slowly, the bookkeeper came to Fallon's desk and withdrew an order form and laid it gently on Fallon's desk. Then his eyes almost bulged out of his head when he saw the money from the craps game still on the desktop. Fallon saw the heading on the paper: Halleck's Mercantile, Hardware, and Sundries.

He looked at the bottom number.

"That's not the price Halleck quoted me," Fallon said sharply, and his eyes bored through the book-keeper's spectacles.

"Y-y-yes," Berrien stuttered. "I . . . I . . . kn-know."

"Did Halleck say why the prices have gone up?"

"A robust economy," Berrien said.

"You mean he's a crook."

The little man shrugged, sighed, and conceded, "He has been known to do this before."

"And I supposed if I went to the lumber mill or Benson's Building Supplies, I'd find that their prices have increased, too—well beyond our means."

"They seem to be in . . . ummm . . . cahoots."

"They ought to be in prison."

"Yes, sir."

Fallon's eyes again met the bookkeeper's.

CHAPTER TWENTY-NINE

"Please," the man begged, "I have no money left. I can't." He glanced at the money from the dice-rolling convicts.

"It's not enough," Fallon told him. He swore and pushed back in his chair.

"I'm sorry."

"Yeah." He stood, sighed, and moved to the hat rack. "I'll be back in thirty minutes, Monty." He stepped outside the door, then came back inside.

"Monty?"

The bookkeeper turned and managed a pathetic smile.

"There's one hundred sixty-five dollars on the desk. It had better all be there when I get back."

John Halleck stood in the giant brick storehouse of Halleck's Mercantile, Hardware, and Sundries, barking orders at the teamsters unloading fresh-cut lumber from one of the sawmills. With the river nearby, and being this close to Missouri, Leavenworth had a lot more trees than what would be found on the western plains that stretched on to the Rockies. That's one thing that made Leavenworth a little more bearable than Cheyenne. The wind blew. It always blew. Probably even blew harder than it did in Wyoming. But you could find trees in this part of the country.

You could also find thieves. John Halleck was one of the biggest, Fallon had learned.

The bald man with big arms and a bigger gut caught a glimpse of Fallon and gave a friendly wave. The kind of wave a dentist might give you before he pulled a tooth. He kept Fallon waiting as he instructed the teamsters, then wiped his hands on his coat and walked toward the waiting warden.

"Good day to you, Mr. Fallon," Halleck said, and held out his hand in what some might think as a peace offering.

Fallon would have rather reached out to grab a coiled rattlesnake.

Instead of shaking the merchant's hand, Fallon handed him the new invoice for the building supplies.

"This price isn't what you quoted me the other day," Fallon said.

Smiling, John Halleck took the invoice while finding his eyeglasses in the pocket of his vest. The vest was made of fine yellow brocade, and the ribbon tie was a high-quality silk. After adjusting the glasses, Halleck read the figures, nodding, finally sighing, and returning the slip of paper to Fallon.

"Yes, yes, those are the right figures. You know how things go, Mr. Fallon. Prices go up. The lumber, the masons, the quarries, even the price of iron. They all go up. They just happened to have gone up after I quoted you the prices last week."

"That's quite an increase," Fallon told him.

Halleck did a little tsk-tsk-ing, and shook his head sadly. "Indeed. I was more shocked than you. After all, I have to pay higher prices to stock my store. It's the sign of a . . ."

Fallon filled in the words, "Robust economy."

"Exactly. You understand economics, I see, especially when you work for the federal government. But I've dealt with the federal government on numerous projects before, and I know they always come up with the money when it's needed."

"I see." Fallon saw. The man was willing to rip off the United States so he could wear an even more expensive vest and silk tie. He had met a few businessmen in Wyoming who felt the same way. He had refused to do business with those men.

"Well, I supposed I could see what prices your competitors are charging."

"You should do that, Mr. Fallon. Talk to Richard, and Mr. Roosevelt. Talk to the Wilson brothers, too."

Yeah . . . it wasn't just John Halleck. All these men were in on a little graft. Cheat the U.S government. Command the market. He wondered how much money Halleck had to pay the other merchants. Did they rotate this around and it just happened to be Halleck's turn to reap the biggest windfall?

"I could go directly to the lumberyards, the sawmills, the quarry, one of the freighters. Try to deal with them directly."

"You could," Halleck said. He removed his glasses

and began cleaning the lenses with a handkerchief he withdrew from his vest pocket. "You could indeed. But I think you'd find their prices would be even higher than mine. They usually don't sell directly to the consumers, you understand, so when they do, they try to make even more money than they have a right to demand. Those men are crooks."

"Thank you, Mr. Halleck. I was unaware of such graft."

"Yes, graft, greed, and green. Greenbacks. That's what drives business."

"So what are the chances that these prices will go up again?"

The man grinned as he returned the handkerchief and then the glasses. "None. For at least six months. I can't make any promises after that. No telling how much the nail factories will increase their prices, you see."

"I see."

Fallon smiled, looked at the invoice, and asked, "So . . . how much is in this for me?"

The man faked his look of shock and surprise.

"Mr. Fallon, I do not know what you mean."

"Sure you do," he said. "But if I'm to buy into this scheme, this fraud, this conspiracy to defraud the United States government, I expect a percentage."

"Mr. Fallon!"

"You've seen my little girl, Mr. Halleck. I'd like to be able to buy her a new doll for Christmas. And my wife . . . well . . . you know how things go these days. With women? Hey, I have two in my house, my daughter and my wife. What about you?"

"I have two women, myself," the man said lecherously. "But no daughter." He winked. "There's a wealthy widow I . . . well . . . you understand."

"Indeed."

They studied one another for a few minutes. Halleck scratched his nose, then looked behind him to make sure none of the employees were close enough to hear what was being said.

"Could I see that invoice again, Mr. Fallon?"

Fallon passed the paper over to him. "How would two hundred dollars sound?"

"It wouldn't sound as nice as four-fifty."

Halleck laughed. "Oh, we're just talking about your first order, Mr. Fallon. You'll need supplies down the way." He winked. "That prison is going to take some time to build."

"Three hundred," Fallon said.

"Two-twenty-five. Don't be greedy, Mr. Fallon. There's enough money being printed in the Denver mint to keep us living high on the hog. And how long do you think it will take to complete the new pen?"

"We shall likely retire before the final nail is driven."

"And we should have a small fortune by the time we retire. Retirement . . . well . . . it does not turn out so well for men who have not saved money for those golden years."

"Two twenty-five," Fallon agreed, and held out his hand.

They shook, and Fallon walked out. He quickly stopped at a water trough, grabbed his handkerchief, soaked it, and washed the filth he felt. He spit out the bile into the trough, threw away the piece of cotton, and stepped into the nearest saloon, walking straight to the bar and putting his boot on the brass rail.

The bartender with a well-greased mustache came down from where two freighters were drinking and asked, "What's your pleasure, Mac?"

"Root beer," Fallon said.

"Root beer?"

"You heard me. I need to get a bad taste out of my mouth."

The barkeep sighed. "Whiskey would do a better job than root beer."

"Root beer." Fallon tossed a nickel on the bar.

"Suit yourself. Let me go see if I can find some."

Back in his office, Fallon saw the cash still on his desk. Preston the clerk and Montgomery Berrien the bookkeeper returned to his office. The clerk asked if Halleck had lowered the price.

Fallon shook his head.

"What does the state code say about businesses conspiring to fix prices or attempt extortion?"

They stared at him blankly. Fallon waved as though he had been funning them. "I could bring this up to the U.S. attorney," he said, sighed, and added. "But that's not the way the American Detective Agency would handle this particular case."

"Sir?" the clerk and the bookkeeper said in unison.

"Nothing."

"Does it mean your plans for the guards and everything will be canceled?" Preston asked.

"I'm trying to think of a way to get justice," Fallon said.

"There are businessmen," the clerk said, "in our town who are worse than many of the men wearing striped suits in our prison. But finding a way to put them behind bars is almost impossible."

"You'd need them to murder somebody. Or rob a store." That's what the embezzling little bookkeeper had to offer.

"Murder is a state crime," Fallon told them. "So is robbing a store. I'd like to get them in federal court."

"Good luck," Preston said.

"Yeah." Fallon was almost ready to give up—on justice, and on his idea to help relieve the pressure and workload on the guards. "Well," he said. "I might as well see if the Reverend Pigate is going to charge me to rent his chapel."

CHAPTER THIRTY

Fallon, Christina, and Rachel Renee had attended the prison services during Fallon's first week on the job—just to see what kind of convicts went to church and what kind of church the chaplain ran. He had been impressed. Levi Pigate was a devout man of the cloth, a believer, but not pushy. He understood what his job was, and he kept his sermons short. They prayed. They sang. They read a bit of Scripture. Fallon did not even know what faith Pigate belonged to, but prisons could not afford chaplains of each denomination. They needed a preacher who could help the Mormons and the Catholics, the Jews and the Baptists, even the atheists and agnostics. Levi Pigate filled the bill.

He was a good man.

"That is an excellent idea," the preacher said after Fallon explained his idea. "I tried that once with the previous warden, but he said there was no need in leading lambs to slaughter. I don't know exactly what he meant, but I knew he was not going to allow me to teach school. And, to be honest, I would have made a lousy schoolmaster."

"I don't know," Fallon told him. "I've heard you preach, and I looked at the convicts sitting on our pew. You had their attention."

"You are too kind." He opened a notebook. "So . . . you are thinking about classes beginning at what time?"

"Nine in the morning," Fallon said. "Till three in the afternoon. Six days a week. Like I said, you'd still have Sundays."

"Guards?"

"Two. Unless you think more would be needed."

"I don't think so, Warden Fallon. If the convicts are serious about learning."

"If they aren't, they'll be back to hard labor all day, and we'll replace them with convicts who want to learn."

The chaplain wished Fallon luck, shook his hand, and saw him to the door. Fallon started back to the office, feeling slightly better about the school. That part was at least settled. Now Fallon just had to figure out a way to get around John Halleck's greed.

He slipped into the alleyway between the solitary cells and the laundry, heading back to his office, when two men appeared at the far exit. Fallon stopped, heard something behind him, and saw another man coming down that way. They wore the striped uniforms of prisoners. No guards could be spotted. The one coming from behind lowered a chain in his left hand, and let it rattle. The bigger of the two coming toward him pulled out a pair of knuckle-dusters and slipped them over the fingers of his right hand. The little cuss with a mangled left ear showed Fallon the homemade knife with the jagged edge.

Fallon waved, smiled, and walked to those in front of him.

"Hey, boys," Fallon called out cheerily. "It's good to see you. I've been looking all over for you." He kept walking. The two men stopped, glanced at each other. Fallon said, "Did Linc Harper send you boys?"

It was the first name Fallon could think of. Linc Harper, the notorious train robber out of mostly Missouri, could not have sent these men to do anything, since Fallon had killed him on the way to Jefferson City to serve time for the American Detective Agency.

"So here's what the plan is, boys, and here's how I'm going to get you out of this hellhole. Yes, sir, we'll be richer than the three kings with Mexican señoritas giving us more than we can handle. I hope you like tequila. I sure do." He picked up his pace because he didn't know how much more stupid banter he could think to say.

The one with the brass knuckles and the one with the shiv separated themselves—which was the smart thing to do—but looked confused, especially when Fallon said, "I know you boys got the money. That was the test. Good job. That proves you're exactly the kind of men we need for this little caper."

He was close enough, so he moved even faster, and kicked the one with the makeshift knife hard in the groin, doubling him over, and bringing up his knee to smash the con's nose and mouth. Fallon whirled then, as the one with the hard fist stepped toward him, swinging. Fallon ducked, and in the close confines of the alley, he heard the man's fist connect against the stone wall. He screamed at the pain from his broken fingers. Fallon grabbed the assassin's ears, jerked, and slammed the man's forehead against stone.

Footsteps pounded on the gravel, and Fallon whirled, dropped to his knees as the running man swung wildly with the chain. It clipped Fallon's head, but just enough to hurt and to make him mad. Fallon had a handful of pebbles in his right hand and he flung them into the man's face. Staggering back, the man tried to raise his arm to slash again with the chain, but Fallon was rolling, over and over, and caught the guy just above the ankles. Down he went, over Fallon's body, landing with a thud and groan.

Fallon came to his knees. So did the convict, only he had let go of his hold of the chain. Fallon drove a fist hard, and heard the jawbone break. The man went down, and now Fallon heard the shrill whistles and more pounding feet. But the one with the knife had recovered after vomiting down the front of his striped shirt. He had the knife and he slashed with it.

Fallon jumped back, feeling the tearing of his woolen vest, and he tripped over the legs of the man who had swung the chain. Down went Fallon, and the man with the knife tried to laugh, but the pain from Fallon's kick just left him wheezing. The knife shifted to his other hand, and he said, "You're dead before they'll kill me."

The guards were running. The convict laughed, but his eyes widened when he saw the chain Fallon had gathered in his right hand. He swung, low, letting go of the chain and watching it wrap around the man's ankles, ripping cloth and skin, and sending him to the gravel. He tried to push his head up, but that was a bigger mistake, because Hank Fallon's boot caught him in the jaw. That one cracked, too.

"You all right, Hank?" Big Tim O'Connor asked.

"Yeah." Fallon looked at his vest, the tear that was likely too deep for Christina to make fashionable again.

"These guys were supposed to be going to get another load of bricks," O'Connor said.

"I think they had something else in mind," Fallon told him. He considered the three men. "But the only one who'll be doing any talking is that one." He pointed to the unconscious man with the swollen knuckles and bloody forehead. "And he looks to be out for a while."

One of the guards laughed. "Guess they won't try to escape when you're blocking their way."

Fallon picked up the knife, tossed it down by the chain still wrapped around the ugly one's legs. "I don't think escape was what they had in mind."

A third guard withdrew a wad of greenbacks from the knuckle-dusting killer's pants pocket. "That's a hell of a lot of cash for Wakefield to be carrying."

O'Connor snatched the money from the guard's fingers and stared. "Bloody hell, that's more money than I make in a month."

Fallon stepped closer. "Check the other prisoners," he ordered, and took a fifty-dollar note from O'Connor's hand.

"Somebody outside these walls wants you dead," O'Connor said.

Fallon nodded at the three assailants. "Those are from inside the walls."

"Yeah." The other guards produced handfuls of green currency. "But," O'Connor went on, "nobody—not a guard and certainly not a scum bucket of a prisoner in Leavenworth—can lay his hands on this kind of money."

Bringing the fifty-dollar bill closer to his face, Fallon studied it. "Let me see another one of those bills, Tim," he said, and took the twenty the big captain held out for him.

"Must be a banker," said the guard named Wilkerson. "Only a banker would have this kind of money."

The other guard said, "I ain't never even seen no fifty-dollar bill before. Didn't know they made them."

Fallon handed both bills back to O'Connor. Then he looked at his fingertips.

Suddenly, Hank Fallon laughed. It all made sense. Hard to believe, but certainly, it all made sense.

CHAPTER THIRTY-ONE

Fallon laid the bills out on his desk, those taken off the men who had tried to assassinate him and those taken from the gamblers. He let Big Tim O'Connor and Montgomery Berrien look at them closely.

"That's a lot of money," the captain of the guards said. "We might find some change, maybe a dollar coin, among the prisoners, but usually it's just a penny or two. They don't use money. Trade is done with mostly tobacco, maybe a pencil and paper, things like that. And I don't know how those dirty sons of strumpets came up with this much money. It has to be coming from the outside."

Montgomery Berrien brought the fifty-dollar note closer to his face, lowered it, turned it over, rubbed his fingers against it, then found another bill of the same denomination. His eyes rose above his spectacles and he let the paper currency fall softly atop the other bills.

"This is counterfeit," Berrien said.

Fallon held up his fingers, revealing the ink stains on the tips. "Certainly. Real American cash doesn't leave your fingers needing some hot water and lye soap."

"Counterfeit." O'Connor came closer, picked up a five-dollar bill, looked it over on both sides, let it fall, and looked at his fingers. "Mine are clean."

"Yeah. Those who attacked me in the alley should have let their cash dry longer. Maybe the man who gave them this fake money told them to let it sit, and they didn't listen. Or their sweat caused the money to lose its color."

"Well," O'Connor said, "Jemez, the Jokester, and Lynde aren't the smartest we have behind the iron here. If they were told, they didn't listen. Which isn't a surprise."

"Lucky break," Fallon said.

"Indeed." The bookkeeper had picked up another bill and was comparing it to one from his wallet. "This is some of the best I've ever seen. Except for the ink stains."

"So," O'Connor said. "There's a damned counterfeiter in Leavenworth." He snapped his fingers. "Well, we can see who came in to visit Jemez, Lynde, or Richards—that's the one we call the Jokester. That'll give us an idea. I doubt if the man making the phony money came himself, but once we know who it was, he can lead the law to the dirty dogs who are making this bad cash."

Fallon smiled. "I don't think a visitor passed the bad money to those three."

O'Connor squinted his eyes. "Then where did it come from?"

"Here," Fallon said.

The timid, embezzling bookkeeper said, "Of course. Of course."

Which caused O'Connor to wet his lips and think. He looked back at Fallon, "You mean to tell me . . . ?"

"Exactly," Fallon said. "Think about it, Tim. Where do you find counterfeiters? In Kansas? Best place, would be right here in the Leavenworth pen, wouldn't you say?" He stepped out of the office and into the hallway, and called for Preston, the clerk. A moment later, the proper man stepped inside and asked how he could be of assistance.

"I want the names of every man here who has been convicted of counterfeiting," Fallon told him. "We'll go through the names and pay a visit to everyone doing time for trying to copy our good old American cash."

Big Tim O'Connor had been working on a new chaw of tobacco. Now the rim of Fallon's cuspidor pinged, and the big man wiped his lip. "Preston," he said, "there's no need for all that. Just bring us the record of Samuel Lippert. You know, Uncle Sam?"

"Certainly." Preston vanished, and Fallon waited for O'Connor's reasoning.

"He's your man," O'Connor said. "If the bad money's coming from here, he's the only one who could pull it off."

"A counterfeiter, I take it," Fallon said.

"No," the little bookkeeper said, and his tone sounded like admiration. "An artist."

Uncle Sam Lippert wasn't lying on the cot in his cell when Big Tim O'Connor unlocked the door and pulled it open. Cot would not describe the bed in the cell. The cherry headboard rose four feet high, and the pillows were plush. Fallon would not call such a bed regulation for a convicted felon. But most inmates in Leavenworth didn't have a matching dresser with built-in mirror and washstand. The desk set in the far cover, and atop it a Regina disc music box of exquisite mahogany box played a polka. The fat man puffed on a Cuban cigar and slowly let his eyelids open.

"Ah, did you bring my steak and potatoes?" he asked.

"Just your change," Fallon said, and closed the gap, turned up the lantern on the marble-topped bedside table, and dropped a few counterfeit bills on the blanket covering Uncle Sam's fat stomach. Then Fallon showed the convict his fingertips.

"Ah," Uncle Sam said.

"Ah," Fallon said, and looked back at O'Connor.

"You know prisons," O'Connor began.

"All too well," Fallon said.

"Well, Uncle Sam here was a favorite of the previous warden, and the warden before him. It was this way when I started. I guess I figured you knew."

"Guessing can be a bad habit, my friend. Sometimes you guess wrong."

"I'll remember that."

"Ah," the fat counterfeiter said. The music box began to slow down to a crawl. When it finally stopped altogether, the man said, "And thus the curtain closes on me."

"I'm pretty sure the other prisoners in this cell block will be thankful when they no longer have to listen to that polka."

"It relaxes me," the counterfeiter said.

"You won't be relaxing for a while, Number Two-Three-Four-Nine. We're building a brand-new penitentiary, and you'd like to be a part of history, I'm sure."

"I already am, Mr. Fallon. I am the most successful counterfeiter in the history of our nation."

"And look where it got you."

"Well, as wise men before me once said, 'All good things must come to an end.'" He winked. "For a while."

"Maybe not," Fallon said.

The man's eyes opened wider. He even managed to sit up in the bed, after doing considerable rearranging of his pillows

"You mean I might stay here . . . with my polka . . . and my . . . comforts?"

Fallon dropped some money on his blanket. "Who wanted this particular order of script?"

The man had a throaty laugh. "You know I can't tell you that. That's why I got such a long term to begin with. I am . . . in my own way . . . honest."

"Well, I figured as much, but it was worth a shot. I imagine the three men who were paid to kill me won't have such loyalty."

"Perhaps. But that is not of my concern."

"I'm sure I'll find the plates under your mattress."

The man shrugged.

"You understand these will have to be destroyed."

"They won't be the first. Sacrifices have to be made. They were good, but all good things must come to an end."

"Yes." He picked up one of the bills. "Captain O'Connor," he said, without taking his eyes off Samuel

Lippert. "How much fake money did we count in my office?"

The commander of the prison guards answered.

Fallon reached inside the pocket of his torn vest, and withdrew the piece of paper from Halleck's mercantile. He stuck that underneath Lippert's nose.

"How good is your math?" Fallon asked.

"My fine young prison commandant, I should let you know that I studied under the best possible tutors at Yale, and attended art school in Paris and Switzerland."

"How much money do I need?"

The big crook's eyes went back to the order form from the mercantile, and his eyes brightened with excitement. "If Captain O'Connor's memory is to be trusted, you need one thousand, six hundred, seventy-nine dollars and fourteen cents more."

"That's what I came up with."

Lippert looked up at Fallon. "Were you educated at Yale?"

"Gads Hill," Fallon said. "And Mr. Berrien has an abacus in his office."

The man laughed a deep, wonderful throaty laugh.

"So . . . would I be correct in assuming that . . ."

"Oh, no, Uncle Sam." Fallon shook his head. "I know a few things about law, and prisons, and what constitutes a crime. You see, I've been in prison myself. So let's just not say one other word. Let's just say that I am going to give you until Wednesday at say five o'clock in the afternoon. Then I'll be coming back here, and I will collect the plates you have been using to print your bad money."

"Bad money?" The fat man grinned. "Tsk, tsk, tsk. You would not insult Rembrandt, would you? I have often seen myself as Rembrandt. Have you ever seen his *Saint Paul in Prison*?"

"I always liked the *Mona Lisa*," Fallon told him.

The fat man yawned. "Leonardo da Vinci did *Mona Lisa*," he said. "Da Vinci is fine, but Rembrandt van Rijn is the greatest artist." He grinned. "He, too, like me, was a master draftsman and etcher. As you will see for yourself."

"I'll be picking up the plates, Mr. Master Draftsman and Etcher. And we'll see how your math is come Wednesday. If the plates are ready, and whatever else you might wish for me to dispose of as I see fit, then perhaps you can finish out your sentence the way my predecessors have seen fit and proper."

"You are a gentleman, scholar, and a true lover of art."

"And you are a good mathematician," Fallon told him. "One thousand, six hundred and seventy-nine. The fourteen cents will be on me."

CHAPTER THIRTY-TWO

The prisoner serving as crew foreman of the cell block construction loved his job and was happy to show Fallon all the progress being made that morning.

"We're gonna have twelve hundred cells here, Warden Fallon, suh," he said in a Texas twang. "And maybe I can get to build 'em all."

Fallon stared at Inmate Number Four-Four-Nine-One. "How long are you in here, Hermann?"

"Six years, seven months to go," he said, smiled, and added. "For the first conviction. Then another fourteen. The judge, he said, there was no way he could justify concurrent sentences. Lucky me, I guess."

Fallon said, "I guess." He looked at the door, and a though struck him. "What about the locks?"

"Oh, I'm glad you asked that," Hermann said. "That ol' miser over at the hardware store, why, the price he said we'd have to pay was . . . well . . . downright criminal, I mean to tell ya, Warden, suh. But we out-foxed that sly ol' fox. Wesley Westinghouse, he agreed to do all the locks for us. He's a locksmith."

"I see."

"A darned good one, by all reports," Hermann added.

"Very good. We'd want good locks."

"Well, you won't find none better."

Fallon waited for Hermann to look him into the eye. It never happened. Wouldn't have happened had Fallon waited ten more years. That's the kind of convict Hermann Schultz was. His eyes locked on Fallon's feet.

"Who's making Wesley Westinghouse's lock?" Fallon asked.

The convict closed his eyes, raised his head toward the clear blue sky as if seeking an answer from the heavens, and finally busted out laughing. "Oh, I get it, Warden, suh. You wuz bein' funny." He slapped his hands together. "By golly, suh, that's a real good one. Yes, suh. Who's makin' the lock for the locksmith? He could just open his own lock real easy and walk all the way back to his wife or his hussy in Iowa City, Iowa." The man howled like a rabid coyote. "Yes, suh. A real good one. Make his own lock." He sniggered.

After shaking his head, Fallon thanked Hermann and left the compound for his office.

Fallon counted the counterfeit money twice, looked up across the desk in his office, and began putting the fake money in an envelope. Without looking up, he said, "What's on your mind, Tim?"

Big Tim O'Connor sighed, shuffled his feet, and began wetting his bottom lip with his tongue.

Fallon sealed the envelope, which he then slipped into his inside coat pocket. "Go on."

"Well," the big Irishman said. "I guess I just never met a warden like you."

Fallon laughed.

"You sure this is what you want to do?"

"You think I'm wrong?"

"I think you might wind up in one of these new cells that are being built."

"It wouldn't be the first time." Standing up, Fallon grabbed his hat off the rack and corrected his statement. "My first time in prison. It would be my first time in the U.S. Penitentiary, of course. But I don't think it'll come to that." He stopped next to the big guard and held out his right hand.

Sighing, Captain Big Tim O'Connor shook the firm hand. Then Fallon reached into his pocket and pulled out a two-bit piece. "Would you happen to have change, Tim? I need fourteen cents."

Luck remained with Harry Fallon. The quarter went into O'Connor's pocket, and Fallon had two nickels, five pennies, and a ten-cent piece.

Afterward, Fallon tilted his head toward his own desk. "Uncle Sam Lippert's printing plates are over on the right-hand side of my desk, with *The Leavenworth Bi-Weekly Record and Messenger* over them. A gentleman named George Goodwin will be meeting you outside the office in fifteen minutes. Give the plates to him. He knows what to do with the plates. And then give Uncle Sam my compliments."

The big Irishman didn't look pleased with either of those assignments.

* * *

The scarlet-haired, green-eyed chirpy hurried out of John Halleck's office at Halleck's Mercantile, Hardware, and Sundries, throwing an overcoat over her unmentionables with the rest of her clothes tucked up underneath the big coat.

"Is she one of your sundries?" Fallon asked.

The man's face turned about as scarlet as the woman's hair, but Fallon figured Halleck's face was natural. The woman probably spent a good deal on dye.

"You don't come bargin' . . ."

Halleck stopped when Fallon withdrew the envelope. He tossed it onto the man's desk, where the chirpy had been . . . sitting . . . or lying down . . . or . . . dancing? He wasn't certain. But the greedy man forgot ever having a woman in his office as he ripped open the paper and let the currency drop heavily onto his desk.

Fallon came over and dropped a dime and four pennies near the bills.

Licking his lips, Halleck quickly tallied the amount of money. "By gawd, sir," he said, "you've done it."

A moment later, Fallon had the receipt out of another pocket. "You'll sign this now, sir."

"You bet," the owner said, and could not help but laugh, a throaty, greedy cackle, as he scribbled his name. Fallon took his copy, and left the other on the desk.

"I expect those supplies will be delivered to the construction site for the new U.S. penitentiary beginning first thing tomorrow morning."

"It's a deal." Halleck extended his hand.

Fallon looked at the man's britches. "You might want to button your fly, sir."

As Halleck quickly went to work on his pants, Fallon pulled out a double eagle. "Can you make change?"

That was easy enough. Halleck handed him two ten-dollar notes and a five. Fallon put those in his pants pocket and walked to the door.

"It has been a pleasure doing business with you, Fallon," the greedy crook said.

"The pleasure will be mine, sir."

After closing the door, Fallon walked outside, bumping into an elderly woman on his way through the front door. The old hag stumbled, but Fallon caught her and immediately apologized.

"Take your hand off me, you fool," the woman snorted, turned, and hobbled over to the counter, where she bought a dozen nails, paying for them with a twenty-dollar gold piece, then started counting the nails on the countertop, examining each as though she were looking for a flaw in a diamond, while the cashier struggled to make change. Finally, as Fallon stared at his pocket watch, the old lady came out and stumbled into a man in a tan sack suit. Her nails and her money scattered on the boardwalk, and the man started picking up money and twelve-penny nails.

Fallon helped the old woman up, who elbowed him in the ribs and snorted, "I ain't no hussy, you young whippersnapper. I'm a proper lady."

"Yes, ma'am," Fallon said.

The man started to hand the woman her money, but stopped and looked at the first note.

"Ma'am," he said in a pleasant, Midwestern tone. "Might I ask you where you got this bill?"

"Yonder," she snapped. "Change for my nails."

Fallon handed her the nails.

"Well . . ." A crowd started gathering in the alcove. The man eyed the next note.

"Is there a problem?" Fallon asked.

"There . . ." The man looked at another bill.

"What's going on here?" A young man wearing a deputy U.S. marshal's badge moved between Fallon and the old hag and the man in the sack suit.

"This." The man handed a bill to the deputy.

"That's my money!" the hag screeched.

"What about . . . ?" The lawman stopped. He lifted his eyes toward the man in the sack suit. "Counterfeit."

"Of exceptional quality," the man said. "Only the paper gives it away."

"I'll be damned," the lawman said.

"I want my money, you Yankee thieves."

At that moment, John Halleck stepped out of the mercantile. "Do you folks mind clearing out of here?" He snapped. "People want to get inside to do their shopping."

The deputy marshal and the man in the sack suit turned to Halleck. "As a matter of fact," the lawman said, "we'd like to do a little shopping in your hardware store, too."

The man in the sack suit withdrew a badge from his pocket. "Yes. I am George Goodwin, operative for the American Detective Agency."

While the lawman and the detective escorted John Halleck back inside his business, Fallon escorted the hag across the street.

"How'd I do?" Christina Whitney Fallon asked.

"You're a pretty good detective for an old hag," Fallon told her.

"Watch who you're callin' an ol' hag, buster," she said in her old hag's voice.

"Where's Rachel Renee?" Fallon asked.

"Helping Janice Jefferson make sugar cookies. I'm supposed to pick her up at two-fifteen."

"You'd better go home and change then," Fallon said. "This getup you concocted might scare her so badly she'll want to sleep in our bed."

Captain Big Tim O'Connor lowered the *Post* onto the table in the mess hall when Fallon brought over two cups of coffee. "You read this?" O'Connor nodded at the newspaper.

"I skimmed it." Fallon sat.

"Convenient," O'Connor said. "A detective and a U.S. marshal finding counterfeit currency in front of that mercantile."

"More in the cash register," Fallon said. "The U.S. solicitor thinks John Halleck was responsible for most of the bad money that has been floating across eastern Kansas the past six months. I guess they brought in the American Detective Agency to help with the investigation."

Fallon slid O'Connor's cup closer, and sipped his.

"Good outfit," O'Connor said. "So I hear." He looked over the paper he had started reading again. "The American Detective Agency."

"I've heard good things about that organization, too." He took another sip and quickly added. "Since

Dan MacGregor took over as president a few years back."

"Un-huh. The plates were found in the warehouse. Counterfeit plates. Those used to print the bad bills."

"What warehouse?"

O'Connor rolled his eyes. "Halleck's."

"Looks like he's guilty then."

"Yeah. Except he said you passed him the bad money."

"Well, crooks often tell fibs." Fallon pointed at the paper. "Keep reading and you'll see that the receipt, which he signed, says he was paid in full in gold coins. The paper money was counterfeit. You don't find too many outfits trying to make bad gold coins."

"We used to try to pass five-cent pieces as five-dollar notes," O'Connor said.

"Tim O'Connor!" Fallon said in mocking shock. "And now you're in charge of prison guards?"

The big man smiled but just briefly. "You think this is fair, Fallon? Ruining a man's life, setting him up for something he didn't do."

"He was trying to defraud the United States government, Tim. He was also conspiring with other merchants to drive up prices for their own profit, and thus hurting families like yours and Elliott Jefferson's, everyone in this part of Kansas."

"But he was no counterfeiter."

"He won't go to prison for this," Fallon said. "They'll settle for a fine. A substantial fine. And the U.S. solicitor will probably work out a deal so that he supplies building materials for the new pen at cost. Meanwhile, the other merchants who were in this with him will see the error of their greedy ways and prices will drop back down to what they need to be, and Leavenworth, Kansas, will be sort of like every other town in the West."

They drank more coffee.

O'Connor said, "I never worked for a warden like you before, Hank."

Fallon managed to grin. "You've never worked for a warden who knows prisons like I do."

CHAPTER THIRTY-THREE

Removing his hat, Fallon pushed open the door to the prison chapel and stepped inside quickly, closing the door behind him and looking at the twenty prisoners scattered about the pews. One guard, Wilson, stood in the pulpit, in the corner, holding a shotgun. The other guard, Raymond, stood in the back corner, close to Fallon, with his shotgun resting leisurely in his arms.

"Good morning, Warden Fallon," Janice Jefferson called out politely and closed her *McGuffey's Reader*. "Class, turn around and tell Warden Fallon good morning." Like she was teaching a bunch of farm and ranch kids about Rachel Renee's age.

But to a man, all of them, black, white, big, small, even old Ben Lawless, turned in their seats and, in unison, spoke in their singsong voices, "Good morning, Warden Fallon."

He had to smile. "Good morning," Fallon told them, and looked up at the pretty young teacher. "I did not mean to interrupt," he said. "Hoped to get here before you started, but I got tied up with a few things. How is everything going, Mrs. Jefferson?"

"I have twenty bright young students who want to learn," she said. "Things could not be any better."

She sounded serious.

"That's fine."

"Now," she addressed her prisoners. "Who had a question?"

Seven hands shot up, and Janice gave her wards a pleasant smile and went to the closest man first. While she started pointing to something in his *Reader* and whispering politely, Fallon watched Wilson step to the pulpit, and bring his shotgun around for easier use. Though none of the students seemed to consider any violent action, Fallon did not like the thought of Janice Jefferson being caught in the middle of a fight with shotguns going off. He slid to the corner and stood next to Raymond.

"How are things going?" he whispered.

"She's learning them their letters," he said, and shouldered the shotgun.

"Maybe," Fallon said, "you should leave the shotguns in the armory and bring rifles. Shotguns . . . well, they tend to be messy."

"To be honest with you, Warden," the guard said. "I don't think we even need anything other than billy clubs."

Janice moved to another prisoner.

Raymond continued. "This is, honestly, like watching over a Sunday-school class at the Johnstown Presbyterian Church back home."

That made Fallon smile. "You learning anything?" he quipped.

"I'm pretty good with my letters," Raymond said. "So I'm waiting till she starts in on geography and arithmetic. Those can be troublesome."

Fallon patted the guard's shoulder. "At least you're out of the heat."

"Yeah. And that woman, well, she's real easy to look at."

"Remember, Raymond. She's married."

Janice moved to another prisoner.

"Yeah. Well, so am I. But I can still look." Fallon gave the guard a smile and a nod, whispered for him to keep up the good work, and turned to leave, stopping when Raymond said softly, "Warden." When Fallon turned, the guard sighed. "I thought this was a damned fool idea, sir. But . . . well . . . this might work after all." He nodded at the pews. "Those convicts, they really want to learn."

"Thanks, Raymond. I hope they keep learning." He was at the door when he heard his name called again. This time it was Janice Jefferson.

She stepped away from the pews to the far side of the chapel and said, "Might I have a brief word with you?"

When Fallon reached her, she turned away from the prisoners and asked, "Could you do me a favor?"

"Sure."

"Well . . ." He inhaled deeply. "Could you . . . well . . . could you sit with Ben Lawless?"

Fallon looked over her shoulder, and saw the one-eyed killer of many Cherokee Indians, sitting on the last pew with his left hand raised. Fallon lowered his gaze back at the schoolteacher.

She sighed. "I . . . I . . . it's fine when I'm teaching

the whole class," she said softly. "I don't have to look directly at him. But . . . but . . . he's . . . well . . . that . . . *eye.*"

He understood. The hole in his head, the scars around it, the ugliness, and that on top of what Ben Lawless had done years and years ago. It unnerved many of the guards, too.

"Why doesn't he wear an eye patch?" she asked.

"I don't know," Fallon said, although he had a good idea. It was the fear that missing eye gave people, those scars, and the legend of all that Ben Lawless had done, had been through. That was why Ben Lawless still reigned as king in the Leavenworth pen. The sight of him alone would put the fear of God in the most fearless of men.

Janice sighed. "I'm . . . well . . . I guess I should just buckle up."

"You help the other prisoners, Janice," he said kindly, and gave her a reassuring smile and then patted her shoulder. "I'll be happy to help Ben Lawless."

He moved to the back pew. Lawless slowly looked up with his one eye.

"How's school, Ben?" Fallon said.

"Fine. I reckon. How's wardenin'?"

"Fine." He sat down beside the man. "Mrs. Jefferson asked if I could help out today, since so many of her students have questions. So . . . what's your question? How can I help you?"

"I want to know how to spell my name," he said.

"Well, Ben, that'll take some time."

"Most of these boys, they at least know all their letters," Lawless complained. "Some I think even know more than that schoolmarm. But I don't know nothin'. Realized I forgot 'em letters my mama taught me, 'ceptin' X, of course."

"Which is why you're here. We all learn, Ben."

"Show me. I ain't got no patience."

"You'll have to have patience, Ben. You don't learn everything overnight."

Lawless hung his head.

Fallon reached over and picked the *Reader* off the convict's lap. He began thumbing through some pages, looking for the alphabet, before he remembered the blackboard the chaplain had brought in.

"Ben," he said. "Look up."

Lawless's head rose.

"Hand me your note pad there. And the pencil." Fallon pointed. "See the second letter on the board." Fallon then wrote the letter B.

He pointed at the letter. "What's your first name?"

"Ben."

"Right. Let's start. This is the letter B. It sounds like . . . B-b-b-b."

"B-b-b-b," Lawless repeated. Fallon handed him pencil and pad. "Now copy that letter." He pointed. "This is the capital B. Which you'd use when you're writing your own name. B-b-b-b."

"B-b-b-BEN." He grinned. And carved a big B in the tablet.

Fallon showed him the E and e, making the "eh" and "eee" sounds, and watched the poisoner of innocent families scratch it next to the B, though not quite on the same line. "That's the letter E," Fallon said. "Now . . . how does your first name sound at the end?"

The man struggled. "B-buh-buh-eh-eh-eeeh . . . ennnnnn." Fallon wrote the capital and lowercase N. The killer carved it deeply onto the page.

Fallon smiled and tapped the crooked BeN. "That's pretty good, Ben. There you have it. B-e-n. Ben. You've written your first name. How's that feel?"

He wasn't certain, but it certainly looked as though a tear welled in the vicious fiend's one eye. "Ben," the man said and drew a circle around his accomplishment.

"Good job." Fallon started to rise. "Now, you keep learning, and you work hard, and you'll be brighter than any of these other twenty students here. You want to learn, Ben. That's the big thing. Keep up the good work."

The man's free hand slammed on Fallon's thigh. "Please, Warden," he whispered. "One more . . ."

Sinking back into the pew, Fallon sighed. "All right, Ben. What else do you want to know?"

"My last name."

Fallon sighed. "Well, Lawless starts with the letter L. El. Lah, lay, l-l-law . . . leh-lee-lehhhh . . . less."

"No. My real last name. MacIntosh."

Fallon looked at him. "Your last name isn't Lawless?"

"Hell, no, Warden. I made it up. Strike fear into those damned Cherokees. Let them know I didn't give a damn about nothin'. That I was the damned law. Coming to kill 'em all."

Fallon asked Ben to keep his voice down. He thought back, but Lawless's outlawry had been decades earlier, yet everything he remembered said the man's last name was Lawless, not MacIntosh. Of course, out here, in the West, men often changed their names.

"MacIntosh."

"Yeah, but don't tell nobody that. Lawless still strikes fear in them."

"I guess so."

"My wife's name was Dirty Feet. That's why I called her Blossom."

"I see."

"She was Shoshone."

"Really."

"Yeah."

"How'd you get a Shoshone woman to move down to the Indian Nations?"

"Because back then I was a charming feller." He laughed. "You know, Warden, I didn't think I could ever talk about Blossom without getting mad."

Fallon patted his leg again.

"All right." He took the pad and paper and wrote L-a-w-l-e-s-s. "That's Lawless. Just so you know. And MacIntosh . . . is that M-c or M-a-c?" He realized the stupidity of his question and said, "Never mind." He wrote a big M.

"This is the capital M. Em-em-em, emmmm. Similar to N as in Ben. And the letters, you see, capital and low-ercase, are a little alike, too. So . . . write the letter M, Ben, and we'll go from there."

CHAPTER THIRTY-FOUR

For a week, Harry Fallon felt good about his life and his job. *Harper's Weekly* had found a correspondent who visited the prison to sketch drawings and interview the teachers, the chaplain, two prisoners, and Fallon about the prison school. Supplies for the new penitentiary began coming in, and Fallon heard people talking in the cafés and other businesses about the change around Leavenworth. He even heard the Widow Daniels—not as bad as Cheyenne's Widow Walkup but a gossiper of the first class—talk about how pleasant the workers at Halleck's store had become. And could you believe how low his prices were these days?

After glancing at his agenda for the day as prepared by Preston the clerk, he had begun his daily routine of opening the mail when the bell began to ring. Fallon stood. The windows to the upstairs office had been opened, because June in Leavenworth had turned hot and muggy. Whistles shrieked. Fallon tossed the letter from Washington, D.C., and the knife he used as a letter opener on the desk, stood, and moved to the window. The clerk and the bookkeeper stepped inside his office as Fallon leaned out the window.

"Is it a riot?" Preston asked.

"My God, we'll all be killed," sighed the bookkeeper, Montgomery Berrien.

"It's not coming from here," Fallon said, and stepped back from the window. The whistles were too faint, and the bell sounded like it came from the fire engine at the kiln. "It's from the new construction site."

He stepped to the filing cabinet, opened the top drawer, and pulled out the top-break Schofield .45. He broke it open and found the box of cartridges nearby. He pushed in five shells, keeping the chamber underneath the hammer empty, and shoved the heavy revolver into the front of his trousers. Then he grabbed his hat and pushed past the two prison employees. "Wait here," he told them, and moved for the stairs.

Citizens, ne'er-do-wells, even two school-age boys playing hooky crowded behind the barricade manned by several guards as Fallon stepped through the cell block construction site. A few reporters from the Leavenworth newspapers asked him what was going on, but Fallon waved them off and saw Elliott Jefferson approaching him. The whistles had stopped long before Fallon arrived, and the engine bell no longer pealed.

Supplies for the construction zone had been delivered, postholes already dug, even a few poles in place, and spools of barbed wire lay on the outer edge, but no one worked on those now. Guards surrounded several prisoners, and a cordon had been put up around the first cell block.

The inmates stood with their hands clasped behind their heads. Fallon recognized two of them, his old enemies, Aaron Holderman and Sean MacGregor, but he knew those two felons, and the others standing erect, staring at the cell block under construction, likely had nothing to do with what had led to the alarm. They were just being held until they could be marched back to their cells. That explained why MacGregor looked so pleased. So did other faces. They'd get out of the work detail early.

"Over here, sir," Elliott Jefferson beckoned. The kid's face had turned white, and he kept swallowing down whatever kept rising up in his throat.

Fallon moved into the stone walls, now about four feet high, and saw the guards standing outside one of the cells. The prison doctor stepped out through the opening for the door, shook his head, and waited for the chaplain to follow. They began whispering.

"It's in there, sir," Elliott Jefferson told him. The kid had no desire to go back into that cell, so Fallon thanked him and moved through the guards. Big Tim O'Connor stepped out, saw Fallon, and waved him in as he returned to the cell.

The floor was stone, thick, the walls rough, hard, well mortared into place. Fallon saw several sawhorses in the five-and-a-half-by-nine-foot triangle, iron doors placed on several, and a few more leaning against the unfinished wall. The body was covered with a white sheet that soaked up blood. A crimson pool already stained what had been a pristine stone floor.

Big Tim O'Connor knelt, waited for Fallon to step

closer, and then withdrew the sheet just over the man's face. Sightless eyes stared up at the sky, and blood had congealed in his mouth, run down his open jaw. "It's Wesley Westinghouse, sir," the captain whispered.

The locksmith. Murdered.

O'Connor lifted his head. "Do you want to see the rest, sir?"

Fallon nodded.

"It ain't pretty," the guard warned.

"It never is." Fallon nodded again.

Standing, O'Connor pulled back the sheet to the dead man's waist. Westinghouse's shirt had been torn open, and then . . . Fallon stepped closer, knelt down, feeling the nausea but mostly the disgust. How could someone do this to another person? He thought, becoming the detective again, that at least two men had grabbed the prisoner's arms, pinned him back, while another, maybe more than one, had ripped open his abdomen with a knife. They had laid him onto the floor and . . . Shaking his head, he stood.

Quickly, O'Connor covered the body.

"Inside his stomach . . . ?" Fallon asked.

"Locks." O'Connor nodded toward the sawhorses. "For the prison doors."

Fallon felt his head bob up and down. "That's what I thought." He spit on the floor.

"Doc says they shoved something into his mouth, to keep him from screaming," O'Connor reported. "He was likely alive when they started shoving the locks into his gut. But not for long."

Fallon pointed to the footprints.

"Yeah," O'Connor said. "One of them wasn't too carcful where he stepped. Marcy Huntt, been a guard here for six years, he found the body. Westinghouse worked alone, and, being a model prisoner, we never posted guards on him. I sent two men following the trail, but the blood stopped, so the trail ended."

"They got away?" Fallon asked.

"No. We knew the prisoners working here. I had all of them lined up. We got the one with bloody soles in the cell over yonder." He gestured with his right arm, and then used the hand to wipe his own mouth. The guard pulled out a greenback from his pocket. "Found this on him."

Fallon stepped closer and picked up the fifty-dollar note. "Uncle Sam's work," he said.

"Yes, sir. But he's not at it again. We got the plates, and this bill is fairly old."

"Let's see what the murderer has to say about who paid him to gut our locksmith and weigh him down with locks."

"He won't say nothing, sir."

"We'll see."

The murderer's name was Winfield McGarry, a hardcase who had done time in territorial and federal prisons. He was already serving life in prison, and because of that, he spit as Fallon approached him and let the smirk form across his face. The guards had taken him from the assembly of men working in the area and put him beside the brick kiln.

"Have all the guards wait outside except you, Tim," Fallon said.

The guard frowned but obeyed, and when they had the work area to themselves, Fallon smiled. "Let's make this easy, McGarry," he said. "You give us the names of the men who acted with you—and the person who paid you—and I see to it that you don't hang."

McGarry spit onto the toes of Fallon's shoes. "You ain't got nothin' on me."

Fallon showed him the fifty-dollar bill.

"Never seen it," the killer said.

Turning the bill around, Fallon shoved it closer to the cocky convict's face. "See that, you idiot. That's a thumbprint. A blood thumbprint. You've been in stir too long, McGarry. People are being identified by fingerprints. A few years back, some copper down in Buenos Aires, Argentina, caught a woman who killed her two boys, then tried to cut her own throat to make it seem as though she were a victim, too."

The killer laughed, shook his head, and said, "Warden, I'm here for life. You can't do nothin' for me. So if you hang me, hell, that means I get out of this place a lot sooner."

Fallon's fist caught McGarry just below the rib cage, doubled him over, and dropped him to his knees. Fallon's quick glimpse showed him that Tim O'Connor was shocked, but he kept his mouth shut, and simply stepped back to avoid McGarry's body as Fallon shoved him to the ground. Before the man could catch his breath, Fallon straddled him, pinning his arms with his knees.

"You . . . can't . . . do . . ." McGarry tried to say.

"I can't do what? *Do nothin' for you.* Isn't that what you said? Oh, but you're wrong, McGarry. You're dead wrong." He pulled the big Schofield from his trousers, eared back the hammer, and put the cold, hard barrel against McGarry's nose. "I can cut your stay here in Leavenworth really short."

The man gasped. His eyes widened.

"You . . . wouldn't . . ."

"Wouldn't I?" Fallon shoved the barrel harder against McGarry's nose. "Are you so deaf you haven't heard? I've been behind bars. I know what it's like in prison. Do you know who I am? Have you ever heard of Monk Quinn? Linc Dalton and his boys? They're all dead, McGarry, because of me. Do you think the president of our United States, the attorney general, anybody in Kansas or the world, would give a hoot if you were found in this kiln with your brains plastered across the bricks?"

He leaned closer. "That's what happens, buster, if I don't hear answers. Look into my eyes. What do you see?"

Fallon was staring into the eyes of McGarry, and he knew what he saw in those pupils.

Fear.

CHAPTER THIRTY-FIVE

Back in the old prison, Captain Big Tim O'Connor stepped in front of the door Raymond had just pulled open and aimed the shotgun at the small man stretched out on the cot, smoking a cigarette.

"There's no smoking in the cells, Hardin," Raymond told the murderer.

"So shoot me," Bowen Hardin said.

Raymond pumped a shell into the chamber. "Don't tempt me."

Behind O'Connor, Fallon watched as the surly man with the shaved head swung his striped britches off the cot and onto the floor, pitched the butt, and stood, casually grinding out the cigarette with the heel of his shoe.

"Hands clamped behind your head, Hardin," Raymond ordered, gesturing with the twelve-gauge. "Now move, eyes forward, fingers locked, and if you even breathe wrong, I'll blow your damned head off."

The black-eyed man stepped around the barrel of the murderous-looking scattergun, saw the five other guards, and laughed when he spotted Harry Fallon. "Well, ain't this something. The warden hisself comes to visit me. What's the matter, Harry, did somebody eat something that made his belly sort of . . . messy?"

Down went Hardin with a curse, to his knees, almost falling flat on his face, but he managed to stick his hands out to break the fall. Fallon never even saw O'Connor slam the butt of the Winchester pump into the back of the convict's head.

"That's enough, Captain," Fallon told the red-faced guard. "You have your orders."

"Raymond," O'Connor barked. "Wilson. Brisbin. Inside."

Bowen Hardin turned his head, saw the guards entering his cell, and he managed to laugh, although Fallon could tell that even cracking a joke pained the man after the blow the powerful captain had landed. "That's right . . ." Hardin shook his head. "It is time . . . for new . . . sheets."

"Stand up," Fallon ordered.

The killer laughed and managed to get to his knees before two other guards jerked him to his feet and shoved him against the outer wall.

Other inmates locked in their cells began hissing, but Fallon silenced that with a reminder: "It's just as easy for me to send all of you to the sweatbox for a month." He stepped in front of Hardin. "Go ahead, Hardin," he said. "Rub your head."

"Thank you, Harry." The convict did just that.

"I heard some bells and whistles," Hardin said after a while. "Don't rightly think it's the Fourth of July already, though it's hot enough to be. Was there some sort of celebration . . . ? We figured it was." He grinned the coldest smile Fallon had seen in years. "That's why we was all cheerin'."

"You're in big trouble, Hardin," Fallon said.

The killer laughed and spit off to the side. "Well, hell, Harry, how much more trouble can I be in? They plan to stretch my neck in a couple of months."

"It'll be a lot sooner," Fallon said.

"My lawyer might have something . . ."

"Your lawyer won't be able to do much for you," Fallon told him. He reached inside his pocket and withdrew the bloodstained money.

"I'm sorry," Hardin said, "but convicts here in Leavenworth ain't allowed to have no currency in their possession."

"Too bad Winfield McGarry didn't remember that rule," Fallon said.

"McGarry. Don't think I know him."

"How about Wesley Westinghouse?"

He appeared to consider the name. "Nah," he said after a moment. "But, see, they don't let me out too much. Me being condemned to a gallows. All a miscarriage of justice, you understand."

"Oh, well, if you were innocent of those crimes that got you here, we can just hang you for the murder of Wesley Westinghouse."

"I don't think I killed him," Hardin said. "Seein' how I was locked up here all today."

"Yeah, but you ought to look closer at that note."

Hardin stretched his head closer.

"Counterfeit," Fallon said.

"Why, I'll be a suck-egg mule. That's against the laws of our United States, ain't it?"

"Yeah. But we won't hang you for passing illegal currency. But for hiring the murder of another inmate . . ."

"Now, how could I do that?"

"Warden." Raymond stepped out of the cell. Hardin turned to see the guard holding a handful of matching fifty-dollar banknotes. Fallon caught a glimpse of uncertainty in the killer's eyes. The man turned back, flashed a quick smile, and said, "I'll say you boys stuck those fake bills in my cell."

Fallon nodded. "And we'll show the confession signed by inmate Samuel M. Lippert that he made those bills for you, for payment of six copies of what the state of Kansas would classify as pornography and four boxes of Cuban cigars. We'll also produce the confessions of the men you hired, who had money that for some reason was an exact match of the fifty-dollar bill that we used to identify Winfield McGarry, who said he was paid by you to kill a man you considered a traitor, a locksmith merely plying his trade."

"Well." He spit again. "If you boys want to delay my execution, I'll be glad to stand trial for having a hand in the death of this belly-aching, traitor to the stripes he wears, fool who got what he deserved, Wesley Westinghouse. Hey, the way courts are runnin' these years, I might live to see the new century roll in. Maybe even the next one."

"You'll be swinging in a week," Fallon told him.

The killer turned around, raising his arms until the barrel of O'Connor's shotgun almost touched the tip of his nose. "I'm to die by firing squad."

"You can't lynch me, you son of a . . ."

"You won't be lynched, Hardin," Fallon told him. "Once the evidence is put in front of the judge who sentenced you, and a copy sent to the attorney general and the president of the United States, your execution date will be moved up. Because of the threat you pose to not only guards, but prisoners."

Hardin's lips began to quiver. His face drained of more color and he raised his right hand to rub the knot forming on the back of his head. "You . . . you . . . you can't do this to me."

"You did it to yourself, Hardin." He stepped away. "No firing squad. You'll swing. Nasty way to die."

Slowly the man turned as the guards exited the cell.

"I'll kill you for this, Fallon," the bitter little man said before Raymond slammed the door shut.

"You have a week to do it," Fallon told him.

Fallon was wrong. Two and a half weeks. That's how long Bowen Hardin had to live. The U.S. government had reduced his time on Earth by three and a half weeks. Well, it was a start, and this time the government did not drag its feet. The judge had issued his ruling the next morning, the U.S. attorney general had telegraphed his affirmation by that afternoon, and the president had refused to intervene or make any comment whatsoever.

On Saturday morning, while Christina was teaching the prisoners in the pen, Fallon was making sure Rachel Renee put on the proper outfit while he straightened his tie.

"Why do I have to go with you, Papa?" the little girl asked.

"Because I couldn't find anyone to look after you?"

"What about Miz Janice?"

"She'll be where we're going."

"To the funeral?"

"Yes, honey, to the funeral."

"Will it be sad?"

"Well." Fallon turned and knelt beside the love of his life. "Yes. It's always sad to say good-bye to a friend. It'll be sadder, of course, for his family. We weren't his family. But we'll also be celebrating his life, telling him good-bye, telling him how much we liked him."

"Did you like him?"

Fallon smiled. Honestly, he hardly even knew Wesley Westinghouse. And he didn't think the old locksmith had any family, but the guards had put up enough money to persuade the Baptists into taking him in, preaching the funeral for him, and burying him in the church cemetery.

"Why isn't he being buried in the prison?" Rachel Renee said.

"Well, honey, when a man is sentenced, he's sentenced for a certain time period. Five years. Ten. Twenty. But no matter what the sentence is, even if it's for the rest of his natural-born life, when that term is over, he's free to walk out of the gate. So in Mr. Westinghouse's case, he has finished his time in the Leavenworth pen. We don't get to keep him after he's dead."

"Oh." She smiled. "Will there be singing?"

"Most likely."

"Papa?" The smile had faded.

"Yes?"

"The Widow Daniels says everybody in the prison are bad men, that none of them should never get out. That ain't true, is it, Papa?"

"No," Fallon said, "I don't think that's true. But remember, Mommy doesn't care much for the word ain't."

"Oh. Right. I'm sorry."

"I won't tell Mommy."

She smiled again.

"So why do people go to prison?"

"Sometimes they just made a bad mistake. Sometimes they're just bad people. It depends." He pulled her close. "Rachel Renee, you're a lucky girl. Because you're usually surrounded by good people all the time."

"Except for the Widow Daniels."

Fallon laughed. "Well, honey, she's not exactly a bad person."

"She ain't exactly good neither."

"Don't say ain't." He figured the double negative would be too much for her five-year-old brain to comprehend. Fallon had trouble with that one himself on occasion.

He kissed her forehead. "At some point, you'll likely come across some people who aren't good. I'd like to keep you from those types of people, but you're bound to meet them when you get older."

"Like the Widow Daniels."

He gave up on trying to save the reputation of that

old biddy. "Well, just remember, that usually there's good in the worst of men, and bad in the best of men."

"There's no bad in you, Papa."

"Well, I try," he said, but he knew he sometimes did not even try. Like when he had to deal with a murdering fiend like Bowen Hardin. "You just remember that. But you look for the good in the bad people. Don't look for the bad in the good people. Does that make sense?"

She shook her head.

He laughed, kissed her forehead again, and hugged her tightly. "I know," he whispered. "I have a hard time trying to sort all that out at work." He released his hold, and rose. "You ready?"

"For the . . . funeral?"

Fallon nodded. He still didn't know if this was a good idea, but Fallon and Christina well remembered they had been at funerals when they were younger than Rachel Renee. Christina recalled that of one of her baby brothers, who had lived but two weeks. Fallon had attended his grandmother's. Then, when he was twelve, his pa had taken him to watch the finest men of Gads Hill lynch a man who had been accused of stealing a mule.

That was something Harry Fallon would never forget. And it might have been why when Judge Parker and the U.S. marshal handed Fallon that deputy's badge five years later, he took it. Thinking now he would work for the law.

And here he was, years later, serving as a warden. Working for the law. And sometimes . . . working for what he figured the law needed to be. "There's no one sentence for one particular crime," Judge Parker told him. "One shoe doesn't fit every foot. Remember that."

"If you get sad, honey," Fallon told his baby girl, "just let me know. It's all right to cry. But if it gets too much for you, we can go wait outside. Don't worry. Everyone will understand."

"All right. Can we go to the ice cream parlor afterward?"

"Absolutely."

CHAPTER THIRTY-SIX

Some of the newspapers didn't know what to make of this new warden the federal pen had. Sometimes, editorials and news articles stated, Warden Fallon came up with these harebrained ideas that made them think he was turning the penitentiary into a Sunday school for killers and traitors to the U.S. government. Other times, they thought he was Genghis Khan.

Two weeks after Wesley Westinghouse's funeral, Fallon had to give a speech at the Leavenworth Opera Hall. For a weekday morning, he figured he had done well to draw a crowd of nineteen people, not including the editor of the *Post*, the only newspaper that figured the warden's speech was worth covering. Which, Fallon thought, it wasn't. He took a few questions from two of the sixteen women in the audience, and one from the Lutheran minister, shook hands, and stopped to make pleasantries with the *Post* editor.

They were walking toward a hack when gunshots ripped through the hot morning air.

"That's coming from . . ." the *Post* editor started.

Fallon already knew. He was running toward the grounds where the new federal pen was under construction.

A gust of wind took the gray bowler off his head as he darted through buggies and freight wagons that had stopped in the middle of the street, but Fallon didn't care. He just ran. Three patrons of a barbershop had gathered their horses from the hitching rail and blocked Fallon's way as they stood holding their reins with left hands and pointing with their right hands. Fallon saw no way around the men and their mounts, so he leaped over the water trough, placing his right foot on the top of the hitching rail, pushing himself up and over, while ducking underneath the awning, and landing on the boardwalk. He barely broke his stride, although if he had to do it nine more times, he would have broken his neck in nine places. Actually, he didn't even remember doing it until the widow Daniels read the article in the *Post* to him after church the following week.

He dodged people, found the road, and ran. Sweating now, tugging loose his ribbon tie. Whistles blared, but the roar of gunfire had faded. The barbed wire surrounding the working section of the new prison glistened in the sun, and through the fence Fallon saw guards taking cover behind lumber and stones. Other guards blocked the gate, yelling at passersby to keep moving, keep their heads down, and get the hell out of there. One of them swung a revolver at Fallon, but quickly recognized him and stepped aside as Fallon raced through the entry port and spotted Captain Big Tim O'Connor at the edge of the pile of stones.

Seeing no sign of arms from the rock wall of the cell block being built, Fallon sprinted forward.

Ten yards from the wall, he saw the muzzle sneak from the doorway to the cell block, heard a laugh, and then he was diving as the shotgun spoke. Fallon landed in front of an overturned wheelbarrow, heard the buckshot bouncing off the iron tub, and rolled over and over. Then O'Connor's meaty mitts grabbed the shoulders of his coat and dragged him behind the wall.

"What the hell are you doing?" O'Connor roared and leaned against the stone.

Fallon didn't answer. He came to his knees, chest heaving, sweat stinging his eyes, and found a spot beside the leader of the guards. After a minute, all he could say was "Report"—and that came out more as a gasp than a command.

"Indianola Anderson got a shotgun," O'Connor said.

"How?" He feared the convict had overpowered a guard.

"Don't know."

"I do." The guard Raymond stood at the other end of their small redoubt, peering around the corner at the cell block. Wilson took his place as the lookout, and Raymond inched his way closer to his two superior officers. "When the crew came in with the supplies, Deke Reno was one of them," Raymond said.

O'Connor swore, first in Gaelic, then in English.

"Who's Deke Reno?" Fallon asked.

"Ex-convict. Spent fifteen years here. Released last December. He's been hanging around Leavenworth, doing odd jobs."

"Did you see him with a shotgun?" Fallon asked.

Raymond shook his head.

Now Fallon cursed, but only in English.

"But," Raymond tried to explain, "another guard, Walter Mitchell, told me that Reno visited Anderson last week."

It was O'Connor's turn to curse.

Fallon wet his lips and tried to put things together. A load of construction materials was being brought inside the compound. Normal. The wagon would be searched, as would the driver. Only one man would be allowed to bring the wagon in, so that one man had to be this Deke Reno. But it would be easy to plant a shotgun in with the lumber and kegs of nails.

"Who unloaded the wagons?" Fallon asked.

"Prisoners."

Fallon swore. "The rule," he said tightly, "is that the wagons are unloaded by employees of the company delivering the supplies. After the wagon has been searched thoroughly." He stared at O'Connor, who shrugged.

After clearing his throat, Raymond said, "Lieutenant Wilder said it was all right since it was only one wagon this time, and hot, and the driver said the four men who were supposed to come out with him today were in jail across the river for getting drunk."

Which confirmed Fallon's suspicion that the driver had been Deke Reno. "I'll have a talk with Mr. Wilder when we've got things under control."

"No," O'Connor said, sighed, and then spit. "That's his body over there." He vaguely motioned to the pile of lumber scraps next to the entryway to the cell block. "They blew his damned head off."

"Do we know how many inmates are inside the block?" Fallon asked.

"Between ten and twenty is our best guess," O'Connor said.

"Hostages?"

O'Connor nodded. "Probably at least two or three guards."

"Which means they have two or three other weapons," Fallon said.

"But maybe not many rounds," Raymond suggested. "They were cutting loose pretty good when this all broke out. Had to be at least eight rounds. Including the shot they took at you."

"No," Fallon said, and rested his head against the stones. "If this Reno managed to get a shotgun in with the supplies, there's a good chance he brought along a box or two of buckshot."

Three shotguns, Fallon thought. Maybe four. The prison outfitted its guards with Winchester Model 1897s, twelve-gauge, special-order twenty-inch barrels, each weapon capable of holding five shells in the tube. Add one in the breech. Twenty-four rounds. In the hands of hardened killers. With a range of . . . Fallon had to guess . . . twenty yards, maybe twenty-five. This day could turn even messier.

"They can't get out of here without us cutting them down," O'Connor said. "It's hopeless."

"Do we know which convicts were working here today?"

O'Connor shook his head. "The lieutenant had the list."

"I recognized Indianola Anderson," Raymond said.

"We know he's there," O'Connor growled. "Why didn't you let us know you recognized Reno?"

"That's enough, Tim," Fallon said. "Reno served his time. He had a job. And the lieutenant let him in."

Raymond whispered. "There's Ben Lawless. And this big cuss named Holderman."

Fallon looked up. "Aaron Holderman?"

"Yeah. I think that's his name. Big dude. Strong. Ugly. Stupid."

Fallon whispered another curse.

"They still can't get out of here," O'Connor said. "Unless they try to sneak out when it gets dark."

Fallon was shaking his head at the captain's naiveté, but before he could explain what was likely to happen, the voice of Indianola Anderson rang out from inside the cell block. "Hey, ya stupid thugs who guard us! We wants to talk at the warden. Right now!"

"I'm here, Anderson!" Fallon called back. "This is Warden Harry Fallon."

"All right, Warden. Here's the deal you best give us. You gonna bring us four horses. Fast horses. Saddled and waitin' fer us outside the gate. An' then all you cur dawgs is a-gonna lay down all yer damned weapons and line up, hands over yer heads, an' jes watch us walk right on past ya. But that ain't all. No. We ain't no fools. Ain't nobody gonna be nowhere on the road. We see anybody, and there'll be hell to pay in triplicate. So you let the laws in town know. I'll give ya fifteen minutes to get the town cleared, the roads emptied, and dem hosses ready for us to ride. Ya see, we just ride outta here, cross the Big Muddy, and nobody follers us, or ya is gonna have to bury one of ya boys."

"Don't listen to him, Warden Fallon!" a voice cried out. "They will just—" The crunch of a shotgun stock ramming into a man's jaw silenced the guard. And left Fallon closing his eyes and lowering his head.

CHAPTER THIRTY-SEVEN

"Them low-down sons of strumpets," Captain O'Connor whispered. "That sounded like Jefferson."

"Yes," Fallon said, his voice barely audible. "It was Elliott."

"Your time, boys, be down to fourteen minutes!"

Fallon spit, yelling back: "Anderson, we'll need longer than fourteen minutes to clear the roads and get people out of harm's way. Give us an hour."

"No."

"Thirty minutes, then, damn it. I have no jurisdiction outside—"

"Thirteen minutes!"

"Dirty dog's watch is fast," O'Connor said.

"All right. I'm going to get your damned horses."

Fallon came into a crouch, turned to O'Connor, and whispered, "Do you have a sidearm?"

"No," the guard said and held out his shotgun.

Fallon shook his head. "They'll see that." He sighed, thinking he should have brought his revolver with him. But who would bring a loaded .45 to a speech at an opera hall in the middle of the morning in a city the size of Leavenworth?

"All right." He came up. "Wait here. If this doesn't work, don't let a one of them out of this yard alive."

"If what don't work . . . ?" the big guard cried out in desperation, but Fallon was already running toward the gate, out of view from the cell block's entrance, then he cut back and ran to the rock wall being built. From this point, he couldn't see O'Connor or Raymond. But he saw the brick trowel lying beside the bucket of mortar. This would have to work. Bending his knees, Fallon reached down and grabbed the handle. The elongated trowel, about eleven inches in length, came to a point at the top, like the point of a spear, just nowhere near as sharp. But this trowel had seen a lot of use, slapped a lot of mortar and untold number of bricks, and as Fallon ran his thumb across the angled heel, the roughness, he hoped, might be enough. The gamble, of course, was to pick which wall to climb over. The only way out of the compound that wasn't fenced in with barbed wire would surely be manned. So Fallon rose and moved to the wall.

He inched his way along the wall, ducking in the places where the wall remained less than three feet high. Moving with hardly a sound, he listened. When he came to the halfway point, he stopped, mopping his face with the sleeve of his shirt. Fallon looked at his shirt and tried to remember when he had removed his suit coat. Staring ahead, through the fence of barbed wire, he watched the armed guards—and the prisoners—all staring in silence. And this was the gamble, he knew. All it would take would be for one of the convicts to shout a warning, let the cons inside the cell block know that Fallon had no intention of getting horses. They'd kill all the hostages. Then come out or let the guards rush in. Either way, these men were hardcases.

They'd die game.

And kill as many guards as they could before being sent to hell.

He crawled along the wall, came to the lowest point, where the stones had been placed no higher than two feet off the ground. But it struck him that this would be the most likely place for Reno and Anderson not to have someone as a lookout. Anyone in this cell would be a sitting duck for a guard with a high-powered rifle.

He lifted his head. He looked into the emptiness, saw no one, heard nothing, and then he rolled over the rock and came down onto the dirt floor, not hard, barely making any sound. No one came after him. No words reached him. He moved hurriedly to the corner, where the walls were higher, and came up.

"You hear somethin', Bootsey?"

That came from the next cell. Fallon brought the trowel up, pressed his back against the wall that came just below five and a half feet high. Eventually, the walls would reach eight feet.

"No."

"Bootsey, ya best go see. I swear I heard somethin'."

"You go," Bootsey said. "I ain't gettin' my head blowed off." The voice, Fallon thought, sounded oddly familiar.

"You're goin', Bootsey."

"Why me?"

A laugh followed. "'Cause I got this here scattergun. You go. It's ain't likely nothin'. But if you don't go,

I'm gonna blow yer head off." The convict laughed like a hyena, and Fallon heard the footsteps on the rock floor. He didn't wait. He came to the hallway, looked down both ways, saw no one, and stepped quickly, seeing the doors waiting for locks to be put on. He found the nook in the wall and shoved himself into it, just as a man in stripes and a cleanly shaved head stepped into the hallway and moved toward the cell Fallon had just left. Fallon came up quickly and pressed the sharp corner of the trowel against the convict's throat.

"One word," he whispered, "Bootsey, and you'll bleed out like a deer before butchering."

The man froze. The smell told Fallon the man had wet his britches. "Drop the shiv."

The handmade knife fell to the floor, rattling just a little, but enough for the man in the other cell with the shotgun to call out, "Bootsey?"

"Answer him," Fallon ordered, and now that he knew who Bootsey was, he whispered his real name. "Holderman."

"Yeah, Dooley," Aaron Holderman said.

"What was that?"

"Tell him the truth." Fallon put the blade closer to the former American Detective Agency operative's throat.

"Dropped my knife."

"You damned idiot. Hurry up."

Fallon didn't have much time. Pretty soon, someone else would step out of a cell. "How many hostages are in there?"

"Jus' the goody-goody yellow dawgs who didn't take no hand in this," Holderman whispered.

"Anyone else who's not a goody-goody yellow dog?" Fallon pressed the trowel's edge tight.

"No, Fallon. But I didn't want to do nothin'. Dooley made me. Swear to God."

Fallon lowered the trowel, brought it around, and then pressed the point hard against a surprised Holderman's back. "Listen to me, Holderman. Do exactly what I say." He was thinking this up as he talked. "Shout out Dooley's name. Tell him to hurry. Then you hurry. You run into that cell, you keep your hands up over your head, and you yell to the guards not to shoot. You might live that way. If you don't, if you don't do exactly what I tell you, I'll gut you like a catfish. And you know I'm not bluffing. Right?"

Holderman's big head nodded.

"Now." Fallon lowered the blade, praying Holderman's cowardice would work in Fallon's favor. For Aaron Holderman had seen Harry Fallon at his best, and his worst, often at the same time.

The big man raised his hands high and roared, "Dooley! Come quick! Hurry!"

Then Holderman ran down the hall, just the few steps, turned into the cell with hardly any outer wall, and Fallon heard the big brute's screams: "Don't shoot! I surrender! Don't shoot! Don't shoot!"

Fallon had turned, rushed, hearing the footsteps of Dooley, and he stepped into the entrance of the cell, and shoved the trowel hard, thrusting up, powering with all his might as the tool sliced into Dooley's abdomen just below the rib cage. Dooley gasped, gagged, and dropped the pump-action shotgun onto the floor. Fallon already was pushing the killer back, twisting while withdrawing the blade, then spinning

Dooley around. He brought the trowel up, but used the angled heel this time, placed it against Dooley's throat. And sliced.

He pushed the dying man forward, letting him fall into the lake of his own blood. The trowel fell as Fallon spun around and grabbed the shotgun. "Stay here!" he roared at the convicts crowded against the unfinished wall. And Fallon stepped into the hallway just as another convict, his head bloody but armed with a scattergun, leaped out of another cell.

Fallon felt the shotgun kick in his arms. He had no time to aim or brace the stock against his thigh. The gun roared, leaving Fallon's ears ringing, and the guard's striped shirt became pockmarked with ragged holes as he slammed against a sawhorse and crashed over onto the floor.

A guard ran out of a cell two doors down. Fallon would have shot him, but he was just pumping another shell into the twelve-gauge, and spotted the uniform. But a blast roared from inside that cell, and the guard went crashing into the wall, twisted around, and caught another load of buckshot in his throat, upper chest, and jaw. He slid down the wall, leaving a trail of blood and gore.

A crazed voice called out from the cell. "You're all gonna die now."

Screams shrieked from the cell, and Fallon ran toward them, hearing another shotgun blast and the groans of someone. He did not stop, just stepped into the doorway, saw the smoke rising from the barrel of another twelve-gauge, saw bodies on the floor, and as the killer with the gun turned toward Fallon, Fallon touched the trigger. This time, he had the shotgun's stock tight against his shoulder, and he took careful aim. The man slammed against the wall, twisted, groaned, and fell to the floor on top of his shotgun.

"Stay right where you are!" Fallon instructed the prisoners. "Keep your hands raised and don't move."

He moved back into the hall, aware that the entire cell block had been turned into chaos.

Ahead of him, two men in stripes leaped out of the cells, turned away from Fallon—not even seeing him—and ran with their weapons into the open. They were met with gunfire. Living up to that outlaws' creed, Fallon figured, dying game. The guards would be rushing the place now. Fallon jumped into a cell, swinging the shotgun right, left, up, down, but this one was empty. He turned, stepped into the hallway, and felt the butt of a revolver split his head open just above the ear.

The next thing he knew, he was on the ground, trying to push himself up, trying to figure out where he had dropped the Winchester pump. Rough hands lifted him to his feet, and Fallon heard the raspy voice.

"Ben . . . give me that pistol."

Fallon's eyes cleared. A forearm pressed against his throat, and blood poured down the side of Fallon's head. "Give me the pistol, damn it."

Now the hallway was filled with guards. Raymond . . . O'Connor . . . all pointing shotguns at the man whose body Fallon was shielding. Fallon felt the blade against his throat.

"Put the knife down, Reno!" Big Tim O'Connor roared.

"No way, man. I ain't comin' back here never again."

The blade tightened. "Give me that pistol, Ben. I need that pistol." The hand jerked, nicking Fallon's throat slightly. "Don't move, I tell ya. I'll kill this man if you don't lower those barrels."

Big Tim O'Connor whispered something to the guards with him, but Fallon could not hear anything, and the muzzles of the shotguns and rifles dropped.

Then Fallon saw one-eyed Ben Lawless, standing against the wall to his left. "I want that pistol, old man," Deke Reno said. "Now." A body lay beside the pistol, but that man was still alive, just unconscious, and Fallon could make out the face on the floor. Indianola Anderson.

"The gun, damn you. Or you'll be washed in the blood of this lamb of a warden."

"Give him the pistol," O'Connor ordered. "But you harm Fallon, Reno, and you'll be blown to hell, you son of a strumpet."

Deke Reno laughed.

Old Ben Lawless stepped over Anderson's body. He reached down, grabbed the heavy revolver, and let it hang by his side as he looked at Deke Reno, waiting for further instructions.

"Give me the gun, now, you damned ol' coot!" Reno roared.

Ben Lawless stepped forward, gun still in his right hand, barrel pointed at the floor. Another step. Another. Deke Reno breathed a sigh of relief.

Which turned out to be his last breath.

CHAPTER THIRTY-EIGHT

Fallon didn't quite see any of it happen. His brain had been so addled by the blow against his head, he didn't see Ben Lawless cock the revolver, raise the barrel, or pull the trigger. He never recalled seeing a muzzle flash or hearing the bullet zip past his head and slam into Deke Reno's forehead. The hand holding the shiv dropped away, and Fallon felt a weightlessness as the body of the dead killer danced away from him and dropped into a heap on the floor, still clutching the prison-made knife.

Fallon felt himself standing there, still not comprehending what had happened, but he did see the smoking Schofield lower in Lawless's right hand, then drop onto the blood-smeared floor.

A second later, Fallon felt himself sinking.

He welcomed blackness, but it did not last long.

When his eyes opened, his head throbbed, and he saw the blurry figures of two men standing over him, while Raymond found a handkerchief and placed it against the cut.

Maybe a minute later, Fallon could hear the words Captain Big Tim O'Connor blasted into the convict Ben Lawless.

"What kind of damned fool stunt was that, you idiot? You could have gotten the warden killed!"

"Well . . ." Ben Lawless shrugged.

"You could have missed. Even if you had not missed, hell, old man, Reno could have cut the warden's jugular. That was foolish. Stupid."

"Captain," Raymond said. "It all worked out."

"That is not the point," Big Tim O'Connor thundered. He wiped his face. Shook his head. Finally, regaining something resembling composure, he said, "I never knew you were a shootist."

"I ain't," old Lawless said. "Never fired no six-shooter before."

"What?" Raymond and O'Connor cried out at the same time.

"No. Hunted with a scattergun and smoothbore. Fair shot with a long gun. Better'n fair. But I ain't no hand with no handgun. Hell, why do you think I poisoned all them red devils I kilt? I ain't no John Wesley Hardin or Wild Bill Hitchcock."

"Hitchcock," Fallon thought he was whispering. "You mean . . . Hickok?"

"See," Lawless said. "I don't even know no gunfighters' names?"

He didn't like lying on these blankets, letting a doctor bandage his head. Not the prison doctor, either, for Fallon figured the penitentiary's sawbones had his hands full.

Fallon kept trying to stand, but the guard Raymond was under orders not to let him stand. And when Captain Big Tim O'Connor told one of his guards to do something, they never shirked their duties.

"Where's Elliott?" Fallon asked.

"Don't talk," the doctor ordered. "Let me finish."

Fallon swore underneath his breath.

The guard Wilson thundered from the gate. "You reporters keep back. Keep back. Nobody's coming in here till we get this place secure."

Fallon found himself focusing on Raymond. "Will you get word to my wife . . . ?"

"Be still and shut up!" the doctor bellowed.

"Let her know I'm all right."

"Damn you. You might have a concussion. Your skull might be fractured. Don't move. Don't speak. Don't . . ." The doctor looked up.

Fallon felt the shadow cross his face. It was not comforting, because when he looked up he saw Big Tim O'Connor.

The doctor quickly tied off the bandage.

"Jefferson?" Fallon asked.

O'Connor shook his head slightly.

"Dead?"

"Not yet." O'Connor swore bitterly and tried to stop the tears. "But . . ."

Fallon tried to rise, but dizziness put him back onto Raymond's lap. "Get me up," he ordered.

He didn't remember anything until he was in the cell, which had been turned into a hospital tent. He had to lean on Raymond for support while following O'Connor to another blanket on the hard floor, and there lay young Elliott Jefferson, his face so white Fallon hardly believed it.

"We think Anderson did it," O'Connor told Fallon.

Fallon cursed. "I got him killed."

"No." Fallon looked down, surprised to hear the young Elliott Jefferson's voice, sounding strong, firm, commanding. It reminded Fallon of the kid's father, Deputy U.S. Marshal Edward Jefferson.

Fallon felt his body being lowered beside the youngster, and he sat on the floor and managed to put his hand on the boy's shoulder. He tried to squeeze, but Fallon wasn't sure he had enough strength to be felt.

"Warden," Fallon heard the kid whisper. "Anderson cut me good. Before any of this . . . started. Laughed." Blood trickled from the corner of the kid's mouth. His eyes closed.

Fallon pressed his lips together.

"Will you . . ." The boy coughed. "Let . . . Janice . . . know . . . ?"

"You'll tell her yourself," Fallon said.

The kid smiled. "They were . . . gonna kill . . . us all," he said after a long silence. "Knew it was . . . hopeless . . . knew . . ." He clenched his eyelids tight, groaned, turned his head left and right, and shuddered. Again, Fallon thought the boy had died, but the eyes opened again, and he attempted a feeble smile.

"They were"—again, Jefferson groaned—"planning . . . to . . . kill every . . . last . . . one . . . of us."

He spit out bloody phlegm. "Started"—he laughed—
"on . . . me . . ."

"Damned butchers," Big Tim O'Connor said.

"I tried . . ." the boy began. "Tried . . . to . . . stop . . ."

"You did fine, Elliott," Fallon said. "Your pa would
be proud."

There was a light in Elliott Jefferson's eyes now.
He grinned. Color seemed to return to his face.

"How'd he die?" the kid asked. "Ma never told me."

Fallon pressed the fingers of his left hand against
the bandage over his ear. He thought back, shook his
head, said, "I don't know, son. I wasn't there when it
happened."

"But you . . . know."

"Yeah," Fallon said. He knew. He remembered.
Edward Jefferson, deputy U.S. marshal with a boy at
home and a loving wife. Edward Jefferson, who had
served in the court even before Judge Parker took
over the district, who had arrested, by his count, seven
hundred and thirty-two felons—including the repeat
offenders—had wounded thirty-nine of those with
gunfire, and had killed another fifteen. Edward Jefferson, who had brought the notorious Cherokee
Chepaney in to hang after the outlaw's murderous,
three-year reign . . . who had outfoxed Linc Harper's
gang at a KATY station near McAllister . . . who had
survived roughly one hundred shoot-outs and knife
fights and countless other brawls with fists, sticks, and
ax handles . . . had died when he turned his back on
a teenage whiskey runner, who picked up a singletree
and broke the lawman's neck.

Fallon grabbed Elliott Jefferson's hand and, this time, squeezed long and hard.

"He died like a man, son," Fallon whispered. "Because he was a man. A brave one. So are you, Elliott. So are you. Your pa is mighty proud. I am, too."

The kid smiled. A moment later, he was dead.

"We can get the chaplain to call on Mrs. Jefferson," Tim O'Connor told Fallon.

"No," Fallon said. "I'll do it. It's my job. My responsibility."

"Boss," the captain protested. "You can't hardly walk. You need to get into bed and . . ."

"Get a wagon. Take me to their house."

"She won't be at home, Hank. She's at the chapel at the old prison. Teaching convicts how to read and write."

Afterward, O'Connor insisted on taking Fallon home, and Fallon was too tired to argue. His head pounded. Maybe he did have a fractured skull. Maybe a concussion.

He made himself stay awake the rest of the day, reading, waiting for newspaper reporters to start pounding on his door, but Christina, he later learned, had stopped that. Two city policemen stood guard at the gate to the house, and nobody was getting through this day, or the next, at least until they had to leave for prison to guard Elliott Jefferson's funeral. There would be several funerals this week, but, from what everyone around the penitentiary and in town was saying, it could have—would have—been much bloodier had the warden not taken immediate and swift action.

"How's your headache?" Christina asked after a late coffee. She had stepped out that afternoon, leaving Fallon with Rachel Renee, who had been instructed not to pester her father and just play and be quiet.

Fallon shrugged.

"It wasn't your fault."

"I know." He looked at his wife. "How's Janice?"

She looked up. "How'd you know?"

He shrugged. "I know you."

Smiling, she set her cup on the table and walked over to him, settling beside him on the sofa.

"Rough day," she whispered. "For everyone in Leavenworth."

"Yeah."

"Do you regret taking this job?" she asked.

"No."

"Good."

They talked for another hour, before Christina went into Rachel Renee's room and put her to bed. Fallon came in, kissed her good night, and told her how much he loved her. She asked if she could touch his bandage. He let her. She kissed the side of his head that hadn't been split with a Schofield's hard grip.

They tucked her in, and went to their own room.

An hour later, just after Christina blew out the lamp, the door squeaked open, and Rachel Renee came up to Fallon's side of the bed.

"Papa . . . can I sleep with you tonight?" he heard her squeaky, frightened voice. "Is that all right, Mommy? I know I'm a big girl but . . ."

Fallon moved over, lifted this bundle of preciousness, and placed his daughter in the middle. Christina rolled over and kissed Rachel Renee's forehead.

"I'm a big boy," Fallon whispered to his daughter. He smiled. "But . . . yeah . . . it's good to have a family. Good to be close together. Sweet dreams."

PART III

CHAPTER THIRTY-NINE

Summer kept its hold on eastern Kansas, so close to the Missouri River, where heat and humidity hung like cockleburs on linen. Life returned to normal, though memories of the bloody escape attempt remained in the thoughts of guards and prisoners. Especially for the condemned killer Bowen Hardin. And Harry Fallon.

The clerk, looking even grimmer than normal, tapped on Fallon's doorjamb and cleared his throat.

Fallon's bandage was gone, the cut scabbed over, the headaches slightly less. He lifted his eyes from the tedious studying of reports and sat up straight in his office chair.

"Yes?"

"This arrived in the morning post, sir." Preston lifted the paper held in his trembling right hand as he stepped out of the hallway and quickly covered the distance between the doorway and Fallon's desk. He slid the paper, facedown, over the myriad reports to Fallon.

"Death warrant?" Fallon knew what it was before he turned it over.

"I'm afraid so," Preston said.

"Don't be," Fallon said. "Bowen Hardin has lived too long already." He lifted his head and stared at the timid clerk. "And you know I don't say that lightly."

"Yes, sir."

"He'll likely have company soon," Fallon said. One of the documents on his desk was the federal trial docket for the following month, when Indianola Anderson would be tried for the murder of Lieutenant James J. Wilder and guard Elliott Jefferson.

Preston withdrew another paper from the pocket of his jacket. "Here are the instructions from Judge Mitchum."

Fallon took that telegraph and frowned. Mitchum. Not McDowell, who Fallon liked as a judge and as a man. Mitchum, who Fallon didn't like, had ordered the immediate transfer of Bowen Hardin and Indianola Anderson to the holding cells in the basement of the federal courthouse. Aaron Holderman, Sean MacGregor, and a piece of trash named Jimmy Calloway were also being ordered to be moved to the court's holding cells. Calloway and Holderman had been charged as accessories to the killings, though Fallon expected Holderman to make a plea and testify against the leaders of what the *Leavenworth Post* was calling "a bloody uprising." But Fallon did not remember the tiny, conniving American Detective Agency president being anywhere near that deadly cell block.

The judge had sent the telegraph from Topeka, the state capital. Fallon looked at the docket and saw that Bowen Hardin's execution was set for the same day the trial of Anderson was to begin. It would be a busy day in Leavenworth.

Fallon looked up at Preston, "Do you know if Mr. Barker is in town yet?" Abe Barker was the federal solicitor in charge of prosecuting the Anderson case.

"I believe he arrived yesterday evening. He's staying at the Prairie Hotel.

Already standing, Fallon thanked the clerk for his attention to detail, then grabbed his Stetson—he had never found the bowler he lost while running from the opry hall, but he had not looked hard for it, either—and his jacket, as well as his revolver. He had decided that he was too old to break habits and didn't want to be caught unheeled ever again.

Fifteen minutes later, he stood in the lobby of the Prairie Hotel.

The bespectacled clerk looked at the rings holding the keys to hotel's thirty rooms, then snapped his fingers, and grinned as he turned back to Fallon. "Warden, sir, I just recalled. I saw Mr. Barker heading to our dining hall not fifteen minutes ago."

Thanking the clerk, Fallon crossed the lobby and pushed through the batwing doors into the darkened dining hall and watering hole. He saw Abe Barker where he expected to find him—and that wasn't at a table.

After bellying up to the bar, Fallon nodded at the bartender and ordered a coffee. Then he smiled up at the ruddy-faced, fat prosecutor and said, "One of these days, the state of Kansas will remember that it passed a prohibition law years ago."

Barker lifted his half-empty glass of Scotch.

"Till that day, Hank, bottoms up!"

The coffee arrived, and Fallon sipped while the bartender refilled Barker's tumbler.

"How you doin', Hank?" Barker asked. "I mean. Your head and all? That was some doin' with that riot and all."

"I'm fine. You know how dense my skull is." Barker was drinking, then wiping his mouth, and asked, "Wife? Kids?"

"Fine. But just one daughter."

"What's keeping you from increasing the size of your herd?"

Fallon made himself smile, but got to the point. "Why do you want to move the prisoners to the courthouse?"

"Bowen Hardin?" Barker laughed and took another sip of Scotch. "Hank, the scaffold for hanging that cretin is in back of the courthouse. A barricade has been put up. Public executions are a thing of the past, ol' hoss. Too gory for common folks. Indecent for kids to see." Fallon started to interrupt, but the prosecutor raised his hand and kept right on talking. "You have to get a special invitation to watch Bowen Hardin swing. Last I heard, a ticket was selling for two hundred and twenty dollars. But you can get in free, of course." He smiled, Fallon opened his mouth, but Barker kept talking. "Anyway, it made sense to get Hardin to the courthouse's cellar. Lock him up there. That way all we have to do is bring him up the stairs, through the door, into the enclosure, and then march him up the thirteen steps to the trapdoor, read the death warrant, and send him on his long drop and short rope to the hereafter."

He needed a drink after that, and took a healthy swallow.

"I understand Hardin. But Indianola Anderson?"

"Security." Barker set the glass down. His face turned serious. "That comes from the A.G., Hank. It wasn't my idea. My understanding is that he—and all of the big to-do's in Washington, D.C.—they were more than a little concerned about the security at the federal pen."

Fallon could even accept that. "And Aaron Holderman?"

"He's a key witness. You should know that, too, Hank. If you can keep a secret, Holderman is going to plead guilty on the first day—reduced sentence, to serve concurrently with what he has left. He'll testify for us. We'll make sure that son of a dog—Indianola Anderson, I mean—swings, too. Maybe we can use the same gallows we put up for Bowen Hardin."

"There are only two holding cells in the courthouse," Fallon said. "Hardin gets one to himself, I hope."

"Yeah." He finished his drink, but, to Fallon's surprise, told the bartender that he was finished . . . at least until after he took his dinner.

"So you're going to put Anderson and Holderman in the same cell?"

"That's right."

"If Anderson knows what Holderman's going to do, Holderman's a dead man."

"He won't know what Holderman has agreed to do for us, Hank. And once Bowen Hardin drops through the gallows, there will be an opening in the other cell." He grinned. "Don't you see? It all works out perfectly. And you don't have to worry about escorting prisoners and witnesses—at least these key ones—to the courthouse from your penitentiary every day. Though I don't think the trial will last more than two days at the most. Should be short and quick."

He drew in a deep breath, held it, and grinned again. His face was ruddier now.

"All right," Fallon said. "So what is Sean MacGregor doing in the holding cell in the courthouse?"

Barker's eyes narrowed.

"Sean MacGregor," Fallon said. "He was in the old penitentiary during the breakout attempt. I checked the records and the log. He works once a week on the new pen. He wasn't working when all that hell broke out."

Barker shook his head.

"Well?" Fallon showed him the judge's order that included MacGregor's transfer. "Why would he testify?"

The prosecutor scowled. "Who the hell is Sean MacGregor?"

Chapter Forty

Troubled, Fallon stepped through the hotel doors, and turned down the boardwalk, moving faster than most of the pedestrians. Something was wrong. Wrong with Judge Lawrence Mitchum's order, and perhaps something wrong with the federal judge himself. But why . . . ? A thought flashed through Fallon's mind, and he ducked inside the alcove of a grocery store and pulled the telegraph from his pocket.

"Idiot." He cursed his casualness, that lack of concentration. Orders from a federal judge. Strictly routine. The warden didn't even have to see them, and, as Fallon read the scribbled line at the top, he knew Judge Lawrence Mitchum had not meant for Fallon to get the telegraph. Preston the clerk probably hadn't even looked at who the telegraph was for, and the clerk from the telegraph office had likely just handed it to the first person he saw in the building.

TO: Montgomery Berrien,
Federal Penitentiary, Leavenworth, Kans.

Poor Monty's path down the straight and narrow had not lasted too long. Maybe he had been blackmailed. The bookkeeper got the order, but he simply passed it on to the guards. No one would have thought anything about it until after. After what? When? Where? He knew this had to mean another breakout, and he figured that Sean MacGregor was among the conspirators. MacGregor was the only person with money, likely stashed away so that only his crooked lawyer had access to it, to pay for anything this big. He'd bring Aaron Holderman because of what little loyalty MacGregor had. And the others because they were just as ruthless as the crooked detective—but a whole lot handier at cold-blooded murder. Exactly the kind of men MacGregor would need to get his sorry hide down to Mexico.

Now all Fallon had to do was stop it. Which would be easy enough, he thought, and he stopped at the corner, about to turn to head back toward the old prison, when he felt the hard jab of steel against his backbone.

"Why don't we walk to the landing instead?" a voice whispered.

Fallon started to turn to his right, but another man bumped against him, casually opening his palm to reveal a derringer. "Ain't this burg seen enough blood on its streets already?" the man whispered, and closed his big hand around the hideaway gun. The revolver in his back pushed harder, and Fallon turned away from the prison and when a beer wagon rolled past, he crossed the street. The man with the derringer stayed at Fallon's right. The one with the gun—likely in a coat pocket—stayed right behind Fallon, although not close enough to press the barrel against Fallon's backbone.

"Kidnapping," Fallon said as he walked with the crowd, but not loud enough for anyone to hear him but the one with the hideaway piece of iron, "is against the law."

"So's murder," the man said with a malevolent grin. "Herzog and me . . . well . . ." He stopped, tipped his Texas-size black cowboy hat to a woman carrying a basket coming at them. She paid no attention. And the man with the derringer did not finish his sentence. Not that he needed to, because Fallon knew what the gunman meant.

The throng thinned, eventually vanishing to only Fallon and the two gunmen, as they proceeded toward the Missouri River's banks. Mosquitoes now buzzed, and the smell of stagnant water, rotting weeds, marsh, and dead fish grew thicker. Smoke belched from a stern-wheeler near the banks, and another large boat was making its way downstream toward Leavenworth, but the man with the derringer said, "This way." And they turned away from the landing.

Getting me far enough away from town so no one will hear the shot, Fallon figured, and tried to think when he should make his play. He wasn't just going to let these vermin put a bullet through the back of his head without something resembling an argument.

The approaching steamboat laid on its horn, and Fallon tensed as he walked. That horn would definitely drown out a gunshot, but now Fallon saw something even more troubling. He heard the singing and the laughter as Fallon and the two killers moved toward the river's edge. A bunch of schoolchildren—no, these boys and girls were no older than Rachel Renee, too young to be in a private or public school in town—splashed in the water as two elderly ladies told them to be careful, not to wade in too deep, and for Billy Joe to quit pulling on Norma's pigtails.

Church group, Fallon figured. Bible school or something like that.

"The boat," the one behind Fallon ordered, and Fallon saw the rowboat on the banks just beyond the kids. He nodded politely and tipped his hat at the two chaperones and stopped twenty yards later in front of the boat. The man with the derringer got in first.

"Your turn," Herzog said, and Fallon felt the pressure of the revolver's barrel again.

He looked up the bank. Still too close to those children. His boots splashed in the water and he climbed into the center row. Then Herzog, bigger than the man with the derringer and big cowboy hat, pulled his hands out of the pockets of his ratty-looking coat, leaned forward and pushed the boat into the current, quickly stepping in and finding a place facing Fallon.

"Don't just sit there like an anchor, Festus," Herzog grumbled. "Row."

The man cursed but pulled a paddle from the boat's bottom. He knew how to row a boat. Fallon figured that out in a hurry. And the current quickly swept them downstream.

The boat bounced off a piece of slow-moving driftwood, causing the men to tilt port and starboard a few times, but not long enough, not hard enough for

Fallon to make a play at survival. "Hellfire, Festus. Watch where you're goin'?"

"Well, tell me what's ahead of me, you damned fool. I can't see through you."

"I gotta keep my eye on our special guest," Herzog said.

The Missouri was wide, and they kept the boat in the middle of the muddy, powerful water.

"How far are we going?" Fallon asked.

"You're going farther than we are, pal." Herzog grinned. Behind Fallon, Festus laughed. "To the depths of this river, and the deepest pit in hell."

Fallon sighed.

Herzog leaned to the right. "Those big paddleboats aren't coming our way. Yet."

Festus brought the oar up and over to the port side. "Let's get around this bend," Festus said. "There's a thicket of woods, real swampy, they'll never find his body." He laughed. "Might even been some gators in there."

"There damned well better not be." Herzog shuddered.

All right, Fallon figured. This was part of the breakout plan. Get Fallon out of town, kill him. The prisoners would be transferred in the morning, before anyone thought enough to realize Harry Fallon was missing. A bit of a gamble. Someone might have spotted Fallon on the banks of the Missouri River, and there was still a chance one of those chaperones of the Bible school would mention it. But in this part of the country, three men getting in a boat and rowing downstream was nothing out of the ordinary. And that's what made Fallon think his luck had soured even more.

"Nobody's fishing this afternoon," Festus said.

Herzog grinned. "Like my ol' pap often said, 'too hot to fish' this time of year."

"Too hot to row this damned boat, too," Festus grumbled.

Herzog turned around as the boat rounded the bend, but not long enough for Fallon to make a move. He was facing Fallon again, the Colt .45 now out of his pocket and resting casually on his leg. "It's clear, Festus," he told his rower. "Make for the shore. We'll get this over with and be back in Westport for breakfast." He grinned at Fallon.

"Hell," Fallon said, and brought his hands off his thighs. "You mind if I smoke?"

"Hell, no," Herzog said. "As long as you roll one for me."

Fallon shook his head. "Sorry. I have a cigar. Not a cigarette."

"Well." Herzog straightened. "I'm partial to that particular weed, too. What about you, Festus? You want a cigar?"

"Don't take your damned eyes off that sneaky bastard," Festus warned.

But by then, Fallon had pulled the Schofield .45 from the back of his waistband. Had Herzog put the barrel of his Colt three more inches to his left, he would have felt the walnut butt of the big revolver. Now he was standing, swearing, rocking the boat while trying to get a better grip on the short-barreled Colt Peacemaker.

"What the hell!" Festus yelled, not seeing either gun. "Sit down, you dumb . . ."

"Nooooo!" Herzog was screaming as his thumb managed to find its proper spot on the Colt's hammer. But he never got the weapon cocked.

CHAPTER FORTY-ONE

The Schofield kicked like a cannon, silencing Herzog's scream. Crimson and carnage exploded from the center of Herzog's shirt and sprayed the rowboat's bow and the muddy water ahead of it with red drops and gore. The Colt arced and spun wildly, splashing in the river, and at the same time Herzog, already dead, was toppling into the river.

Keeping his balance proved awkward, but Fallon managed to turn, seeing Festus, face grim, eyes hardening. He was smarter than Herzog. That much Fallon knew because the oarsman knew better than to try to find the derringer in his coat pocket. Instead, he brought the oar up and swung. He didn't have enough time, or strength, for a crushing, killing blow, but the wet hickory paddle's thin side slammed hard into Fallon's hip, a stinging, painful blow that likely would leave a bone bruise—if he lived long enough.

His feet slipped on the wet bottom of the boat. Fallon felt himself suspended in air, wondering if he would hit the water. Instead, the boat managed to catch him. His shoulder throbbed. He rolled over, aware that he still held the Schofield in his right hand, but had not had enough time to thumb back the hammer. And the boat rocked violently, a ship in a gale in the North Atlantic.

The paddle came down again, but Fallon twisted his head away and felt the shudder of the blow just inches from his ear. That blow, and the boat's violent actions, caused Festus to lose his own footing. He came down on his knees, cursing, his teeth cracking hard against one another. And he lost his hold on the long end of the paddle. It bounced on the bottom, but the bottom was now filled with at least four inches of water from the Big Muddy.

Fallon came up, began thumbing back the hammer. Festus was reaching for the derringer he had slipped inside a pocket, but realized he'd never be able to get it. So he dived, extending both arms, lunging and cursing and praying. The Schofield came to half cock, then Festus's river-hardened mitts clasped on the big .45 and Fallon's right hand. The hammer slipped, ripping off a chunk of skin below Fallon's pinky. They rolled, and that caused the water-logged boat to capsize, sending Fallon and Festus, locked together, into the dark, deep, dangerous waters of the Missouri River.

Head-first they disappeared into murkiness, then blackness, dropping into the depths like a heavy anchor. Festus wrestled with the Schofield, tried a punch into Fallon's exposed ribs, but that had no effect. Fallon opened his mouth, tried to breathe, but quickly stopped. His eyes opened, but he saw what appeared to be bubbles and nothing more. They kept going down, as though Festus was driving with his legs, pushing them deeper and deeper and deeper.

The pressure built in Fallon's head. In his lungs. He wasn't sure how much longer he could hold his breath, and for a Missouri boy in the hills, he never had been much of a swimmer. Decent. Enough to save himself. But in the creeks and streams and ponds. Not in anything like this impenetrable ugliness.

Suddenly he was freed. Festus had lost his hold, or was trying to swim back to the surface. Fallon felt himself twisting in the current, and he kicked his legs, reached out with his arms, grabbed water, and pulled and pulled. He realized he still held the Schofield. His mind told him to get rid of that extra weight. His fear made him unable to work the muscles and joints in his fingers. He swam. Swam. Until he realized he wasn't swimming to the sky, the beautiful air, but to the depths of the Missouri. To the muddy bottom.

To his own watery grave.

He stopped, somersaulted in the mud and thick and wetness, and kicked hard. Up now. His lungs almost exhausted, his arms and legs spent. The pressure screaming in his head. But faint light appeared ahead. Almost. Almost. Just keep grabbing that water and pulling it back. Don't stop kicking.

He stopped so suddenly he felt he had been hooked. And soon realized he had, but not by a fisherman. A hand grabbed his ankle, pulling him down, down, down again.

Panic rose so quickly, he almost breathed in water. Almost drowned. Another hand grabbed his waistband, jerked. And Fallon realized he was dancing in the dark deep water with Festus. The killer was trying to force him down, make him give up. Festus, Fallon realized, was the seaman, the man of the water, the swimmer. Fallon was doomed. He couldn't see the killer's face, could hardly make out anything about the man's body, but he knew Festus was pulling him down. Festus could outlast Fallon under the water. Festus had all the advantages.

But Harry Fallon still held the Schofield.

The hammer cocked. He shoved the barrel into what he thought was Festus's belly.

Fallon squeezed the trigger.

For a moment, Fallon wasn't sure what had happened. In water, he didn't know if the gun would fire or not. Yes, the Schofield fired brass cartridges, not the paper cap-and-ball bullets that Fallon had used as a boy. Those would never work when wet. But a brass cartridge sometimes protected the powder. Sometimes. Not always.

Yet his hand shuddered, and whatever had been holding Fallon stopped. Now he dropped the Schofield. It was like cutting loose the ball and chain bringing him down. He pushed up, using his hands against the shoulders of the sinking corpse of Festus, forcing Fallon up, and Festus's body down. He reached up, brought water back. Kicked. Kicked. Fallon kicked as hard as he could, wanting to scream, to pray, wanting to reach that whiteness that he could just make out.

His head and arms and shoulders emerged into bright sunlight. He sucked in air, and dropped beneath the water. He came up again, and this time he was above the water long enough to scream: "HELP!"

Back below, but once again, Fallon splashed through the surface. He saw the bend of the river ahead of him, and realized he remained in the middle of the Missouri. An eternity to the west bank. Even farther to the east. He'd never make it.

And one of those damned steamboats was coming right at him.

Fallon closed his eyes, started to sink below, at least drowning would be a better death then being cut apart by the bow of a sternwheeler.

Then reason returned. He kicked, pushed forward, and reached out, grabbing a firm hold on the branches of that piece of driftwood that had almost capsized the boat. More than a chunk of wood, or a branch, this seemed to be a whole damned tree. But it was as sound as a boat. Solid. Unsinkable. And all Fallon had to do was not let go. Just drift. Drift with the Big Muddy.

He turned around, getting a better hold on the waterlogged branches that scratched his face and arms, and ripped his coat. He thought he made out the capsized boat. And the body of Herzog. Maybe if the captain of the steamboat that had to be coming this way at some point noticed that, he would send word, and a rescue party would come looking for . . . survivors.

But by then, Fallon would be . . . where?

And he had to get back to Leavenworth. He had to stop Sean MacGregor and those vicious killers from escaping.

First, Fallon decided, he had to get rid of this coat. It was weighing him down, waterlogged so much it felt like a dead man's shroud. By the time the coat was floating, then sinking, the river had twisted again. Next he tried to kick off his waterlogged boots. That probably took him at least a quarter of a mile. Or did they measure by knots in a river?

"Hell," he said, just to say something, "you're not a damned sailor."

But he remembered all the marching he had done in prison, all the walking, walking, walking. He did a lot of walking as a warden, too, and his legs had to be strong. The legs had kicked him up from the depths of this river. So now, as the uprooted remains of the tree floated into what would pass for narrows in this country, Fallon began kicking, steering it toward the bank. He knew he couldn't turn it toward the west bank, on the Kansas side, closer to Leavenworth, but he also knew he didn't have enough strength to swim to that bank. He needed the wood to keep from drowning. And he needed to reach that bank before he slipped off and let the Big Muddy carry him to a grave downstream from the two men he had shot to death in the river.

CHAPTER FORTY-TWO

As soon as his feet began dragging on the bottom, he pushed himself away from the drifting tree and managed to crawl out of the river, where he collapsed on the bank, feeling the sand caking to his cheek, hair, hands, and clothes. Breathing in and out deeply through his mouth, he rested for just a few minutes. Fallon could have lain here for hours, maybe days, but there was no time to rest. He rolled over and eventually managed to sit up.

The capsized boat was out of view, either below the surface, past the next turn in the river, or in the jam of trees, brush, trash, and driftwood. The bodies of the two kidnappers were gone, as well. The Missouri River had a way of keeping its secrets hidden for a long, long time.

One of the steamboats was rounding the bend, the paddle wheels splashing—about the only sound in the eerie stillness. Groaning, Fallon pushed himself to his feet and began waving his arms over his head, trying to signal the captain or any of the deckhands and passengers. Moving his arms hurt like blazes after all the swimming Fallon had done. He shouted, coughed, and cleared his throat and yelled again, but this time music blasted from the rear deck of the paddle-wheeler, boisterous to the point of being ear-splitting.

Fallon swore. He had never understood the appeal of the calliope, the organ that made what some people, though certainly not Harry Fallon, called music through its steam-powered pipes.

He tried to yell, but nothing could be heard over the racket from the deck, not even laughter, waves, or birds. It moved down the river, hardly leaving a wake, making Fallon feel invisible. The passengers on the rear deck never looked his way, just stood around listening to that horrible screeching that came from the calliope.

So Fallon turned and stared upstream. There was another boat, he remembered, but how long it would stay moored along the landing he didn't know. Hours. Maybe even a day. And it could be one of the short-liners, just moving upstream to Weston and Atchison, then back. He could find another sturdy enough piece of driftwood to carry him to the western bank, but the current would take him farther downstream. Time became critical. So Fallon started moving up the banks, barefoot. The current had swept off his socks. His shirt and pants felt twenty pounds heavier because of the water. In Cheyenne, with the wind and the dry air, he would likely be dried off by now. But here . . . with the humidity stifling, he felt as heavy as Aaron "Bootsey" Holderman.

Still, it wasn't like they had traveled the length of the Missouri River. They hadn't even neared Kansas

City. Maybe five miles. If that. All Fallon had to do was hike to the ferry. He could be back in Leavenworth in an hour or ninety minutes.

Or so he thought.

Until he came to the dam of debris, one of nature's impenetrable blockades of timber and trash and dirt, in one of the Missouri River's crevasses. It stretched out like a finger, a good hundred and fifty yards, so tall—perhaps twenty-four feet high—that Fallon could not see how wide it was, for he had not noticed it on his rowboat ride down the Big Muddy. He reached up and pulled down a branch, which snapped easily from rotting and drying over the years.

That meant it wasn't sturdy enough to support his weight. If he tried to grab hold of it in the water, it might disintegrate, and he'd risk drowning or floating downstream for who knew how far—away from Leavenworth. Most certainly, there was no way he could climb over it. That meant . . .

Fallon looked inland.

With a curse, he began to walk.

The first thirty yards were easy enough, ducking through trees. Then he found a branch, good, strong, and sturdy, and he used it like a scythe, crushing the vine and briars as best he could. He had no idea how many years of driftwood, wreckage and rot had been accumulating here, but he saw the rotting hull of a lifeboat seventy-five yards deep into the woods, a rusted coffeepot a short while later, and even the faded name of a ship, though he could not clearly make out the name or the company that had built her. Fallon's bare feet burned from cuts and the spines of twigs that had pierced his skin. He had taken off his shirt, using the sleeves to tie around his waist. He chopped. He moved. If he had dried off the water from his plunge into the river, sweat had replaced it.

But he had to find a way back to Leavenworth.

Now his legs sank into the swampy, murky, vile stagnant water of the marsh, but he had found the end of the giant mess of the casualties of the river, of the floods, of the storms for fifty or a hundred years, maybe even longer. Mosquitoes hummed about him, biting his neck, his face, his arms, and bare chest. What were his chances of catching yellow fever? Spiderwebs brushed his face. A snake swam past him. His feet sank deep into the mud, past his ankles, sometimes up to his calves. He trudged on.

The water never came higher than his waist, but the gaseous foulness often caused him to gag, turn his head, and spit. When he reached the edge, he had to toss the probing stick he had been using onto the carpet of rotting leaves and pine needles, then grab a vine and pull himself out of the marsh. He rolled over on his back, sat up, and began pulling the smelly, soaking legs of his trousers up to his knees.

He counted seven leeches, four on the right, three on the left. They didn't hurt. No stinging, nothing but disgust and annoyance. No matches to burn them off. No salt to pull them off. And while it wasn't like they were filling his body with venom, Fallon wasn't going to leave those nasty parasites on till he reached town, and let them suck his blood for hours. Chances are the leeches would suck till they were fat, then just drop off and wait for some other unlucky animal to pass by.

Fallon ran the finger of his right hand down to the thinnest end of the closest leech. He ran the fingernail of his pointer finger to the leech's mouth and carefully pushed the head and mouth sideways. With his other hand, he plucked the fatty end of the leech off. Blood flowed easily from the bite, but Fallon had removed leeches before. The wounds would bleed a while, but there was no danger. And he had not pulled the mouth off, which could leave the mouth under the skin. That sometimes would cause itching and swelling and take a long time to heal. He flung the leech into the pile of debris and went to work on the next disgusting present from the swampy hell he had managed to ford.

When the last leech was finding a perch on some fat leaf, Fallon stood, dropped his trousers and summer underwear, and did a cursory check to make sure no other bloodsuckers had found a part of him they liked. Clear, he hoisted the trousers, pulled the suspenders back over his shoulders, and moved back through brambles and thick forest, until he moved back to the bank.

After hours in the darkness of the thick, miserable woods, the brightness of the sun refreshed him. But still he saw no sign of help along the river. So he kept marching, determined now, free of the obstacles. Where there was not much of a bank, at least there was enough of a path for him to move at a steady clip.

Twenty minutes, maybe a mile, maybe not nearly a mile, later, he came to a sandy part of the river, and heard the braying of a mule. Fallon peered around into a cutbank, and saw the white mule, which lifted its ears, snorted, and pawed the ground.

He must have been delirious, because he asked the mule, "Can you swim?"

And the mule looked him in the eyes and said, "This mule don't swim."

Fallon turned, reaching for a gun that wasn't there, understanding that—obviously—a mule doesn't talk. A man sat on a bucket by the river, holding a cane pole in his right hand. He brought the pole up, and saw the hook remained on the line, and a minnow wiggled as bait. The man let the weighted line carry the hooked minnow about twelve feet into the Missouri, plop on the surface, and sink till the cork floated.

The fisherman, a black man with white hair and a salt-and-pepper Abraham Lincoln beard, did not look at Fallon, just kept his eyes on the floating cork. He wore Civil War–era Army trousers covered with patches, black boots, and a loosely fitting muslin shirt, the sleeves torn off around the shoulders, exposing the massive muscles of his arms.

"I need to get to Leavenworth," Fallon told the back of the Negro's head. "It's an emergency."

CHAPTER FORTY-THREE

"I done tol' ya," the black man said without looking at Fallon. "That mule don't swim." He pulled the pole a little to his right, dragging the cork a few inches, then let it settle and float. "Ain't much good for walkin', neither."

Fallon sank to the sand, just to rest, to relieve his legs of the weight of carrying the rest of his body. At least he had met another human being—unless he was suffering from sunstroke and was imagining everything.

"How . . . far . . ." He swallowed. All this water around him and he had not had anything to drink since . . . he didn't want to think about that. "To . . . Leavenworth?"

"Never been. I live in Missouri."

The mule brayed.

"Fish biting?" Fallon asked.

"Nah. Too hot."

"Yeah."

Fallon pushed himself back to his feet. "Maybe they'll start biting." He looked at the sky. "Yeah. There some clouds coming. If they go in front of the sun, you might get some supper."

Now the man lifted his head and looked at the sky. "Maybe," he said. "Maybe not. You done some fishin' I guess."

Fallon tried to laugh, but doubted if he had succeeded. "It has been a long time, but yeah. Only not in the Missouri River." He gestured off to the southeast. "But I'm a Missouri boy myself. I'll be seeing you."

He walked past the man and the mule, and kept walking, staring at the bank, watching how it curved up and ran into another mess of brambles. He'd have to barge through that, too, and probably another after that, and he glanced at the river and wondered if he could just swim. But the banks looked no more promising on the Kansas side than they did on the eastern edge. He walked, feeling the world spin and then sinking to his knees. The last thing he remembered was the rotting leaves and driftwood on the bank rushing up to stop his fall.

He floated, serene, at peace, most likely dead. The sun warmed his face, and when Fallon managed to force his eyes open, he found himself staring into the blue skies. The clouds he remembered telling the big black fisherman about must have vanished, or, perhaps there were no clouds in heaven.

No. Fallon shook the cobwebs from his addled mind and felt the stiffness and aches in practically every muscle from his neck down. He heard the gentle, soothing rippling of water, and felt the motion underneath his body. An oar stroked the water, followed by the wonderful sound of water dripping into water, then over wood, and pushing through water. He was in a boat.

Fallon lifted his head to see the big black fisherman working the oar, again on his left side. Fallon tested the joints in his legs. The ones in both knees appeared to work, so Fallon brought his calves and legs up, and shoved himself into a seated position at the bow of the boat. He glanced around.

"Mule ain't here," the big man said. "He don't swim. And he don't like ridin' in boats."

Fallon looked at his legs. No leeches. Hardly a sign of where the parasites had been sucking his blood.

"Where are my pants?" Fallon asked.

"Had to charge you somethin'," the black man said. "They won't fit me. But I'll gets some use outs of them, for shore." He pointed at his old Civil War trousers. Yeah, Fallon thought, his pants would be fine for patches.

Twisting around, Fallon looked up the river. Black smoke rose around the river's bend, and he knew that would be a waiting steamboat at the landing. He looked back at his savior. "How long have you been rowing?"

The man shrugged. "Don't keep much track of time. Hard, though. Paddling ag'in' da current. But"—he grinned—"I am right strong for an ol' veteran of the War a'g'in' da South."

"Well, I thank you."

The old man nodded. "It's all rights, suh. Be real easy for me to get back to the mule. And by den, well, suh, I figure dem fish might be bitin'."

Fallon turned completely around, because the

weight of the big rower in the boat's stern reduced the rocking to almost nothing. He could see the banks coming closer as the old man turned the boat and headed for shore. The steamboat was being loaded with barrels and crates. Passengers crowded around the gangplank that led to the deck. Vendors still hawked peanuts and popped corn for passengers to take on their voyage. Fallon looked up toward town. He could only guess the time, but he had made it in plenty of time. At least, that's what he hoped.

Due to the old Union soldier's weight, the boat touched ground before reaching the banks. But Fallon did not mind. He stepped over the edge and into water up to his knees, and moved down the boat, to extend his right hand toward the big man.

"My name's Fallon," he told the rower. "Harry Fallon. But you can call me Hank. Any time. I'd like to pay you more than just those pants, though."

"Shucks, Mistuh Fallon," the man said, as a grin brightened his ebony face. "I don't need nothin' mo'. Why, when I tells my family and all my friends how I come to get these here britches, I'll be rich with the laughter I'll be hearin'. Good luck to you, suh. Good luck. And iffen you even needs another ride up the Big Muddy . . ."

He used the oar to push away into deeper water, then turned the boat around. Fallon thought he'd just row away, back to the mule and the fish that weren't biting, but he did turn his head and wave. "I reckon I wasn't thinkin' too good. My Pa and my Ma would raise a conniption for bein' so ignorant and rude. My name's Noah, Mr. Fal— I mean, Mr. Hank.

My name's Noah. And that ain't no joshin'. It's writ down in the family Bible back home."

He waved again. Fallon waved back, watched the old man and the boat find the current, and then Fallon turned and ran along the landing to the stairs.

The stairs weren't much. More gradual because Leavenworth was just a smidgen higher than the Missouri, and the streets closest to the river often flooded. But there were steps, and those steps sat close to the steamboat. Fallon heard the gasps first, but he didn't care. He saw women turning around after their faces brightened with embarrassment and outrage. Some ladies pointed. One, wearing a brightly colored dress and a finely painted face, laughed.

A priest crossed himself.

A sailor swore and pointed a gnarled finger as Fallon ran past him with hardly a glance.

"Have you no shame?"

"You scoundrel!"

"Of all the indecencies!"

One woman staggered, put her elbow against her forehead, and collapsed into her husband's arms.

A deckhand roared, "Put on some pants, you damned freak!"

"This is a God-fearing town, you demon."

The man hawking peanuts stepped in his way, yelling for the police. Fallon knocked him into the cart, which toppled over, showering the grass and shell-lined path with paper sacks and kernels of corn, some parched or popped, others waiting to be cooked.

He was past them now, moving up the walkway between docks, moorings, and warehouses to the road that ran alongside the river. His bare feet really hurt now, from the briars and the sticks and stones, and now the hard cobblestone street along the waterfront. He had to get to the federal courthouse first. Or maybe the police station. It was closer.

"For God's sake, you pervert. Get off the street and put some clothes on!"

It wasn't like Fallon was naked as a baby or that proverbial jaybird. His underbritches remained on, wet, stained, torn, maybe hanging on by threads, but still preventing him from sending churchgoing Kansas women into seizures.

There was no time to stop. No time to try to talk a merchant into loaning him a pair of britches. He rounded the corner, apologized for almost pushing a young brunette into the streets, and stepped into a big man in a dark blue coat. Fallon hardly saw him, but his left hand pressed against a familiar piece of tin. A badge.

He pushed back and saw the ruddy face and the coarse black walrus mustache and the green eyes underneath a police officer's cap.

Fallon sucked in a deep breath, exhaled. "Officer," he said. "Am I glad to see you. I'm Fallon. Harry Fallon. And . . ."

He thought one word, an expletive that would have had his mother washing out his mouth with lye soap, back in his childhood years in Gads Hill. He saw the nightstick swinging from the mustached policeman's hand. No time to duck. No time to scream. Fallon tried to shout a warning and a plea.

"There's a plan to break the prisoners out of the federal courthouse!"

But the world turned into an ugly, cold darkness.

And Harry Fallon didn't know if he had managed to say anything before he fell into the depths of midnight, something darker, colder, and more threatening than being thirty feet deep in the roaring undercurrent of the Missouri River.

CHAPTER FORTY-FOUR

Foul-smelling wet strings from the mop swept across Fallon's face, causing him to roll over with a moan. The side of his head throbbed, but the blurriness slowly faded ,and he saw the ceiling. He had been lying on the cold, hard floor, his face pressed against the iron bars to the city jail. Some trusty was mopping the hallway floor, which explained why the beard stubble on Fallon's face now stunk like urine.

Rolling back toward the bars, he reached up and grabbed hold of the bar running horizontal and pulled himself up.

He remembered the policeman with the billy club. Fallon swore and yelled at the trusty with the mop.

One of the men in his cell swore at Fallon that it was too early in the morning to be yelling. Fallon turned back and stared at the window high up on the wall. Light shone in. Morning light. He had arrived in Leavenworth in the afternoon. That meant today was the day. He had been out all night. Now Fallon swore and pulled himself to his feet.

"Hey!" His voice thundered down the corridor.

The trusty, a thin old man with a ragged white beard, turned and frowned.

The man in the cell rolled over in his bunk and said, "Mistuh, you don't shuts your trap—"

Fallon turned back to him and said, "Open your mouth again and I'll close it."

He knew he didn't look tough at all, not with the lump on his head, his filthy shirt and underpants, no socks on his battered feet, and no pants. But his face, and that voice, gave the tough nut in the bunk a moment's pause. The six other men in the cell simply found some other place to stare or just closed their eyes and tried to sleep off their hangovers.

Fallon twisted again. The old man in the corridor scratched his beard.

"My name's Fallon. I'm warden at the federal pen here in town. Get Andrew Cameron down here immediately."

That ended the silence. The men in the cell, and even those across the corridor, began sniggering.

"Ya hear that, mate? He's the warden."

"Telly, it must be hard times over at the pen. When the warden can't afford pants, socks, or even boots."

Ignoring them and the laughter, Fallon kept his eyes trained on the old mopper. "You heard me. Get Andy down here. He's the chief of police."

When the man didn't move, Fallon pushed his head against the bars. "There's going to be an attempted breakout today at the federal courthouse, from the holding cells. And if you don't get the chief of police down here immediately, every one of you will be indicted as accessories." Still, no one moved, except the mopper's picking at his filthy beard. So

Fallon exploded with a stream of profanity that felt as if the entire cells quaked. That at least got the old man with the mop to step back and caused a policeman beyond the locked door that led to the cells to open it and bellow. "What is all this racket? Keep it quiet—"

Fallon roared. "Get Andy Cameron down here right now. I'm Harry Fallon, warden at the federal pen, and blood will be rolling through the streets of this town if we don't get some armed officers to the federal courthouse."

The cop stepped inside. "What?"

"You heard me. Get Andy down here, or let me out now."

The cop and the mopper stared at each other. Fallon screamed, "Do you want Bowen Hardin roaming free in Kansas? With Indianola Anderson with him?"

The police officer shut the door. Fallon turned around, kicked at a roach crawling across the floor.

"I think he must be the warden," said the red-mustached man in the corner of the cell.

"I think he's drunk," said another.

Five minutes later, the door opened, and Fallon turned back, grabbing the bars, leaning to see. He swore. It wasn't the police chief, only the sergeant. The sergeant stepped lively, turned to face Fallon through the iron barns, and assumed the Army stance of at ease.

"You say you are Warden Fallon?" the cop said in thick Irish brogue.

"I am."

"No identification was on him, Paddy," the first cop

said. "Kellogg brought him in late yesterday afternoon. Indecent exposure, disturbing the peace."

"Kellogg might find himself under federal indictment, too," Fallon said. "You don't rap a man over the head with a nightstick when he isn't resisting arrest."

"He didn't have any identification on him," the first cop said.

"You can find it in my pants and coat at the bottom of the Missouri River a few miles downstream. Get Andy here."

"He's . . ." one of the cellmates decided to say, but the sergeant cut him off.

"Fallon's wife was here," the sergeant said. "She said he didn't come home last night. Thought he might be at the federal courthouse. Or working late at the pen. But he wasn't."

"Her name's Christina," Fallon said. He described her. "There's a five-year-old daughter. Her name is Rachel Renee."

The sergeant looked at the cop beside him, and Fallon described his daughter, then cited the address where the lived. "You won't find it in the city directory," he added. "We haven't been here long enough."

Turning to the cop, the Irish sergeant said. "Go upstairs. Fetch Chief Cameron." He stepped back and yelled to the open door. "Benji. Get the keys. Now." His head turned and he studied Fallon. "If this is your idea of a joke, you'll find it really hard to laugh with your bloody jaw busted in ten places."

Before the cell door was unlocked, one of the prisoners pulled off his brogans and gave them to

Fallon. Not be outdone, a man across the corridor removed his Levi's, bragged that they had hardly been worn, that he had just stolen them a few days ago from a store in Missouri and that he didn't think he'd get extradited from Kansas for a pair of blue denim britches. Fallon stepped into the jeans as soon as he was out of the cell, while the sergeant carried the shoes. By the time Fallon sat in the chief's office, he had also been gifted a pair of thick socks. He was pulling those on when Chief of Police Andrew Cameron stepped into the office.

"Harry—you look like hell—what the hell is going on?"

Fallon laced up the first shoe. "Andy, there's hardly any time to explain. But you need to get every officer you have to the federal courthouse." He found the other shoe. "Telephone the federal pen. Tell Preston, the clerk, to have as many guards as can be spared sent to the federal courthouse. Give them shotguns and as many boxes of shells as they can carry. Tell Preston the order is coming from me, and I'm taking full responsibility. And if Monty Berrien is still in his office, tell Preston to keep him there. And if he moves, blow his head off."

He tied the laces of the other brogan and stood. "We'll need to arrest Judge Mitchum. Don't look at me that way, Andy, there's no time to explain."

He stood. The pants fit fine. The shoes were too big, but with the thick socks, they'd do. And those socks were just what he needed as badly as the bottoms of his feet had been scraped, poked, jabbed, and ripped walking through the hellishly thick forest along the river.

"I don't know how this is going down, Andy." Fallon tried to comb the mess of hair with his fingers. "But there's a plot to get Hardin and Anderson out of the holding cells in the courthouse's basement. Three other prisoners are likely breaking out with them."

The sergeant brought over a gray bowler. "Here," he said. "This was found in the street a while back."

Fallon almost laughed. It was his old hat. He couldn't even lose the damned thing.

The other policeman was on the telephone. Andrew Cameron yelled across the office to break out the Winchesters and to send a runner to the courthouse to clear the streets immediately.

"Let's go," Fallon said, jamming the bowler over his head.

"Wait." Andrew Cameron moved to the desk, opened a bottom drawer, and pulled out a .41-caliber double-action Colt Thunderer. He checked the cylinder before handing the revolver butt forward to Fallon.

"You might need this," the police chief said.

CHAPTER FORTY-FIVE

Knowing how important time was, they did not bother trying to find a hack or get into one of the police wagons. They ran, ten city policemen—including the chief and desk sergeant—and Fallon, guns in their hands. Men, women, and children on the sidewalks gave them a wide berth. Drivers of wagons stopped in the middle of streets. Horsemen reined up and sat deep in their saddles, keeping a tight grip on the reins, and watched with faces drawn and pale.

When the federal courthouse came into view, so did a stream of men Fallon recognized instantly. Guards from the federal pen, brandishing pump-action Winchester shotguns, stopped at the courthouse steps. Raymond pushed back his hat. He was sweating and out of breath. "Good to see you, sir," he said.

"Good to see you," Fallon said. O'Connor, Fallon figured, would have been minding the prisoners on the work detail at the new facility. But Raymond had proved himself time and time again.

A church bell chimed. Nine o'clock. The judge

would be talking to the attorneys. The witnesses and defendants would be getting ready to be led to the courthouse. Fallon had fifteen men at his disposal.

He turned to the city police chief. "Andy, take six men to the courtroom. Arrest the judge, and don't let anyone leave until you've checked them out." He looked at the other city officers. "The rest of you, find a position at every corner of this building. Make your presence known, but don't be flashy about it. And keep your heads down if this place turns into a turkey shoot."

He nodded at the guard named Wilson, who like most of those who rotated between duty at the old prison and the one under construction, had likely figured he'd have an easy job this day. "Wilson, take half the men around back. Get some cover and wait. If they come out running, I have to think they'll come out that way. If people are already there, slap the manacles on their wrists and gag them. We'll worry about their protests and threatening to sue us later. If someone flashes a gun, kill him."

He thumbed back the hammer of the Colt that Cameron had given him, but he kept his finger out of the trigger guard. He smiled without humor at Raymond. "You men, come with me."

They followed him up the steps and through the door.

A federal deputy marshal put his hand on the holstered Remington and walked stern-faced to Fallon.

"Warden . . . ?" he managed to say, but could not keep the tremor out of his voice.

"Fred," Fallon told him. "We've got a potential problem. Have Bowen Hardin or Indianola Anderson been moved out of the holding cells to the courtroom yet?"

"No." He looked up the stairs that led to the courtrooms. "Waiting on orders. What's going on?"

"There's a breakout planned."

"God." The man's face turned ghostly pale. He thought of something else. "Your wife was just here, looking for you."

Fallon felt the cold fear strike him. This was not something he had thought about, though it certainly made sense, knowing Christina as well as he did. "She wondered . . . well . . . you hadn't come . . ."

"I know." He nodded toward the door that led to the stairs. "Let's go."

"Was Christina alone?"

"Yeah. She said she left your girl with . . . oh . . . the widow of the guard who got killed during that bloody mess . . ."

Fallon breathed easier. Christina would be out of harm's way if this morning turned ugly. She'd be with Janice Jefferson and Rachel Renee.

The door opened, and Raymond stepped inside first, swinging the twin barrels of the shotgun in all directions. "Nobody around, sir," he announced, and moved down the steps. Fallon was next, followed by the deputy marshal and the rest of the assembled men, packing enough iron to start a war.

Raymond led the way down to the first landing,

swung around, nodded, and continued to the basement. Fallon followed, with the rest of the guards behind him. Boots hammered against the stairs, echoing up and down the cavernous chamber, but Fallon hoped the noise could not be heard beyond the heavy doors.

They stopped on the bottom, sweating. Fallon shifted the .41, still cocked, to his left hand, wiped his palms against the stolen jeans, and took the revolver again in his right. He pushed himself against the wall near the door, nodded. Slowly, Raymond took the handle in his left hand, clutching the twelve-gauge in his right, and cracked the door open.

Fallon could see the gas lamp flickering in the drafty hallway. No one in view. He ordered the door opened with a nod, and Fallon stepped into the damp hallway, looking up and down the hall. Nobody in view. The chair by the door was empty, and that could be a problem. With prisoners about to be escorted to the courtroom, a deputy marshal should have been here. But he could also be checking the cells past the door, maybe even relieving his bladder.

"Let's go," Fallon whispered, and the men followed him to the door that led to the holding cells.

He looked through the circular hole in the center of the door, through the bars, and breathed a sigh of relief. The guard was there, talking to the prisoners. Fallon stepped back and told Raymond to open this door. When he did, Fallon called out to the guard, "Deputy. This is Warden Harry Fallon. Is everything all right in there?"

He could see the deputy, stepping back, startled. "Ummm . . . yes, sir, Warden. Just a routine check."

Fallon moved into the doorway, keeping the revolver pressed against his leg, and walked down the corridor. Raymond and two of the others entered the holding area with him. The rest remained outside.

"What's going on?" the deputy said. With his job of guarding prisoners, he had no weapon. Men with close contact with men in holding cells were not allowed to carry firearms or any type of weapon. It was a sound policy. You didn't want a convict to be able to get a lawman's weapon.

"Are you armed, Deputy?" Fallon asked as he covered the twenty yards.

The man looked as if he had taken an ax handle across his stomach. "No . . . no . . . sir."

Good, Fallon thought. For if the man presented a gun, Fallon would have drilled him with a slug from the Thunderer.

"Are you men here to escort some witnesses and defendants to the courtroom?" the guard asked. "I mean . . . you're not here for Bowen Hardin, are you?"

Even better, Fallon thought. Bowen Hardin was still in his cell, too. Waiting for his date with the executioner. Maybe this had all been some sort of wild rumor, that there never was going to be a breakout. It would have taken some doing . . .

No, no. Fallon knew that was wishful thinking. This had been planned. This was proceeding, most likely. Men did not kidnap wardens and take them downstream in a rowboat planning to murder them and dispose of their bodies. No. You didn't do anything like that if you were bluffing or would even consider backing out of the murderous scheme.

"All right." Fallon exhaled. He turned to the guards and saw doubt creeping into their faces, and he even briefly considered the chance that perhaps that knot on his head, the one either given him by the Leavenworth policeman or the men who had kidnapped him, had rattled his mind and compromised his faculties.

He looked into the cell at one of the prisoners, turned back to say something to Raymond, and then spun, and rushed to the door, gripping the bars and looking at the little man sitting on a cot.

"Who the hell is this?" Fallon thundered.

The deputy stepped closer and said, "It's the notorious murderer Bowen Hardin."

Turning viciously, Fallon thundered, "That is not Bowen Hardin." He rushed to the cell across the narrow hall and looked inside. "And these men are not Aaron Holderman, Sean MacGregor, Jimmy Calloway, or Indianola Anderson." Raymond rushed to the cell that allegedly housed Bowen Hardin. Raymond's savage curse confirmed to Fallon that he had not lost his mind. None of the cells housed any of the men they were supposed to be holding.

Fallon spun to the deputy. "When were these men delivered to you?"

"Early this morning," the deputy said. "I swear on a stack of Bibles, Warden, that these were the men the marshals brought here."

Fallon stepped toward Raymond.

"Six federal marshals arrived before dawn," Fallon said, "with the proper paperwork. They took the five prisoners, shackled them, loaded them into a wagon, and headed away from the prison, sir."

The man in Bowen Hardin's cell laughed. "Well, if we're not supposed to be here, y'all better let us go." Across the hall, the other four men laughed like howling coyotes.

CHAPTER FORTY-SIX

Fallon let out a breath, calmed himself, and stepped closer to the cell housing the impostor. The man who looked nothing like Bowen Hardin leaned back on his cot, putting his hands behind his head and resting against the stone wall.

"I hope," Fallon said in a calm, collected voice, "that they paid you handsomely. Because Bowen Hardin is scheduled to hang at noon today."

That straightened him. He sat upright, and his face turned white. "You . . . can't . . ."

"I imagine the judge upstairs is finalizing your death warrant as we speak."

"But . . . but . . . you . . . you can't." He swallowed. Then Fallon saw the wetness forming in the crotch of his tan britches—the courtroom suit for prisoners. "You can't hang me!" he shrieked. "I'm not Bowen Hardin."

"Deputy," Fallon said, and the guard stepped over quickly.

"You better tell this marshal everything you know, and I mean details and descriptions." He stepped to the next cell and stared down the four frauds in that room, turning to the nearest guard and taking the shotgun from him. "And you four are going to do the exact same thing. You'll tell this guard exactly what happened. And if you make one slip, you'll wish you were hanging in Bowen Hardin's place before I'm through with you. Because you don't know what hard labor is, but, by thunder, you'll find out."

Before he got to the door to the stairs, it swung open, and the chief of police rushed into the hallway. "Harry," he said, trying to catch his breath. "Judge Mitchum isn't in the courtroom. He hasn't been seen since yesterday evening."

"Andy," Fallon said. "We've got bigger problems. Bowen Hardin. Indianola Anderson. All the others. They're not here."

"What the . . . !"

"I'll explain on the way out," Fallon said and started for the stairs.

His mind tried to take it all in, figure things out. The six men, likely posing as federal marshals, had arrived at the pen before dawn. Bowen, Holderman, MacGregor, Anderson, and Calloway would have swapped places with the hired imposters. That would have taken some time, not long, but a few minutes. Then what? No train would be running, not that early in the morning, and with the hanging scheduled, Bowen Hardin's likenesses had been put in newspapers and magazines across the frontier. There was no way Hardin would risk being recognized on a train.

"Raymond," Fallon said. "Go to the prison. I told Preston to keep Montgomery Berrien from trying to leave the prison or Leavenworth."

"That little pipsqueak," the guard blurted out. "You mean he was in this conspiracy."

"Yes, he was," Fallon said. "I doubt if Berrien knows much, but just in case."

Raymond left. Fallon stopped. "We need to check every livery stable. See if anyone rented five or more horses this morning."

"They could have had the horses ready, waiting on the outskirts of town, or even in some vacant lot," Cameron said.

"I know," Fallon said. "But someone might have seen the horses."

"A steamboat?" another guard suggested.

"Doubtful," Fallon said. "For the same reasons as the train. But we can't just dismiss the possibility." He nodded at the guard who had mentioned the steamboat route, and that guard shifted his shotgun under his shoulder and took off at a dead run toward the landing.

Fallon looked back at the police chief. "There's no sense in putting this off," he said. "We need to send telegraphs out to every county sheriff in the state, plus Kansas City and the federal marshal's office there. Iowa. Nebraska. Arkansas. Colorado. Texas and the Indian Nations. Then telegraph the attorney general's office in Washington D.C. This is huge. We'll need all the help we can get."

Another city policeman was running toward them, pale and exhausted. He slid to a stop, bent forward, holding his hands against his thighs, and gasped. "Chief . . . it's . . . the . . . judge . . ."

"Mitchum?" Andy Cameron asked.

The officer's head nodded once. He kept sucking in breath after breath. "Yes." His eyes lifted. "He's . . ."

Fallon knew before the officer finished the sentence or his next breath.

"Dead."

Cut throat. In his own bathtub.

"Maybe . . ." the officer said. "Sui-cide."

"Maybe." But Fallon doubted that.

"They can't get away," the chief said.

"They have four hours, maybe more, of a head start," Fallon said, but then he stopped. He turned to the closest man he saw, a city policeman with a fuzzy mustache. The kid couldn't have been older than twenty-one. "What would you do? How would you try to escape?"

"Shoot," the kid said. "I'd just ride as fast as I could for the Indian Territory."

Fallon nodded. "Right." He turned to Cameron. "We'd send every posse we could outfit in every direction there is."

Cameron straightened. "There wouldn't be a peace officer left in Leavenworth."

"You think they're still in town?" a guard asked. "That's crazy."

"Like a fox," Fallon said. "Or Sean MacGregor." He grinned. Now he knew why desperate men like Bowen Hardin and MacGregor had let him tag along. Fallon knew all the tricks, how to sneak men out . . . what was the saying . . . hide in plain sight? And detectives knew quite a lot about disguising.

"Search the hotels," Andrew Cameron ordered. "Every one. Every room. Every rooming house."

"Livery stables, too," Fallon suggested.

"They can't be still here," whispered another police officer. "That's just . . ."

"Yeah," Fallon said. He nodded at Cameron. "Get those wires sent out as quickly as you can. There's still a very good chance those boys are halfway to the Indian Nations by now. Telegraph the law in Baxter Springs first. That's the first place they'd shoot for . . . if they're going south."

He walked away, calling back, "I'll meet you at your office, Andy, in half an hour."

"Where are you going?" the chief asked.

"To see my wife and daughter. Let them know I'm alive. And put on some shoes and socks that actually fit." He picked up the pace. "I have a feeling that I'll be on my feet for quite a long time."

He let his guard down. Didn't give Sean MacGregor enough credit. After pushing open the door and calling out Christina's name, he saw the gun barrel aimed at his head.

"Hello, Hank." Aaron Holderman grinned.

Hiding in plain sight. Fallon felt his stomach turn. *Hiding in my own home.*

Then, the blood rushed to his head.

"Your wife and child are fine." Sean MacGregor, looking even older, rounded the corner, and grinned. "Let's keep them that way, all right, Harry?" He turned his head and yelled, "Miss Whitney." He stopped, laughed, and shook his head. "I'm sorry. I just can't get used to that. Mrs. Fallon!"

The door to Rachel Renee's bedroom opened, and Christina emerged, looking tired but beautiful, carrying Rachel Renee in her arms. Jimmy Calloway, holding a Winchester repeating rifle, followed them but stayed in the doorway.

"Good to see you," Christina said softly.

Fallon answered the same way, but smiled at his daughter. "How you doing, sweetheart?"

"Papa," his daughter said, sounding more sleepy than scared. That was good. "Who are these men?"

"We're friends of your old man." Bowen Hardin stepped around, wearing trail duds, looking more like a cowboy than a man who should have been dropping through the trapdoor of a gallows right about now. Hardin looked at MacGregor. "I told you there was no way those two goons could kill Warden Harry Fallon. I told you he'd come right back here."

"You told me," the former private detective said.

Then the door to the master bedroom opened, and Indianola Anderson threw Janice Jefferson out. Her hair was disheveled, her bottom lip puffy and discolored. She had put up a fight.

"You all right?" Fallon asked.

She didn't answer. But Anderson did. "Of course, she's all right."

Fallon looked back at Hardin, knowing MacGregor might have come up with the plan and paid most of the money to get this all set in motion, but Bowen Hardin was the leader.

"What's the plan?"

"We had two plans." The killer reached for a cup on a bookshelf, lifted it in a mock toast. "One was we stay here. Till the town cleared out of lawmen. Then ride to Omaha." He sipped the coffee. "But since that's not going to happen, we're going to the landing.

All of us. Right now. We're going to get into a boat. And just take a ride down the river. All of us."

Fallon nodded. "Leave the women and child here. I'll go with you."

"Oh, you're going with us, Hank," the killer said. "But so are the lovely ladies."

Calloway laughed. "If we see dust or anybody on either side of the river, some of our passengers will become supper for the catfish."

Fallon looked around his home then back at Hardin. "What did you do with your federal marshals?" he asked. "You know, the ones who were escorting you to the courthouse?"

The killer finished his coffee, and let the cup fall on the floor, shattering. "I had Calloway pay them off, Hank."

"Like you paid off Judge Mitchum?"

The man grinned evilly. "And how we'll pay you off when you've finished your job for us, Hank. But you know one thing about me. I won't harm the hair on the head of a woman or a child. So long as you do what I say, exactly what I say. Savvy?"

Fallon nodded.

CHAPTER FORTY-SEVEN

Hardin turned to Sean MacGregor. "Now what?" the murderer asked.

"We get changed," the old detective said. "Bootsey and I'll go first." Both men disappeared into Fallon's bedroom. Calloway went to the front door, peaking through the curtains.

"Quiet neighborhood you got here," he said and chuckled. "That's one reason we picked this place."

After clearing her throat, Christina said, "How about coffee?"

"Good idea," Indianola Anderson said, but when Christina stepped toward the kitchen, the murderer stepped in front of her, put his hand on her shoulder, and grinned. "But I like the way I make coffee." He pushed her back gently. "You, darlin', I figure might be inclined to poison us all."

Hardin swore. "Let her make the coffee, Anderson," he barked. "They never let you work in the mess hall for good reason. She won't poison us. But keep the door open, and keep an eye on her." He nodded at Christina. "Go ahead."

She stepped, and Rachel Renee ran to her, grabbing the side of her skirt. "Let me help, Mommy."

With his family in the kitchen, Janice Jefferson sitting on the sofa, Fallon tried to think of some way out of this trap. Surely, these men didn't think they could just walk to the landing, take a boat. They'd be recognized instantly, and there was no way the authorities would let them go—even with hostages. Fallon looked through the open doorway and saw Christina making coffee.

Then the door to his bedroom opened, and Holderman and MacGregor stepped into the parlor.

They wore the uniforms of the U.S. Army, Holderman becoming a sergeant in the infantry, and MacGregor a lieutenant colonel.

"What do you think?" Holderman said with a snort.

"You should be fighting in Cuba or the Philippines," Fallon told them.

"Take over for Calloway," Hardin ordered Holderman, then Bowen Hardin and Calloway entered Fallon's bedroom, while MacGregor took Hardin's revolver and aimed it casually at Fallon's chest.

"I planned this pretty good, don't you think?" MacGregor said with a smile.

"You're not out of Leavenworth yet," Fallon told him, his voice icy.

"You better hope we are soon," MacGregor said. "Or nobody gets out of Leavenworth alive."

By the time Calloway and Hardin emerged, dressed in Army attire, the coffee was ready, so Indianola Anderson took his mug and stepped into the bedroom for the last of the uniforms.

The plan might work. Fallon had to concede that

argument. With everyone running around, civilians scared out of their wits, lawmen and prison guards trying to get posses together, the sight of the prison warden marching with soldiers to the riverfront would make a certain amount of sense. Why wouldn't federal soldiers be involved in the effort to round up the escapees from a federal pen? Few would look at the faces of the soldiers. The uniforms would comfort them. This was another reason Bowen Hardin had brought MacGregor into the fold. The crooked old detective had people on the outside, men who could get him Army uniforms that fit, as well as guns.

But how would they explain two women and a five-year-old girl?

Indianola Anderson came out of the bedroom. The kepi didn't fit, for the killer had a small head compared to the rest of his hard, tough body.

"How's it look?" Bowen Hardin asked Holderman, still at the door looking through the curtains.

"Nobody on the street or in the yards," the big brute said.

Hardin walked up to Fallon. "The women and kid walk ahead of us. If they run, yell, do anything, they die first," he whispered. "You get to see that, right before I put a bullet in your spine. I'll be right behind you. One mistake, and everybody pays the extreme penalty." He walked to Christina and Rachel Renee and, smiling, whispered the instructions to them, patted Rachel Renee's head, and came back to Fallon.

"Let's go," Hardin said, and Aaron Holderman opened the door.

* * *

The escaped convicts looked like soldiers. They also marched like them. That was another thing prison had taught these scum. And since nobody saw them leave Fallon's home, by the time they were out of the neighborhood and turning onto the nearest street that ran straight to the Missouri River landing, Fallon guessed that these killers had a good chance to get out of the city.

People ran this way and that—citizens, preachers, drummers, women with their children, even lawmen. Fallon kept his head straight, but his eyes darted north, south, and east, trying to find some friendly face.

One old, one-eyed drunk sat up from where he had crumpled in front of a vacant building, brushed himself off, snapped his heels together, and grinned as he saluted sharply, slurring out, "Sergeant Major Christianson, Seventh Ohio Infantry. All present and accounted for, Gen'ral. Welcome to Gettysburg, sir."

A woman across the street pointed, and whispered something to another woman standing next to her, but they just gave them a moment's consideration, and then went back to gossiping.

He caught glimpses of faces of men he knew, but none was a person he needed, a person willing to put his life on the line. They stopped to let a fire wagon pass, crossed the street. A policeman rounded the corner and, ahead of Fallon, Christina, holding Rachel Renee's hand, and Janice Jefferson stopped and shuffled closer to the millinery shop's window.

"Pardon me," the officer said. "Pardon me. Emergency. Let me through." It was the same copper who had hammered Fallon's head with the nightstick, had arrested him and knocked him out for indecent exposure. He didn't even notice Fallon, probably could not have told anyone he passed a few soldiers on the boardwalk.

"Ladies first," Bowen Hardin said, and doffed his hat at the two women and girl.

Christina glared, but picked up her daughter and carried her across the street. Janice walked beside her. One more block, and they'd be heading down to the Missouri.

"Where's the boat?" Hardin asked MacGregor once they hit the final boardwalk.

"Tully will be there," MacGregor said.

"Who the hell's Tully?"

"An informant of mine from years back," the old detective said. "Worked for us on a lot of cases in Kansas City, Westport, Omaha, Lawrence, Leavenworth. He arranged for those uniforms and weapons. He's a good man."

"I thought he'd just leave us the boat."

MacGregor laughed. "Not before he gets paid."

"What do we have to pay him with?"

MacGregor said: "That's your department, Hardin. But I wouldn't pay him till he gets us downstream to the horses."

"Shut up."

Fallon couldn't see MacGregor or Hardin, since he walked in front of them, but he pictured MacGregor grinning as he said, "But I wouldn't pay him off here, unless you know how to work a boat on the Missouri River. The Big Muddy can be right treacherous."

"I said shut your trap."

"Be careful who you're talking to, Hardin." MacGregor was feeling like he had returned to power, that he was in command of forty detectives and ruled Chicago with an iron fist. "You wouldn't be here without me."

"And you wouldn't be here without me," Hardin whispered. "You didn't have the guts to do any of this. You just had the money and the connections."

A horseman rounded the corner, loped down the street. Fallon saw and smelled the black smoke from a steamboat on the landing, getting ready to sail, but he knew that wasn't the boat these men wanted.

His chances were getting slimmer. They had reached the end of the boardwalk. One more street to go. One slight slope to descend, but surely the city police would have plenty of officers wandering the landing, just in case the convicts tried to gain passage on a riverboat.

"Move," Hardin barked.

They crossed the cobblestone street, and Fallon looked left and right but saw just more of the same. Strangers moving. People talking. Peddlers trying to sell their wares. A newspaper boy crying out the headlines of today's *Times*. No one paid any attention to Fallon and his party.

Then, with only the descent to the landing before them, Fallon saw maybe his last chance at keeping his family, Janice Jefferson, and himself alive.

CHAPTER FORTY-EIGHT

Levi Pigate, chaplain at the federal pen, came up from the landing and grinned as he saw Fallon. He swept his flat-crowned, flat-brimmed straw hat off his head and bowed at the ladies, then stepped toward Fallon and extended his hand.

"Good day, Warden." He looked back at Bowen Hardin, then at Sean MacGregor. Fallon watched his wife, Janice, and Rachel Renee descend.

"Escort the ladies, Sergeant," MacGregor sang out, startling the preacher, but Holderman stepped forward and raced after the two women and girl.

"Busy day," Pigate said. "A tragic day." He smiled at Holderman. "But it's good to see the Army is helping us in these desperate times."

"What brings you to the landing, Reverend?" Fallon asked.

"I was seeing my brother off on the ferry. He's returning home to Independence."

He looked again at MacGregor. "Major, I don't believe I've had the pleasure. You must be new to the fort."

"Indeed," MacGregor lied, extending his hand and shaking briefly. "Arrived two days ago."

"Well, let me welcome you to Leavenworth."

MacGregor bowed.

"Beggin' your pardon, sir," Bowen Hardin said, keeping his head down, "but we do have a boat to catch."

"Yes. Chaplain." MacGregor cleared his throat. "I'm sending this patrol across the river. In case the vermin that escaped have made it to Missouri."

"Very good, Major. Very good." The man of the cloth looked at Fallon. "Good luck. I shall pray for you, for our deliverance." As he walked away, he said, "Major, please come to my services Sunday. My sermon will be on Jacob and Esau."

He crossed the street and began whistling.

"Move," Bowen Hardin mumbled.

On the landing, Holderman waited with Janice, Christina, and Rachel Renee.

The steamboat, the *Muddy Queen*, was pulling out, and people were hurrying away from the river and back toward town. Fallon was right. The police chief had sent men to check the boats, but now that the paddleboat was moving downstream for Kansas City, the officers figured there was no threat. None paid any attention to Fallon or the fake soldiers.

"That was close," Anderson said. "If that preacher had any sense . . ." He wiped his face with the wool sleeve of his Army uniform.

"This is the trick of disguise," MacGregor gloated. "He has seen me countless times in prison, but because I wore the uniform of a . . ." He stopped, wet his lips, and looked up the landing toward the street. "A major."

"What of it?" Indianola Anderson growled.

"I am a lieutenant colonel."

"I don't give a damn if you're General Nathan Bedford Forrest," Bowen Hardin said. "Find that monkey of yours who has the boat, and let's get moving in a hurry."

Then Calloway laughed. "That sky pilot knows about as much 'bout military ranks as you boys know about your Scripture. Don't read the Old Testament much, do you?"

"Spill it out, Calloway," Hardin ordered.

"Joshua and Esau," Calloway began, and Fallon stepped forward to lay the convict out, but felt the barrel of Holderman's pistol, hidden in his Army coat, pressed against his back.

Calloway finished. "Two brothers. One fools his pa to get the blessing by throwing a lamb's skin, or something like that over his arm. See, Esau was a hairy son of a gun. So Esau gets shortchanged, and Joshua gets . . ."

"Calloway," Hardin said and stepped forward. "Find that preacher. Give him a taste of Old Testament vengeance before he finds a lawman or prison guard."

Then the killer ordered MacGregor. "Let's get on that boat. Pronto."

"This is a boat?" Bowen Hardin spit into the shallows of the Missouri.

"What do you want, buster?" the fat, scrappy man named Tully said. "The *Monitor* or the *Merrimack*?"

"I'd take a canoe," Hardin shot back. "Who the hell are you? Huckleberry Finn?"

Which proved one thing to Fallon. The damned killer at least visited the prison library every once in a while.

The raft, complete with a lean-to, and, even two anchors in the center, rested in the sand, the tiller and oars in the rear. It was big enough to hold most of them, Fallon figured, providing they weren't going far. But Sean MacGregor had given Fallon enough information to know they wouldn't go downstream too far. The raft confirmed that.

"The price of this raft—since I'm the only one who knows exactly where those horses are—just went up." Tully leaned back and laughed.

"If we don't shove off now," Indianola Anderson pointed out, "you'll be swinging pretty soon, Bowen, and you"—he nodded at the fat river man—"well, you'll be paid in a lengthy sentence at the new prison them fools are building west of here."

"Right." Bowen Hardin shoved Janice toward the raft. "Ladies first."

"What about Calloway?" Holderman said.

"What about him?" Hardin answered, and Holderman grinned. He had the foresight to tell Tully the river raft man, "Name your price. You'll get it. But if you don't start sailing, we can kill you here or leave you to build a big-arse jailhouse with Calloway."

* * *

"I don't want to go on a boat ride, Mommy!" little Rachel Renee wailed.

"It's all right," Christina tried.

"But we're rocking. I'm scared."

Fallon felt that fear, too. Indeed, with all the movement—Tully seemed the only man comfortable on the river—water splashed over the logs that appeared to be held together with nothing but strips of rawhide. The big man of the Missouri found his place at the stern, one hand on the tiller, and laughed as the others sought, fruitlessly, to find their so-called "sea legs."

The others found spots that would keep the raft from listing to one side, and the current shot them downstream. Fallon wasn't moving too much, for Holderman and Indianola Anderson had wrapped his hands together with a strip of rawhide, lashing him to one of the anchors.

Fallon looked at Janice, Christina, and little, innocent, beautiful Rachel Renee, huddled between the two shivering women—women shaking from fear, not sickness from the motion of the raft in the current—and Fallon felt that old familiar feeling. The one from prison riots. Gunfights in the Indian Territory. Working for that lout Sean MacGregor. But all he could do was ball his hands into fists and feel the leather thongs bite into his flesh.

The raft raced toward the Mississippi.

Gunshots sounded from somewhere upstream in Leavenworth. Indianola Anderson laughed. "I guess Calloway didn't make it."

Bowen Hardin, who had found a place in the shade in the lean-to, grinned.

"Let's hope he died game," MacGregor said. "And didn't tell the authorities—"

"All the secrets you gave away," Hardin concluded. "For a detective, I figured you might have learned to keep your trap shut."

"These people are mean, Mommy," Rachel Renee cried out and tried to hug Christina tighter. "They are really, really mean."

Janice pointed to a bird, sitting on a branch on the other side of the river, trying to distract the child. The results were not all that anybody wanted.

The raft floated downstream.

The *Muddy Queen* shot past them, rocking the raft in the wake, and people on the decks, crewmen and passengers alike, waved and blew kisses, and then the only thing Fallon could see was the sternwheeler's paddle moving the riverboat closer to Kansas City, Missouri, and leaving the lives of Fallon and—more important—his wife, his daughter, and an innocent woman in Fallon's hands.

Fallon's hands . . . tied to an anchor.

"What do you think?" Indianola Anderson asked as soon as the *Muddy Queen* had put a decent-enough length past Tully's ramshackle raft.

Bowen Hardin emerged from his shady spot underneath the lean-to, grabbing hold of a crossbeam to pull himself to his feet. He looked upstream, then downstream, and on the banks on the Kansas and Missouri side.

"This will do," he said at length, and gave a nod with a malevolent grin.

"What are y'all boys doin'?" Tully said from the stern.

"Shut up, and just get us to where we can pay you off," Hardin told the raft captain.

Aaron Holderman and Indianola Anderson stood, and began gingerly maneuvering their way to where Fallon sat, secured to one of the anchors—an anchor, he suddenly realized, that was not connected to a rope.

That's when Fallon understood.

The men positioned themselves on either side of Fallon and took hold of the lengthwise-running bar at the anchor's top. Grunting, they dragged steel and Fallon toward the bow's port. That caused the captain to yell at the other passengers: "Y'all quick. Quick now. Get to the starboard side. That side. Away from those fools. Hurry. Or we'll capsize and have to swim to shore!"

Janice grabbed Rachel Renee's shoulders, and Fallon saw both the widow and Fallon's baby girl being dragged by Sean MacGregor to the other side of the raft. The rawhide bit into his wrists, and his shoes tried to find some traction on the slippery, soaking poles that made up the bottom of the raft. His heart pounded. He twisted, turned, kicked his legs, trying to find some way he could prevent what the men meant to do.

Then he saw Christina lunge, and Holderman let go of Fallon and buried his shoulder into the stomach of the woman. The breath must have been knocked out of Christina, for she fell on the raft's bottom, heaving, trying to find oxygen. Which is what Fallon knew he would be desperately trying to find—but unlike sweet Christina, he would have no chance.

The last thing he saw was his dearest child, lovely Rachel Renee, crawling toward him as the raft rocked furiously.

Then the anchor pitched over the side, and Fallon felt the coldness, and the brutality, of the muddy, and mighty, and treacherous Missouri River. He caught a glimpse of sky before the darkness and the silt of the river closed in all around him.

The weight of the anchor carried him to the bottom of the Big Muddy.

To his own watery grave.

CHAPTER FORTY-NINE

When he understood what the vermin intended, he had sucked in as much oxygen as he could, and he held his breath when the anchor toppled off the side of the raft and sent him into darkness.

Down he went, but Fallon also knew what worked in his favor. Tully, the raft master, had kept his ugly, barely watertight vessel close to the shore—the Kansas shore—rather than steer his passengers in the center of the wide river. When Fallon hit bottom—and he reached the muddy mess quickly—he knew he wasn't all that far from safety, the banks of the Big Muddy, but reaching even the shallows was impossible.

And a man's lungs can hold only so much air for a short time, a time made even shorter when an anchor sinks deep in the dark, foul, mud-clogged bottom of a mighty river.

He could count more luck. The anchor had not pinned him in the mud. Holding his breath, vision obscured by the darkness and the filth of the bottom, he pushed himself toward the surface, and began sawing the cords left and right against the iron stock.

But the leather was tight, strong, and hard. His eyes remained open, but the soot and silt and mess that flowed this deep in the river hampered his vision.

Seeing doesn't matter, he thought. Just work. Cut these binds loose. If you don't, you're dead. Worse than that, if you don't, Rachel Renee, Christina, and Janice are dead, too. And those sons of, as O'Connor would say, "strumpets" will be free for a while to wreak havoc on innocent people.

The cords moved against the iron. His head ached. His lungs strained.

Then he saw her, though he made out nothing more than a blur, an angel swimming down toward him, ready to raise him into paradise. And for a moment, he felt reassured, that death is not the end—not if you believe—and that heaven awaited even a sinner like Harry Fallon.

But almost instantly, he felt terrified.

Because what came closer to him was not an angel from Heaven. It was a young girl, a baby really. She did not swim. She pulled herself toward him on the anchor's short line that she must have grabbed.

Fallon could barely fathom what had happened. They had pushed him and the anchor off the rocking raft, and Fallon's precious daughter, Rachel Renee, had leaped out, trying to save her father. At the last moment, she had latched hold of a chain, a small length of maybe four feet, not attached to a cable or rope or anything. Fallon had plunged with the anchor to the muddy bottoms of the river.

To his horror, he suddenly realized that he had brought his baby girl with him.

They would drown together.

Fallon wanted to scream in rage.

He wanted to yell at his daughter, tell her to let go of the chain, to forget her father. He wanted to beg her to let the current and her lightness raise her from the depths of hell back to the surface. This close to the shore, she could float to the banks, crawl to dry land. *Live, baby.*

Just live.

Maybe say a prayer for your father in the years to come.

Yet he could not open his mouth.

The mud, the debris, the trash, and the filth from the roiling bottom clouded Fallon's vision, but Rachel Renee pulled herself toward him and the anchor. The current was furious, and her little hands desperately clutched the chain as she pulled herself closer. Closer, closer, and there she was, holding the chain, with the current jerking her every which way like a cork or a minnow being whipped in a mountain stream. Fallon wanted to scream at her to let go, swim away, but he could only try urgently to saw the cords loose. If he could save himself, then he could save precious Rachel Renee.

She let go, and Fallon almost opened his mouth and screamed in terror. Rachel Renee, all of five years old, released her left hand, hanging on with only her right, which was affixed like a Gila monster's jaws on that chain. She brought her tiny legs up, bending at the knee, and used the left hand to move toward her little boot. The next thing Fallon saw in his daughter's hand was a knife, a knife from their kitchen cabinet, and then she managed to bring the blade to the leather cord.

He watched her saw. Saw and cut, though in the darkness of the depths and the swirling mud, he only caught glimpses of a tiny hand holding a table knife.

The pressure in his lungs, against his temples, tripled, quadrupled, and Fallon knew he could not keep his lungs closed for much longer.

Suddenly . . .

He felt freed.

His hands parted from the anchor, and the current started to sweep him away. In desperation, he reached out with his left hand, swiped, missed, came back, and through some miracle, some burst of light that shown from the heavens to the bottoms of the Big Muddy, he saw Rachel Renee. He grabbed her tiny wrist and began kicking as hard as he could. He reached above him with his free hand, grabbed at water, and pushed the water behind him. Rising. Fallon kept rising, bringing his daughter with him. Swimming. Swimming toward the light.

He burst through, and strained with all his might, bringing his daughter into the clearness of daylight. Rachel screamed and sucked in a deep breath. Fallon's lungs worked hard, breathing in, exhaling, again and again. He caught a glimpse of the raft as it rounded a bend, and then Indianola Anderson, Bowen Hardin, the raft captain named Tully, and Fallon's old nemesis Sean MacGregor and his ruthless brigand, Aaron Holderman, were out of his view.

But for the time being, that really didn't matter. Fallon kicked and brought Rachel Renee closer.

They treaded water as the current carried them downstream.

"Hey," Fallon said, spitting out water. "Sweetheart, wrap your arms around my neck."

His daughter obeyed, and he clung to her as his legs worked, and he felt the current and his own strength carrying him to the banks. A moment later, his feet dragged through the mud, and his knees sank into the wet loam underneath the mighty Missouri. The current slackened, and Fallon and Rachel Renee were in the shallows. Alive. Somehow alive.

Fallon rose, lifting Rachel Renee with him. She hugged him tightly, and Fallon moved through the ugly water, up the banks, and onto the narrow shoreline.

"Papa," Rachel Renee said. "Are you all right?"

"I'm fine, pumpkin," he told her. "Thanks to you."

He held her back, looked at his daughter with love in his eyes, and realized that his face had to show shock and confusion. "Honey," he asked, "when did you learn how to swim?"

She giggled. "Mama said living this close to the river, I needed to learn. So we've been going when you've been working."

But her face turned sad, and she looked down the river. "But Papa, where is Mommy going? And Mrs. Janice? What will happen to them with them bad, bad—"

Fallon swept her into his arms and stood. "You don't worry about your mother, honey," he whispered, even though his stomach had turned sick with dread. "I'll bring your mother back. And Mrs. Janice, too."

"Promise?"

"Promise." He kissed her cheek.

Her arms and her wet weight felt not like an anchor, but something comforting. He turned up the river, and walked back toward the landing at Leavenworth.

"How did you get that knife, sweetheart?" Fallon asked.

"I took it," she said. "I know I shouldn't have. Miss Janice told me to take it. When them mean ol' men come to our house. She told me to keep it. To use it only in an emergency."

Fallon pulled her tight to his chest. He saw men running down the banks, now, and one of them, he recognized from the hat and the man's frame as none other than the federal pen's chaplain, the Reverend Pigate. Fallon's heart started to slow down.

"Did I do wrong, Papa? Mama says little girls ought not to play with knives."

Fallon kissed her wet, sand-coated cheek, one more time.

"Your mother," he told his pride and joy, "was a pretty fair hand with a knife before you were born—and a whole lot of other things. Maybe she'll tell you about it when you're a wee bit older."

CHAPTER FIFTY

Lowering Rachel Renee, Fallon extended his right hand as the chaplain slowed, out of breath, sweating. Lawmen from the city police force and county sheriff's office circled around, and a few even ran down the river, carrying rifles, as though they might be able to stop the prison escapees—but the raft had rounded the bend by then.

"Good to see you, Reverend," Fallon said.

"And you as well." The chaplain smiled at Rachel Renee. "And I'm especially glad to see you, little girl." Rachel Renee hugged Fallon's leg. When Pigate raised his head to look at Fallon, his face turned serious. He looked at the two soaking bodies.

"It'll take too long to explain," Fallon said. "They sent a man with a knife after you."

"He found me." Pigate grinned. "Convict Calloway learned that before I heard the Call, I was boxing champ at Fort Griffin. Mr. Calloway ran after feeling my left-right-right-left. Deputies fired warning shots. He stopped. Raised his hands. They're holding him in the city jail."

"I'm familiar with the jail." He turned to Rachel Renee, dropped to his knee, and put his hands on her shoulders. "Sweetheart, I have to go bring your mom and Mrs. Janice home now. So I want you to go with the Reverend Pigate. He'll just sit with you at his house. He has a grandson living with him, just a few years older than you. So you'll be fine. And I'll be back shortly. But till then, you need to be strong, like your mother, and just wait and be the great girl you always are. Is that all right?"

She tried to stifle the tears, but a few leaked down her wet face. Fallon hugged her, then stood, and watched his daughter take the preacher's hand. "What's . . . your . . . grandson's . . . name?" she said between sniffs.

"His name is Timothy. He likes trains."

Fallon nodded his thanks at Pigate, and called out, "I love you, Rachel Renee." Let the other lawmen hear him say that. He didn't give a damn.

"I love you, too, Papa," his daughter said.

Then Fallon turned to the police sergeant, started to say something to him, but Andy Cameron, the chief of police, was hurrying down the landing.

Fallon said, "Let's go," and walked to cut the distance.

He explained on the way off the landing and into the city, which was still reeling from the turmoil of the day.

"They're in Army uniforms, on a raft. Anderson, MacGregor, Hardin, Holderman. The man working the raft is a big man, smells like the river, called Tully."

"We can telegraph Kansas City—"

"They'll be off the river long before Kansas City. Hardin's not dumb enough—and MacGregor's no idiot either—to try to escape from prison on a raft that's barely waterproof."

"We can—"

Fallon snapped, "They have two women hostages, Andy. You close in on them, these men won't hesitate to kill them."

They were walking now with urgency, headed for the city jail. "I need some trail clothes, Andy. A revolver. And a Winchester."

"I have a Marlin. Repeater."

"Caliber?"

"It's one of the new big-bore models, .45-70."

"That'll do the job."

"Harry, my jurisdiction ends at the city limits."

"I know that, Andy, and I thank you for all you're doing. Dry clothes. Horses. Ammunition. That's all I need."

"We can go with you," one of the sheriff's deputies said. "At least as far as the county line."

"And I appreciate that, but I think this is a job for federal peace officers." He felt better at the sight of Captain Big Tim O'Connor hurrying down the street. "And prison guards."

Two policemen brought Calloway to Cameron's office as Fallon changed into dry, comfortable, but durable clothes. After Fallon nodded, all of the city policemen walked out of the room, leaving Fallon and O'Connor alone with the squirming convict.

Fallon slipped the suspenders over his shirt, then sat down and pulled on the right sock first. A good woolen sock that came up high. Good for boots and a saddle.

"Listen . . ." Calloway sniffled.

After Fallon's nod, O'Connor's well-placed backhand left Calloway on the sofa against the wall, wiping his split lip with the back of his hand.

"Breaking out of prison adds at least a year to your sentence." Fallon pulled on the other sock. "The reverend will testify that you tried to knife him to death. I'll verify that I heard you agree to kill the reverend on orders from Bowen Hardin. That's not just attempted murder, Calloway, it's murder for hire."

The nervous man straightened, and let his lip, now quivering, bleed.

"You broke out of prison with two hardened convicts, Calloway." Fallon pulled on the right Wellington—a little loose, but it would work fine in the saddle and break in fairly quickly. "You have kidnapping charges, too, including the abduction of a five-year-old girl." Fallon grabbed the other boot and stared at Calloway for the first time as he pulled it on and rose from the chair.

"Let's face facts, son." He grabbed the bandana and tied it around his neck, then pulled on a vest. "Anderson and Hardin have nothing to lose. Someone will die. Some innocent person. The U.S. solicitor will add an accessory to murder charge to everything else you're looking at, Cameron, when one of those killers puts down an innocent victim. With everything else, I think you'll be facing the gallows."

Now he moved across the room, buckling on the gunbelt. By the time Fallon stood in front of the sofa, he has pulled out the long-barreled Colt Peacemaker, and was rotating the cylinder and checking the .45-caliber cartridges.

"But you probably already know this, Calloway," he said, losing the conversational tone and letting his voice fall into a deadly whisper. "If something happens to my wife, or the widow of Elliott Jefferson, you won't go to trial." He pulled back the hammer and squeezed the trigger. The snap of the hammer landing on the empty chamber must have sounded like a cannon going off, because Calloway let out a shriek and jumped. "You'll be back in the federal pen here as soon as we can transfer you," Fallon said. "And you know how easy it is for a man to die in the pen. You've been around enough to see that for yourself."

"You can't . . ."

"I don't have time to dicker with you, Calloway. You tell me where Hardin's going, and you tell me in six seconds or your life is over."

"He didn't tell us nothin'. Come on, Warden, you know Bowen Hardin. He don't trust nobody."

"I'm extending the time you have," Fallon nodded. "But MacGregor and Holderman aren't so tight-lipped."

The man wiped his bloody lip now, thinking.

Fallon let him think, but after half a minute, he whispered, "They're getting farther down the river, Calloway. My patience has its limits."

"I'm . . . tryin' . . ." The man almost burst into tears, but then his eyes brightened, and he said, "Tully."

"The raft man," Fallon said.

"Yeah."

"MacGregor mentioned him."

"I met the son of a . . ." He choked off the curse, saw O'Connor, and concluded the sentence with "strumpet." Seething, he said, "I was on the raft . . ."

"I know, Warden, Honest, I know all that. MacGregor said Tully would get them there."

"There?"

"Yeah. And then Holderman . . . he said . . . he said . . ." He trembled and turned ashen. "Sin. It's a bar. A saloon or something. Yeah. Tully must run a bar. Sin A Bar. That's what he called it. MacGregor said it was the perfect place to hold up for a while."

"Sin A Bar." Fallon kicked the trash can across the room. "Sin A Bar. That river rat wouldn't own a bar." His memory triggered something, though, and he stopped, looked at Big Tim O'Connor. "Sni-A-Bar. Sni-A-Bar."

Calloway's head was shaking. "No, boss, I swear to the Lord, that big cur named Holderman, Bootsey we call him, he said, 'Sin A Bar.'"

"Because Holderman's a moron." Fallon hurried to the police chief's desk, grabbed the heavy Marlin repeating rifle and his hat, nodded at O'Connor, and went through the door.

"He's all yours, Andy," Fallon said. "Lock him up and keep him."

CHAPTER FIFTY-ONE

U.S. marshals, federal troops, and state peace officers had agreed to put a cordon from Kansas City, beginning ten miles north of the city on both sides of the river, then moving southwest through Olathe, Ottawa, Osage City, Emporia, Cottonwood Falls, then back up toward Council Grove, Alma, St. Mary's, Holton, and Atchison.

Posses would be sent out, with orders to follow, not fight if they came across the kidnappers and their two hostages. The U.S. marshal and the colonel from the fort were coordinating those plans with the county sheriff and a representative from the U.S. marshal's office across the river in Missouri.

Fallon let them go about their business. He and Big Tim O'Connor went back to the federal pen. "We need a tracker," O'Connor said. "I'll fetch Ol' Buffalo Bones."

"No," Fallon said. "Not Buffalo Bones. I have someone else in mind. Someone even better."

* * *

The cell was decorated with hangings of the letters he had drawn, one with the entire alphabet, capital and small letters, and another, above the head of his cot, printed and in cursive letters:

Benjamin James MacIntosh

Benjamin James MacIntosh "Warden," the convict said without rising from his bunk.

"Ben. How would you like to get out of this hell-hole for a few days?"

One-eyed, scar-faced Ben Lawless pushed his cap back, shook his head, and spoke sadly, "I figured you'd pay me a visit. You know I had no knowledge of what those pieces of trash was plannin'."

"I know that."

He sat up, looked at the letters, and pointed to them. "Those were two mighty fine teachers, boss. Good ladies. Real patient."

"They still are, Ben."

MacIntosh sighed and began to shake his head sadly.

"Boss," he said, "I can't help you."

"I need a tracker."

Now he looked up, the hardness replacing sympathy in his eyes, and he said coldly, "Boss, you won't want your wife back after them dogs is through with her or the other gal."

Fallon's response came quickly, as though he expected something like that from the poisoner of Cherokee Indians decades earlier. "Before you discovered strychnine, Ben, and before you gave up on yourself behind these walls, you were a damned good tracker. And you were a man. I'd like to see you become that man again."

For the first time since they had left the boat in the swampy creek that drained into the Big Muddy, Bowen Hardin let the men rest. But it was not like anyone could find comfort in this hell, a wooden inferno of humidity with mosquitoes and gnats tormenting the escaped convicts and the two women.

All Christina knew was that they were in Missouri. She had thought the men would head to the western bank, shoot across Kansas. It was closer to the Indian Territory, and traveling would be a whole lot easier. But now she understood the logic, maybe even the genius of Bowen Hardin's—or rather, Sean MacGregor's—plan. Just about everyone would think these felons would move across Kansas. The posses would not be able to bring dogs to sniff them out, not until they found out where they had landed, and that could be anywhere between Leavenworth and Kansas City.

She was certain that Missouri lawmen would be combing the banks, but few would think to look into the depths of this hellish wooded maze.

"This ain't nothin'," Tully the raft master said with a laugh when Aaron Holderman began bellyaching at how hard it was to move through the muck and the brambles and the briar patches, while fighting bloodsucking insects with both hands. "Wait till we hit the Sni-A-Bar."

That had also surprised Christina. She thought for certain that either Indianola Anderson or Bowen

Hardin would have sliced Tully's throat from ear to ear as soon as he had landed the raft, but now she understood. Tully knew where the horses were, and the horses were bedded down somewhere along the Sni-A-Bar.

She remembered Tully boasting on the raft: "The price of this raft—since I'm the only one who knows exactly where those horses are—just went up."

Now she wished her geography was a little better. She didn't know anything about this Sni-A-Bar, except that, within all reason, it had to be in Missouri. How far? Well, a good distance, she reasoned. They wouldn't leave the horses too close, or too easy for someone to find. They had moved fast since leaving the river, but that, she guessed, was to put distance between them and the Big Muddy. Get farther from the river, where search parties would be fewer. Find the horses. And ride . . . to . . . wherever.

Janice came over, sweating, hair disheveled, mosquito bites already forming on her cheek, neck, arms, and hands. She sank beside Christina, sniffing, and whispered, "I'm . . . so sorry . . . Christina . . ." Tears mixed with the sweat. "Poor Rachel Renee."

"They're fine, Janice," Christina said. She knew it. Her heart told her that.

"Christina," Janice said.

But she reached over and put her right hand on Janice's forearm, then squeezed. "You gave her the knife, Janice. Remember?" She somehow managed to smile. "You helped me teach her how to swim. And you don't know my husband all that well, Janice, but let me tell you something. He never quits. He never gives up. And people have been trying to kill him for a damned long time. And most of those who tried . . . they're the ones who are dead." She looked up, because Indianola Anderson and the raft man, Tully, were moving toward them. "Or," she quickly added, "soon will be."

Tully came up behind Christina, put his meaty paws on her shoulders, and began rubbing. If Christina thought having a gorilla try to break her collarbones romantic, she might have been moved. Instead, she spit at the feet of Anderson, who had dropped to his knees, pinning her against the walls of the small sinkhole they had dropped into to catch their breaths.

Anderson ignored her. Tully whispered, "It's 'bout time you and me got better acquainted, don't you think?"

She didn't answer. Her eyes locked on Bowen Hardin, who now stood over them and barked, "Get back, eat some salt in that pouch over there. Wash it down with a swallow of water and get ready to move."

"In a little bit," Anderson said and winked.

But Tully's hands shot off Christina's shoulders, and the cocking of the revolver caused Indianola Anderson to turn away from Janice.

"I don't give orders twice," Hardin said.

The two thugs moved away from the women.

Bowen Hardin turned briefly to Janice. "You, too," he said. "Salt'll be good for you." Janice did not move. "Go," Hardin said, raising his voice. "They won't touch you."

When she climbed out of the hole, Hardin looked at Christina.

"If you want my thanks," she said after a while, "you'll have to do better than that."

He managed a slight smile.

"I didn't do that for your . . . reputation." A glance over his shoulder told him no one was listening, but he lowered his voice anyway. "If they have you, you'll be insane. If you're crazy, I'd have to kill you. And if I kill you, I won't have any bargaining chips when they catch us."

Christina tilted her head, trying to comprehend what the killer had said. "What makes you think you'll be caught?"

"We're always caught."

"Then why bother?"

"Because this time, they might kill us rather than take us back to that hellhole. When that happens, you might as well know, I plan on taking you and your friend to hell with me."

"What have we done to you?"

"Nothing. It's just a matter of revenge."

"Revenge for what?"

"For me living this long."

"How well do you know the Sni-A-Bar?" Fallon asked.

Ben Lawless pulled up a pair of chaps over his newly issued jeans. "When I was working for Missouri marshals, I had to track some men through that country." He grabbed a vest, slipping his arms through the holes. "It's rough. Bushwhackers took to that country during the War Between the States. Outlaws hid out there before, during, and after the war."

"Ever heard of a man named Tully?"

"Nope."

"Well, we can question a few . . ."

"No, boss, you can't say nothin'." He picked up a gunbelt, held it up for Fallon's inspection, and when the warden nodded, Ben Lawless looked amazed. Quickly, he buckled the rig on before Fallon changed his mind. "You mention this guy Tully's name, and he'll know you're after him in the time it takes a crow to fly over his head. It's tough country, but word spreads fast. Especially word that the law's coming to pay a call on some resident."

"Can you find him?"

"Boss." He moved across the display of guns in the mercantile, and finally pointed to an old cap-and-ball percussion Navy half-buried under a wheat sack. The clerk pulled out the ancient weapon and handed it to him butt first. Lawless deftly lifted from the young man's hand, spun the .36 around, cocked it, uncocked it, rotated the cylinder, listened to the action, and smiled as he handed it back to the young man. "Load it for me, buddy," he said. "But I'll put the caps on my ownself."

Then he turned to Fallon.

"Yeah, I can find them, boss. I can find a fart in a hurricane. Let me do the askin', my way. But all I'm doing, boss, is findin' them. Killin' 'em. That'll be your department. Is you fine with that?"

Fallon nodded. "Yeah," he said. "I'm fine with that."

CHAPTER FIFTY-TWO

"Warden Fallon," Captain Big Tim O'Connor said when Fallon and Lawless emerged from the mercantile. "Sir, I think it's my duty to come with you. I can get Wilson, Raymond, a few other of my best men."

"Tim," Fallon said. "I appreciate the gesture and your volunteering. But I need someone to look after the pen. And too many men puts Janice and Christina in harm's way."

"Two men's too many," Ben Lawless said. "But I don't reckon you'll turn me loose on my own."

Fallon didn't smile. He didn't even look back at the old killer. What he did, though, was reach out and shake O'Connor's massive hand. "Thank you, Tim. Thank you for everything."

O'Connor, if Fallon wasn't mistaken, had wetness in his eyes, but he nodded as they shook, stepped back, and snapped a salute at his boss. "Thank you . . ." He even managed a smile as he added, "Hank." Before turning away he said, "I'll see you boys when you get back."

* * *

After crossing the ferry into Missouri, Fallon and Lawless rode in silence. An hour east, Lawless twisted in the saddle and studied the warden for a long while. Finally, he spit tobacco juice, wiped his mouth, and said, "You ain't concerned that I might just blow you out of the saddle and skedaddle?"

"You wouldn't do that," Fallon said.

"Why not?"

"Because you know I'd blow you out of the saddle before I died."

The killer chuckled, and another hour passed.

This time it was Fallon who broke the silence. "Where exactly are we headed?"

"Sni-A-Bar." Lawless shifted the chaw, snorted, and scratched his chin. "Or around there."

"What makes you think we're on their trail?"

"We ain't." He kicked free of the stirrups and stretched his legs. "You ain't got no idea, Fallon, how long it's been since I been in a saddle. And, hell, we got sixty, seventy or so miles to go. Hope I ain't crippled by the time we meet those bad boys."

Fallon took time to grab his canteen and drink. It was hot. Miserably hot.

"Before you ask," Lawless said after spitting to his right. "We got no idea where 'em boys got off the Big Muddy. My guess is it wasn't too far south. And they'd take to the woods, the swamps and cricks, to make it hard going for anyone who follows 'em. Make it hard goin' for themselves, too. So here's what we got goin' for us, boss. They'll be lookin' over their shoulders, watchin' the back trail. They ain't likely to expect someone headin' 'em off, catchin' 'em in front."

His feet returned to the stirrups, but now he dropped the reins over the horse's neck and began rubbing his shoulders. "I figure we'll get close to Liberty. Ride in to that burg in the morn. You telegraph your pals back home, see if they've caught the bastards—which then won't have—then we turn southeast. Cross the Big Muddy ag'in the next day. Find you another place to telegraph, while we rest our horses. Make our way to the Sni-A-Bar. Be there . . ."

"Three days." Fallon heard the anxiety in his own voice.

"And a little more."

Leaning back in his saddle, Fallon felt sick to his gut, and figured he was sweating even more. Three days. Three nights. Janice and Christina would have to spend that long with those murdering scum—if they didn't kill them long before they ever reached the Sni-A-Bar.

Ahead of him, Ben Lawless looked comfortable in the saddle despite his constant stretching and spitting and shifting his butt. But then, what did the killer have to worry about? He was out of prison, riding free, with nothing—certainly not a wife or friend—to lose.

"Fallon," Lawless said without looking back.

It took a while before Fallon answered. "Yeah."

"You served a long while in Joliet, didn't you?"

"Long enough."

"And before you even went to trial, there was a long stay in the hell they had for a jail at Fort Smith. Right?"

"Yeah."

"And how many days did you spend behind the iron workin' for that crook MacGregor?"

"Enough."

Now the killer turned back and grinned. "Then you know how to survive. You know better than count the days or count the hours. That drives the fresh fish crazy. Why so many are broke in a week, sometimes just after that first night. You need patience to survive in the pen, boss. Patience of an oyster. That's what you need right now. Those two ladies, they're safe. They're alive. Bowen Hardin done a lot of bad things, Fallon, but you look at his record and you'll see that he never harmed no woman. Indianola Anderson, he ain't got that reputation. But Anderson, well, he ain't no Bowen Hardin."

Maybe. Fallon let out a sigh. But there were also snakes, wild animals, and, for all Fallon knew, other hardcases between the Missouri River and the Sni-A-Bar. Anything could happen in three days. Still, Fallon knew that Ben Lawless was right. You could not worry. You had to find that resolve, that patience, and you had to focus on getting to the Sni-A-Bar first. The first obstacle appeared on the path about a hundred yards ahead.

Six men, farmers by the looks of them, four on horses, one on a mule, one afoot. But all of them carried shotguns, and those were aimed at Fallon and Lawless.

Fallon eased his horse alongside Lawless, who rode

without concern toward what Fallon figured would be a local posse.

"Who are ya?" one of the shotgun-wielding farmers hollered.

Fallon answered with his name and title, and they kept riding until they came to where the posse blocked the trail, reining up, and allowing Fallon the opportunity to say, "Who are you?" Though he had a pretty good idea.

"You got any proof of that?" the leader asked.

"You haven't answered my question," Fallon said.

The men shifted, and the one with the mule spit out a well-chewed cigar, and grinned. "We're citizens. Protecting our families."

"If I were you," Fallon said, "I'd be home. If you want to protect your families, stay close. Because the killers that broke out of the Leavenworth pen surely won't be riding on a trail in broad daylight. Don't you think?"

"Then why are you?" said the one on foot, a man wearing decades-old Confederate-gray trousers, well frayed and patched here and there with calico. He was barefoot. But his left hand gripped an old Enfield, and his right hand was hooked in the waistband, near the butt of an old horse pistol that bulged down his pants.

"We figured to get ahead of the killers." Fallon stressed the word killers, hoping it might help convince the men that their best bet—if their families came first and they weren't out here hoping to reap some massive reward the state of Kansas and the U.S. government would issue for the capture and return, dead or alive, of the fugitives—would be to go home. Look after the families there.

The leader did not seem interested in going home. He shifted in the saddle, spit, and said, "Now we've answered your questions. So how about proving to us that you is who you say you is?"

"As a warden, I don't carry a badge," Fallon said. "And if I had a card, I'd have to reach into my pocket. That would mean my hand would be away from the Colt I'm packing. And, well, boys, you fellows don't look all that trustworthy."

"But there's six of us." The leader grinned.

Then Ben Lawless spit out his wad of tobacco, and grinned. "You boys is rude. You ain't asked who I be?"

"Well," said the former Rebel from the ground. "Who the hell be you?"

"I be Ben Lawless."

Fallon's shoulders relaxed, for he saw the fear, the dread, in the men's faces, although the ex-Confederate with the .44 horse pistol laughed. "Like they'd let Ben Lawless out of the pen."

"Why wouldn't I?" Fallon said. "If you were after Bowen Hardin and Indianola Anderson and some other hard rocks, wouldn't you bring along the best tracker and the best killer with you?"

Lawless scratched the scars under the eyeless socket. "You boys think anybody but Ben Lawless has a face like this?" He smiled.

"You gonna p'i's'in 'em, Ol' Ben?" the one on the mule said with a laugh.

"Hell," Lawless said. "You poison a passel of Cherokees and folks forget of how many Rebels I kilt in the

Rebellion. How many lawbreakers I brought in for the courts over a packsaddle. Ruins a fellow's reputation. Sometimes, I wish I'd kilt all 'em red scum faceup, like I'm about to do you white scum."

The leader's face had paled, but he managed to ease down the hammer of his single-shot sixteen-gauge, and he said, his voice higher than it had been. "I think these men are who they claim to be," he said, trying to make it seem that he was still in command. "Let's . . . umm . . . let's give them the road."

Chapter Fifty-three

When Fallon stepped out of the telegraph office on the Liberty town square, Ben Lawless, leaning against a column to a business across the corner, began untying the reins to Fallon's horse. He was in his own saddle by the time Fallon crossed the street. Lawless leaned down from the saddle and handed Fallon the reins.

"I figured it was pointless," Lawless said. "What did they say?"

Fallon pitched the telegraph paper into the trash can. "No trace," Fallon said and mounted his horse and looked at Lawless. "On either side of the river. How'd you know?"

"Your face."

They backed their horses out and left the bustling city.

Lawless began working on a new plug of tobacco. "So, boss, you didn't tell 'em law dogs in Kansas about the Sni-A-Bar and what Calloway tol' you."

"They were set on the assumption that Hardin

would make for the Indian Nations by way of Kansas. But Missouri officials are on the lookout, too. You saw that with those farmers yesterday afternoon."

"Uh-huh."

"You could be wrong, too. They could be in Kansas."

"Yep. That's a fact."

They rode side by side, and Fallon turned and looked the killer in the eye. "Their posses are too big. If they did the same in Missouri, and Hardin got surrounded, Christina and Janice would be dead. You know that better than I do. I think the two of us have the best plan—even if it's a long shot."

"All right."

"Besides," Fallon added. "They escaped from a federal pen. All four of them are my responsibility. And since this man Tully's helping them, he's my responsibility, too."

Lawless spit, shook his head, and laughed. "Like ever'body in Leavenworth keeps sayin', 'You ain't like no warden we've ever seen before.'"

"Like I keep telling all you cons, I'm the only warden you've ever seen who knows what it's like behind bars and walls."

They rode southeast.

From the edge of the woods on the other side of the ditch, Christina watched in fear. Just beyond the small pasture, where four cows and three goats grazed, a family sat at a table outside their hardscrabble home, taking their noon meal. Well, it was likely hotter inside the log cabin than outside.

The girl, though likely a few years older than Rachel Renee, reminded Christina of her daughter. A puppy yipped around while the coonhound mother lounged without paying attention. A teenage boy came down the road in a wagon pulled by two mules and stopped between the barn and a corral.

"What are we waiting here for?" Indianola Anderson said, then swatted at a buzzing horsefly. "Let's kill them now, get that wagon, make haste for the Sni-A-Bar." Then he laughed. "But maybe we won't kill them all . . . just yet."

An older girl, red hair flowing, wearing a Sunday dress, stepped out of the cabin. And the boy in the wagon whipped off his straw hat and waved it back and forth, shouting, "Hey, Lucy. You look real pretty in that dress. Is it Easter already?"

The girl laughed, and the bearded man at the head of the table yelled, "Don't unhitch them mules, Connor. Food'll be cold by then. Let them blow and cool down. We can take care of 'em after we've et."

"I don't see no guns on any of them," the river rat, Tully said. "But I'm of the same mind as Anderson here. Kill . . . *most* . . . of 'em. First."

"Shut up," Bowen Hardin said in a hoarse whisper.

They had shed the woolen blouses of their Army uniforms, and they now wore muslin or linen shirts. The pants were still Army, but no one would recognize those filthy garments as belonging to soldiers.

Sean MacGregor sidled up next to the killer. "We'll

make better time on that wagon," he said. "And they likely have more animals inside the barn."

"You want us to just ride right through Richmond or some other burg, bold as brass?" Hardin said in an icy voice.

"It's a right far piece to Sni-A-Bar," the old detective told him. "And we spent enough time—too damned long—in those thickets and swamps. The posses are behind us now, most likely. Hell, most of them are in Kansas, just like we thought."

"And when we don't show up, they'll start looking at Missouri—and not east of Kansas City."

MacGregor nodded his head. "Which is why we need to make better time now."

The killer looked at the revolver in his hand, frowned, and watched the family and the boy— obviously a beau to pretty Lucy—stand around the rough-hewn table and hold hands. Their heads bowed. Christina couldn't hear the prayer, but she could make out the one Janice Jefferson was whispering on Christina's right.

"They're out of range for a pistol," Hardin said. "And we don't know how far the neighbors are."

"Right." Anderson grinned. "So here's my plan. Me and big ol' Aaron Holderman, we come out of these thicket. I'm leaning on the big boy, dragging my leg. Aaron, he waves at them, and says something like I been hurt . . . snakebit . . . yeah, that'll do it. We was looking for them cutthroats that . . ."

"No," MacGregor said. "That'll make them nervous, suspicious. And hicks that these folks are, they might not have heard of the breakout." But MacGregor liked the concept of Anderson's plan. "So you were trapping. Lots of critters in these woods. Remember that big trap that Tully almost stepped on yesterday?"

"Trappers." Anderson nodded. "I like that idea."

Hardin rolled over and listened. Christina knew he would agree to the plan. It wasn't like he had much of a choice. These men would follow him only so far. And even Bowen Hardin couldn't take on four men by himself.

"I'll say, 'We mean y'all no harm,'" Holderman said, liking this kind of detective work. "That we just need some help."

"Yeah," Anderson said. "And once we get close enough . . ."

"The knives," Holderman said. "Quieter that way."

Anderson nodded his head and grinned. "Yeah. But the girl, the ripe one, we let her live . . . for a while anyway."

She knew Bowen Hardin was about to say fine, so Christina said, "I have a better idea."

All of them, even Janice, looked at her in amazement.

"You kill them," Christina said, "and there's still the problem of neighbors. What are you going to do? Throw their bodies in a well?"

"That is," Anderson said, "exactly what I'm thinking."

"Then neighbors see the buzzards. Or they come calling. That boy . . . he doesn't live here. Young enough, I'd say he has a ma and pa around. When he doesn't come home for supper, they'll come here.

Then you'll have every lawman in this part of Missouri coming after you. Is that what you want?"

Hardin seemed to be looking at Christina with new-found respect. "How would you go about it?"

She turned to Anderson. "Take off your shirt."

"Why, ain't you a forward little tart," he said with a lecherous grin.

"Take it off," she said.

"Ladies first."

"Take it off," Bowen Hardin said, and cocked the hammer on the revolver. "I'm curious to hear her plan."

The killer frowned but slipped off the linen shirt that had once been white. Christina took it, detesting the smell and the man who had handed it to her, and refused to look at the shirtless killer. Instead she tied the sleeves tight around the neck, then stuffed leaves into the shirt, leaves and straw—as much as she could—before tying the tails together. After untucking her own filthy blouse, she rammed the ball of linen and straw and leaves under her shirt, tucked her own back in, and began smoothing the bulge in her belly. Janice stared at her in disbelief. Bowen Hardin tilted his head and waited for her to explain.

Indianola Anderson sniggered and said, "Didn't know a gal could get in the family way just like that. Damn, I'm like a stud hoss."

"I'm pregnant," Christina said. "I'm coming down the road. About to deliver. Have to get to the doctor . . . he's waiting for me . . . it's twins."

"I don't get it."

"They loan us the wagon. It's already hitched." Christina studied the faces.

"Us?" Tully said.

"You're not going to trust me to go down there by myself," Christina said. "And they'd wonder where my husband was." She looked at Aaron Holderman. "Well, he'll be with me."

"What if they ask to come along?" Hardin said. "The man. The boy."

"They might, but Aaron will say no, no, just the wagon. This nice family should finish their dinner. Aaron will get the wagon back."

"But they don't know you . . ."

"Because we just moved in. Other side of the creek. We have to get to that doctor." She feigned anxiety. "I couldn't stand to lose another child like this."

Holderman laughed. "She always was a real fine detective. Good actress. Ain't that how you come to . . ."

"We're wasting time," Christina said and looked directly at Bowen Hardin. "Either my way. Or Anderson's. Which do you think is likely to lead to more lawmen on your trail?"

"What happens," said Anderson, "when that wagon ain't returned, when the doc in the nearest settlement says he ain't delivered no baby since November?"

"They won't know which way we've gone," she said.

"I don't like it," Anderson said. "What do we do with the wagon? Take it all the way to this river rodent's hideout where he's got our horses? The laws'll be on us quicker than I can spit."

"Didn't you see what's in the back of that wagon?" Christina said.

"Yeah. Straw. Or hay. I ain't blind, hussy."

"Shut up," Hardin said. But he knew what Christina was getting at.

"One man bringing hay to his farm in a wagon," Hardin said. "They'll be looking for a man and a woman. And that man and that woman will be in the hay. With all of us but . . ."

"Tully," Christina finished. "Tully is heading home. And Tully knows the quickest way to get to the Sni-A-Bar from here. That wagon's like all the others in this country. I doubt if anyone will be able to identify it as the boy's."

"Maybe," Hardin said. "Maybe not. But the mules are likely branded. The mules will be checked."

"Mules," Christina argued. She felt right pleased with herself, that the instincts of lying came naturally, that she could make this all up after more than five, closer to six, years now away from the American Detective Agency. She was still a damned fine operative. "Mules can be replaced. Traded or stolen. Easy as that."

Hardin turned to MacGregor. "I hear tell she worked for you," the killer said. "So what do you think?"

"It ain't foolproof," Tully interrupted. "That'll be me on that seat, a sittin' duck for any lawman or angry farmer with a rifle."

"No plan's foolproof," MacGregor said with a certain amount of humility in his voice. Prison had changed him. "I know that better than all of you criminals. But her plan is solid. It might get us out of here and into Mexico. Alive."

"All right," Hardin said. "How do we get in that wagon with you and Bootsey?"

Christina nodded. "Head a mile down the road. We'll be traveling fast. Have to. I need to get to the doctor. We'll pick you up."

She wasn't sure if she should have suggested this, because it might just be death warrants for her and Janice. But at least she thought she had saved the lives of these innocent, God-fearing, poor farmers.

CHAPTER FIFTY-FOUR

Sni-A-Bar Creek flowed through Jackson and Lafayette counties on its way to the Missouri River, meandering through the small but rough Sni-A-Bar hills. It wasn't much of a waterway, more stream than creek, often little more than a ditch, and the hills weren't high or treacherous. But the country was. The thickets proved dense, and the people who settled here were hard as the cedar, and sharp as the briars that could rip the skin off a squirrel or jackrabbit. During the Civil War, William Quantrill's bushwhackers often hid in the hills between murderous raids. The country was filled with Confederate sympathizers. More than three decades after the war's end, it still was.

Unionists and federal troops had always kept their distance from Sni-A-Bar. So did lawmen.

"Disgusting." Ben Lawless spit tobacco juice at a cricket but missed. "This country has tamed down since I last seen it."

Fallon swatted a mosquito on his neck. The air felt heavy, dense, and the humidity seemed suffocating.

Riding on the single-track path through trees that seemed more like a fort than forest, he had to ride behind Lawless. It was like riding in a cave, the foliage proved to be so thick, and vines, briars, and branches hung close to the trail, scratching chaps and shoulders, but the horses plowed on.

"Can you find Tully's hideout?" Fallon asked, lowering his head and letting his hat deflect a low, leafy limb.

"We'll find out at O'Neal's grog shop about a mile down this path," Lawless said.

Fallon blinked sweat out of his eyes. "You haven't been here in years. What makes you think O'Neal's grog shop is still in business?"

"Because a place like O'Neal's never goes out of business. Not in this country."

Roughly one mile later, they saw the lean-to, the corral, the hitching rail, and the rough-timbered one-story dogtrot cabin in what amounted to a clearing. An ass, two mules, three horses, a goat, a ewe, and a milk cow stood listlessly in the corral, which hadn't been cleaned in months, maybe years. A mule and three horses were tethered to the hitching rail, but Lawless and Fallon found room for their mounts.

Lawless tugged on the gun in the holster, pulled his hat low, and looked at Fallon after the warden followed him onto the warped, rotting porch. "You just watch my back, pard," the murderer said. "Don't get all uppity about law and order. This is my play. You savvy?"

Fallon made sure his revolver could be drawn smoothly from the holster, let it slide back into the leather, and looked Ben Lawless in his lone dark eye. "I'm an ex-con, Ben. Don't forget that." And he walked to the heavy door, pulled it open, and held it for Ben Lawless to enter first.

The place was dark, lighted only by candles, the windows shuttered. The smell of sour beer and cigar smoke filled the room, though no one was smoking, and the drinks being served came from a jug that contained corn liquor. The bearded bartender poured two glasses with the clear liquid when Fallon and Lawless stepped toward the walnut plank that stretched over old chicken crates.

Fallon flipped a silver dollar that the bartender caught. This was the kind of bar where there was no choice in what you drank.

Lawless found his glass, and shot down the whiskey, coughed, sniffed, and chuckled. "Not as potent as it used to be," he said, and nodded at the bartender for a refill. Fallon picked up his glass in his left hand, and turned to look at the other patrons. Two men, one old, one middle-aged at one table, a big man in the corner, drinking alone, and the last man, tall, lean, leathery dealing solitaire by a cold stove.

"Where's O'Neal?" Lawless asked.

"Who's that?" the bartender said.

"This is O'Neal's place. Or used to be."

The old man at one of the tables laughed. "O'Neal. Hell, he got gut shot . . . hmmm . . . fifteen years back."

"That ain't no surprise," Lawless said.

"Been two, three, maybe four owners since," the middle-aged man sitting with the old-timer added.

Lawless killed another shot, nodded at the barkeep, who filled the glass, surprised that one man could drink that much rotgut. "You the current owner?" he asked.

"Who wants to know?"

Lawless laughed, drew the gun, and broke the bartender's jaw with the butt, spun around, and shot the man in the corner, who was standing up, pulling a hogleg from his pants pocket. The man toppled back into his chair, and held his broken, bloody arm, whining.

"Ben Lawless wants to know," Ben Lawless said.

Fallon slid his untouched whiskey toward the killer, who lifted it with his free hand and raised it to the patrons in salute.

"Ben Lawless," said the middle-aged man. "Ain't he dead?"

"Nah," the old man said. "But he's in prison."

"He ain't now, is he, pard?" Lawless said with a grin, and killed the whiskey with his free hand, then thumbed back the hammer of his revolver.

"He ain't," Fallon said casually.

"Look into my eye—no look into my eye where there ain't no eye—and tell me I ain't Ben Lawless." He laughed. "Now, since that rude bartender ain't likely to be able to answer me so that I can understand, I'll give you folks time to satisfy my curiosity. I'm lookin' for the location of a feller from these parts. What's his name?"

"Tully," Fallon answered.

"Right. Tully. Knows these creeks, knows this country, and knows the Big Muddy."

When no one answered, and the gambler kept playing solitaire, Lawless shot him in the left foot. He crumpled to the nasty floor, whining, cursing, trying to stanch the blood coming from the hole where his big toe once was. Lawless walked over to him, and kicked him in the head. He rolled over, knocking the table and chairs to the floor, and lay still.

"You boys still think I ain't Ben Lawless?" Lawless said. And came to the old man. He cocked the pistol, and put the barrel between the middle-aged man's eyes. "Your son?" he asked the old man.

"Grandson," the man said.

Lawless laughed. "You look good for a feller your age."

The old-timer bowed his head in thanks. "You look pretty good for a man who's been in prison all these years," he said.

"That's because I ain't in that hellhole. And I'm sowin' my oats. So, I come here for information, mostly just to ask directions, and that's what I'm doin'. So far, I ain't been pleased with the lack of cooperation. Now, here's what we're all gonna do. I'll ask a question, again, and if I don't get what I want, I'm gonna go behind the bar, and I'm gonna mix my own drinks. And you folks is gonna drink them one at a time, till someone tells me what I want. And y'all remember ol' Ben Lawless. The Cherokees down in the Indian Nations shore does. That ol' skinflint behind the bar, he might have trouble swallowin' with his jaw busted to hell. But it won't be painin' him after a shot of Ben Lawless's Cherokee liquor."

He laughed, raised the revolver, and put a ball into the ceiling.

"Tully." Lawless spoke to the old man as he returned the revolver's hot barrel close to the middle-aged man's nose. "Or you won't never have no great-grandsons."

"P-p-Pa," the now white-faced middle-aged man said. "If we tell him, he leaves. And there ain't no man here to charge us for the whiskey."

The old man sighed. "Place don't bring in the same kind of men as it done when O'Neal run this joint."

"Ain't that the gospel truth," Ben Lawless said. The gun did not move an inch.

"Ain't seen Tully in a while," the old man said.

"He had business in Leavenworth. Should be home directly. If we see him, you don't have to worry about ever seein' him ag'in."

"That'd be fine." The old man nodded. "Real fine."

"You done good in there, Hank," Ben Lawless said as they rode down the track.

Fallon managed a short laugh that held no humor and said seriously, "What if Tully and the others stop at O'Neal's first?"

Lawless was busy tearing off a chunk from a twist of tobacco he had stolen from O'Neal's. "We're east of Tully's place. He won't go there."

"Other men might," Fallon said. "And come after us."

"They won't." Lawless remained confident.

"How do you know?"

"Because nobody, not even folks livin' in the Sni-A-Bar hills, would come after Ben Lawless." He shifted the mouthful of tobacco, shoved the rest of the twist into his saddlebags, and looked Fallon directly in the eye. "Would you?"

CHAPTER FIFTY-FIVE

From the woods, they looked down the hill at the shack, corral, and barn in what amounted to a clearing in a dense pocket of timber. Eight horses wandered around in the corral. No smoke rose from the chimney in the shack. The horses looked to be hungry, but then, from the looks of Tully's hideout, no one had been around to feed them for days.

"I'd hate to have to depend on those mounts to get me anywhere," Fallon whispered.

Ben Lawless spit. "Well, when you're runnin' from the law, you can't be too particular." Lawless rolled over and looked up at the warden. "I got you here. So this is your play from here on out."

"If Hardin actually gets here," Fallon said.

"There's a chance he might not. Ain't no rules in life."

Fallon let himself smile. "I've learned that the past few days. No rules. No laws."

"Not in the Sni-A-Bar," Lawless said.

"And not behind the walls of the Leavenworth pen."

Now Lawless shook his head. "Maybe before you

come, Hank. But not now. Those things you done, helpin' me learn my letters, changin' things aroun'. Those are good ideas. You might even be able to re-habilitate some of us hardened criminals. And 'em younger convicts, well, when they get released, they might even have a chance. Wasn't like that before you come. And I think you know it. You're a pretty good fellow, boss, and a fine warden. This is a job that suits you."

But he drew his revolver and showed it to Fallon.

"But some folks is beyond rehabilitation. I reckon I'm one of 'em. There ain't nothin' you can do for a fellow like Bowen Hardin—it's way too late for him—and there sure ain't nothin' to be done for a low-down sneak and rat like Indianola Anderson. Except kill 'em. You ready to do that, hoss? Or you want to leave it to me?"

"You said you were tracking, the killing was up to me," Fallon reminded him.

"Yeah, well, maybe I changed my mind. This fresh air. Does somethin' to a man. Hell, I ain't kilt more'n a couple in twenty years. More'n twenty. And I ain't hardly shot nobody in nigh thirty . . . till today."

Fallon did not hesitate. "We need to get these horses out of here," he said. "They whicker, we're dead."

"If it was just me," Lawless said, "I'd slit their throats."

"And bring the buzzards and wolves out in droves."

With a grin, Lawless spit, wiped his mouth, and ges-tured to the northeast.

"Remember that drainage ditch about a mile back?" Seeing Fallon nod, he continued. "You just follow that deer path. Picket 'em so they can drink, loosen the cinches, but don't unsaddle 'em. If some of them get away, we'll have a hard time catching up with 'em—especially if we have to saddle those horses once we get to that ditch. Think you can handle that?"

"You handle it," Fallon told him. "After all, this is my wife, and those are my responsibility." Fallon pointed to the barn. "I'll be in there when you get back. Where will you be? So I don't shoot you by mistake."

Lawless pointed. "Up here. I like bein' high up. That'll give me a clear shot at any fool who tries for the horses. That is, if you'll loan me that big Marlin."

"It's in the scabbard," Fallon told him.

Lawless drew his revolver, handed it butt forward. "Take it," he said. "You won't have much time to reload, and a short gun won't do me no good up here."

Fallon shoved the pistol in his waistband.

"How far ahead of them do you think we are?" Fallon asked.

"Depends. If they're still afoot. Maybe a day. Even more. If they ain't dead. But, on the other hand, they may have killed Tully and lit out for the Nations. Life's a gamble. I hope we bet on the right hand."

Both men stood. It was Ben Lawless who extended his hand and grinned as they shook.

"Good luck," Lawless said.

"Don't miss your aim," Fallon told him.

"I never have," Lawless replied, and moved quickly for their horses. "And I don't have to close one eye to line up my sights these days."

His instincts had been sharpened through years as a federal lawman in the Indian Nations and Arkansas, and even more as a convict in Joliet—not to mention those tours for the American Detective Agency in Yuma, Jefferson City, and Huntsville. You learned to have patience as a lawman. Even more so in prison. But Fallon did not wait long after Lawless left with the horses. He knew enough from watching Tully's place for the past hour or more that no one was around. He picked a patch that would give him cover in case the killers showed up. And he took his time, so not to alert the horses, or anyone in the woods around them doing the same thing Fallon and Lawless had been doing.

At the edge of the clearing—the Tully homestead, farm, whatever you want to call it ("dung heap" came to mind)—Fallon caught his breath, wiped the sweat off his forehead, and looked. The horses caught his scent and began prancing around the stinking corral. He could see the ribs on those poor animals and had to fight back the urge, that humanity, to go give the horses some grain or hay. Instead, he breathed out, breathed in, and ran lightly to the well, ducking behind the crumbling stone.

He glanced back. Good. No tracks to make out from where he had come. The barn door was closed, but cracks were prominent in the walls, and he noted a big hole in the wall facing the east. That would be his entrance point. His head inched to the side of the well, and he looked at the wooded hills, saw a trail— a real path, wide enough for horses, even wagons, not one made by animals—that wound up those hills. That would be, in all likelihood, the way from which Hardin—and Janice and Christina—would be coming down. Once he got the layout of the barn, he could figure out which way he could have the best chance to set up his ambush. Although with only six-shooters, his range would be limited.

Seeing nothing, he pulled his head back behind the well. He looked up the other hills, trying to see if he could spot Lawless or the horses, but he knew he wouldn't. Ben Lawless was too savvy to make that kind of greenhorn error.

Fallon looked again at the barn, and that hole in the side of the wall. He drew in a deep breath, came to his knees, and prepared to run.

That's when one of the horses in the corral whinnied.

And a moment later, Fallon heard an answering whinny.

That came from the wide path coming down the western hills.

He sank, feeling his heart pounding and the sweat bathing his armpits, neck, and forehead. He had to wipe his clammy hands on the chaps.

The horses ran to the edge of the corral, staring at the hills behind Fallon, snorting, whickering, and neighing.

Next came the faint jingling of a trace chain.

The horses loped around the corral, excited, and Fallon realized that now it was he who was in the tight spot. They were coming down the hill—most likely Tully and the others—and Fallon was caught behind the well. Tully. Hardin. Anderson. Holderman. Mac-Gregor. Providing this was indeed the party they were after, and not just some worker or neighbor.

Like anyone would work for a miserable and disgusting pig like Tully. Or any neighbor would come calling.

All right, Fallon thought. They couldn't have killed Tully. They couldn't find this place without him. Holderman. MacGregor. Hardin wouldn't have killed them, either. Not yet. Once he sees the condition of the horses, he might kill them to save himself. But for now . . . five men. One can keep Christina and Janice covered. It won't take them long to find a way to get me in a cross fire.

Fallon glanced up the eastern hills. How far away would Lawless be? How soon could he get back? And what if they threatened to put a bullet in the head of Janice or Christina?

This was going to be hell, he knew, but he did not move, except to draw the Peacemaker from the holster and cock it now, while Hardin's men were too far away to hear to clicking. Next he pulled Lawless's smaller Colt from his waistband. He checked the percussion caps and breathed a little easier as he thumbed back the hammer of the .36. Ben Lawless had filled all six chambers. So had Fallon. A lot of men kept the chamber under the hammer empty, or without a percussion cap on the nipple, for safety reasons. But when a man was facing killers like Indianola Anderson and Bowen Hardin, every shot counted.

The escapees had found a wagon. Had made better time than either Fallon or Lawless had expected. The wagon had reached the clearing.

"You call this a homestead?" That was Sean MacGregor's voice.

"You call them horses?" Bowen Hardin raged.

CHAPTER FIFTY-SIX

He didn't know how far away Tully had stopped the wagon. At least, he assumed Tully would be driving, since Tully knew the way.

"Those hosses is what you need," Tully said. He must have set the brake on the wagon. "It's called disguise. Like them Army duds y'all wore. Ain't nobody gonna think you're runnin' from the law ridin' mounts like that." He laughed and hopped to the ground. "I'll get some coffee on, and we can settle up, and you boys can be on y'all's way."

Fallon bit his lip. *You boys.* He had not heard anything resembling a woman's voice.

"You got any grub?" Indianola Anderson asked.

"Grub wasn't in the price," Tully said. "But I reckon I can fix up some grits, and they's probably some corn pone that ain't too hard. Got some otter jerky, too. Ever et otter jerky? It ain't half bad. Which means it ain't half good, neither. But it'll fill you up, if it don't jerk out your teeth."

He could hear feet, men brushing off their duds, one of the animals urinating. Fallon looked again at the hills, saw only the woods and the sky, and wet his lips. He had no plan. No need of making a plan. At some point, someone would come to the well. Then hell would erupt.

"You ladies," Tully said. "The facilities is over yon. It's a two-seater, too."

Now Fallon breathed easier. *Ladies. Plural.* At least Janice and Christina were still alive.

Fallon looked toward the barn. The outhouse was past that, near the edge of the woods. They'd come right past him. If they could get that far, that close to the woods . . . if they didn't gasp when they saw him behind the well. But . . . no . . . that wasn't going to happen. Bowen Hardin wasn't an idiot.

"Holderman," Hardin said. "Go with them."

"Good," Holderman said. "I need the use of that there facility myself." He laughed.

"Piss on the ground while they're inside," Hardin barked. "You're not letting them out of your sight."

"But . . . that ain't what I gotta do. Piss, I mean."

"Then hold it till they're back here. Or dig a hole and squat."

Fallon heard the footsteps. Approaching from the barn side. He wondered if it might be possible to slip to the other side, toward the shack that served as Tully's home. If the men were standing closer to the barn, if no one moved for the shack, he might be able to slide over, hug the wall. No.

Tully announced he'd go see what he could cook up. He started for the shack. Then Indianola Anderson said, "I'm thirsty. How's the water here?"

No one answered, but Fallon heard more steps, coming to the well.

"Bootsey!" Hardin barked.

All the footsteps halted.

"Those two gals might whup your arse," Hardin said, softer now, but firm. Indianola Anderson began sniggering, revealing his distance to the well. "And since your bowels is troubling you, take one of the ladies. Like you said, it's a two-seater. Just don't let the gal catch you with your pants down."

All the men laughed at the lousy joke.

"You can't mean that," Christina said, and Fallon felt relief sweep over him from just the sound of his wife's voice.

"Oh, I mean it, ma'am. You got to answer nature's call, you do it with my man with you. You get into them woods, we'd have the dickens of a time to find you. So it's onc at a time. With Bootsey this time. Or . . ."

"I reckon I might need to see the facilities myself," Indianola Anderson said, and chuckled with great malevolence.

"Go!" Hardin barked.

One step. Then nothing. Anderson cackled again.

"I said go," Hardin said. "There's nothing to stop me from killing you two right now. But it's your call."

Then those footsteps started. Behind Fallon. Behind him and to his left. And off toward his right, near the shack that passed for a house. Fallon listened, keeping the guns in both hands, turned silently, and crouched, knees bent, ready to spring forward. He did not even think about the odds.

Five against two. Those were the odds. But Fallon had surprise working in his favor. They didn't know he was here.

Footsteps. Closer. Closer. He saw them, moving

toward the privy, maybe fifteen yards away from him, half the distance between the well and the barn. Then Janice Jefferson turned. She must have caught him out of the corner of her eye, and she gasped, and stepped back against Aaron Holderman.

That's when Fallon leaped from behind the well, boosting himself with his strong legs, and ran straight at Holderman and the girl. But he wasn't looking at the big brute. Fallon shoved the .45 in his holster, and aimed the Navy at Indianola Anderson. The .36 barked.

Anderson yelped and dived behind the well as the bullet whined off the top stones.

"Son of a—" Bowen Hardin yelled, and drew his own pistol. But Christina dived, grabbed the killer's right arm, and jerked it down. Fallon fired at him, missed, then he turned and shot Aaron Holderman in the shoulder as the big man reached for a pistol on his hip.

Janice Jefferson screamed, stepped away, and Fallon charged toward her, turned back, saw Hardin kicking Christina, who rolled away. Fallon triggered the .36. Hardin turned and dived toward the wagon, but the big draft horses, stolen like the wagon, began bucking in their harnesses.

Fallon felt a bullet tear through the left side of his chaps. By then he met Janice Jefferson, and he lowered his left shoulder and caught her hard in the abdomen. His legs kept pumping. Another bullet whined off an old, rusted horseshoe a few feet in front of him. Janice fell over his shoulder like a sack of grain, and Fallon kept running even as she vomited all over his back.

A bullet singed his right ear. And he was at the barn, diving into the hay and pulling Janice behind him.

Hay wouldn't stop a bullet, of course, and Fallon had no plans to stay where he was as two more bullets thudded into the barn wall. He fired the Navy again, shoved it into his waistband, feeling the heat singe his skin. He grabbed Janice's arms and dragged her ten feet to that hole in the wall. Another bullet splintered the wall. Fallon dropped to his knees, dived through the opening, turned around, came back, crawled out just far enough to grab both of Janice's arms.

That's when he saw Aaron Holderman. The man was dazed, but he had found his feet. More important, Holderman had found a Remington revolver. And he was weaving, maybe twenty yards from Fallon and Janice. The gun barked. The bullet kicked up mud and manure into Fallon's face and mouth. He began backing into the barn, as fast as he could, but pulling Janice was like pulling nothing but dead-weight.

And now Aaron Holderman stood over Fallon, his shoulder bleeding.

"Stop!" Holderman yelled. "Stop or I kill the girl, Fallon. Hell, you know I'll do it."

And at this range, with the big criminal having covered the distance, Fallon knew even Aaron Holderman, wounded like he was, would not miss. The revolver was pointed at the widow's chest. Fallon's guns were in his waistband and his holster. He could see Anderson coming from behind the well, and big Tully moving through the open land with a repeating rifle.

He stopped moving.

Aaron Holderman smiled. He wasn't delirious enough to turn toward Anderson or Bowen Hardin, but he yelled, "I got him. I got Fallon. He's right here in my gunsights." Though for the time being, those sights were lined up on Janice Jefferson.

Out of Fallon's view, toward the front of the barn, Bowen Hardin yelled, "Well, stop talking and dilly-dallying with him. Kill him, Holderman. Put a bullet through his damned brains."

Laughing, Holderman raised the revolver, so Fallon tried to draw the .45 from the holster.

All the while knowing he did not have any chance at all.

CHAPTER FIFTY-SEVEN

A second later, a gush of crimson exploded from the center of Aaron Holderman's chest, and the big Remington fell, still in his hand, at his side. Holderman stared at the gore, confused, as the report of a rifle sounded from the hills.

"What the hell!" Indianola Anderson was beside the barn, running toward Fallon and the others. Now he stopped, turned to the woods, and dived beside the hay pile.

Holderman staggered to his left, and his eyes rolled back in his head as he fell into the manure and mud.

Another roar sounded, and a hole appeared in the side of the barn behind Indianola Anderson. "Rifle!" he shouted. "Rifle in the woods! Top of the hill!"

That's when Anderson remembered Harry Fallon, and he spun around, seeing Fallon charging him, with the Navy in his left hand and the .45 in his right.

The killer leaped up, brought his pistol level, but Fallon shot him twice, and both pistols aimed true.

The man fell against the wall, dropped his pistol, and staggered toward the yard.

"Hell's bells!" Tully cried.

Fallon saw the river rat beside the well now, and snapped a shot just as Indianola Anderson died. The bullet punched the bucket at the top of the housing, and Tully leaped behind the well. Another blast from the hills echoed.

"I'm hit," Tully yelled from behind the well. "No. I . . . am . . . kilt."

Fallon found himself at the edge of the barn. He could`see Indianola Anderson staring at him with sightless eyes, see the two holes in his dirty shirt. Fallon tossed the Navy away. He hadn't been counting his shots, but he had to figure it was empty. And Fallon liked the .45 better.

"Fallon." It was Sean MacGregor's voice.

Fallon kept quiet.

"Tell your boy in the woods that if he fires one more shot, Christina's dead."

Bowen Hardin echoed MacGregor's threat. "I got a gun to her head, Fallon. You know me, I won't hurt a woman . . . lessen I have to. Right now. I figure I have to."

Fallon looked at the hills before tossing the .45 out toward the well.

"Good boy," MacGregor said. "Now step out here so we can see you. And have your boy start down the hills. No gun. Ask him to join us."

Fallon yelled up at the hills. "Hey! They've got a gun on Christina! Come on down!" From the hills, a long object was tossed down the hill, and Ben Lawless stepped from the thicket, put his hands on top of his hat, and began coming down the hill. Fallon knew Lawless would be too smart to actually throw away that Marlin. That would be his chance.

"Your turn, Hank," Sean MacGregor ordered.

Only my friends call me Hank.

Fallon gave himself another chance. Bending, he picked up Indianola Anderson's revolver and shoved it behind his back. Then he stepped around the corner and smiled at Christina.

"Well, honey," he said. "We did pretty good for a while."

"Yeah," she said. Bowen Hardin released his hold on her and shoved her aside. He started to raise his revolver, but MacGregor barked for him to stop.

"Let the one with the rifle get closer," MacGregor said. "Then we kill them all. You start shooting too soon, and that man'll run. And grab that cannon he's been shooting with."

"All right," Hardin said.

MacGregor stepped closer, and Christina leaped at him, grabbing his right hand that held a pepperbox pistol and bringing it down.

Bowen Hardin spun, aiming his gun, but caught the movement of Fallon out of the corner of his eye, and quickly snapped a shot that tore through Fallon's collar. Fallon held Anderson's gun now and squeezed the trigger as he ran toward Hardin. The hammer snapped, striking an empty cylinder. Hardin tried firing his pistol, but it, too, was now empty. Both men hurled the pistols, but both targets ducked underneath the somersaulting revolvers. Then Fallon slammed into Hardin, driving him into the side of the wagon. They went down, and Fallon was on top of him. Rage. Rage like he had never known—not even when he had found the man who had murdered his first wife and child—not even after all the abuse he had endured as a convict in all the hellholes he had been in.

His hands locked on Bowen Hardin's throat. And he squeezed. Squeezed as hard as he could.

He did not see MacGregor shove Christina off him. He did not see MacGregor run, run as fast as his thin old legs could carry him and the pepperbox. He did not see Sean MacGregor turn around the corner of the barn, and he did not even hear the pistol shot that punched a hole in Sean MacGregor's forehead, driving him back into the farmyard, spread-eagled and dead. Fallon did not even see Janice Jefferson walk around the corner, look at Sean MacGregor's dead body, look at Aaron Holderman's smoking revolver that she held in her hands, then toss the revolver onto the dirt, move to a shady spot, and sit down.

And he did not hear his wife, Christina, standing over his shoulder, saying, "Let him go, Harry. Let him go. He's not worth it."

No, somehow Harry Fallon came to that conclusion himself. The rage did not vanish, but it faded enough for him to push himself away, spit out the gall, and find reason and calmness slowly returning.

Christina offered him her hands, and he let her help him to his feet, while Bowen Hardin rolled over on his side, clutching his bruised throat, trying to get enough oxygen in his lungs.

The next thing Fallon realized was that Ben Lawless

was walking into the farmyard. He grabbed a string around his shoulder and pulled the Marlin rifle that was hanging from his back. "Tossed a tree limb," Lawless said. "Figured I might need this thing later." He looked at the dead men. "But I reckon I was wrong."

CHAPTER FIFTY-EIGHT

As the guards escorted Bowen Hardin to his cell in solitary, Big Tim O'Connor looked at Harry Fallon and Ben Lawless and shook his head.

"Berrien?" Fallon asked.

"He confessed," the big guard said. "Locked up in the federal courthouse for the time being."

Fallon nodded.

Big Tim O'Connor spit tobacco juice and grunted. "Hank, I know you mean well, but you and your humanity," the guard captain said. "But when will you learn that these sons of strumpets can't be rehabilitated?"

Lawless also spit tobacco juice and saw the guards coming to escort him to his cell. He grinned at Fallon, and said, "Tell your wife, I look forward to learnin' my letters, an' even doin' some cipherin'. And tell Miss Janice, too. She's a fine teacher. And a dead shot." They shook hands, and Lawless winked at O'Connor. "Capt'n," he said. "That's the only reason I come back to these walls."

"You won't be here long, Ben," Fallon said. "I'll see to that."

"What the blazes was that all about?" O'Connor asked as the guards led Ben Lawless away.

"Some men will surprise you, Captain," Fallon answered. "And if you can save one, well, that's a start."

"Well, the governor's screaming his head off," O'Connor said. "So is the U.S. marshal, and you won't believe all the telegrams that have been coming in, from Washington and Topeka. And the reporters . . ." He sighed, wiped his mouth, and watched the prisoners being led to their cells.

"I still say we ought to lock them all up and throw away the key."

"They said the same thing about me," Fallon said. "Several times."

But he shook O'Connor's hand before excusing himself. The hack had stopped outside the prison gate, and Fallon pushed through it. He smiled as he raced to meet Christina, who stepped out of the hack and put Rachel Renee on the ground.

The five-year-old screamed, "Papa!" She ran into Fallon's arms, which swept her up, and held her tightly, as Christina hurried to join the embrace.

*Keep reading for a special preview
of your next Western adventure!*

A MacCallister Christmas

From bestselling authors William W. *and* J. A. Johnstone
*comes a special action-packed holiday western tale of
peace on earth and bad will toward men . . .*

Ever since he left Scotland to start a new life in
America, Duff MacCallister has stayed true to the
values and traditions of his clan in the Highlands.
But as Christmas approaches, he yearns to
reconnect with his family—even the ones he hasn't
met yet. This year, two of his American cousins—
twins Andrew and Rosanna—will be joining Duff
for the holidays at the Sky Meadow Ranch.
That is, if they manage to get there alive . . .

The twins' train is held up by not one but *two* vicious
outlaw gangs. The Jessup gang has been using the
Spalding gang's hideout to plan the robbery. The
Jessups just lost two of their brothers in a bank job
gone wrong—courtesy of Duff MacCallister—and
they're gunning for revenge. Together, these two
bloodthirsty bands of killers and thieves are teaming
up to make this one Christmas the MacCallisters will
never forget. But Duff's ready to deliver his own
brand of gun-blazing justice, holidays be damned . . .

**Look for *A MacCallister Christmas* this November
wherever books are sold.**

PROLOGUE

Dunoon, Argyll, Scotland, present day

"'Tis because o' that television show that yer here, isn't it, lassie?" the old woman asked as the young American couple came up to the counter to pay for the lunch they'd enjoyed in this picturesque little café.

The young woman smiled and said, "Is it that obvious?"

"Ye look a wee bit like the girl who plays the daughter, ya ken."

"You really think so?" The young woman blushed, obviously pleased by the comparison.

"Oh, aye. In fact, ye look as if ye have some Scots blood a-flowin' in yer veins."

"I do! A little. I don't really know how much."

"Enough that I'd consider ye a good Scottish lass. We need to figure out what clan. Once we ken what yer colors are, ye can go next door to me sister's shop, where she sells all sorts o' goods decorated with all the clan colors . . ."

While that conversation was going on, the young man had handed over his credit card. He took it back from the old woman now as she handed him his receipt along with it. His wife said eagerly, "I don't really know anything about the clans. Well, other than what I've learned from watching TV."

"Then ye've come t' the right place. I'll teach ye everything ye need to ken. What is't ye Americans call it? A *crash course*?"

"Yes, that's right."

While his wife leaned over the counter to continue the spirited conversation with the woman who ran the café, the young man stepped through the door to the narrow cobblestone street to wait for her. He had a hunch it might be a while.

"Snagged another'un, did she?"

The voice came from the young man's left. A burly older man sat there, puffing on a pipe, bundled up against the day's chill with his cap pulled down on his gray hair.

"I beg your pardon?" the young man said.

The older man took the pipe out of his mouth and pointed with the stem at the café entrance. "Aileen in there. She can spot the tourists and the TV fans and manages to send about half of 'em in her sister Isobel's shop. 'Twouldn't surprise me if she gets what you Americans call a *kickback*."

"Annabel really does enjoy that show," the young man said with a smile. "We've been all over the Highlands during the past week. Saved up to take this trip for a couple of years."

The older man moved over on the bench and nodded curtly to the empty space. The young American sat down and held out his hand.

"I'm Richard van Loan."

"Is that an English name?"

"Dutch, I believe. I've never been into genealogy all that much."

"I've nothin' against the Dutch, so I'll shake yer hand. Graham McGregor is me name. 'Tis a pleasure to meet ye, lad."

"Likewise," Richard said. He looked around at the old buildings that fronted the narrow street. Eastward, between some of those buildings, a narrow slice of the Firth of Clyde was visible, the water a deep, deep blue on this cloudy day.

"You have a beautiful city here."

"'Twas not always so large. Me grandfather told me it grew like wildfire after the port was put in and the steamers began comin' up the firth, and James Ewing built Castle House next to old Dunoon Castle. A'fore that, 'twas just a country town, Dunoon, spelled a bit different than today. Me great-great-grandfather Ian McGregor had a pub here, the White Horse."

"Sounds like it would have been a wonderful place to visit," Richard said.

"Dinna ye go talkin' about such things! Ye would never believe how many tourists show up in the High-lands searchin' for some magical place where they can go travelin' through time!"

Richard laughed. "Really? Well, people take these things seriously, I suppose."

"Aye, they do. Yer wife . . . I'd wager she's a wee bit in love wi' tha' braw laddie on the TV."

"Oh, I don't know about that—"

"But he's not the only hero t' come from Scotland,

ye ken. Why, there was once a lad from right here in old Dunoon who was every bit as big and bold and handsome, an' even better in a fight! Me great-great-grandfather Ian was his friend, ye ken, before he left to go t' America and become a famous frontiersman, like in yer Western movies."

"Your great-great-grandfather became a frontiersman in America?"

"No, th' lad I'm tellin' ye about! Duff MacCallister, tha' was his name. Duff Tavish MacCallister. Did ye ever hear of him?"

Richard shook his head slowly and said, "No. No, I don't think so."

Annabel came out of the café, pointed at the shop next door, and said, "Richard, I'm going to be in there for a while looking around. Are you all right out here?"

"Yes, I'm fine," he told her. "Take your time."

"She will, ye ken," Graham McGregor said after Annabel had vanished into the shop. "Take her time, that is. Lassies always do."

"Yes, I've been married long enough to know that. You were saying about this fellow Duff . . . Tell me more about Duff MacCallister."

"I reckon I can do that," Graham said, nodding. "Old Ian filled me grandfather's head wi' stories, and he passed 'em on to me when I was naught but a tyke." He paused, obviously thinking about which story to tell, then went on, "I know a good one. Lots o' ridin' an' shootin' an' fightin', like in them movies I was talkin' about. It started in th' month o' December, long, long ago, in a frontier settlement, Chugwater, Wyomin' . . ."

CHAPTER ONE

Chugwater, Wyoming . . . back then

Duff MacCallister took off his hat and raised his arm to sleeve sweat off his rugged face.

"If I dinna ken what day 'tis, I'd say 'twas the middle o' summer, not December!"

"Not that long until Christmas," Elmer Gleason agreed. "It's unseasonably warm, that's for sure."

The two men had just finished loading a good-sized pile of supplies, including heavy bags of flour, sugar, and beans, into the back of the wagon they had brought into town from Sky Meadow, Duff's ranch farther up the valley. Both were in shirtsleeves, instead of the heavy coats most men normally wore at this time of year in Wyoming. In fact, Duff had rolled up the sleeves of his shirt over brawny forearms.

He was a tall, broad-shouldered, tawny-haired young man, originally from Scotland, but now, after several years here in Wyoming, a Westerner through and through. He had established Sky Meadow Ranch when he arrived on the frontier, brought in Black Angus cattle, like the ones he had raised back in Scotland, and built the spread into a large, very lucrative operation that took in thirty thousand acres of prime grazing land.

Elmer, a grizzled old-timer who had lived a very adventurous life of his own, had been living on the land when Duff bought it, squatting in an old abandoned gold mine at the northern end of the property. People believed the mine was haunted, but what they had seen was no ghost, just Elmer.

Since Duff had made that discovery, the old-timer had become one of his most trusted friends and advisors. He worked as Sky Meadow's foreman, and Duff had even made him a partner in the ranch with a ten percent share.

Now, with the supplies Duff had purchased from Matthews Mercantile loaded, Elmer licked his lips and said, "I reckon we'll be headin' down to Fiddler's Green to wet our whistles before startin' back to the ranch? A cold beer'd taste mighty good on a day like today."

"Aye, the same thought did occur to me," Duff said. "Go ahead, and I'll catch up to ye. I'll be makin' one small stop first."

"At the dress shop?" Elmer asked with a knowing grin.

"Perhaps . . ."

"Go ahead. I'll be down there yarnin' with Biff when you're done. We can talk about the weather, like ever'body else in town is probably doin'."

Duff lifted a hand in farewell and turned his steps along Clay Avenue toward the shop where Meagan Parker sewed, displayed, and sold the dresses she made, which were some of the finest to be found anywhere between New York and San Francisco, despite the unlikely surroundings of this frontier cattle town. Meagan's talents were such that she could have been in high demand as a designer and seamstress anywhere in the country, but she preferred to remain in Chugwater.

Duff MacCallister was a large part of the reason she stayed.

Duff and Meagan had an understanding. Neither of them had a romantic interest in anyone else, and because of financial assistance she had rendered him in the past, she was also a partner in Sky Meadow.

The ranch was named after Skye McGregor, Duff's first love back in Scotland. The young woman's murder had been part of a tragic chain of circumstances that resulted in Duff leaving Scotland and coming to America. A part of Duff still loved her and always would. Meagan knew all about Skye and Duff's feelings for her, and she accepted the situation, so it never came between the two of them.

Someday they would be married. Duff and Meagan both knew that. But for now, they were happy with the way things were between them and didn't want to do anything to jeopardize that.

Now that Duff wasn't lifting heavy bags and crates into the wagon, the day didn't feel quite as warm to him, although the sun still shone brightly in a sky almost devoid of clouds. A couple of times earlier in the fall, a dusting of snow had fallen, but it wouldn't have been unusual for several inches to be on the ground by now.

A little breeze kicked up as Duff walked toward Meagan's shop. He lifted his head to sniff the air. There was a hint, just a hint, of coolness in it.

Maybe that was a harbinger, Duff thought, an indication that the weather was going to change again and become more seasonable. Even though a man would have to be a fool not to enjoy the pleasant weather—it wasn't a raging blizzard, after all—with Christmas coming, it needed to *feel* like winter. That little tang he had detected put some extra enthusiasm in Duff's step. He was in a good mood, and he didn't think anything could change that.

Four men reined their horses to a halt in front of the Bank of Chugwater, swung down from their saddles, and looped the reins around the hitch rail there. Hank Jessup, the oldest of the group, turned to the other three and said, "All right, Nick, you'll stay out here with the horses."

They all had the same roughly dressed, rawboned appearance, and their facial features were similar enough that it was obvious they were related. Hank, with his weather-beaten skin and white hair, could have been father to the others, based on looks, but in actuality he was their older brother. Half brother, anyway. Late in life, their father had married a much younger woman and somewhat surprisingly sired the other three—Logan, Sherm, and Nick.

They had willingly followed Hank into the family business of being outlaws, and they had come to Chugwater to help themselves to an early Christmas present of however much loot was in the bank's vault.

"You said I could go inside this time, Hank," Nick complained. "I always have to watch the horses."

Sherm said, "It's an important job, kid."

"You're our lookout, too," Logan added. "You've got to warn us if any blasted badge-toter comes along and starts to go in the bank."

"Yeah, yeah," Nick muttered. "I guess so."

Hank said, "And you're watching the horses because I say so, that's the most important thing." He squared his shoulders, nodded to Logan and Sherm. "Come on."

The three of them stepped up onto the boardwalk and headed for the bank's front door. They didn't draw their guns yet, because they didn't want to alert people on the street that anything unusual was going on.

Nick lounged against the hitch rail, handy to the spot where the reins were tied so he could loosen them in a hurry if he needed. This wasn't the first bank robbery he and his brothers had pulled. Sometimes the boys came out walking fast, still not wanting to draw attention, and sometimes they came on the run, needing to make as rapid a getaway as they could.

Inside the bank, Hank glanced around quickly, sizing up the situation without being too obvious about it: two tellers, each with a single customer, one man and one woman. A bank officer, probably the president, was seated at a desk off to one side behind a wooden railing. The man had a bunch of papers spread out on his desk and was making marks on one of them with a pencil, pausing between each notation to lick the pencil lead.

No guard that Hank could see, but it was entirely possible those tellers had guns on shelves below the counter, and the bank president probably had an iron in his desk drawer, too.

Question was, would they be smart enough not to try to use them?

Hank wouldn't mind gunning them down if it came to that. Wouldn't mind at all.

He exchanged a glance with his brothers and nodded. No time like the present.

Hauling the gun from the holster on his hip, Hank yelled, "Stand right where you are! Nobody move, or we'll start blasting!"

Meagan was sitting at a table with several pieces of cloth in front of her when Duff came into the shop. She had three straight pins in her mouth, taken from a pincushion close to her right hand. She looked up at him and smiled.

"Careful there, lass," he cautioned. "Ye dinna want t' be stickin' pins in those sweet lips o' yours."

Deftly Meagan took the pins out of her mouth and returned them to the pincushion, which allowed her to smile even more.

"I certainly wouldn't want to hurt my lips," she said, "when I have such an important use for them."

"Oh? And what would that be?"

Meagan stood up and came toward him, a sensually shaped blond beauty. Because of the unseasonably warm weather, she wore a lightweight dress today that hugged her figure, instead of being bundled up.

"This," she said as she put her arms around Duff's

neck and lifted her face so he could kiss her. He did so with passion and urgency.

After a very enjoyable few moments, Duff stepped back and said, "I have some news this morning. Elmer and I stopped at the post office on our way t' the mercantile, and a letter was there waiting for me."

"Well, don't keep me in suspense," Meagan said. "Who is it from?"

"My cousin Andrew. Ye've heard me speak of him many times."

"Of course. He's the famous actor. He and his twin sister, both."

Duff nodded and said, "Aye, Rosanna. The pair o' them were actually the first of my American cousins I ever met, when they came to Glasgow to perform in a play called *The Golden Fetter*. Andrew had written to me then, introducing himself and asking me to come see the play and meet him and Rosanna. Fine people they are."

"Being MacCallisters, how could they be anything else?"

"Aye, 'tis true, we are a fine clan. I've seen them a number of times since then, in New York and elsewhere, and back in the summer, I wrote to Andrew and invited him and Rosanna to spend Christmas at Sky Meadow if they could arrange their schedule to make it possible. In his letter I received today, he says they've been touring, but they're ready t' take a break from it and pay me a visit for the holidays."

"Duff, that's wonderful news," Meagan said. "I'm looking forward to meeting them. When will they be here?"

"Andrew is no' sure yet, but 'twill not be for another few days, at least. He assures me they'll arrive before Christmas."

"And what about your cousin Falcon? Didn't you tell me that he's coming for Christmas, too?"

Duff grinned and said, "Falcon told me he would *try* to make it. Wi' Falcon, ye never can tell what wild adventure might come along an' drag him away. So if he shows up, I'll be mighty glad t' see him, of course, but I willna be surprised if circumstances prevent that."

"Well, I hope he's able to come," Meagan said. "It would be almost like a family reunion. Isn't he Andrew and Rosanna's brother?"

"Aye, youngest brother. Falcon is the baby of the family, although I doubt he'd appreciate bein' referred to as such. Andrew and Rosanna are ten years or so older than him."

"Aren't there other brothers and sisters?"

Duff waved a hand and said, "Aye, spread out all over the country, they are. One o' these days, they need to have a proper MacCallister family reunion."

"I'll bet that would be exciting," Meagan said with a smile. "There's no telling what might happen."

"Och, lass, are you for sayin' that th' MacCallisters attract trouble or some such?"

"Well, now that you mention it . . ."

Duff chuckled and pulled Meagan back into his arms for another hug and kiss. He stroked a big hand over her blond hair and said quietly, "'Tis something else I'd rather be attractin'."

"Oh, you do, Duff. You definitely do."

He was about to lower his lips to hers for another kiss when gunshots suddenly rang out somewhere down the street. The sounds shattered the warm, peaceful day and made Duff jerk his head up again.

Those shots were concrete proof of what Meagan had just said. No MacCallister could go very long without running into a ruckus.

"I'll be back," Duff said over his shoulder as he charged out of the dress shop.

CHAPTER TWO

As president of the Bank of Chugwater, Bob Dempster's job usually involved making sure all the numbers
added up and all the other day-to-day details were
attended to. But as a frontier banker, he knew that
sometimes he might be called upon to perform other
tasks as well.

For that reason, a .45 revolver rested in the middle
drawer of his desk. As the three rough-looking strangers
entered the bank, Bob took note of them and carefully
eased the drawer out so that the gun came into view.

When the three men pulled their guns, and the
oldest one shouted for everybody not to move, Bob
reached for his own weapon and closed his hand
around it.

Unfortunately, the boss outlaw swung sharply toward
Bob and lined his revolver on him.

"When you take your hand outta that drawer, mister,
it better be empty, or I'll put a bullet right through
your brain."

Bob wasn't going to throw his life away by betting
on his own rudimentary gun-handling skills. Slowly

he opened his hand and lifted it away from the drawer. He raised his other hand at the same time.

"Now you're bein' smart," the outlaw said. "Stand up and move over here, careful-like."

While Bob was doing that, another of the robbers herded the two customers away from the tellers' windows at gunpoint. The third man menaced the tellers with his gun and told them, "You fellas come out of those cages. We want everybody together. And make it pronto!"

Soon the robbers had the five people in the bank lined up along the railing in front of the president's desk. The leader jerked his head toward the counter and told his companions, "Get everything in the tellers' drawers, and then we'll clean out the vault."

"You got it, Ha—"

The man who started to reply cut it short just as he started to say the leader's name. Looking a little embarrassed by his near slipup, he hurried to carry out the orders.

Bob Dempster looked at the others and nodded confidently, hoping they would take his meaning that they should cooperate with the bank robbers and maybe they would all come through this all right. Bob hated to think of the monetary loss, but it was more important that these innocents survived.

The female customer was an elderly widow named Mrs. Hettie Richardson, who raised chickens and made a small but livable income by selling their eggs. Cloyd Nelson was the other customer, who had driven a freight wagon for R. W. Guthrie in the past, but currently worked in Guthrie's building supply warehouse. He was a short, brawny, middle-aged man known to have a bad temper, and if anybody was going to fly off the handle and cause a problem, Bob knew it would be him.

Unfortunately, Bob was wrong about that, because while he was watching Nelson warily, Mrs. Richardson reached into her bag and hauled out an old cap-and-ball pistol that had been converted to percussion. She held the gun in both hands, hooked bony thumbs over the hammer, and hauled it back to full cock.

"You scoundrels, get away from my money!" she cried, and the next instant she pulled the trigger.

The booming report was thunderously loud inside the bank. The boss outlaw's hat flew off his head. The gun in his hand came up toward the five people gathered along the railing.

Cloyd Nelson yelled, "Mrs. Richardson, get down!" and lunged at her, apparently intending to grab her and pull her to the floor, out of the line of fire.

That put his back toward the outlaw, and the shot the man fired struck Nelson squarely between the shoulder blades. The slug's impact threw the man forward into Mrs. Richardson.

Both of them toppled over the railing and sprawled on the floor behind it.

The two tellers dived for the floor, no doubt thinking that now the shooting had started, the air would be full of flying lead. That was highly probable.

Bob Dempster turned and dashed back through the gate in the railing. Another shot boomed. He heard the ugly, high-pitched whine of a slug passing close beside his ear.

After the outlaws had gotten the drop on him, Bob would have cooperated in the hope that no one would be hurt. Now, with the fat in the proverbial fire, his best chance seemed to be to fight back.

He flung himself behind his desk, snatched the .45 out of the still-open drawer, and triggered twice in the general direction of the bank robbers. His two employees were on the floor, as well as Mrs. Richardson and Nelson, so he didn't have to worry about hitting any of them.

Return fire blasted at him. He heard the bullets thudding into the desk, but the heavy piece of furniture stopped them. He stuck the gun up and risked another shot without having any idea if he'd hit anything.

"Hank's hit!" one of the outlaws yelled. "Let's get outta here!"

"I got the money from the drawers!" another man shouted.

Boot soles slapped the polished wooden floor as the men rushed out of the bank.

Bob Dempster waited a couple of heartbeats to make sure they were gone, then looked over the desk. A haze of powder smoke floated in the air. Bullets had shattered the frosted glass that flanked the tellers' windows, and there might be other damage he couldn't see yet. He pushed himself up and called, "Mrs. Richardson! Are you all right?"

"Get this big ox off me!" the old woman wailed.

That *big ox* probably had saved her life, Bob thought, but with Nelson's considerable weight pinning her to the floor, she wasn't thinking about that. She had to be worried that he would suffocate her, which he just might. Bob hurried around the desk and called to the tellers, "Give me a hand here!" Both young men appeared to be unhurt.

They were trying to lift Cloyd Nelson's limp form off Mrs. Richardson when more shots roared outside.

When Duff reached the street, he could tell the shots were coming from the direction of the bank. He pulled his gun from its holster and started running along the street toward the impressive brick building.

As he approached, he saw Thurman Burns, the deputy town marshal, hurrying toward the bank from the other direction. A young man stood near four horses tied at the hitch rail in front of the building. He didn't seem to have noticed Duff, but he had seen the deputy. Using the horses to shield his movements, he drew his gun and aimed over the saddles at Burns.

"Look out, Thurman!" Duff shouted. The warning caused Burns to veer to the side just as the man behind the horses fired. Burns didn't appear to be hit.

Duff paused to line up a shot of his own. He wasn't a fast draw, but he was remarkably accurate in his aim. Not even Duff could hit every mark, though. Just as he squeezed the trigger, the man pivoted, so Duff's bullet missed narrowly and struck one of the saddle horns instead, blasting it to pieces and spooking the horse on which the saddle was cinched. The animal started to caper around and pull against the hitch rail. That made the other mounts skittish, too.

The young man snapped a shot at Duff that kicked up dirt in the street a good twenty feet to Duff's right.

He grabbed the reins and tried to get the horses under control as three more men came barreling out of the bank, throwing shots behind them. One of the robbers was unsteady on his feet and had blood on his shirt.

Duff dropped to a knee behind a water barrel and leveled his revolver. Confident that the men had at least attempted to rob the bank and might have committed who knew how much mayhem inside, as well as taking shots at him and Deputy Burns, Duff felt no hesitation in shooting to kill. He squeezed the trigger as one of the outlaws tried to swing up into his saddle. The gun roared and bucked in Duff's hand.

Blood and brain matter sprayed in the air as the bullet blew a fist-sized chunk out of the man's head. His momentum carried him on over the horse's back, where he spilled into an ungainly heap in the street. The horse broke away and stepped on him a few times in stampeding away with reins trailing in the dust.

Thurman Burns had taken cover in an alcove where a doorway was located. He fired around the edge of that alcove, not hitting any of the outlaws but coming close enough to distract them. That gave Duff an opportunity to aim again. His best shot was at the man who was already wounded, but still on his feet, and spraying lead around. He was hatless and had striking white hair, although he didn't move like an old man.

Duff triggered two rounds. Both bullets pounded into the outlaw's chest and drove him toward the boardwalk. The back of his boots hit the edge of the walk. He sat down, but didn't fall over. Slowly his head slumped forward and he bent over until it looked like he was going to fall on his face, but he didn't.

"Hank!" one of the remaining two outlaws shouted. "Hank, no!"

"Come on!" the other one urged. "Let's go!"

They leaped into their saddles despite being caught in a cross fire between Duff and Burns. Desperation had given them wings. Bending low, they slashed at their horses with the reins and sent the animals charging into the middle of the street. Wild shots flew from their guns. All the bystanders on the street and the boardwalks had scurried for cover as soon as the shooting started. Duff hoped none of that flying lead found any of them.

The fleeing men were bouncing around so crazily in their saddles and the horses ran in such a jerky fashion that drawing a bead on them was next to impossible, even for Duff. He fired a few more times, then grimaced in disgust as the two outlaws galloped out of Chugwater without ever slowing down. He straightened from his position behind the water barrel and walked toward the two fallen outlaws, keeping his gun trained on them, just in case.

The man Duff had shot in the head was clearly dead. Nobody could survive having so much blood and brains leak out of his shattered skull. The other man, the white-haired hombre, hadn't moved since sitting down on the edge of the boardwalk. He had dropped his gun, which now lay between his feet.

Duff kept his gun ready while he reached out cautiously with his other hand and prodded the outlaw's shoulder. That was enough to make the man flop over backward onto the boardwalk. The glazed, unseeing look in his eyes was unmistakable as he stared up at the awning over the walk.

"Are they both dead?" Deputy Burns called from the alcove.

"Aye," Duff replied. "Dead as ever can be."

Burns emerged from cover and blew out a relieved breath. He said, "That was some mighty good shooting, Duff, as usual."

Duff ignored the compliment and asked, "Where's Marshal Ferrell?"

"Rode down to Cheyenne on some business and left me in charge." Burns rolled his eyes. "Sure enough, that's when somebody tries to rob the bank." He paused, then said, "The bank! Has anybody checked in there yet?"

"Just about to," Duff said.

"No need," Bob Dempster said as he stepped through the open doors. He was pale and obviously shaken, but didn't seem to be hurt. "They killed one of the customers, Cloyd Nelson, and the other customer who was inside, old Mrs. Richardson, may have a broken rib from Cloyd falling on her, but the tellers and I are all right."

"Did they get away with much money?" Burns asked.

"Just what was in the tellers' drawers. A few hundred dollars, more than likely. I'll have to make an exact count, to know for sure."

"So, three men dead and an old woman hurt, all for th' sake of a few hundred dollars," Duff said.

Dempster nodded and said, "I'm afraid so. Greed has a high price."

"Aye, 'tis true." Duff looked at the white-haired outlaw with the empty stare and thought about poor Cloyd Nelson. "And all too often, 'tis the innocent who have t' pay."

Connect with

Visit us online at
KensingtonBooks.com
to read more from your favorite authors, see books
by series, view reading group guides, and more.

for sneak peeks, chances to win books and prize packs,
and to share your thoughts with other readers.

facebook.com/kensingtonpublishing
twitter.com/kensingtonbooks

Tell us what you think!

To share your thoughts, submit a review,
or sign up for our eNewsletters, please visit:
KensingtonBooks.com/TellUs.